ANNE OF GREEN GABLES

broadview editions
series editor: L.W. Conolly

ANNE of
GREEN GABLES
By
L. M. MONTGOMERY

ANNE OF GREEN GABLES

L.M. Montgomery

edited by Cecily Devereux

broadview editions

National Library of Canada Cataloguing in Publication

Montgomery, L. M. (Lucy Maud), 1874–1942.
    Anne of Green Gables / L.M. Montgomery ; edited by Cecily Devereux.

(Broadview editions)
Includes bibliographical references.
ISBN 1-55111-362-7

    I. Devereux, Cecily Margaret, 1963– II. Title. III. Series.

PS8526.O55A63 2004   C813'.52   C2004-903032-9

Broadview Editions

The Broadview Editions series represents the ever-changing canon of literature by bringing together texts long regarded as classics with valuable lesser-known works.

Advisory editor for this volume: Colleen Franklin

Broadview Press Ltd. is an independent, international publishing house, incorporated in 1985. Broadview believes in shared ownership, both with its employees and with the general public; since the year 2000 Broadview shares have traded publicly on the Toronto Venture Exchange under the symbol BDP.

We welcome comments and suggestions regarding any aspect of our publications–please feel free to contact us at the addresses below or at broadview@broadviewpress.com / www.broadviewpress.com

North America
PO Box 1243, Peterborough, Ontario, Canada K9J 7H5
Tel: (705) 743-8990; Fax: (705) 743-8353
email: customerservice@broadviewpress.com
3576 California Road, Orchard Park, NY, USA 14127

UK, Ireland, and continental Europe
NBN Plymbridge
Estover Road
Plymouth PL6 7PY UK
Tel: 44 (0) 1752 202 301
Fax: 44 (0) 1752 202 331
Fax Order Line: 44 (0) 1752 202 333
Customer Service: cservs@nbnplymbridge.com
Orders: orders@nbnplymbridge.com

Australia and New Zealand
UNIREPS, University of New South Wales
Sydney, NSW, 2052
Australia
Tel: 61 2 9664 0999; Fax: 61 2 9664 5420
email: info.press@unsw.edu.au

Broadview Press Ltd. gratefully acknowledges the financial support of the Government of Canada through the Book Publishing Industry Development Program for our publishing activities.

PRINTED IN CANADA

Contents

Preface

Really, when I first penned *Anne of Green Gables* so many years
ago I had no idea what would spring from it all (Montgomery
to G.B. Macmillan, 27 December 1936; Bolger and Epperly 183).

L.M. Montgomery's *Anne of Green Gables* is among the world's
best-known and most enduringly popular novels in English. First
published in 1908 by a Boston firm, L.C. Page and Company,
Anne went into ten editions within a year, and it has remained in
print ever since. Indeed, new editions have appeared in greater
numbers than ever since the novel entered the public domain in
the United States in 1983 and in Canada in 1992.[1] In 1998, *Books
in Print* (Bowker's) lists forty-one editions of the novel, eleven of
which are new; in 2001–02, forty-two are listed, five of which are
new. These numbers do not include related texts, such as adaptations for younger children, cookbooks, paper doll books, and
daybooks, which, while text-based, are also collateral commodi-
ties representing the massive and growing types of "Anne"
merchandise that are such potent indices of the continuing appeal
of Montgomery's novel.[2] It might thus seem rather unnecessary

---

[1] See "It All Began with Anne" by Molly Colin, *Publishers' Weekly* (19 Oct. 1992):
27–28. *Anne of Green Gables* is still protected by copyright in some locations.

[2] "Anne" merchandise goes well beyond dolls and is far too varied and numerous to
describe in detail here. See Jeannette Lynes, "Consumable Avonlea: The
Commodification of the Green Gables Mythology," in *Making Avonlea: L.M. Montgomery
and Popular Culture* (Toronto: U of Toronto P, 2002) 268–279; Cecily Devereux,
"'Canadian Classic' and 'Commodity Export': The Nationalism of 'Our' *Anne of Green
Gables*," *Journal of Canadian Studies* 36.1 (2001): 11–28; Grieg Dymond and Geoff Pevere,
Mondo Canuck: A Canadian Pop Culture Odyssey (Scarborough, ON: Prentice-Hall, 1998)
12–15. For a discussion of the imaginary Avonlea represented in the Sullivan
Entertainment series *Road to Avonlea*, see Aspasia Kostopoulos, "Our Avonlea: Imagining
Community in an Imaginary Past," *Pop Can: Popular Culture in Canada*, ed. Lynne Van
Luven and Priscilla L. Walton (Scarborough, ON: Prentice-Hall, 1999) 98–105. See also
the range of articles in *Making Avonlea: L.M. Montgomery and Popular Culture*, ed. Irene
Gammel, Toronto: U of Toronto P, 2002. An important document of the value of the
"Anne" commodity is the report of the decision in "Anne of Green Gables Licensing
Authority Inc. et al. v. Avonlea Traditions Inc.," Court File No. 95-CU-89192, Ontario
Superior Court of Justice, Wilson J. Heard, November 15–19 and 21–26, 1999.
Judgement rendered March 10, 2000. *Canadian Patent Reporter*, 4th ser. (Aurora, ON,

to add yet another edition to this throng. The need, however, for an edition that can be used, like the elegant and comprehensive *Annotated Anne* published in 1999 by Oxford University Press, for informed reading, as well as for secondary and post-secondary teaching, has been apparent for some time: the appearance in the past few years of study guides suggests that *Anne of Green Gables* is figuring increasingly on pre-university curricula; and Carole Gerson has recently shown that *Anne* is also appearing more frequently in university literature courses (see Gerson, "Anne Goes to University," in *Making Avonlea*, ed. Irene Gammel, U of Toronto P, 2002). This edition is intended to provide a usable scholarly text of the novel with relevant contextual materials for reading and teaching.

Canada Law Book, 2000) 289–370. This judgement upheld the validity of the trade-marks of "Anne of Green Gables" and images of "Anne."

Acknowledgements

This edition of *Anne of Green Gables* owes a great deal to a great many people. Debbie Muttart, Kevin Rice, and Judy Simpson at the Confederation Centre for the Arts in Charlottetown, Prince Edward Island, were extremely helpful and generous in making the manuscript available to me, answering many questions, and finding places for me to work. I am also grateful to the librarians and staff at many libraries and archives, including the Public Archives of Prince Edward Island; the University of Prince Edward Island Library, Special Collections; the National Library of Canada and the National Archives of Canada; the Thomas Fisher Rare Book Library; the Osborne Collection in the Toronto Public Library; the Metro Reference Library in Toronto; the L.M. Montgomery collection in the Archives at the University of Guelph; the University of Alberta Library and the Bruce Peel Special Collections at the University of Alberta, as well as the L.M. Montgomery Institute. I would like to thank graduate assistants Jennifer Chambers and Tasha Ausman for carefully checking the text, and Archana Rampure and Paul Chafe for preliminary research. Family, friends and colleagues supported this project in many ways: thanks to Benet, Jeremy, Joan and Joanna Devereux, Chris Gittings, Susan Hamilton, Michelle Jackson, Connie Langille-Rowe, Benjamin Lefebvre, Jennifer Litster, Jo-Ann Wallace and Stephanie Wood; thanks to Kate Macdonald Butler and Sally Cohen; special thanks to Scott, and to my daughters, Lucy and Susan Wright. Finally, I wish to express my gratitude to the University of Alberta Faculty of Arts for generously supporting this project. Material from the introduction appeared in different forms in *The Journal of Canadian Studies* and *Canadian Children's Literature*, and is included here with permission. All errors are my own.

Cecily Devereux
University of Alberta

Abbreviations

AGG   *Anne of Green Gables*; all references are to this edition

AA   *The Annotated Anne of Green Gables*

AP   *The Alpine Path*

OED   Oxford English Dictionary

R/W   *A Preliminary Bibliography of L.M. Montgomery*, by Ruth Weber Russell, D.W. Russell, and Rea Wilmshurst (1986)

SJ   *The Selected Journals of L.M. Montgomery*, ed. Mary Henley Rubio and Elizabeth Waterston

Introduction

Anne of Green Gables, still L.M. Montgomery's best-known novel, was published in 1908 by American publisher L.C. Page and Co. Although it was Montgomery's first novel to appear in print, when Page printed and distributed copies of the book that would be registered for copyright and issued in July, Montgomery had published at least two hundred and ninety-four short stories (*R/W* 654–948) and two hundred and fifty-nine poems (*R/W* 1152–1411).[1] Thus, while *Anne* is a first novel, it is also the work of a writer who had been serving what Montgomery described as her "apprenticeship" for many years. For almost two decades, Montgomery had been practicing narratives and representations in short stories, and finding the genre within which she preferred to work, or, at least, the genre that proved to have for her the greatest popular appeal: romantic stories of girl orphans (or children who were "virtually" orphans) in established settler communities in the "New World."

Montgomery's journals and *The Alpine Path*, her 1917 professional autobiography, drawn largely from the early journals and published in the Toronto magazine *Everywoman's World*, notably conflict in their accounts of the writing of *Anne*.[2] Montgomery indicates in the 1917 version that she had found a "faded entry" in an old notebook with the idea for the novel in the spring of 1904 (72); the earlier journals present the date as spring 1905 (*SJ* I 330). In *The Alpine Path* she records finishing the book in October 1905 (72); in the journal, she says it was (she "think[s]") January 1906 (*SJ* I 331).[3]

---

1 It should be noted that the numbers of stories and poems indicated in the Russell/Wilmshurst bibliography are based on early assessments of the published material: there may be more stories and poems from this period for which there is no record in Montgomery's ledger or in her scrapbooks, and there are stories and poems of uncertain dates.

2 Montgomery's journals have been published in four volumes to date since 1985 by Oxford University Press, edited by Mary Rubio and Elizabeth Waterston. A fifth and final volume is forthcoming in 2004.

3 The confusion in the dates may be simply a result of carelessness in the proofreading of the 1917 article, or it may be that Montgomery wanted to prolong the period of its writing. She wrote many years later to Macmillan that it had only taken her five months to write the novel (Bolger and Epperly 177); perhaps in the early years of its success she felt this would not appear to have been long enough to produce the best-seller that *Anne* had become.

Adding to this confusion, in a letter to her correspondent Ephraim Weber, she claims to have written it "last fall and winter" (Eggleston 51), or during the later part of 1906.[1] The most accurate account of *Anne's* writing seems to be a journal entry of 1914, in which Montgomery claims that she "remember[ed] well" writing "the opening paragraph of *Green Gables*" (*SJ* II 147):

> It was a moist, showery, sweet-scented evening in June ten years ago. I was sitting *on the end of the table*, in the old kitchen, my feet on the sofa, beside the west window, because I wanted to get the last gleams of daylight on my portfolio. I did not for a moment dream that the book I had just begun was to bring me the fame and success I had long dreamed of. So I wrote, [sic] the opening paragraphs quite easily, not feeling obliged to "write up" to any particular reputation or style. Just as I had finished my description of *Mrs. Lynde* and her home *Ewan* walked in. He had just moved to Cavendish from Stanley, where he had previously been boarding and this was his first call since moving. He stayed and chatted most of the evening, so no more of *Green Gables* was written that night. (*SJ* II 147)

The "Ewan" to whom Montgomery refers here is Presbyterian minister Ewan Macdonald,[2] to whom she would become engaged in 1906, and whom she would marry in 1911 following her grandmother's death. This passage suggests that the book was begun in 1904, but it may be that Montgomery's "ten years" is a bit general. She notes in her journal in 1906 that Ewan did not "get a boarding house in Cavendish so he boarded in Stanley until the spring of 1905" (*SJ* I 321). If this account is accurate, then the "five months" she claims in a letter to her correspondent George Boyd Macmillan for the writing of the book ran from June to October in 1905 (Bolger and Epperly 177).

It is difficult to validate the exact date for the writing of *Anne*

---

1   Montgomery wrote to Weber telling him about the acceptance of the novel for publication on 2 May, 1907.

2   Ewan Macdonald's name appears on his gravestone in Cavendish, PEI as *both* "Ewan" and "Ewen." Mongomery usually used "Ewan."

not only because of the differences in these two primary accounts, but because Montgomery's record of writing it was generated only after the fact of its acceptance. On 16 August, 1907, Montgomery noted that she had, earlier that year, "received a letter from the L.C. Page Co. of Boston accepting the MS of a book and offering to publish it on a royalty basis" (*SJ* I 330). Prior to this entry, there are no references to the account of the writing of *Anne* that is now so familiar to most of Montgomery's readers, of her discovery of a "faded entry" in one of the notebooks in which she scribbled ideas for her writing—"Elderly couple apply to orphan asylum for a boy. By mistake a girl is sent them" (*AP* 72, *SJ* I 330)[1]—nothing of the process of writing it, nor of typing it out, nor of her hopes for the book. There are no entries that convey her disappointment when the manuscript was repeatedly returned by publishers as she later wrote that it was. There is nothing of the story that has now become a major part of the Green Gables mythology, of Montgomery's putting the manuscript away in a hatbox in a closet after what she indicates in her journal in 1907 were four rejections,[2] and of finding it again the following year, sending it off to the Page Company in Boston, and, in April 1907, receiving their acceptance of the book with a request that she write a sequel. Montgomery simply summarized this story in the 16 August entry and revisited this first summary for her readers in the 1917 account. Her desire to keep the completion and fortunes of her work prior to acceptance secret, even from her journal, certainly problematizes Montgomery's position in relation to her personal writing; but it does seem to operate on the same principle she articulated

---

[1]   Montgomery identifies this notebook in her journal as one she had written "ten years before" (*SJ* I 330); this would date the notebook to 1895, her year at Dalhousie. This notebook does not appear to exist, and there is some confusion as to whether or not it was based on a newspaper clipping, or, as has been suggested, on the actual event of Montgomery's relations Rachael and Pierce Macneill's adoption of a "Home" child in 1892, having been sent a girl, according to John Willoughby, when they were expecting a boy. The Ellen connection is a bit obscure; but Montgomery herself does indicate in her journal in 1910 that, in fact, the adoption of Ellen by the Macneills was the source of the scribble in her notebook: "The idea of getting a child from an orphan asylum was suggested to me years ago as a possible germ for a story by the fact that Pierce Macneill got a little girl from one, and I jotted it down in my note book" (*SJ* II 40).

[2]   Montgomery notes five rejections in *The Alpine Path*.

with regard to her very first publication, in 1890.[1] She wrote then in her journal, "I did not dare hope it would be printed, so I never squeaked a word about it to anyone" (*SJ* I 35). She would repeat this sentiment to Weber in 1907, with reference to *Anne*: "I didn't squeak a word about it," she told him, "because I feared desperately I wouldn't find a publisher for it" (Eggleston 51).

According to the after-account of the book in *The Alpine Path, Anne of Green Gables* had initially been conceived as a "short serial for a certain Sunday School paper" (*AP* 72). Montgomery had been publishing stories in such serials since the late 1890s, and many of her short stories between 1900 and 1905 appeared in "Sunday School" papers, magazines directed at young people and concerned with the reinforcement of Christian ideas. (Four stories are included in this edition in Appendix A.) The story of Anne, Montgomery suggests, grew into a novel when, after she had written the first seven chapters, she found herself wanting to develop her heroine's story beyond the conventional Sunday School serial length. "I began to block out the chapters, devise, and select incidents and 'brood up' my heroine," she indicates in *The Alpine Path*. "Then the thought came, 'Write a book'" (72). The manuscript of *Anne of Green Gables* appears to confirm this process, seeming to have been written sequentially, chapter by chapter, with very few amendments (see A Note on the Manuscript 47). Montgomery comments in *The Alpine Path* that, after *Anne's* repeated rejections, she put it away, planning to "take her and reduce her to the original seven chapters of her first incarnation" (75–76), thus ending the story with the chapter "Anne Says Her Prayers," or before Marilla tells her she will stay at Green Gables. Montgomery's journal account again differs slightly here, noting as it does that she planned to "cut her down to the seven chapters of [her] original *idea*" (*SJ* I 331; emphasis added), or the length of the projected serial, which this entry implies had not already been written in that form. These seven chapters are, it is worth noting, the most "Sunday Schoolish," bringing Anne

---

[1] Montgomery is referring to her first publication, a poem, "On Cape Leforce," that appeared in *The Charlottetown Patriot*.

to the point of saying her first prayer, and are thus perceptible as the body of the text as she had originally imagined it.[1]

Although *Anne of Green Gables* would be Montgomery's first published novel, she had, by her own account, already written what she describes as a Sunday School novel of the kind *Anne* was to be. In 1925 Montgomery wrote in her journal that, prior to writing *Anne*, she had produced a "book whereof no record remaineth" (*SJ* III 240); that is, she destroyed it.[2] This book, like its successor, was repeatedly rejected (*SJ* III 240). The earlier text, or at least Montgomery's account of it, makes an interesting counterpart to *Anne*, because Montgomery did for it what she would later plan to do for her second novel: she indicates that she "boiled the book down to seven or eight chapters and sent it out to several Sunday School papers in the hope of having it taken as a serial" but "[n]obody would have it at any price" (*SJ* III 240). Finally, she writes, she "burned it," as she did for so much of her writing, such as her early journals and many of her letters (*SJ* III 240). This unsuccessful book would represent a significant turning-point for Montgomery. The acceptance of this novel, she maintained, "would have been the greatest misfortune that ever happened to '[her] literary career' [... since] it would probably have committed [her] to a lifetime of writing 'series' similar to it" (*SJ* III 240). Indeed, she makes the point that the rejection of the novel she called *A Golden Carol* was a *good* thing in that it compelled her to "vow[] that never again would [she] try to create a Sunday School heroine" (*SJ* III 240). "It was the re-action [sic]," she wrote, "that drove me to 'Anne' and probably kept me from making a dummy of her" (*SJ* III 240). The result of

---

[1]   The editors of *AA* have noted that Chapter VII of *AGG*, "Anne Says Her Prayers," is evocative of a popular text of the nineteenth century, *Jessica's First Prayer* (1867), by "Hesba Stretton" (Sarah Smith, 1832–1911). See *AA* 97, note 1.

[2]   As is the case for *Anne*, Montgomery does not mention this novel in her journal during the years that she was actually writing it, during the last year of the nineteenth century, in '99 or '00. I intended it for a "Sunday School Library book"—thinking that if I could get it accepted by one of the religious publishing houses I might make a few hundreds out of it. I modelled it after the fashion of the "Gypsy" and "Pansy" books of my childhood and had no idea of attempting anything beyond a pot-boiler. It was called *A Golden Carol*—a title punned from the name of the heroine, "Carol Golden," who was a girl at Halifax Ladies' College when the story opened. (*SJ* III 240)

Montgomery's reaction to *A Golden Carol* and her subsequent "vow," as she presents it here, was one of the best-known and most beloved characters in literature, and one of the most popular novels ever to have been published in North America. *Anne* sold over a million copies in Montgomery's life, and has been translated into many languages. New editions of the novel continue to appear; new translations continue to be made; the tourist and merchandising industries relating to Anne continue to expand in Canada and globally. Indeed, Anne's popularity is as strong as ever, and critics continue to investigate the reasons for and the implications of the extraordinary longevity of her appeal.

One persistent explanation of Anne's attraction to readers is her putative "realism." Montgomery herself made this claim, writing in her journal in 1907 that she had "cast 'moral' and 'Sunday School' ideals to the winds and made her 'Anne' a real human girl" (*SJ* I 331). Similarly, she maintained to Macmillan in 1909 that her "other [styles of writing] [we]re only skilfully assumed garments to suit the particular story being 'built'" (Bolger and Epperly 44). "I wrote *Anne* in my *own* style," she stated, "and I think that is the secret of her success" (Bolger and Epperly 44). In *The Alpine Path*, in a comment that is frequently quoted as an index of Montgomery's desire to see all her fiction as anti-didactic, she cited an earlier journal entry: "I write a great many juvenile stories," she observed, and

> I like doing these, but I should like it better if I didn't have to drag a "moral" into most of them. They won't sell without it, as a rule. So in the moral must go, broad or subtle, as suits the fibre of the particular editor I have in view. The kind of juvenile story I like best to write—and read, too, for the matter of that—is a good, jolly one, "art for art's sake," or rather "fun for fun's sake," with no insidious moral hidden away in it like a pill in a spoonful of jam! (*AP* 61–2)

While Montgomery deplores here the editorial imperative that she "drag a 'moral'" into most of her stories, she did not ever take a position on her own or any other writing that effectively functions outside of what can be understood to be a "moral" framework. As Clarence Karr has observed, it is clear that "she expected her readers to be more than simply entertained. There were hidden messages that would instruct and guide—messages more likely to be received by a modern, secular audience than if she had highlighted and preached them" (126). Montgomery's sense of "art for art's sake" seems, then, to have to do with her ability to write what she wanted, rather than the freedom to produce a literature that was *not* at some level comprehensible in "moral" terms.

Anne of Green Gables is no exception. Although presented as "a real human girl," Anne remains, as we are regularly reminded throughout the novel, extraordinary. She is more winning and has a "brighter face, and bigger, starrier eyes, and more delicate features" (231) than those of her more "common" acquaintance. She is naturally clever and articulate: in only a few months of school during her eleven years prior to arriving at Green Gables, she has absorbed most of the material in the *Royal Readers* that were used, as the editors of *The Annotated Anne* point out, in Nova Scotia and P.E.I. schools at the end of the nineteenth century and the beginning of the twentieth (*AA* 89, note 20), and that represent the literary context from which much of the quoted material in *Anne of Green Gables* is drawn. Anne is naturally polite, despite having spent all her early years, from only a few weeks of age, in an environment that is presented as being peopled exclusively with uneducated and abusive guardians. While much is made of her never having said a prayer before, she is shown to be much more spiritual than the other little girls in her Sunday School class. She makes funny mistakes, but she is never actually miscreant; she does not, it is made clear in the story, lie or steal or show disloyalty to her friends. As a reviewer in *The New York Times Saturday Review of Books* observed in 1908, Anne has been remarkably able to transcend the environments and circumstances in which she has grown up (see Appendix E 391).

Indeed, despite the representation of the various pitfalls on the path to young adulthood that is charted in the novel, Anne is a model of intelligent virtue; in this she is not, in fact, unlike the spirited "Pansy" heroines produced by Isabella Macdonald Alden (1841–1930), upon which Montgomery indicates she had modeled her reported first novel's heroine, Carol Golden.[1] There is a lot of Sunday School—and "Pansy"—about Anne, not only in the original seven chapters, but throughout the book. Anne is not the "dummy" that Carol Golden putatively was, but her story is nonetheless directed toward an exemplary and "moral" conclusion. When Anne chooses to give up the Avery scholarship and to stay instead with Marilla after Matthew's death, this decision is clearly framed in terms of what is represented in the novel as a responsibility and an obligation. Once she decides to stay at Green Gables, she is shown with "a smile on her lips and peace in her heart" (326). "She had," we are told, "looked her duty courageously in the face and found it a friend—as duty ever is when we meet it frankly" (326). In *Green Gables*, Anne learns that "duty" supersedes ambition and that responsibility to others is more important than the satisfaction of individual and personal desires. Not necessarily a "lesson" of the Sunday-School-text kind (catechism, for instance, or paraphrases) that, it is pointed out in the novel, Anne learns by rote, this is the culmination of the story that structures the narrative of the heroine's education. It is, moreover, a very "Pansy" lesson, framed in ways that are evocative of Macdonald Alden's novels, notably in the positioning of the lesson in relation to life experience and spiritual growth, and in questioning the value of mechanical Sunday-School instruction (see Appendix D).

Montgomery observed in her journal shortly after the publication of *Anne*, in a period of profound depression, that she was

---

[1] "Pansy," pen-name of American writer Isabella Macdonald Alden (1841–1930); Alden's novels for children, including the popular "Pansy" series, are of the Sunday School variety. *The Feminist Companion to Literature in English* notes that Macdonald published more than 120 books, mostly for children, as well as, from 1874, editing a Sunday school magazine called *Pansy*. See *AGG* 160, note 2. See also Appendix D. The "Pansy" connection is an interesting one. For instance, in Alden's *Links in Rebecca's Life* there are several suggestive convergences with the language of *AGG*. The heroine Rebecca is concerned, as Anne is, with her "besetting sins" (151); Rebecca's husband Frank refers to her as a "Job's comforter" (154), the phrase Montgomery uses in reference to Mrs. Lynde's comments on Matthew and Marilla's adoption of an orphan; Rebecca writes in her journal of knowing that something she did not want to do "would be a cross" (163), the phrase Anne uses in reference the burden of bearing names which do not appeal to her. There are several similar echoes in *Ruth Erskine's Crosses*, notably in the use of the term "kindred spirit" (30). See 84, note 1 on the sources for this phrase.

grateful for her ability to "keep the shadows of [her] life out of [her] work": "I would not wish to darken any other life—I want instead to be a messenger of optimism and sunshine" (*SJ* I 339). She would later present this impulse as an imperative in a 1915 article for *Everywoman's World*, "The Way to Make a Book" (see Appendix B). "[I]f we have something to say," she maintained there,

> that will bring a whiff of fragrance to a tired soul and to a weary heart, or a glint of sunshine to a clouded life, then that something is worth saying, and it is our duty to try to say it as well as in us lies. (366)

Art, in other words, in Montgomery's view, is to be spiritually uplifting (as well, clearly, as "fun"). These comments serve as a reminder that Montgomery did not significantly alter the representation of her heroine when she decided to turn her Sunday School story into a novel. They also emphasize that Montgomery's "own style" is not, after all, as different from her earlier work as she would have her readers see. Indeed, she reworks in *Anne* some material she had already developed in earlier stories, notably the liniment cake and the jumping on Miss Barry incidents, both of which she had treated in stories, in the latter case in "Our Uncle Wheeler" (1898), and in the former case in at least three versions: "A New-Fashioned Flavoring" (1898), "Patty's Mistake" (1902), and "The Cake that Prissy Made" (1903) (see Appendix A). Although she often maintained, as she did to Macmillan in 1909, that *Anne* was her first truly characteristic work, *Anne*, in fact, represents the maturation of the "style" and the kinds of stories she had been developing since the 1890s and from which she would not significantly depart—although she certainly wished she could, on occasion—for the rest of her career.

★   ★   ★

Gender and the "Feminism" of Anne

Montgomery's clearly stated sense of an author's duty is best understood in relation to early twentieth-century social constructions of gender in North America. That is, although it is certain that Montgomery saw morality in fiction as an imperative for all writers, male and female, it is also certain that her perception of duty for writers was based at least in part on gender. She directs her comments, in *Everywoman's World* at any rate ("The Way to Make a Book"), primarily to women and much of her writing to girls. It is not hard to see that an idea of woman's authorial duty comes into play in the structuring of the narrative of *Anne of Green Gables* around issues of gendered identification and a growth towards the "right" performance of femininity. When Anne gives up her education and, in the later novels, her ambition to write, the implication is that these sacrifices have been made *because* she is a girl, whose responsibility is to remain at home and care for her husband and children. The first novel ends with Anne's having matured to the point of recognizing that her duty as a girl is more important and will ultimately be more rewarding than either her education or her ambition. The position of the narrative at the moment of Anne's transformation from ambitious girl to responsible woman is clear: she has, as virtually everyone in the novel who matters also affirms (Marilla, Mrs. Lynde, Mrs. Allan, Gilbert), done the right thing when she accepts her "duty."

The situating of Anne's duty in the performance of femininity is emphasized in the prefacing of *Anne of Avonlea*, the first sequel to *Green Gables*, published in 1909 but begun well before the first novel appeared, with an epilogue quoted from American poet John Greenleaf Whittier's settler-narrative poem "Among the Hills" (1868):

> Flowers spring to blossom where she walks
> The careful ways of duty,
> Our hard, stiff lines of life with her
> Are flowing curves of beauty.[1]

Anne's story, it is suggested in the opening of *Anne of Avonlea*, will continue to develop with reference to the idea of feminine duty

---

[1]   *The Complete Poetical Works of Whittier* (Boston: Houghton Mifflin, 1894), 88.

that ends *Anne of Green Gables*; and Anne will, in other words—
as the subsequent sequels in fact show she does—move increasingly away from the public and professional career of her early
dreams and more insistently towards domesticity and the "beau-
tifying" of life that is presented as woman's work in Whittier's
poem. As she does so, moreover, her immediate environment will
be improved, as "flowers" and "beauty" alter the "hard, stiff lines
of life" *in* the novels, as well as *through* them—or in other words,
in both the narrative representation of women's work and the
author's performance of it in the writing of her novel.

Gillian Thomas articulates a widespread and popular view
when she argues that the seven sequels Montgomery wrote after
Anne of Green Gables become "progressively unsatisfactory" (23) as
Anne moves from being an appealingly "spirited individualist" in
the first novel to "a rather dreary conformist" in the last (24). For
Thomas, Anne's "decline" is marked in her shifting away from her
early writerly ambitions to taking up motherhood as a profession
to the exclusion of all other activities: she becomes, Thomas
observes, a "matron" (23). But the culmination of Anne's story in
motherhood should not be surprising. Anne has already chosen
this direction by the end of *Green Gables*, which is concerned with
her education precisely *as* an incipient mother. Like many of
Montgomery's early short stories (such as "Patty's Mistake" and
"A New-Fashioned Flavoring," reproduced in Appendix A), *Anne*,
as Patricia Kelly Santelmann observes, pays a good deal of attention to the heroine's training and eventual skill in housewifely
work (65–66). Thus, when Anne accepts her role as Marilla's care-
giver at the end of a novel that was initially written without a
sequel in mind, the implication is not only that everything else has
been directed towards her making this decision, but that the decision itself marks a crucial recognition by Anne of what Gilbert
describes as "destiny" (408). Although Gilbert is referring here to
Anne's long refusal to be friends with him, his comment empha-
sizes the extent to which the conclusion of the first of the *Anne*
books reproduces a narrative that is comprehensible in terms of
the contemporary North American constructions of gender and
race that also figure in Whittier's poem. As Montgomery would
suggest in a later interview should be the case for all women,

Anne's work as a teacher should not conflict with her domestic obligations (See Appendix C.2 379).

Eve Kornfield and Susan Jackson have suggested that *Anne of Green Gables* belongs to a nineteenth-century American genre of female coming-of-age novels that work to inculcate girls into an ideology of domesticity while offering, in the context of the fiction, a temporary respite from "the bonds of womanhood" (150). Like Louisa May Alcott's *Little Women* (1868) and Margaret Sidney's *Five Little Peppers and How They Grew* (1878), *Anne*, they maintain, is a "female *Bildungsroman*," a novel that marks a narrative resistance to the limitations imposed upon women in the nineteenth century while ultimately reaffirming the perceived importance of women's acceptance of these limitations. T.D. MacLulich takes a similar position when he discusses *Anne* and the later *Emily* books as female "portraits of the artist," or *Kunstlerromane*: he argues that, "[i]n her fiction, Montgomery demonstrates a strong awareness of the limitations that hedge a woman's life, but she seems unable to imagine any escape for her characters from a conventional role" (89).

Such a narrative impulse might well situate Montgomery's fiction—and *Anne* in particular—in relation to the idea of realism MacLulich discusses, and thus to the frequently bleak "New Woman" fiction produced by some of Montgomery's English-Canadian contemporaries, such as Sara Jeannette Duncan, Maria Amelia Fytche, and Joanna Wood. That is, *Anne*'s decision to stay at Green Gables might have been represented far more negatively than it is, as a grim reminder, as in so much "New Woman" fiction in Canada at any rate, of the gendered limitations the novel seems to foreground. The romantic and happy ending of *Anne*, however, situated as it is in the affirmation of what Kornfield and Jackson describe as "the womanly virtue of self-sacrifice" (150), conveys another "message" altogether than "New Woman" fiction does even when it too, as Misao Dean has suggested it does, forecloses the possibility of radical change or female "advancement" (Dean 75–76). *Anne* does appear, as MacLulich and Kornfield and Jackson have all observed, to endorse as "duty" and implicitly as biological imperative or "destiny" the heroine's choice of what is conventional and expected.

The "feminism" of *Anne* does not seem to have been an issue for readers at the time of its publication: there is scarcely any reference to gender politics in contemporary reviews of the novel (see Appendix E). It has, however, become one for readers since the so-called second wave of feminism in the 1960s and '70s, also the moment, significantly, that scholarly attention began to be focused in a consistent way on the text. While not all of this scholarship has been feminist in its interpretive positioning, it has collectively drawn attention to the function of *Anne* as an important and popular work that represents and negotiates in problematic ways early twentieth-century tensions between restrictive ideas of femininity and first-wave feminist politics. Critics have been notably polarized in their valuing of the novel on these terms. One school of thought has tended to adopt the stance articulated by MacLulich, Kornfield and Jackson, and Thomas, that the novel demonstrates a desire for greater freedom and social responsibility for women, but ends up foreclosing the possibility of such freedom and thus reinforcing Montgomery's own "limited" position as a professional woman writer who fulfilled her domestic obligations first. Another has held that the novel presents a heroine who shows young female readers the way to independence and self-representation: Temma F. Berg, for instance, has argued that the novel is feminist and "empower[ing]" (155), in "subtle" but important ways subverting the patriarchal framework in which Anne is located. Anne is "feminist" for critics such as Berg because she is configured in terms of agency. From this perspective, Anne is not seen to be submitting passively to ideological imperatives, but to be turning them to her own advantage, choosing what is represented as her "duty" while, as Santelmann has suggested, taking on a new and important position as a subject and as a self-sufficient and self-determining member of the Avonlea community. Anne thus might be seen to represent a desire for gendered authority—as a writer of her own romantic narratives, as the heroine of her own self-constructed adventures, as a young girl whose development to adulthood is shown by her female teacher to be a matter of social and cultural significance.

Other readers have found the same kind of feminist "empower[ment]" in *Anne*. The editors of the 1998 *Annotated*

Anne have suggested that the framing of the novel between two quotations from the poetry of Robert Browning signals its incipient concern with female agency. The epigraph, from "Evelyn Hope," "gives an impression of [...] a female persona that can act also as an agent of fate and is acted on by fate" (460); the closing line, from "Pippa Passes," evokes, they argue, a heroine who "profoundly affects the feelings and actions of others whom she unknowingly encounters" (461). Elizabeth Epperly has made a case for *Anne*'s resistance of dominant romantic narratives as an indication not only of the novel's impulse towards "realism," but of its foregrounding of "Anne's voice and [...] her point of view" (28). In her discussion of Chapter XXVIII, "An Unfortunate Lily Maid," as it responds to and reproduces Tennyson's idyll *Lancelot and Elaine*, Epperly notes that Anne's romantic vision of herself as heroine is comically inverted in the incident (26). What is implicit in the inversion Epperly describes is the novel's resistance to a genre of romance in which the heroine's sacrifice is presented as an erotic spectacle. This scene works to reconfigure the role of the woman in the piece, and to question in important ways how it is that gender is performed: in this case, Anne "directs" the scene and stars in it. That the scene goes awry is important, not because it shows her to have been disempowered on the basis of gender (Gilbert, after all, does rescue her), or trapped within particular notions of romantic love, but because, as Anne comes to recognize, those notions are themselves faulty, at least in the twentieth-century North American context Anne inhabits and the novel represents.[1]

In these readings of the novel, Anne represents an idea of equality in terms of social and cultural value. While the novel reinforces biological difference and concomitant divisions of labour (Anne is unquestionably "feminine"), it also posits an equal intellectual and physical development in boys and girls. Anne is smarter than all the boys but Gilbert, who is her intellectual equal; she runs faster than all the boys, as we see when she arrives at school amongst them in the episode of Mr. Phillips' punishment. Boys and girls in Avonlea, it is suggested, contribute

---

[1] On romance in the novel, see also Ahmansson 101–114.

equally if differently to the successful functioning of community, and the work of one is not less valuable than that of the other. The key to Anne's story, after all, as is demonstrated in the opening chapters and in Montgomery's construction of the novel around the reference to the scribbled entry in the notebook, is that she is not a boy. Matthew's last talk with Anne significantly returns the narrative to this fact. Having seen that Matthew is growing older, Anne says "wistfully," "If I had been the boy you sent for, [...] I'd be able to help you so much now and spare you in a hundred ways. I could find it in my heart to wish I had been, just for that." "Well now, I'd rather have you than a dozen boys, Anne," Matthew responds. "Just you mind that—rather than a dozen boys. Well now, I guess it wasn't a boy that took the Avery scholarship, was it? It was a girl—my girl—my girl that I'm proud of" (318). What is suggested here is that it is precisely her gender that makes her so important to Matthew and Marilla, and, by extension, to her world. When Anne takes up her "duty" at the end of the novel, she is thus doing a work that is understood to be not an index of gender limitations but itself vital to the sustenance and the future of the community. In the narrative of *Green Gables*, gender difference is affirmed; inequality is not. It may be that the feminism of *Anne*—and at least part of its long appeal—inheres in this affirmation.

Although second-wave feminist readings have foregrounded a conception of the heroine's agency and of the extent to which *Anne of Green Gables* demonstrates its concern with restrictive ideologies of gender, the categorization of the novel in terms of feminist politics (the idea that it is a "feminist" novel) is nonetheless complicated by Montgomery's own frequently articulated position outside of early twentieth-century feminism. Montgomery never aligned herself with first-wave feminism; in fact, she often strove to establish a distance between herself and women who were continuing the late nineteenth-century struggle for equal civil and social rights on the basis of gender. Her often oppositional and seemingly anti-feminist position tended to be embedded primarily in her strong sense that women should not, in fact, have any career other than wife and mother, unless they could accomplish their work, as she herself did, without interrupting or in any way adversely affecting what she clearly saw as the first responsibility of women, to home and family.

Montgomery articulated this position in an interview that appeared in *The Toronto Star Weekly* on 28 November, 1925 (see Appendix C). Earlier, in 1910, she had distanced herself from woman suffrage, the touchstone of first-wave feminism, in an interview published in the Boston *Republic* when she was in Massachusetts visiting her American publisher L.C. Page at his home. Mollie Gillen has cited this interview in *The Wheel of Things*, observing that "in the [article's] ensuing discussion of women's work and ideals, Miss Montgomery was revealed as 'distinctly conservative [....] She has no favour for woman suffrage; she believes in the home-loving woman'" (Gillen 85–86). Montgomery would affirm this lack of "favour" later and repeatedly. For example, she wrote to Weber in 1909:

> As for the woman suffrage question, I feel very little interest in it. But I *do* believe that a woman with property of her own should have a voice in making the laws. Am I not as intelligent and capable of voting for my country's good as the Frenchman who chops my wood for me, and who may be able to tell his left hand from his right, but who cannot read or write? (Eggleston 91)[1]

Montgomery's apparent lack of interest in woman suffrage and her endorsement of "the home-loving woman" who should not have a public career would seem to place her at odds with the feminist politics of her contemporaries, and thus to reinforce that notion that the culmination of Anne's career in motherhood, in the later novels, indicates her position *outside* of feminist politics. But when Montgomery's comments—and, importantly, her fiction—are aligned with those of her feminist contemporaries (notably, for instance, English-Canadian novelist Nellie L. McClung), although there is some distance in the sense of the extent to which women ought to operate in the public sphere as

---

[1]   See also *SJ* II 234. The engagement of this argument with ideologies of Anglo-Saxon "racial" identity will be evident.

well as in the home, there is actually remarkably little difference in terms of gender ideologies as they pertain to ideas of biological responsibility and particularly to the prevailing feminist ideology of maternalism.[1]

In fact, *Anne of Green Gables* is pervasively and didactically maternalist. That is, the novel is concerned primarily with the development of a young girl from prepubescent child to young adult, charting her development in terms of her academic as well as moral and domestic education in maternal womanliness. It is, as Kornfield and Jackson have observed, a novel of feminine education that is focused on the kind of work performed by Miss Stacy for the girls of Avonlea, of laying "the foundation [...] for [their] whole future [lives]" (272). As Anne tells Marilla, Miss Stacy teaches the girls that they "couldn't be too careful what habits [they] formed and what ideals [they] developed in their teens, because by the time [they] were twenty [their] characters would be developed" (272). However, while the novel is focused on the education of girls to right womanhood, it is also concerned with the promotion of maternalism in a broader sense. As Margaret Atwood has observed, the novel can be seen to be as much Marilla's story of maternal development as it is Anne's toward responsible womanhood (Atwood 335–36). Marilla, after all, discovers her "untapped springs of mother-love" through Anne's affection and in the process becomes a "better and happier" (315), more "mellow" person (407); such, at any rate, is the implication in the representation of Anne's mistakes as most often the result of Marilla's. For instance, Marilla fails to notice the amethyst brooch on her shawl before she puts it away; she forgets that she has put the bottle of raspberry cordial in the cellar; she neglects to tell Anne about the liniment in the vanilla bottle. Her role in Anne's trials strongly suggests that the older woman is to learn from them, as Anne does. But Marilla's lesson is not exactly the same as Anne's: Anne is innately maternal, knowing, apparently instinctively, how to care for children. She learns how to choose the putatively correct path towards womanhood, when

---

[1] See Cecily Devereux, "Writing with a 'Definite Purpose': L.M. Montgomery, Nellie L. McClung, and the Politics of Imperial Motherhood in Fiction for Children," *Canadian Children's Literature* 99 26.3 (2000): 6–22.

there are other options presented to her. Marilla, conversely, learns how to find the "maternity she had missed" and how to be a responsible example of what would be designated in the early twentieth century as the "mother-woman."

Arguably, Marilla's transformation suggests that *Anne* should be understood in relation to the principles of feminism of the so-called first wave or, loosely, the period between the 1870s and the 1930s. By the first decade of the twentieth century, feminism had come to be associated less with the hazardous, anti-patriarchal figure of the "New Woman" who appeared to resist the representation of gender in terms of biological imperatives, and more frequently with a politics of "advancing" women towards political and social agency on the basis of a nationally and, usually, racially identified maternity. Feminism by the early 1900s in Canada was characteristically maternal. Indeed, feminism in Great Britain and in Canada had begun as early as the 1880s to adopt the rhetoric of maternalism that was circulating then in the discourse of "race" improvement, in Anglo-imperial contexts and *for* the empire. The context for this burgeoning rhetoric of racialized maternalism was the expansionist impetus motivating the growth of the British and other empires. As empires competing for dominance acquired more and more territory during and after the 1870s, the need to fill the territories with racially identifiable colonial presence became, as Anna Davin has noted in her important study, "Imperialism and Motherhood," increasingly pressing. To ensure reproduction, Davin observes, motherhood "was to be given new dignity: it was the duty and destiny of women to be the 'mothers of the race,' but also their great reward" (13)—as of course it is for Marilla, and as it eventually will be for Anne.

In Anglo-imperial locations, such as in Canada, women were to be empowered in society *because* they were potential mothers, whose role in bearing children had come by the end of the nineteenth century to be represented as the crucial work for the preservation of what was usually referred to as "the race." Feminists such as Charlotte Perkins Gilman in the United States and Nellie McClung in Canada would argue that women had to be empowered politically and socially in order to protect their own work of child-bearing and to be enabled to direct their maternal "instinct" towards society as a whole, "to serve and save the race," as McClung put it in her 1915 feminist manifesto, *In Times Like These* (100). The feminist "mother of the race" was not imagined by feminists as simply the passive reproductive vessel or breeder conceived in some of the period's eugenicist rhetoric, but a social and political agent who would mother "the race" at large and keep it from moral and physical degeneration. In early twentieth-century Canada, the "mother of the race" would in effect *become* what was also called the "New Woman," the imagined representative of feminist politics and women's social "advancement": the two terms would be used in English-Canadian feminism interchangeably.

Montgomery is clearly well on the conservative side of the early twentieth-century feminist spectrum. She is nonetheless engaging with feminism when she speaks of suffrage and of maternal "duty," and she is also engaging with it when she writes a novel like *Anne of Green Gables* for which gender is the crux. Although many of the "lessons" Anne learns must be seen to be embedded in an idea of female domesticity, and to be leading her toward the ideal of duty which ends the novel, it is also clear that gender issues figure in *Anne*, not only in the crucial issue of Anne's not being a boy, but in the way the narrative draws attention to issues of gender inequality. Marilla and Mrs. Lynde are both important figures in the representation of these issues in *Green Gables*. Mrs. Lynde is shown on the one hand to be the dominant figure in her home: Thomas Lynde is identified as "Rachel Lynde's husband" (54). She is also a "red-hot politician" (179)—far more so than her husband—and she is evidently on the side of suffragism, arguing in a very McClungian way that "Canada [was] going to the dogs the way things [were] being run at Ottawa, and that [...] if women were allowed to vote [Canada] would soon see a blessed change" (181). On the other hand, Mrs. Lynde opposes the ordination of female ministers, a contentious issue through the nineteenth century, and a topic that was prominent in Presbyterian and subsequently United Church debate in North America in the early twentieth century; she also opposes higher education for women.

Mrs. Lynde's views, however, are not presented as themselves dominant. While her comments indicate the extent to which the novel is concerned with the implications of gender ideologies—particularly for girls, and particularly as they grow up and situate themselves in their world—they are contested and sometimes undermined by other views. Marilla, who is more ambivalent about women preachers and the vote, strongly supports the idea of education, at least for the purposes of "a girl being fitted to earn her own living whether she ever has to or not" (274). Montgomery, who demonstrated in her journal her sense of anxiety that she could well find herself in this situation after the death of her grandmother, was certainly aware of the immediate obstacle posed by gender for women not only in terms of the pursuit of their ambitions but of their ability to earn enough to support themselves when careers were limited and remuneration was so much less for women than for men even for the same work. It is clear that Montgomery was herself, like Marilla and Anne, an advocate of higher education for women; she desired it for herself, and she wrote about it in her 1896 article for the *Halifax Herald*, "The Thirty Sweet Girl Graduates of Dalhousie University" (see Appendix C). It is also clear that she, like Mrs. Lynde, did not think women ought to preach. Montgomery would present her early ideal of the minister's wife in *Anne of Green Gables*, and she would not diverge from that ideal in her own practice or thinking.

Anne, as is later emphasized in the 1936 novel *Anne of Windy Poplars*, is "not one of those dreadful new women" (*AWP* 187), but she is not unlike one of those *other* "New Women" of the early twentieth century, the maternal feminists.[1] The same might be said of Montgomery herself. Not a political activist, Montgomery is nonetheless addressing complex gender issues in her first published novel in ways that she would continue to do throughout her career. Despite her disavowals of feminist thinking, she shows her awareness and sometimes her resentment of social codes of gender in a good deal of her personal writing as well as in her fiction. While she certainly achieved her childhood

---

[1] See Cecily Devereux, "'Not One of Those Dreadful New Women': L.M. Montgomery and the Politics of Imperial Motherhood," in *Windows and Words: A Look at Canadian Children's Literature*, ed. Susan Cooper and Aida Hudson (Ottawa: U of Ottawa P, 2003) 119–130.

goal of becoming a writer, it is not clear that she ever felt she had reached the point of being satisfied with the work she produced and with the critical acceptance of her writing as something "worth while." Her fiction was immensely popular, and she was for most of her adult life one of the best-known women in Canada and one of the most popular writers of fiction in English in the world. Still, as Mary Rubio has observed, she was conscious and resentful of remaining outside of the largely male, modernist literary establishment in English Canada, even though she was much better-known and her work much more widely read than that of almost any other author in Canada.[1] She also resented the restrictions on education and income that affected the ability of women to be self-sufficient, and she was aware that her gender made her vulnerable in some business affairs, such as, in her view, her contracts with her first publisher.

There are clear contradictions in the way Montgomery presented herself as a public figure. While a professional writer and what Carole Gerson describes as a "canny businesswoman" ("'Dragged at Anne's Chariot Wheels'" 51), Montgomery was a woman who appeared to the public as a minister's wife and the mother of two sons. She did not always identify herself as "L.M. Montgomery" outside her writing, and she always maintained that her work as "Mrs. Macdonald" came before her work as a writer. Yet she clearly had ambivalent feelings about the politics of feminism, about the involvement of women in public spheres, and about their professions. She saw women as mothers first and professionals second, and had a strong sense of herself as exceptional. In Montgomery's representations throughout her career, from the 1896 *Halifax Herald* article to her late writing, only remarkable and highly motivated women such as herself had any business venturing beyond motherhood. She thus presents a model of gendered success and configures a range of potentially "feminist" heroines such as Anne at the same time that she seems

---

[1]   Rubio has suggested that Montgomery "was mostly angry at not being respected by the literary establishment, [that] Toronto literary mafia who put upon her as being a woman writer. It caused [a] severe depression and gave her enormous emotional and mental strain" (Rubio qtd. in *Today's Senior* [July 1999], clipping in Special Collections, University of Guelph).

to limit these possibilities for most women, reinforcing in her life what critics have seen in her fiction, and, importantly, drawing attention to the kinds of conflicts professional women had, of necessity, to negotiate in the late nineteenth and early twentieth centuries—and arguably still negotiate in the twenty-first.

★   ★   ★

A Note on Montgomery's Literary Allusions

Montgomery's writing in *Anne of Green Gables* is highly and almost constantly allusive, both in direct quotations and in other less overt references. There are two primary sources for the references in *Anne*. Many of the quotations and allusions are biblical, or relate to catechism, hymns, translations, and paraphrases, as well as to standard texts of religious education for children, such as the *Peep of Day* series (see 102, note 1). Montgomery's family and her community, as her biographers have shown, were staunchly Presbyterian, and Montgomery grew up with a strong awareness of these texts. Many more of the quotations are drawn from material included in the series of readers used in Nova Scotia schools: Montgomery indicates in her journal that these readers were used in her education in Prince Edward Island. Related to this set of allusions are other quotations and references which pertain to works not in these readers but which are written by canonical writers whose works do figure in the readers. Montgomery quotes extensively from Sir Walter Scott; Alfred, Lord Tennyson; Felicia Hemans; John Greenleaf Whittier; Henry Wadsworth Longfellow; James Russell Lowell; George Gordon, Lord Byron; Robert Browning; Elizabeth Barrett Browning; and Robert Burns. She also quotes from numerous poets who are frequently categorized as "lesser" or "minor" poets of the nineteenth century, but whose work figured prominently in readers until well into the twentieth century: these writers include Thomas Campbell, William Edmonstoune Aytoun, and Caroline Sheridan Norton. Montgomery does not allude to much English-Canadian writing in *Anne*, although she increasingly will in her later work.

Most of the literary texts Montgomery quotes in *Anne* appeared in anthologies—not only school readers but also elocution readers and other kinds of collections that were widely available in the late nineteenth century. Ten of the works quoted, for instance, can be found in *Bell's Standard Elocutionist*. In the same vein, Montgomery cites several Shakespearean sources, and her references are primarily to excerpts from the plays that appeared in the readers as well as in collections of dialogues and elocution pieces: the famous "Seven Ages of Man" speech of Jacques in *As You Like It* is one example, and Mark Antony's speech on the death of Caesar is another.[1] More obscure references may have come from popular collections of the period. It is possible, for instance, that Montgomery was familiar with Edmund Clarence Stedman's *An American Anthology, 1787–1900*.[2] Although there is a common post-Romantic vocabulary shared by much popular nineteenth-century poetry in certain genres, there are also indications in *Anne* that Montgomery had read some of the poems selected by Stedman, especially some of the more sentimental ones; certainly, she seems to echo some of them, sometimes ironically, in Anne's speeches.

It will be evident that most of the quoted material draws upon sources that are curricular and didactic. The references in *Anne* indicate Montgomery's own educational context and, in most cases, do not range far beyond it. However, the allusions in *Anne* arguably have more to do with the narrative than with Montgomery herself. The story is of Anne's education in a P.E.I. school and in a Presbyterian homestead; Montgomery returns to the texts of her own childhood and adolescence because her story is about a girl's education in the same context, and most of the references thus function primarily as didactic markers and part of the moral work of the narrative as a whole.

Anne's allusions, with their emphasis on prescribed texts, also

---

[1]   New Ed. 1892. The texts in *Bell's* are "The Battle of Hohenlinden" (238); "Mary, Queen of Scots" (299); "The Battle of Flodden and the Death of Marmion" (312); "Edinburgh after Flodden" (313); "Elegy in a Country Churchyard" (325); "The Downfall of Poland" (337); "Bingen on the Rhine" (376); "The Seven Ages of Man" (from *As You Like It*) (396); "Henry V at Harfleur" (from *Henry V*) (406); "Antony over Caesar's Body" (from *Julius Caesar*) (435). There are also excerpts from *The Lady of the Lake*, Byron's "Childe Harold," and John Home's *Douglas*.

[2]   1900, 1968.

function as indices of location, situating the novel in relation to P.E.I. and to the English-Canadian and Anglo-imperial curriculum. The tendency to cite writing that is clearly rooted in an imperial and sometimes emigrationist context, especially Scots, has been noted in *The Annotated Anne* (420). There are also references to American settler writing, such as, for instance, Whittier's "Cobbler Keezar's Vision." Other works cited suggest Montgomery's interest in constructing a didactic novel directed at girls and feminine education, the solid foundation to which Miss Stacy refers when she instructs the teen-age girls. As I have suggested, this education is not concerned only with domesticity but also with individual intellectual and social equality. The many references to the works of Felicia Hemans strongly suggest this feminist impulse: most of these references pertain to Hemans' configurations of heroic women. The embedding of the novel between quotations from Robert Browning has already been noted (see Introduction 24–25); the references to Charlotte Brontë's *Jane Eyre* reinforce the novel's focus on the education of young girls to self-sufficient womanhood; the cultural specificity of the book suggests that what is being constructed in the text is ultimately an ideal of heroic womanhood, largely in an imperial context, and specifically in the "New World."

Works Cited

Ahmansson, Gabriella. *A Life and Its Mirrors: A Feminist Reading of L.M. Montgomery's Fiction*. Stockholm: Uppsala, 1991.

Atwood, Margaret. "Afterword." *Anne of Green Gables*. L.M. Montgomery. 1908. Toronto: McClelland and Stewart, 1992. 331–36.

Barry, Wendy E., Margaret Anne Doody, and Mary E. Doody Jones, eds. *The Annotated Anne of Green Gables*. L.M. Montgomery. New York and Oxford: Oxford UP, 1997.

Bell, David Charles. *Bell's Standard Elocutionist*. London: Hodder and Stoughton, 1892.

Berg, Temma F. "*Anne of Green Gables*: A Girl's Reading." Reimer 153–64.

Bolger, Francis. *The Years Before "Anne."* 1974. Halifax: Nimbus, 1991.

——— and Elizabeth Epperly, eds. *My Dear Mr. M: Letters to G.B. Macmillan from L.M. Montgomery.* Toronto: Oxford UP, 1992.

Colin, Molly. "It All Began with Anne." *Publishers Weekly* 19 Oct. 1992: 27–28.

Davin, Anna. "Imperialism and Motherhood." *History Workshop Journal* 5 (1978): 9–65.

Dean, Misao. *Practising Femininity: Domestic Realism and the Performance of Gender in Early Canadian Fiction.* Toronto: U of Toronto P, 1998.

Eggleston, Wilfrid. *The Green Gables Letters, from L.M. Montgomery to Ephraim Weber, 1905–1909.* Ottawa: Borealis, 1981.

Epperly, Elizabeth R. "Approaching the Montgomery Manuscripts." Rubio 1994 74–83.

———. *The Fragrance of Sweet-Grass: L.M. Montgomery's Heroines and the Pursuit of Romance.* Toronto: U of Toronto P, 1992.

Gammel, Irene and Elizabeth Epperly. *L.M Montgomery and Canadian Culture.* Toronto: U of Toronto P, 1999.

Gerson, Carole. "'Dragged at Anne's Chariot Wheels': The Triangle of Author, Publisher, and Fictional Character." Gammel and Epperly 49–63.

Gillen, Mollie. *The Wheel of Things: A Biography of L.M. Montgomery.* Toronto: Fitzhenry and Whiteside, 1975.

Heilbron, Alexandra. *Remembering Lucy Maud Montgomery.* Toronto, Oxford: Dundurn, 2001.

Karr, Clarence. *Authors and Audiences: Popular Canadian Fiction in the Early Twentieth Century.* Montreal and Kingston: McGill-Queen's UP, 2000.

Kornfield, Eve and Susan Jackson. "The Female *Bildungsroman* in Nineteenth Century America: Parameters of a Vision." Reimer 139–52.

MacLeod, Anne Scott. "The Caddie Woodlawn Syndrome: American Girlhood in the Nineteenth Century." *A Century of Childhood: 1820–1920.* Ed. Mary Lynn Stevens Heininger. Rochester NY: Margaret Woodbury Strong Museum, 1984. 97–119.

MacLulich, T.D. "L.M. Montgomery's Portraits of the Artists: Realism, Idealism, and the Domestic Imagination." Reimer 83–100.

McClung, Nellie L. *In Times Like These*. Toronto: McLeod and Allen, 1915.

"Major Lucy Maud Montgomery Acquisitions at the National Library of Canada." *National Library News* 31.6 (June 1999): 1.

Montgomery, L.M. *The Alpine Path: The Story of My Career*. 1917. Markham, ON: Fitzhenry and Whiteside, 1997.

———. *The Selected Journals of L.M. Montgomery*. 4 vols. Ed. Mary Rubio and Elizabeth Waterston. Don Mills, ON: Oxford UP, 1985–2000.

Pansy (Isabella Macdonald Alden). *Links in Rebecca's Life*. London: Ward, Lock and Co. n.d.

———. *The Man of the House*. London: Ward, Lock, n.d.

———. *Ruth Erskine's Crosses*. London: Routledge, n.d.

Reimer, Mavis, ed. *Such a Simple Little Tale: Critical Responses to L.M. Montgomery's* Anne of Green Gables. Metuchen, NJ and London: Scarecrow, 1992.

The Royal Readers. Halifax: A. & W. MacKinlay, 1882.

Rubio, Mary Henley. "L.M. Montgomery: Scottish Presbyterian Agency in Canadian Culture." Gammel and Epperly 89–105.

———. "L.M. Montgomery: Where Does the Voice Come From?" *Canadiana: Studies in Canadian Literature. Proceedings of the Canadian Studies Conference, Aarhus, 1984*. Ed. Jorn Carlsen and Knud Larsen. Aarhus: Canadian Studies Conference, 1984.

———, ed. *Harvesting Thistles: The Textual Garden of L.M. Montgomery, Essays on Her Novels and Journals*. Guelph, ON: Canadian Children's Press, 1994.

Russell, Ruth Weber, D.W. Russell, and Rea Wilmshurst. *Lucy Maud Montgomery: A Preliminary Bibliography*. Waterloo, ON: University of Waterloo Library, 1986.

Santelmann, Patricia Kelly. "Written as Women Write: *Anne of Green Gables* Within the Female Literary Tradition." Rubio 1994 64–73.

Spadoni, Carl and Judy Donnelly. *A Bibliography of McClelland and Stewart Imprints, 1909–1985: A Publisher's Legacy*. Toronto: ECW, 1994.

Stedman, Edmund Clarence. *An American Anthology, 1787–1900.*
1900. New York: Greenwood, 1968.

Thomas, Gillian. "The Decline of Anne: Matron vs. Child."
Reimer 23–28.

Tiessen, Paul and Hildi Froese Tiessen, eds. *L.M. Montgomery's
Ephraim Weber Letters, 1916–1941.* Waterloo, ON: Mir, 1999.

Waterston, Elizabeth. *Kindling Spirit: L.M. Montgomery's* Anne of
Green Gables. Don Mills ON: ECW, 1993.

Whittier, John Greenleaf. *The Poetical Works of Whittier.* 1894.
Boston: Houghton Mifflin, 1975.

Willoughby, John H. *Ellen.* Charlottetown: John H. Willoughby,
1995.

Lucy Maud Montgomery: A Brief Chronology

1874   30 November, Lucy Maud Montgomery born in the village of Clifton (now New London) in Prince Edward Island, Canada.

1876   14 September, Montgomery's mother, Clara Woolner Macneill Montgomery, dies of tuberculosis; Montgomery remains with her maternal grandparents, Lucy Woolner and Alexander Maquis Macneill; her father, Hugh John Montgomery, eventually moves west to Saskatchewan.

1889   21 September, Montgomery begins the journal she will keep for her whole life, now published in four volumes as *The Selected Journals of L.M. Montgomery*, ed. Mary Henley Rubio and Elizabeth Waterston.

1890   Summer, Montgomery travels with her grandfather to join her father and his new family in Saskatchewan; 26 November, poem, "On Cape Leforce," printed in the Charlottetown *Daily Patriot*, first recorded publication by Montgomery (see *SJ* I 35); in the fall of 1891, Montgomery returns to P.E.I.

1893–94   Montgomery records first remuneration for writing, receiving subscriptions to a magazine as payment for a poem, "The Violet's Spell."

1895–96   Montgomery attends Dalhousie University in Halifax, Nova Scotia for a year.

1896–98   Montgomery teaches in P.E.I.

1898   5 March, death of grandfather Macneill; Montgomery returns to homestead to live with her grandmother.

1900   Death of her father, Hugh John Montgomery.

1901–02   Montgomery works as proofreader and weekly "society" writer for the Halifax *Morning Chronicle* and *Daily Echo*; she subsequently returns to P.E.I and remains with her grandmother at the Macneill homestead until 1911.

1905	June-October, Montgomery writes *Anne of Green Gables*. In the same period, her relationship with her future husband, Presbyterian minister Ewan Macdonald is developing.
1905–06	Probable period in which the manuscript is typed and sent to American publishers (according to her journal, Bobbs-Merrill of Indianapolis; MacMillan of New York; Lothrop, Lee and Shepherd of Boston; Henry Holt Co. of New York), all of whom reject it.
1906–07	Probable period in which the manuscript is sent to L.C. Page and Company in Boston.
1907	14 April, manuscript accepted by L.C. Page and Company; Page suggests Montgomery begin writing a sequel; shortly after this letter she begins writing what will be published by Page in 1909 as *Anne of Avonlea*.
1907	22 April, Montgomery signs contract with L.C. Page Company.
1908	12 June, L.C. Page registers copyright of Anne in U.S.; first edition of *Anne* appears, with illustrations by M.A. and W.A.J. Claus.
1908	December, *Anne* goes into seventh impression.
1908	Pitman publishes *Anne of Green Gables* in Great Britain.
1909	May, Montgomery corrects page proofs of *Anne of Avonlea*.
1911	Death of her grandmother Macneill; Montgomery marries Ewan Macdonald; after a honeymoon in Great Britain, they move to Leaskdale near Toronto, Ontario.
1911	May, Grosset and Dunlap popular edition of *Anne of Green Gables*.
1916	Montgomery leaves Page; signs Toronto company McClelland, Goodchild and Stewart as literary agents, publishing *The Watchman and Other Poems* in 1916 and *Anne's House of Dreams* in 1917.
1918	Montgomery sues Page for having sold the popular edition rights to Grosset and Dunlap in 1914

without her consent and for failing to pay her $1000 for this edition (see *SJ* II 284). Her suit is successful (in 1919); but she sells all rights to first seven books to Page for approximately $18,000, providing her at this time with settlement of nearly $20,000.

1919 Immediately after obtaining rights to *Anne*, Page licenses rights for silent screen adaptation to Famous Players-Lasky for $40,000.

1919 First film adaptation of *Anne of Green Gables*, Famous Players-Lasky silent picture, starring Mary Miles Minter, directed by William Desmond.

1920 January, 48th impression, 344th thousand; April, 49th impression; 349th thousand; "The Mary Miles Minter Edition," "illustrated with 24 half-tone reproductions of scenes from the motion picture production, and a jacket in colors with Miss Minter's portrait."

1920 June, 50th impression 354th thousand.

1920 Montgomery undertakes second lawsuit against Page, this time for his unauthorized publication of *Further Chronicles of Avonlea*.

1925 New plates for *Anne* made in U.S. Page issues new edition with illustrations by Elizabeth R. Withington.

1925 Harrap edition in Great Britain: Pitman license evidently concluded.

1933 Page issues "Silver Anniversary" issue, with 8 illustrations by Sybil Tawse.

1933–34 Oct. 1933–Dec. 1934, 68th to 71st impressions.

1934 RKO talking picture; actress Dawn O'Day, who plays role of Anne, changes her name to Anne Shirley, and continues to act under that name for the rest of her life.

1935 Grosset and Dunlap large cloth edition.

1935 14 June, original copyright renewed in U.S. (after 28 years); entered in name of Lucy M. Macdonald.

1937 Dramatization by Alice Chadwicke (Wilbur Braun).

1942 First Canadian edition of *Anne*. This issue of the first Canadian edition follows Montgomery's death on 24 April.

A Note on the Text

The publishing history of *Anne of Green Gables*, as Molly Colin has put it, is "byzantine" (27). *Anne* was first published in the United States in 1908 by L.C. Page (Boston), with illustrations by M.A. and W.A.J. Claus. In the same year, the British firm Isaac Pitman issued a British edition, using the Page plates. Page issued review copies in April of 1908; the copyright was registered in the U.S. and the official first editions were issued in June 1908. The Page printings are recorded in most editions during the early years, up to and including the May 1914 Popular Edition that New York company Grosset and Dunlap produced in a limited run (150,000 copies), using the Page plates and the frontispiece from the 1908 edition (but not the rest of the illustrations). This Popular Edition was the thirty-eighth Page impression of *Anne*, although it appeared with the Grosset and Dunlap imprint.[1] After 1914, Page continued to produce editions using the 1908 plates, including a tie-in edition that was issued following the 1919 Famous Players-Lasky silent picture starring Mary Miles Minter. This edition used stills from the film in place of the Claus illustrations. By 1919, Page owned *Anne of Green Gables* completely, having bought the rights to it and Montgomery's six other early books for $17,880 in that year. Although the records of impressions continue to appear in subsequent editions, Montgomery's own involvement with its sale ceases, and she kept no records of her own of the novel's publication in the U.S. during this period.[2] Page's papers in the Farrar, Straus and Giroux records at the New York Public Library are incomplete, and it is impossible to ascertain from them a precise history of the publication of *Anne*.

Ronald I. Cohen, who in 1999 donated his important collection of L.M. Montgomery editions to the National Library of Canada, has suggested that, in "the absence of a descriptive bibli-

---

[1] This Popular Edition was at the centre of an early action taken by Montgomery against Page. See 40–41; see *SJ* II 284.

[2] Montgomery did, however, record her earnings from *Anne* between 1908 and 1919 in a ledger, now held in the Special Collections at the University of Guelph.

ography of the works of [...] Montgomery," their publishing history is a "jigsaw puzzle in which only the edge pieces, namely, the titles of the books, are clear":

> Once beyond the early L.C. Page editions of Montgomery's first seven books (published between 1908 and 1915), the publishing priorities of which are clear, things become murky, if not utterly inscrutable [...] The establishment of the priority of editions and even printings is uncertain, to say the very least.[1]

Although there do not seem to be pirated editions of *Anne* in English from the early years, there are numerous translations licensed by Page, and dozens of editions have appeared since the novel more or less entered the public domain in the U.S. in 1983 and Canada in 1992.[2] The details even of the early editions are difficult to trace because of the absence of records as well as of their sheer numbers, but also because a book as beloved as *Anne of Green Gables* has been since its first appearance tends to be well used, to be kept by owners, and thus to be difficult to find.

---

1 *National Library News* (June 1999) 31.6:3

2 Since *Anne of Green Gables* entered the public domain in the United States in 1983 and in Canada in 1992, editions have proliferated, and, increasingly, adaptations of the book have been produced and marketed. Many of these editions use the 1908 Page first edition, and indicate the text on which they are based (like the McClelland and Stewart New Canadian Library edition of 1992, and the 1997 Running Press edition, which also includes an excerpt from the *Selected Journals*); some do so inaccurately. For instance, the 1998 Nimbus edition (based on the 1992 Nimbus hardcover edition, and reissued in paper in 1998 as "The Green Gables Edition, Produced exclusively for the Boutique Green Gables Gift Shop" in the National Park in Cavendish, P.E.I.) indicates that it is a reprint of *Anne of Green Gables* "as it originally appeared," but it is clearly a reproduction of the 1925 Harrap edition, rather than the 1908 Page edition.
   The most important edition of *Anne* to appear in recent years is the *Annotated* Oxford University Press edition of 1998, edited by Wendy Barry, Margaret Anne Doody, and Mary E. Doody Jones. This text is the first version of the novel with explanatory notes and textual apparatus noting variants between the manuscript and the editions of 1908, 1925, and 1942; it provides, in addition, an interesting range of photographs from Montgomery's and other archives. Its text is to some extent new: in many cases the editors have restored the manuscript, based usually on connections between the manuscript and the 1925 text, and in some cases on the manuscript alone. As I have already suggested, the process of restoring the manuscript on the basis of the 1925 or any edition of *Anne* is a difficult one, and it is not undertaken here.

The editors of the 1998 *Annotated Anne* have suggested that there are three main "families" of editions in English of Montgomery's novel: the 1908 first edition published in the U.S. by L.C. Page; the 1925 first "true" British edition by Harrap (first "true" because it was not made with the original Page plates, which by then had had to be replaced, in any case, and it seems to have followed a new licensing agreement); and the 1942 first Canadian edition by Ryerson Press.[1] These three groups of editions differ in numerous minor ways, primarily having to do with British and American conventions of spelling and punctuation, and it seems clear that they do not originate from the same source or that there was considerable editorial intervention in some of the cases. The 1908 edition is certainly based on a typescript sent to Page by Montgomery. The copy-text used for the Harrap edition is obscure: this edition differs from the 1908 text, primarily in its Anglicizing of some constructions and usages, while maintaining many of Page's British spellings. The variants suggest either that the Harrap edition was not based on the Page text, or that the editors at Harrap wanted to de-Americanize the text for British readers. The *Annotated Anne* prefers the 1925 Harrap text because of the number of points at which the first English edition matches the manuscript, suggesting, the editors argue, Montgomery's having had more "input" into the production of the 1925 edition than she may have had into the 1908 Page edition (399). This is a compelling argument, but it is also possible that the editors of the 1925 text simply reverted to Montgomery's British conventions of punctuation and in some cases of usage: Montgomery did not, after all, have any financial interest in *Anne* after 1919, and it would be odd for her to play a part in the arrangement made between Page and Harrap.

The 1942 Canadian edition also differs from the Page text, although it almost certainly uses the Page text as its source, since it was published by a limited-term licensing agreement with the

---

[1] It should be noted that, among the "families" of English editions of *Anne*, the Australian editions are also important: Russell/Wilmshurst notes the two main versions—the Cornstalk Publishing edition in 1924 and the Angus and Robertson in 1934. This latter edition has been reprinted many times. As copy-texts, however, the Australian editions may be as problematic as any of the post-1908 editions.

L.C. Page Company, and usually agrees with it. Since 1916, Montgomery's Canadian publishers had been McClelland, Goodchild and Stewart, and, while they held the rights to all of Montgomery's books published after 1916, it was the Ryerson Press that published the first Canadian edition of *Anne of Green Gables*. McClelland and Stewart, as the firm would later be known, would not publish an edition of *Anne* until 1981, when they issued a paper edition as McClelland and Stewart-Bantam Ltd.[1] It is possible, moreover, that the Ryerson edition used a later Page impression, issued after the 1908 plates had been replaced in 1925. The pagination changes at this point for standard editions of *Anne*. An edition with new illustrations by Elizabeth Withington was issued in 1925; these illustrations use the same captions as the Claus illustrations of the first edition. Always alert to a marketing opportunity, Page also issued a Silver Anniversary edition in 1933, in a larger size, with illustrations by Sybil Tawse. The first licensed "popular" edition that was not produced from (although it was still based on) the Page plates seems to have been the Grosset and Dunlap large edition in 1935. Grosset and Dunlap had earlier, in 1914, produced a limited, licensed edition; the licensing agreement between Grosset and Dunlap and Page may have been reactivated on at least one other occasion; and other "popular editions" produced and distributed, were also based on Page texts.[2]

This text uses the 1908 L.C. Page first edition. It was checked against the manuscript of *Anne of Green Gables* at the Confederation

---

[1] The McClelland-Bantam edition used the Bantam sheets, from the edition of 1976 (see Spadoni and Donnelly, *A Bibliography of McClelland and Stewart Imprints, 1909–1985* [3264]; this Bantam edition was published simultaneously in Canada and the U.S.). McClelland and Stewart's subsequent issuing of *Anne* in their New Canadian Library series in 1992 uses the 1908 Page text. The McClelland and Stewart paper edition of 1981 was not, however, the first Canadian paperback of *Anne of Green Gables*: Ryerson had officially issued that in 1968, although an earlier unauthorized paper edition by Ryerson had also been marketed for some time. The early paper editions have a rather complex history: the Ryerson edition was also in conflict with a Grosset and Dunlap paper version, published in 1964 under the insignia of Tempo, and distributed in Canada despite an agreement that it not be distributed there. The Tempo edition is the first official paper edition of *Anne of Green Gables*.

[2] Grosset and Dunlap still produce an edition of *Anne of Green Gables* for their Illustrated Junior Library Series.

Centre for the Arts in Charlottetown, P.E.I., as well as the first British edition (the 1925 Harrap text), and the first Canadian edition (the 1942 Ryerson text). There are scores of minor variants between these texts, very few of which are in any way substantive. The text is amended only for consistency where the 1908 edition uses two spellings or versions of a word or phrase (e.g., Lovers' Lane, pedlar, gypsy, sear).

There are many reasons to use the 1908 edition before any of the others, not least of which is that it has circulated for nearly half a century in North America. Although, as the tumultuous relationship Montgomery describes in her journal between herself and her first publisher may suggest, the political value of an amended text that puts the manuscript before the Page edition will be evident, the manuscript, without a typescript to consider with it, is probably not the best copy-text. While the manuscript represents, of course, *Anne of Green Gables* as Montgomery wrote it, it may not represent it as she sent it to any publishers, including L.C. Page. It is not clear that there was ever more than one typescript, but this is a possibility since she claims to have sent the novel to four or five publishers. However, until a typescript or corrected page proofs should turn up, the Page text is arguably the closest to Montgomery's original text for publication. Moreover, the variations between the manuscript and the 1908 text do not indicate high-handed editing on the part of the company: changes tend to be made at the level of the comma, on whose placement Page's staff and Montgomery may have disagreed, and of national conventions of spelling. The few phrases in the 1908 edition that do not occur in the manuscript text may have been included in a typescript. Some changed words may be typesetting errors; a few may represent editorial interventions (see A Note on the Manuscript 47).

Page's 1908 edition of *Anne of Green Gables* is something of a cultural curiosity, foregrounding as it does its own—and Montgomery's—transcultural position between Canada, the U.S., and Great Britain. As has already been indicated, the 1908 text uses British and English-Canadian conventions of spelling, particularly in the case of *-or/-our* words such as *parlour* and *neighbour*, where Montgomery, who had written for so many years for American magazines, tended to use the American spellings in her own writing. Page may have used these spellings in order to facilitate the publication of the first edition in Britain in 1908 by the firm Isaac Pitman. Other explanations are more obscure. It is possible that Montgomery changed these spellings in the typescript; it is possible, although hard to imagine, that Page replaced the American spellings that appear in the manuscript in order to reinforce the Canadianness of the novel's context. This is certainly an effect of the use of British conventions in the 1908 edition, although it is perhaps offset by the "Americanizing" of some idioms (e.g., "dreadful" for "dreadfully") and other spellings in the novel. The differences between these spellings and what they connote, however, are not less problematic than Montgomery's having written her novel with explicitly English-Canadian references, but sending it only to American publishing houses. And, again, it is not clear that these spellings persisted in the typescript or page proofs.

A Note on the Manuscript

The manuscript of *Anne of Green Gables* is held at the Confederation Centre for the Arts in Charlottetown, Prince Edward Island. A photocopy of the manuscript is generously made available for use at the Centre. Both the copy and the manuscript are occasionally illegible, as is the case for much of Montgomery's writing, originals as well as photocopies and microcopies. The manuscript is blotted in a few places with water or ink, and when Montgomery appears to be writing very quickly it is sometimes difficult to decode. There are 716 numbered pages of story in the manuscript, and 137 of notes, numbered from A to S19, with some numbers repeated. Some of these notes are quite long (Elizabeth Epperly has observed that the "longest additions [...] are made to the raspberry cordial scene");[1] some are only a few words. The notes are written and inserted sequentially. The early sections of the book are written on the backs of manuscript pages from other, earlier stories; it is only about a third of the way through that Montgomery shifts

---

[1]   Rubio, *Harvesting Thistles* 75.

to fresh paper, when, as she writes in her journal, she realized that the "serial" was becoming something else.

The primary variations between Montgomery's manuscript (MS) and the 1908 edition are to be found, as noted above, in punctuation and particularly in commas, on the placement of which Montgomery and Page's editors seem to have differed at several points in *Anne of Green Gables*. One difference is evident in the refiguring of Matthew's favourite phrase which appears in the MS as "Well, now...". This phrase has no comma in 1908, with only a couple of exceptions. In many cases, 1908 replaces a comma of Montgomery's with a colon in structures in which a quotation follows a verb of expression (e.g., "said brusquely": [1908]; "said brusquely," [MS] [123]). Changed commas in 1908, both those that seem to have been added in the 1908 text and those that seem to have been deleted from the MS, are pervasive, and their enumeration may not be productive except in a manuscript-based edition. Indeed, it is often not possible to tell where commas are intended to appear in the MS, if they have been overwritten, for instance, or the page is blotted, or a word, phrase, or sentence has been inserted, either above the text or in a manuscript note. Montgomery may have changed much of her punctuation in a typescript.

The second major cluster of variations between 1908 and MS has to do with the placement of hyphens in nominal and adjectival compounds. Montgomery is inconsistent in her use of a hyphen in words such as "to-day," "to-morrow," "to-night": with the exception of what are a few probably typographical errors or editorial oversights, 1908 always hyphenates. Similarly, 1908 always hyphenates "up-stairs," "down-stairs," "out-of-doors," etc. while MS usually does not, preferring to use one word (i.e., "upstairs," "downstairs") or a phrase (i.e., "out of doors"). 1908 always, with few exceptions, hyphenates tree names: e.g., "cherry-tree." MS does not usually hyphenate trees as 1908 does, but occasionally hyphenates other compounds (e.g., "tea-rose") which 1908 does not. MS almost always uses "Sunday School" with no hyphen (except, sometimes, in its adjectival form); 1908 always hyphenates (and uses a lower-case *s* for "school.") However, Montgomery does prefer to use "good-night," while 1908 prefers two words (i.e., "good night"). These variations are not, however, indicators of significant differences between the MS and the first edition: Montgomery is inconsistent in her usage, and it is often impossible to discern from the MS whether or not a word is actually hyphenated. Montgomery's MS *t*'s are often crossed past the word, and the cross looks like a hyphen in some cases; in other cases, the MS is blotted or there are crossings and overwritings which obscure the place of a hyphen; in some cases, a word is hyphenated in the MS because it falls at the end of a line. In some cases, however, the removal of MS hyphens in compounds does affect the meaning or at least the way Montgomery appears to have wanted to present the adjective or noun compound. For instance, 1908 removes the hyphen from "bloom-white" and "white-lace," but Montgomery almost always hyphenates such compounds in her MSS, and their linking seems important to the way such adjectives function in her writing.

Related to this set of variations are the differences between compounds that can be used either as one word or as two. For instance, the MS tends to use "daresay" as one word, where 1908 prefers "dare say." Similarly, the MS uses "forever," while 1908 prefers "for ever"; "anymore," where 1908 uses "any more"; "anyone," where 1908 uses "any one"; "someone," where 1908 uses "some one"; "faraway," where 1908 uses "far away."

There are also some discrepancies in the use of certain words in both MS and 1908: "Hopeton/Hopetown" is one example. As in the case of "pedlar/peddler" and the rather more contentious "Lovers' Lane/Lover's Lane," both texts use both forms. This edition maintains one usage for each for the sake of consistency. In the case of "Hopeton/Hopetown," I have followed the first occurrence. For "Lover's/Lovers' Lane," I have followed the version that is used most often in 1908 ("Lovers"). *AA* uses "Lover's Lane" with the argument that it could be a place for a single lover (*AA* 399), but it seems clear that Montgomery saw it as a place for plural lovers, despite her inconsistent placement of the apostrophe. Anne and Diana, after all, "imagine the lovers into it" (149). For pedlar/peddler, I have not followed the first occurrence in 1908, but have again used the version that appears most often in the first edition (pedlar).

There are other minor textual issues that are arguably attributable to the nature of MSS in general and to Montgomery's speed in writing *Anne of Green Gables*. 1908 tends to add "that" to many of Montgomery's sentences. The MS often uses numbers instead of words (e.g., 5:30 instead of five thirty) and a plus sign (+) in place of "and." It frequently leaves out apostrophes, question and exclamation marks, closing quotation marks, and dashes; it is also inconsistent in the placement of a period after chapter titles. Although the MS, as Epperly notes, is relatively tidy, Montgomery's writing is frequently a challenge to decipher. It is often difficult to distinguish between "would" and "could," for instance. It seems, too, that she could not read her own writing on occasion: this may explain the repetition of some MS notes, as well, possibly, as some of the differences in 1908, given that some of those misreadings of her own writing may have appeared in a typescript.

ANNE OF GREEN GABLES

By
L. M. MONTGOMERY

Illustrated by
M. A. and W. A. J. CLAUS

" The good stars met in your horoscope,
Made you of spirit and fire and dew."
— *Browning.*

BOSTON ❧ L. C. PAGE &
COMPANY ❧ MDCCCCVIII

CHAPTER I

MRS. RACHEL LYNDE IS SURPRISED

MRS. RACHEL LYNDE lived just where the Avonlea main road dipped down into a little hollow, fringed with alders and ladies' eardrops and traversed by a brook that had its source away back in the woods of the old Cuthbert place; it was reputed to be an intricate, headlong brook in its earlier course through those woods, with dark secrets of pool and cascade; but by the time it reached Lynde's Hollow it was a quiet, well-conducted little stream, for not even a brook could run past Mrs. Rachel Lynde's door without due regard for decency and decorum; it probably was conscious that Mrs. Rachel was sitting at her window, keeping a sharp eye on everything that passed, from brooks and children up, and that if she noticed anything odd or out of place she would never rest until she had ferreted out the whys and wherefores thereof.[1]

There are plenty of people, in Avonlea and out of it, who can attend closely to their neighbours' business by dint of neglecting their own; but Mrs. Rachel Lynde was one of those capable creatures who can manage their own concerns and those of other folks into the bargain. She was a notable housewife; her work was always done and well done; she "ran" the Sewing Circle, helped run the Sunday-school, and was the strongest prop of the Church Aid Society and Foreign Missions Auxiliary. Yet with all this Mrs. Rachel found abundant time to sit for hours at her kitchen window, knitting "cotton warp"[2] quilts—she had knitted sixteen of them, as Avonlea housekeepers were wont to tell in awed voices—and keeping a sharp eye on the main road that crossed the hollow and wound up the steep red hill beyond. Since

---

[1] In the MS, this long first sentence is two sentences, the second beginning, "But by the time..."

[2] A type of cotton yarn that is strong enough to be used as warp yarns, or those which, as Verla Birrell points out in *The Textile Arts* (New York: Schocken, 1959, 1973), "run the long way of the loom and of the fabric. Weft yarns are woven through and across the warp" (n.2, 44).

Avonlea occupied a little triangular peninsula jutting out into the Gulf of St. Lawrence, with water on two sides of it, anybody who went out of it or into it had to pass over that hill road and so run the unseen gauntlet of Mrs. Rachel's all-seeing eye.

She was sitting there one afternoon in early June. The sun was coming in at the window warm and bright; the orchard on the slope below the house was in a bridal flush of pinky-white bloom, hummed over by a myriad of bees. Thomas Lynde—a meek little man whom Avonlea people called "Rachel Lynde's husband"—was sowing his late turnip seed on the hill field beyond the barn; and Matthew Cuthbert ought to have been sowing his on the big red brook field away over by Green Gables.[1] Mrs. Rachel knew that he ought because she had heard him tell Peter Morrison the evening before in William J. Blair's store over at Carmody that he meant to sow his turnip seed the next afternoon. Peter had asked him, of course, for Matthew Cuthbert had never been known to volunteer information about anything in his whole life.

And yet here was Matthew Cuthbert, at half-past three on the afternoon of a busy day, placidly driving over the hollow and up the hill; moreover, he wore a white collar and his best suit of clothes, which was plain proof that he was going out of Avonlea; and he had the buggy and the sorrel mare, which betokened that he was going a considerable distance. Now, where was Matthew Cuthbert going and why was he going there?

Had it been any other man in Avonlea Mrs. Rachel, deftly putting this and that together, might have given a pretty good guess as to both questions. But Matthew so rarely went from home that it must be something pressing and unusual which was taking him; he was the shyest man alive and hated to have to go among strangers or to any place where he might have to talk. Matthew, dressed up with a white collar and driving in a buggy, was something that didn't happen often. Mrs. Rachel, ponder as she might, could make nothing of it and her afternoon's enjoyment was spoiled.

---

[1]   Gable: "The vertical piece of wall at the end of a ridge roof, from the level of the eaves to the summit" (OED).

"I'll just step over to Green Gables after tea and find out from Marilla where he's gone and why," the worthy woman finally concluded. "He doesn't generally go to town this time of year and he *never* visits; if he'd run out of turnip seed he wouldn't dress up and take the buggy to go for more; he wasn't driving fast enough to be going for a doctor. Yet something must have happened since last night to start him off. I'm clean puzzled, that's what, and I won't know a minute's peace of mind or conscience until I know what has taken Matthew Cuthbert out of Avonlea to-day."

Accordingly after tea Mrs. Rachel set out; she had not far to go; the big, rambling, orchard-embowered house where the Cuthberts lived was a scant quarter of a mile up the road from Lynde's Hollow. To be sure, the long lane made it a good deal further. Matthew Cuthbert's father, as shy and silent as his son after him, had got as far away as he possibly could from his fellow men without actually retreating into the woods when he founded his homestead.[1] Green Gables was built at the furthest edge of his cleared land and there it was to this day, barely visible from the main road along which all the other Avonlea houses were so sociably situated. Mrs. Rachel Lynde did not call living in such a place *living* at all.

"It's just *staying*, that's what," she said as she stepped along the deep-rutted, grassy lane bordered with wild rose bushes. "It's no wonder Matthew and Marilla are both a little odd, living away back here by themselves. Trees aren't much company, though dear knows if they were there'd be enough of them. I'd ruther look at people. To be sure, they seem contented enough; but then, I suppose, they're used to it. A body can get used to anything,[2] even to being hanged, as the Irishman said."

With this Mrs. Rachel stepped out of the lane into the backyard of Green Gables. Very green and neat and precise was that yard, set

---

[1] "House with its dependent buildings and offices; esp. a farm-stead" (*OED*). Although the term is used to refer to homes in a general sense, it is used here in the context of settlement; the founding of the Cuthbert homestead is a mark of the migration and settlement of Anglo-imperial culture in P.E.I.

[2] *The Oxford Dictionary of American Proverbs* (New York: Oxford UP, 1992) notes the occurrence of a similar proverb in Ontario, Canada: "One can get used to anything— even hanging" (278).

about on one side with great patriarchal willows and on the other with prim Lombardies. Not a stray stick nor stone was to be seen, for Mrs. Rachel would have seen it if there had been. Privately she was of the opinion that Marilla Cuthbert swept that yard over as often as she swept her house. One could have eaten a meal off the ground without overbrimming the proverbial peck of dirt.[1]

Mrs. Rachel rapped smartly at the kitchen door and stepped in when bidden to do so. The kitchen at Green Gables was a cheerful apartment—or would have been cheerful if it had not been so painfully clean as to give it something of the appearance of an unused parlour. Its windows looked east and west; through the west one, looking out on the back yard, came a flood of mellow June sunlight; but the east one, whence you got a glimpse of the bloom white cherry-trees in the left orchard and nodding, slender birches down in the hollow by the brook, was greened over by a tangle of vines. Here sat Marilla Cuthbert, when she sat at all, always slightly distrustful of sunshine, which seemed to her too dancing and irresponsible a thing for a world which was meant to be taken seriously; and here she sat now, knitting, and the table behind her was laid for supper.

Mrs. Rachel, before she had fairly closed the door, had taken mental note of everything that was on that table. There were three plates laid, so that Marilla must be expecting some one home with Matthew to tea; but the dishes were every-day dishes and there was only crab-apple preserves and one kind of cake, so that the expected company could not be any particular company. Yet what of Matthew's white collar and the sorrel mare? Mrs. Rachel was getting fairly dizzy with this unusual mystery about quiet, unmysterious Green Gables.

"Good evening, Rachel," Marilla said briskly. "This is a real fine evening, isn't it? Won't you sit down? How are all your folks?"

---

[1] The reference is to the quantity of dirt one might be expected to consume with other food over a lifetime, i.e., the dirt on food or associated with it. The proverb itself is obscure. *The Oxford Dictionary of American Proverbs* suggests a first citation in 1603, in Chettle, Dekker, and Haughton, *Patient Grissel*; it also notes that the proverb circulated in the U.S. and Canada with a range of variations (151). *The Macmillan Book of Proverbs, Maxims, and Famous Phrases* (New York: Macmillan, 1948) notes several occurrences from 1709 to the late nineteenth century.

Something that for lack of any other name might be called friendship existed and always had existed between Marilla Cuthbert and Mrs. Rachel, in spite of—or perhaps because of—their dissimilarity.

Marilla was a tall, thin woman, with angles and without curves; her dark hair showed some gray streaks and was always twisted up in a hard little knot behind with two wire hairpins stuck aggressively through it. She looked like a woman of narrow experience and rigid conscience, which she was; but there was a saving something about her mouth which, if it had been ever so slightly developed, might have been considered indicative of a sense of humour.

"We're all pretty well," said Mrs. Rachel. "I was kind of afraid *you* weren't, though, when I saw Matthew starting off to-day. I thought maybe he was going to the doctor's."

Marilla's lips twitched understandingly. She had expected Mrs. Rachel up; she had known that the sight of Matthew jaunting off so unaccountably would be too much for her neighbour's curiosity.

"Oh, no, I'm quite well although I had a bad headache yesterday," she said. "Matthew went to Bright River. We're getting a little boy from an orphan asylum in Nova Scotia, and he's coming on the train to-night."

If Marilla had said that Matthew had gone to Bright River to meet a kangaroo from Australia Mrs. Rachel could not have been more astonished. She was actually stricken dumb for five seconds. It was unsupposable that Marilla was making fun of her, but Mrs. Rachel was almost forced to suppose it.

"Are you in earnest, Marilla?" she demanded when voice returned to her.

"Yes, of course," said Marilla, as if getting boys from orphan asylums in Nova Scotia were part of the usual spring work on any well-regulated Avonlea farm instead of being an unheard of innovation.

Mrs. Rachel felt that she had received a severe mental jolt. She thought in exclamation points. A boy! Marilla and Matthew Cuthbert of all people adopting a boy! From an orphan asylum! Well, the world was certainly turning upside down! She would be surprised at nothing after this! Nothing!

"What on earth put such a notion into your head?" she demanded disapprovingly.

This had been done without her advice being asked, and must perforce be disapproved.

"Well, we've been thinking about it for some time—all winter in fact," returned Marilla. "Mrs. Alexander Spencer was up here one day before Christmas and she said she was going to get a little girl from the asylum over in Hopetown in the spring. Her cousin lives there and Mrs. Spencer has visited her and knows all about it. So Matthew and I have talked it over off and on ever since. We thought we'd get a boy. Matthew is getting up in years, you know— he's sixty—and he isn't so spry as he once was. His heart troubles him a good deal. And you know how desperate hard it's got to be to get hired help. There's never anybody to be had but those stupid, half-grown little French boys; and as soon as you do get one broke into your ways and taught something he's up and off to the lobster canneries or the States. At first Matthew suggested getting a Barnardo boy.[1] But I said 'no' flat to that. 'They may be all right— I'm not saying they're not—but no London street Arabs[2] for me,'

[1] Marilla seems to be using "Barnardo boy" in a general way to refer to the many children from Britain—often, but not always, orphans—who were sent to the settler colonies as labourers throughout the nineteenth century. In *Barnardo Children in Canada* (Peterborough, ON: Woodland, 1981), Gail Corbett notes that London-based doctor Thomas Barnardo had become well known by the 1870s as a social reformer whose greatest concern was with the homeless and destitute children in London. Corbett indicates Barnardo had begun as early as 1868 to send groups of children with other child-emigration organizations. By 1870, he had opened his first home; by 1882, "he determined to launch a comprehensive scale for the emigration of Barnardo children into Canada" (Corbett 25). According to Kenneth Bagnall in *The Little Immigrants: The Orphans Who Came to Canada* (Toronto: Macmillan, 1980), Barnardo "emigrated" around 30 000 children to Canada. Given Joy Parr's observation that around 77 000 British children were relocated to Canada between 1868 and 1915 (*The British Child Migration Movement*, Ottawa: National Museum of Man, 1979 np), Barnardo children represented almost half of the number of juvenile migrants to Canada. Corbett records the final emigration of Barnardo children to Canada in 1939 (122). See also Joy Parr, *Labouring Children: British Immigrant Apprentices to Canada, 1869–1924* (London: Croom Helm, 1980).

[2] The term *street Arabs* or *City Arabs* is used throughout the nineteenth century to refer to homeless children living in the streets of a city—often, but not always, London. Its origins are unclear, but it implies a kind of nomadic or wandering existence. It is clearly a racializing term: it marks homeless children in urban contexts as being outside of the category of whiteness, and thus marks racial prejudices common in Anglo-Saxon cultures of the period, as well as indicating prejudices that pertained specifically to orphaned children, such as Marilla invokes here.

I said. 'Give me a native born at least. There'll be a risk, no matter who we get. But I'll feel easier in my mind and sleep sounder at nights if we get a born Canadian.' So in the end we decided to ask Mrs. Spencer to pick us out one when she went over to get her little girl. We heard last week she was going, so we sent her word by Richard Spencer's folks at Carmody to bring us a smart, likely boy of about ten or eleven. We decided that would be the best age—old enough to be of some use in doing chores right off and young enough to be trained up proper. We mean to give him a good home and schooling. We had a telegram from Mrs. Alexander Spencer to-day—the mail-man brought it from the station—saying they were coming on the five-thirty train to-night. So Matthew went to Bright River to meet him. Mrs. Spencer will drop him off there. Of course she goes on to White Sands station herself."

Mrs. Rachel prided herself on always speaking her mind; she proceeded to speak it now, having adjusted her mental attitude to this amazing piece of news.

"Well, Marilla, I'll just tell you plain that I think you're doing a mighty foolish thing—a risky thing, that's what. You don't know what you're getting. You're bringing a strange child into your house and home and you don't know a single thing about him nor what his disposition is like nor what sort of parents he had nor how he's likely to turn out. Why, it was only last week I read in the paper how a man and his wife up west of the Island took a boy out of an orphan asylum and he set fire to the house at night—set it *on purpose*, Marilla—and nearly burnt them to a crisp in their beds. And I know another case where an adopted boy used to suck the eggs—they couldn't break him of it. If you had asked my advice in the matter—which you didn't do, Marilla—I'd have said for mercy's sake not to think of such a thing, that's what."

This Job's comforting[1] seemed neither to offend nor alarm Marilla. She knitted steadily on.

"I don't deny there's something in what you say, Rachel. I've had some qualms myself. But Matthew was terrible set on it. I

---

[1]   According to *Brewer's Concise Dictionary of Phrase and Fable* (Oxford: Helicon, 1995), a Job's comforter is "One who means to sympathize with you in your grief, but says that you brought it on yourself, thus adding to your sorrow. An allusion to the rebukes Job [in the Old Testament *Book of Job*] received from his 'comforters.'"

could see that, so I gave in. It's so seldom Matthew sets his mind on anything that when he does I always feel it's my duty to give in. And as for the risk, there's risks in pretty near everything a body does in this world. There's risks in people's having children of their own if it comes to that—they don't always turn out well. And then Nova Scotia is right close to the Island. It isn't as if we were getting him from England or the States. He can't be much different from ourselves."

"Well, I hope it will turn out all right," said Mrs. Rachel in a tone that plainly indicated her painful doubts. "Only don't say I didn't warn you if he burns Green Gables down or puts strychnine[1] in the well—I heard of a case over in New Brunswick where an orphan asylum child did that and the whole family died in fearful agonies. Only, it was a girl in that instance."

"Well, we're not getting a girl," said Marilla, as if poisoning wells were a purely feminine accomplishment and not to be dreaded in the case of a boy. "I'd never dream of taking a girl to bring up. I wonder at Mrs. Alexander Spencer for doing it. But there, *she* wouldn't shrink from adopting a whole orphan asylum if she took it into her head."

Mrs. Rachel would have liked to stay until Matthew came home with his imported orphan. But reflecting that it would be a good two hours at least before his arrival she concluded to go up the road to Robert Bell's and tell them the news. It would certainly make a sensation second to none, and Mrs. Rachel dearly loved to make a sensation. So she took herself away, somewhat to Marilla's relief, for the latter felt her doubts and fears reviving under the influence of Mrs. Rachel's pessimism.

"Well, of all things that ever were or will be!" ejaculated Mrs. Rachel when she was safely out in the lane. "It does really seem as if I must be dreaming. Well, I'm sorry for that poor young one and no mistake. Matthew and Marilla don't know anything about children and they'll expect him to be wiser and steadier than his own grandfather, if so be's he ever had a grandfather, which is doubtful. It seems uncanny to think of a child at Green Gables somehow; there's never been one there, for Matthew and Marilla

---

[1] "A highly poisonous vegetable alkaloid" (*OED*).

were grown up when the new house was built—if they ever *were* children, which is hard to believe when one looks at them. I wouldn't be in that orphan's shoes for anything. My, but I pity him, that's what."

So said Mrs. Rachel to the wild rose bushes out of the fulness of her heart; but if she could have seen the child who was waiting patiently at the Bright River station at that very moment her pity would have been still deeper and more profound.

CHAPTER II

MATTHEW CUTHBERT IS SURPRISED

MATTHEW CUTHBERT and the sorrel mare jogged comfortably over the eight miles to Bright River. It was a pretty road, running along between snug farmsteads, with now and again a bit of balsamy fir wood to drive through or a hollow where wild plums hung out their filmy bloom. The air was sweet with the breath of many apple orchards and the meadows sloped away in the distance to horizon mists of pearl and purple; while

"The little birds sang as if it were
The one day of summer in all the year."[1]

Matthew enjoyed the drive after his own fashion, except during the moments when he met women and had to nod to them—for in Prince Edward Island you are supposed to nod to all and sundry you meet on the road whether you know them or not.

Matthew dreaded all women except Marilla and Mrs. Rachel; he had an uncomfortable feeling that the mysterious creatures were secretly laughing at him. He may have been quite right in thinking so, for he was an odd-looking personage, with an ungainly figure and long iron-gray hair that touched his stooping

---

[1]   Properly, "The one day in summer of all the year." See American poet James Russell Lowell (1819–91), "The Vision of Sir Launfall" (1848); 1.2.3–4. *AGG* alludes again to this poem; see 168, note 1.

shoulders, and a full, soft brown beard which he had worn ever since he was twenty. In fact, he had looked at twenty very much as he looked at sixty, lacking a little of the grayness.

When he reached Bright River there was no sign of any train; he thought he was too early, so he tied his horse in the yard of the small Bright River hotel and went over to the station-house. The long platform was almost deserted; the only living creature in sight being a girl who was sitting on a pile of shingles at the extreme end. Matthew, barely noting that it *was* a girl, sidled past her as quickly as possible without looking at her. Had he looked he could hardly have failed to notice the tense rigidity and expectation of her attitude and expression. She was sitting there waiting for something or somebody and, since sitting and waiting was the only thing to do just then, she sat and waited with all her might and main.

Matthew encountered the station-master locking up the ticket-office preparatory to going home for supper, and asked him if the five-thirty train would soon be along.

"The five-thirty train has been in and gone half an hour ago," answered that brisk official. "But there was a passenger dropped off for you—a little girl. She's sitting out there on the shingles. I asked her to go into the ladies' waiting-room, but she informed me gravely that she preferred to stay outside. 'There was more scope for imagination,'[1] she said. She's a case,[2] I should say."

"I'm not expecting a girl," said Matthew blankly. "It's a boy I've come for. He should be here. Mrs. Alexander Spencer was to bring him over from Nova Scotia for me."

The station-master whistled.

"Guess there's some mistake," he said. "Mrs. Spencer came off the train with that girl and gave her into my charge. Said you and your sister were adopting her from an orphan asylum and that you would be along for her presently. That's all *I* know about it—and I haven't got any more orphans concealed hereabouts."

---

[1] This phrase circulates in a good deal of writing in English throughout the late eighteenth and nineteenth centuries. An early occurrence is found in *A Sentimental Journey* (1768; Penguin, 1967) by Laurence Sterne (1713–68); see 97. Cf. also *The Mill on the Floss* (1860; OUP, 1980) by George Eliot (1819–80) (147), and *The Rights of Women* (1792; Penguin 1982, 1992) by Mary Wollstonecraft (1759–97) (163).

[2] Nineteenth-century American slang for a "character" or an odd person.

"I don't understand," said Matthew helplessly, wishing that Marilla was at hand to cope with the situation.

"Well, you'd better question the girl," said the station-master carelessly. "I dare say she'll be able to explain—she's got a tongue of her own, that's certain. Maybe they were out of boys of the brand you wanted."

He walked jauntily away, being hungry, and the unfortunate Matthew was left to do that which was harder for him than bearding a lion in its den[1]—walk up to a girl—a strange girl— an orphan girl—and demand of her why she wasn't a boy. Matthew groaned in spirit as he turned about and shuffled gently down the platform towards her.

She had been watching him ever since he had passed her and she had her eyes on him now. Matthew was not looking at her and would not have seen what she was really like if he had been, but an ordinary observer would have seen this:

A child of about eleven, garbed in a very short, very tight, very ugly dress of yellowish gray wincey.[2] She wore a faded brown sailor hat and beneath the hat, extending down her back, were two braids of very thick, decidedly red hair. Her face was small, white and thin, also much freckled; her mouth was large and so were her eyes, that looked green in some lights and moods and gray in others.

So far, the ordinary observer; an extraordinary observer might have seen that the chin was very pointed and pronounced; that the

---

1   A reference to Daniel 6.16–28 (see also 197, note 1, and 208, note 1), this is also one of many references in *AGG* to *Marmion: A Tale of Flodden Field* (1808) by Sir Walter Scott (1771–1832), here VI. xiv. 23–25. *AGG* cites *Marmion* several times: see 251, note 1; and 262, note 1. Scott's poem, a popular text in the nineteenth century, is later presented in *AGG*, like the Tennyson idyll in Chapter XXVIII, "Unfortunate Lily Maid," as prescribed reading for Avonlea schoolchildren. It also figured in readers and many other anthologies in English Canada throughout the nineteenth century and into the twentieth. Part of the canto cited here and later was included as "The Parting of Marmion and Douglas" in the *Fifth Royal Reader*, the series to which Montgomery refers throughout *AGG* (See *Fifth Royal Reader* 64–65).

2   According to *Fairchild's Dictionary of Textiles,* 7th ed. (New York: Fairchild, 1996), a wincey is "a plain weave cotton flannelette made from fine yarns, piece dyed, and given a napped finish. Better qualities were made with an admixture of wool. Originally a fabric made with wool filling and a linen or cotton warp. Derived from linsey-woolsey. Used for men's shirts, winter underwear." Here the suggestion is that Anne's dress is made of poor quality wincey.

big eyes were full of spirit and vivacity; that the mouth was sweet-lipped and expressive; that the forehead was broad and full; in short, our discerning extraordinary observer might have concluded that no commonplace soul inhabited the body of this stray woman-child of whom shy Matthew Cuthbert was so ludicrously afraid.

Matthew, however, was spared the ordeal of speaking first, for as soon as she concluded that he was coming to her she stood up, grasping with one thin brown hand the handle of a shabby, old-fashioned carpet-bag;[1] the other she held out to him.

"I suppose you are Mr. Matthew Cuthbert of Green Gables?" she said in a peculiarly clear, sweet voice. "I'm very glad to see you. I was beginning to be afraid you weren't coming for me and I was imagining all the things that might have happened to prevent you. I had made up my mind that if you didn't come for me to-night I'd go down the track to that big wild cherry-tree at the bend, and climb up into it to stay all night. I wouldn't be a bit afraid, and it would be lovely to sleep in a wild cherry-tree all white with bloom in the moonshine, don't you think? You could imagine you were dwelling in marble halls,[2] couldn't you? And I was quite sure you would come for me in the morning, if you didn't to-night."

Matthew had taken the scrawny little hand awkwardly in his; then and there he decided what to do. He could not tell this child with the glowing eyes that there had been a mistake; he would take her home and let Marilla do that. She couldn't be left at Bright River anyhow, no matter what mistake had been made, so all questions and explanations might as well be deferred until he was safely back at Green Gables.

"I'm sorry I was late," he said shyly. "Come along. The horse is over in the yard. Give me your bag."

"Oh, I can carry it," the child responded cheerfully. "It isn't heavy. I've got all my worldly goods in it, but it isn't heavy. And if it isn't carried in just a certain way the handle pulls out—so I'd better keep it because I know the exact knack of it. It's an extremely old carpet-bag. Oh, I'm very glad you've come, even

---

1   "A travelling bag, properly one made of carpet" (*OED*).
2   Cf. song by Alfred Bunn (1796–1860) ("I dreamt I dwelt in marble halls") from *The Bohemian Girl* (1843), a comic opera.

if it would have been nice to sleep in a wild cherry-tree. We've got to drive a long piece, haven't we? Mrs. Spencer said it was eight miles. I'm glad because I love driving. Oh, it seems so wonderful that I'm going to live with you and belong to you. I've never belonged to anybody—not really. But the asylum was the worst. I've only been in it four months, but that was enough. I don't suppose you ever were an orphan in an asylum, so you can't possibly understand what it is like. It's worse than anything you could imagine. Mrs. Spencer said it was wicked of me to talk like that, but I didn't mean to be wicked. It's so easy to be wicked without knowing it, isn't it? They were good, you know—the asylum people. But there is so little scope for the imagination in an asylum—only just in the other orphans. It *was* pretty inter-esting to imagine things about them—to imagine that perhaps the girl who sat next to you was really the daughter of a belted[1] earl, who had been stolen away from her parents in her infancy by a cruel nurse who died before she could confess. I used to lie awake at nights and imagine things like that, because I didn't have time in the day. I guess that's why I'm so thin—I *am* dreadful thin, ain't I? There isn't a pick on my bones. I do love to imag-ine I'm nice and plump, with dimples in my elbows."

With this Matthew's companion stopped talking, partly because she was out of breath and partly because they had reached the buggy. Not another word did she say until they had left the village and were driving down a steep little hill, the road part of which had been cut so deeply into the soft soil that the banks, fringed with blooming wild cherry-trees and slim white birches, were several feet above their heads.

The child put out her hand and broke off a branch of wild plum that brushed against the side of the buggy.

"Isn't that beautiful? What did that tree, leaning out from the bank, all white and lacy, make you think of?" she asked.

"Well now, I dunno," said Matthew.

---

[1] OED notes that *belted* can refer, as it does here, to "the distinctive cincture [belt or girdle] of an earl or knight [...] worn as a mark of rank or distinction." OED cites Sir Walter Scott's poem, *The Lay of the Last Minstrel* (1805) and his novel, *The Abbot* (1820), as well as Scottish poet Robert Burns (1759–96), "A Man's a Man" ("For 'A That and A' That") (1795): "A prince can mak a belted knight" (25).

"Why, a bride, of course—a bride all in white with a lovely misty veil. I've never seen one, but I can imagine what she would look like. I don't ever expect to be a bride myself. I'm so homely nobody will ever want to marry me—unless it might be a foreign missionary. I suppose a foreign missionary mightn't be very particular. But I do hope that some day I shall have a white dress. That is my highest ideal of earthly bliss. I just love pretty clothes. And I've never had a pretty dress in my life that I can remember—but of course it's all the more to look forward to, isn't it? And then I can imagine that I'm dressed gorgeously. This morning when I left the asylum I felt so ashamed because I had to wear this horrid old wincey dress. All the orphans had to wear them, you know. A merchant in Hopetown last winter donated three hundred yards of wincey to the asylum. Some people said it was because he couldn't sell it, but I'd rather believe that it was out of the kindness of his heart, wouldn't you? When we got on the train I felt as if everybody must be looking at me and pitying me. But I just went to work and imagined that I had on the most beautiful pale blue silk dress—because when you *are* imagining you might as well imagine something worth while—and a big hat all flowers and nodding plumes, and a gold watch, and kid gloves and boots. I felt cheered up right away and I enjoyed my trip to the Island with all my might. I wasn't a bit sick coming over in the boat. Neither was Mrs. Spencer, although she generally is. She said she hadn't time to get sick, watching to see that I didn't fall overboard. She said she never saw the beat of me for prowling about. But if it kept her from being seasick it's a mercy I did prowl, isn't it? And I wanted to see everything that was to be seen on that boat, because I didn't know whether I'd ever have another opportunity. Oh, there are a lot more cherry-trees all in bloom! This Island is the bloomiest place. I just love it already, and I'm so glad I'm going to live here. I've always heard that Prince Edward Island was the prettiest place in the world, and I used to imagine I was living here, but I never really expected I would. It's delightful when your imaginations come true, isn't it? But those red roads are so funny. When we got into the train at Charlottetown and the red roads began to flash past I asked Mrs. Spencer what made them red and she said she didn't know and for pity's sake not to ask her any more questions.

She said I must have asked her a thousand already. I suppose I had, too, but how are you going to find out about things if you don't ask questions? And what *does* make the roads red?"[1]

"Well now, I dunno," said Matthew.

"Well, that is one of the things to find out sometime. Isn't it splendid to think of all the things there are to find out about? It just makes me feel glad to be alive—it's such an interesting world. It wouldn't be half so interesting if we knew all about everything, would it? There'd be no scope for imagination then, would there? But am I talking too much? People are always telling me I do. Would you rather I didn't talk? If you say so I'll stop. I *can* stop when I make up my mind to it, although it's difficult."

Matthew, much to his own surprise, was enjoying himself. Like most quiet folks he liked talkative people when they were willing to do the talking themselves and did not expect him to keep up his end of it. But he had never expected to enjoy the society of a little girl. Women were bad enough in all conscience, but little girls were worse. He detested the way they had of sidling past him timidly, with sidewise glances, as if they expected him to gobble them up at a mouthful if they ventured to say a word. This was the Avonlea type of well-bred little girl. But this freckled witch was very different, and although he found it rather difficult for his slower intelligence to keep up with her brisk mental processes he thought that he "kind of liked her chatter." So he said as shyly as usual:

"Oh, you can talk as much as you like. I don't mind."

"Oh, I'm so glad. I know you and I are going to get along together fine. It's such a relief to talk when one wants to and not be told that children should be seen and not heard. I've had that said to me a million times if I have once. And people laugh at me because I use big words. But if you have big ideas you have to use big words to express them, haven't you?"

"Well now, that seems reasonable," said Matthew.

"Mrs. Spencer said that my tongue must be hung in the middle. But it isn't—it's firmly fastened at one end. Mrs. Spencer

---

[1]   Anne learns later in school what makes the roads red, but it is not indicated in the novel that the colour is attributable to the high iron-oxide content in the soil in P.E.I. See also 181, note 1.

said your place was named Green Gables. I asked her all about it. And she said there were trees all around it. I was gladder than ever. I just love trees. And there weren't any at all about the asylum, only a few poor weeny-teeny things out in front with little whitewashed cagey things about them. They just looked like orphans themselves, those trees did. It used to make me want to cry to look at them. I used to say to them, 'Oh, you *poor* little things! If you were out in a great big woods with other trees all around you and little mosses and Junebells growing over your roots and a brook not far away and birds singing in your branches, you could grow, couldn't you? But you can't where you are. I know just exactly how you feel, little trees.' I felt sorry to leave them behind this morning. You do get so attached to things like that, don't you? Is there a brook anywhere near Green Gables? I forgot to ask Mrs. Spencer that."

"Well now, yes, there's one right below the house."

"Fancy! It's always been one of my dreams to live near a brook. I never expected I would, though. Dreams don't often come true, do they? Wouldn't it be nice if they did? But just now I feel pretty nearly perfectly happy. I can't feel exactly perfectly happy because—well, what colour would you call this?"

She twitched one of her long glossy braids over her thin shoulder and held it up before Matthew's eyes. Matthew was not used to deciding on the tints of ladies' tresses, but in this case there couldn't be much doubt.

"It's red, ain't it?" he said.

The girl let the braid drop back with a sigh that seemed to come from her very toes and to exhale forth all the sorrows of the ages.

"Yes, it's red," she said resignedly. "Now you see why I can't be perfectly happy. Nobody could who had red hair. I don't mind the other things so much—the freckles and the green eyes and my skinniness. I can imagine them away. I can imagine that I have a beautiful rose-leaf complexion and lovely starry violet eyes. But I *cannot* imagine that red hair away. I do my best. I think to myself, 'Now my hair is a glorious black, black as the raven's wing.' But all the time I *know* it is just plain red, and it breaks my heart. It will be my lifelong sorrow. I read of a girl once in a novel who had a lifelong sorrow, but it wasn't red hair. Her hair was pure gold, rippling back from her alabaster brow.[1] What is an alabaster brow? I never could find out. Can you tell me?"

"Well now, I'm afraid I can't," said Matthew, who was getting a little dizzy. He felt as he had once felt in his rash youth when another boy had enticed him on the merry-go-round at a picnic.

"Well, whatever it was it must have been something nice because she was divinely beautiful. Have you ever imagined what it must feel like to be divinely beautiful?"

"Well now, no, I haven't," confessed Matthew ingenuously.

"I have, often. Which would you rather be if you had the choice—divinely beautiful or dazzlingly clever or angelically good?"

"Well now, I—I don't know exactly."

"Neither do I. I can never decide. But it doesn't make much real difference for it isn't likely I'll ever be either. It's certain I'll never be angelically good. Mrs. Spencer says—oh, Mr. Cuthbert! Oh, Mr. Cuthbert!! Oh, Mr. Cuthbert!!!"

That was not what Mrs. Spencer had said; neither had the child tumbled out of the buggy nor had Matthew done anything astonishing. They had simply rounded a curve in the road and found themselves in the "Avenue."

The "Avenue," so called by Newbridge people, was a stretch of road four or five hundred yards long, completely arched over with huge, wide-spreading apple-trees, planted years ago by an eccentric old farmer. Overhead was one long canopy of snowy fragrant bloom. Below the boughs the air was full of a purple twilight and far ahead a glimpse of painted sunset sky shone like a great rose window[2] at the end of a cathedral aisle.

Its beauty seemed to strike the child dumb. She leaned back in the buggy, her thin hands clasped before her, her face lifted rapturously to the white splendour above. Even when they had passed out and were driving down the long slope to Newbridge she never moved or spoke. Still with rapt face she gazed afar into the sunset west, with eyes that saw visions trooping splendidly

---

[1] "A term applied to fine translucent varieties of carbonate or sulphate of lime, especially to the pure white variety used for vases, ornaments, and busts" (*OED*).

[2] "A circular window, *esp.* one divided into compartments by mullions radiating from a centre, or filled with tracery suggestive of the form of a rose" (*OED*).

across that glowing background. Through Newbridge, a bustling little village where dogs barked at them and small boys hooted and curious faces peered from the windows, they drove, still in silence. When three more miles had dropped away behind them the child had not spoken. She could keep silence, it was evident, as energetically as she could talk.

"I guess you're feeling pretty tired and hungry," Matthew ventured at last, accounting for her long visitation of dumbness with the only reason he could think of. "But we haven't very far to go now—only another mile."

She came out of her reverie with a deep sigh and looked at him with the dreamy gaze of a soul that had been wondering[1] afar, star-led.

"Oh, Mr. Cuthbert," she whispered, "that place we came through—that white place—what was it?"

"Well now, you must mean the Avenue," said Matthew after a few moments' profound reflection. "It is a kind of pretty place."

"Pretty? Oh, *pretty* doesn't seem the right word to use. Nor beautiful, either. They don't go far enough. Oh, it was wonderful—wonderful. It's the first thing I ever saw that couldn't be improved upon by imagination. It just satisfied me here"—she put one hand on her breast—"it made a queer funny ache and yet it was a pleasant ache. Did you ever have an ache like that, Mr. Cuthbert?"

"Well now, I just can't recollect that I ever had."

"I have it lots of times—whenever I see anything royally beautiful. But they shouldn't call that lovely place the Avenue. There is no meaning in a name like that. They should call it— let me see—the White Way of Delight. Isn't that a nice imaginative name? When I don't like the name of a place or a person I always imagine a new one and always think of them so. There was a girl at the asylum whose name was Hepzibah Jenkins, but I always imagined her as Rosalia DeVere. Other people may call that place the Avenue, but I shall always call it the White Way of Delight. Have we really only another mile to go before we get home? I'm glad and I'm sorry. I'm sorry because this drive has

---

[1] MS uses *wandering*.

been so pleasant and I'm always sorry when pleasant things end. Something still pleasanter may come after, but you can never be sure. And it's so often the case that it isn't pleasanter. That has been my experience anyhow. But I'm glad to think of getting home. You see, I've never had a real home since I can remember. It gives me that pleasant ache again just to think of coming to a really truly home. Oh, isn't that pretty!"

They had driven over the crest of a hill. Below them was a pond, looking almost like a river so long and winding was it. A bridge spanned it midway and from there to its lower end, where an amber-hued belt of sand-hills shut it in from the dark blue gulf beyond, the water was a glory of many shifting hues—the most spiritual shadings of crocus and rose and ethereal green, with other elusive tintings for which no name has ever been found. Above the bridge the pond ran up into fringing groves of fir and maple and lay all darkly translucent in their wavering shadows. Here and there a wild plum leaned out from the bank like a white-clad girl tiptoeing to her own reflection. From the marsh at the head of the pond came the clear, mournfully-sweet chorus of the frogs. There was a little gray house peering around a white apple orchard on a slope beyond and, although it was not yet quite dark, a light was shining from one of its windows.

"That's Barry's pond," said Matthew.

"Oh, I don't like that name either. I shall call it—let me see— the Lake of Shining Waters. Yes, that is the right name for it. I know because of the thrill. When I hit on a name that suits exactly it gives me a thrill. Do things ever give you a thrill?"

Matthew ruminated.

"Well now, yes. It always kind of gives me a thrill to see them ugly white grubs that spade up in the cucumber beds. I hate the look of them."

"Oh, I don't think that can be exactly the same kind of a thrill. Do you think it can? There doesn't seem to be much connection between grubs and lakes of shining waters, does there? But why do other people call it Barry's pond?"

"I reckon because Mr. Barry lives up there in that house. Orchard Slope's the name of his place. If it wasn't for that big bush behind it you could see Green Gables from here. But we have to go over the bridge and round by the road, so it's near half a mile further."

"Has Mr. Barry any little girls? Well, not so very little either—about my size."

"He's got one about eleven. Her name is Diana."

"Oh!" with a long indrawing of breath. "What a perfectly lovely name!"

"Well now, I dunno. There's something dreadful heathenish[1] about it, seems to me. I'd ruther Jane or Mary or some sensible name like that. But when Diana was born there was a schoolmaster boarding there and they gave him the naming of her and he called her Diana."

"I wish there had been a schoolmaster like that around when *I* was born, then. Oh, here we are at the bridge. I'm going to shut my eyes tight. I'm always afraid going over bridges. I can't help imagining that perhaps, just as we get to the middle, they'll crumple up like a jack-knife and nip us. So I shut my eyes. But I always have to open them for all when I think we're getting near the middle. Because, you see, if the bridge *did* crumple up I'd want to *see* it crumple. What a jolly rumble it makes! I always like the rumble part of it. Isn't it splendid there are so many things to like in this world? There, we're over. Now I'll look back. Good night, dear Lake of Shining Waters. I always say good night to the things I love, just as I would to people. I think they like it. That water looks as if it was smiling at me."

When they had driven up the further hill and around a corner Matthew said:

"We're pretty near home now. That's Green Gables over—"

"Oh, don't tell me," she interrupted breathlessly, catching at his partially raised arm and shutting her eyes that she might not see his gesture. "Let me guess. I'm sure I'll guess right."

She opened her eyes and looked about her. They were on the crest of a hill. The sun had set some time since, but the landscape was still clear in the mellow afterlight. To the west a dark church spire rose up against a marigold sky. Below was a little valley and

---

[1] Matthew is referring to the association of Diana's name not with a Christian figure but with the Roman divinity. Diana was identified with the Greek goddess Artemis, and was goddess of the moon.

beyond a long, gently-rising slope with snug farmsteads scattered along it. From one to another the child's eyes darted, eager and wistful. At last they lingered on one away to the left, far back from the road, dimly white with blossoming trees in the twilight of the surrounding woods. Over it, in the stainless southwest sky, a great crystal-white star was shining like a lamp of guidance and promise.

"That's it, isn't it?" she said, pointing.

Matthew slapped the reins on the sorrel's back delightedly.

"Well now, you've guessed it! But I reckon Mrs. Spencer described it so's you could tell."

"No, she didn't—really she didn't. All she said might just as well have been about most of those other places. I hadn't any real idea what it looked like. But just as soon as I saw it I felt it was home. Oh, it seems as if I must be in a dream. Do you know, my arm must be black and blue from the elbow up, for I've pinched myself so many times to-day. Every little while a horrible sickening feeling would come over me and I'd be so afraid it was all a dream. Then I'd pinch myself to see if it was real—until suddenly I remembered that even supposing it was only a dream I'd better go on dreaming as long as I could; so I stopped pinching. But it *is* real and we're nearly home."

With a sigh of rapture she relapsed into silence. Matthew stirred uneasily. He felt glad that it would be Marilla and not he who would have to tell this waif of the world that the home she longed for was not to be hers after all. They drove over Lynde's Hollow, where it was already quite dark, but not so dark that Mrs. Rachel could not see them from her window vantage, and up the hill and into the long lane of Green Gables. By the time they arrived at the house Matthew was shrinking from the approaching revelation with an energy he did not understand. It was not of Marilla or himself he was thinking or of the trouble this mistake was probably going to make for them, but of the child's disappointment. When he thought of that rapt light being quenched in her eyes he had an uncomfortable feeling that he was going to assist at murdering something—much the same feeling that came over him when he had to kill a lamb or calf or any other innocent little creature.

The yard was quite dark as they turned into it and the poplar leaves were rustling silkily all round it.

"Listen to the trees talking in their sleep," she whispered, as he lifted her to the ground. "What nice dreams they must have!"

Then, holding tightly to the carpet-bag which contained "all her worldly goods," she followed him into the house.

CHAPTER III

MARILLA CUTHBERT IS SURPRISED

MARILLA came briskly forward as Matthew opened the door. But when her eyes fell on the odd little figure in the stiff, ugly dress, with the long braids of red hair and the eager, luminous eyes, she stopped short in amazement.

"Matthew Cuthbert, who's that?" she ejaculated. "Where is the boy?"

"There wasn't any boy," said Matthew wretchedly. "There was only *her*."

He nodded at the child, remembering that he had never even asked her name.

"No boy! But there *must* have been a boy," insisted Marilla. "We sent word to Mrs. Spencer to bring a boy."

"Well, she didn't. She brought *her*. I asked the station-master. And I had to bring her home. She couldn't be left there, no matter where the mistake had come in."

"Well, this is a pretty piece of business!" ejaculated Marilla.

During this dialogue the child had remained silent, her eyes roving from one to the other, all the animation fading out of her face. Suddenly she seemed to grasp the full meaning of what had been said. Dropping her precious carpet-bag she sprang forward a step and clasped her hands.

"You don't want me!" she cried. "You don't want me because I'm not a boy! I might have expected it! Nobody ever did want me. I might have known it was all too beautiful to last. I might have known nobody really did want me. Oh, what shall I do? I'm going to burst into tears!"

Burst into tears she did. Sitting down on a chair by the table,

"'MATTHEW CUTHBERT, WHO'S THAT?' SHE EJACULATED."

flinging her arms out upon it, and burying her face in them, she proceeded to cry stormily. Marilla and Matthew looked at each other deprecatingly across the stove. Neither of them knew what to say or do. Finally Marilla stepped lamely into the breach.[1]

"Well, well, there's no need to cry so about it."

"Yes, there *is* need!" The child raised her head quickly, revealing a tear-stained face and trembling lips. "*You* would cry, too, if you were an orphan and had come to a place you thought was going to be home and found that they didn't want you because you weren't a boy. Oh, this is the most *tragical* thing that ever happened to me!"

Something like a reluctant smile, rather rusty from long disuse, mellowed Marilla's grim expression.

"Well, don't cry any more. We're not going to turn you out-of-doors to-night. You'll have to stay here until we investigate this affair. What's your name?"

The child hesitated for a moment.

"Will you please call me Cordelia?" she said eagerly.

"*Call* you Cordelia! Is that your name?"

"No-o-o, it's not exactly my name, but I would love to be called Cordelia. It's such a perfectly elegant name."

"I don't know what on earth you mean. If Cordelia isn't your name, what is?"

"Anne Shirley," reluctantly faltered forth the owner of that name, "but oh, please do call me Cordelia. It can't matter much to you what you call me if I'm only going to be here a little while, can it? And Anne is such an unromantic name."

"Unromantic fiddlesticks![2] said the unsympathetic Marilla. "Anne is a real good plain sensible name. You've no need to be ashamed of it."

"Oh, I'm not ashamed of it," explained Anne, "only I like Cordelia better. I've always imagined that my name was Cordelia—at least, I always have of late years. When I was young I used to imagine it was Geraldine, but I like Cordelia better now.

---

[1] Mock-heroic allusion to Shakespeare's *Henry V* 3.1.1–2. The passage from which the phrase is taken appears in the *Sixth Royal Reader* as "Speech of Henry V at the Siege of Harfleur" (242–243).

[2] Nonsense.

But if you call me Anne please call me Anne spelled with an *e*."

"What difference does it make how it's spelled?" asked Marilla with another rusty smile as she picked up the teapot.

"Oh, it makes *such* a difference. It *looks* so much nicer. When you hear a name pronounced can't you always see it in your mind, just as if it was printed out? I can; and A-n-n looks dreadful, but A-n-n-e looks so much more distinguished. If you'll only call me Anne spelled with an *e* I shall try to reconcile myself to not being called Cordelia."

"Very well, then, Anne spelled with an *e*, can you tell us how this mistake came to be made? We sent word to Mrs. Spencer to bring us a boy. Were there no boys at the asylum?"

"Oh, yes, there was an abundance of them. But Mrs. Spencer said *distinctly* that you wanted a girl about eleven years old. And the matron said she thought I would do. You don't know how delighted I was. I couldn't sleep all last night for joy. Oh," she added reproachfully, turning to Matthew, "why didn't you tell me at the station that you didn't want me and leave me there? If I hadn't seen the White Way of Delight and the Lake of Shining Waters it wouldn't be so hard."

"What on earth does she mean?" demanded Marilla, staring at Matthew.

"She—she's just referring to some conversation we had on the road," said Matthew hastily. "I'm going out to put the mare in, Marilla. Have tea ready when I come back."

"Did Mrs. Spencer bring anybody over besides you?" continued Marilla when Matthew had gone out.

"She brought Lily Jones for herself. Lily is only five years old and she is very beautiful. She has nut-brown hair. If I was very beautiful and had nut-brown hair would you keep me?"

"No. We want a boy to help Matthew on the farm. A girl would be of no use to us. Take off your hat. I'll lay it and your bag on the hall table."

Anne took off her hat meekly. Matthew came back presently and they sat down to supper. But Anne could not eat. In vain she nibbled at the bread and butter and pecked at the crab-apple preserve out of the little scalloped glass dish by her plate. She did not really make any headway at all.

"You're not eating anything," said Marilla sharply, eying her as if it were a serious shortcoming.

Anne sighed.

"I can't. I'm in the depths of despair.[1] Can you eat when you are in the depths of despair?"

"I've never been in the depths of despair, so I can't say," responded Marilla.

"Weren't you? Well, did you ever try to *imagine* you were in the depths of despair?"

"No, I didn't."

"Then I don't think you can understand what it's like. It's a very uncomfortable feeling indeed. When you try to eat a lump comes right up in your throat and you can't swallow anything, not even if it was a chocolate caramel. I had one chocolate caramel once two years ago and it was simply delicious. I've often dreamed since then that I had a lot of chocolate caramels, but I always wake up just when I'm going to eat them. I do hope you won't be offended because I can't eat. Everything is extremely nice, but still I cannot eat."

"I guess she's tired," said Matthew, who hadn't spoken since his return from the barn. "Best put her to bed, Marilla."

Marilla had been wondering where Anne should be put to bed. She had prepared a couch in the kitchen chamber for the desired and expected boy. But, although it was neat and clean, it did not seem quite the thing to put a girl there somehow. But the spare room was out of the question for such a stray waif, so there remained only the east gable room. Marilla lighted a candle and told Anne to follow her, which Anne spiritlessly did, taking her hat and carpet-bag from the hall table as she passed. The hall was fearsomely clean; the little gable chamber in which she presently found herself seemed still cleaner.

Marilla set the candle on a three-legged, three-cornered table and turned down the bedclothes.

"I suppose you have a nightgown?" she questioned.

---

[1] Clichéd expression for profound grief. Cf. American poet Winnifred Howells (1863–1889), "A Wasted Sympathy," in *An American Anthology: 1787–1900* (1900), ed. Edmund Clarence Stedman (New York: Greenwood, 1968) (702).

Anne nodded.

"Yes, I have two. The matron of the asylum made them for me. They're fearfully skimpy. There is never enough to go around in an asylum, so things are always skimpy—at least in a poor asylum like ours. I hate skimpy night-dresses. But one can dream just as well in them as in lovely trailing ones, with frills around the neck, that's one consolation."

"Well, undress as quick as you can and go to bed. I'll come back in a few minutes for the candle. I daren't trust you to put it out yourself. You'd likely set the place on fire."

When Marilla had gone Anne looked around her wistfully. The whitewashed walls were so painfully bare and staring that she thought they must ache over their own bareness. The floor was bare, too, except for a round braided mat in the middle such as Anne had never seen before. In one corner was the bed, a high old-fashioned one, with four dark, low-turned posts. In the other corner was the aforesaid three-cornered table adorned with a fat, red velvet pincushion hard enough to turn the point of the most adventurous pin. Above it hung a little six by eight mirror. Midway between table and bed was the window, with an icy white muslin[1] frill over it, and opposite it was the wash-stand. The whole apartment was of a rigidity not to be described in words, but which sent a shiver to the very marrow of Anne's bones. With a sob she hastily discarded her garments, put on the skimpy nightgown and sprang into bed where she burrowed face downward into the pillow and pulled the clothes over her head. When Marilla came up for the light various skimpy articles of raiment scattered most untidily over the floor and a certain tempestuous appearance of the bed were the only indications of any presence save her own.

She deliberately picked up Anne's clothes, placed them neatly on a prim yellow chair, and then, taking up the candle, went over to the bed.

"Good night," she said, a little awkwardly, but not unkindly.

Anne's white face and big eyes appeared over the bedclothes with a startling suddenness.

---

[1]   "A large group of firm, plain weave cotton and cotton blend fabrics in a wide range of qualities and weights from lightweight sheers to heavyweight sheetings" (*Fairchild's Dictionary of Textiles*).

"How can you call it a *good* night when you know it must be the very worst night I've ever had?" she said reproachfully.

Then she dived down into invisibility again.

Marilla went slowly down to the kitchen and proceeded to wash the supper dishes. Matthew was smoking—a sure sign of perturbation of mind. He seldom smoked, for Marilla set her face against it[1] as a filthy habit; but at certain times and seasons he felt driven to it and then Marilla winked at the practice, realizing that a mere man must have some vent for his emotions.

"Well, this is a pretty kettle of fish,"[2] she said wrathfully. "This is what comes of sending word instead of going ourselves. Robert Spencer's folks have twisted that message somehow. One of us will have to drive over and see Mrs. Spencer to-morrow, that's certain. This girl will have to be sent back to the asylum."

"Yes, I suppose so," said Matthew reluctantly.

"You *suppose* so! Don't you know it?"

"Well now, she's a real nice little thing, Marilla. It's kind of a pity to send her back when she's so set on staying here."

"Matthew Cuthbert, you don't mean to say you think we ought to keep her!"

Marilla's astonishment could not have been greater if Matthew had expressed a predilection for standing on his head.

"Well now, no, I suppose not—not exactly," stammered Matthew, uncomfortably driven into a corner for his precise meaning. "I suppose—we could hardly be expected to keep her."

"I should say not. What good would she be to us?"

"We might be some good to her," said Matthew suddenly and unexpectedly.

"Matthew Cuthbert, I believe that child has bewitched you! I can see as plain as plain that you want to keep her."

"Well now, she's a real interesting little thing," persisted Matthew. "You should have heard her talk coming from the station."

"Oh, she can talk fast enough. I saw that at once. It's nothing in her favour, either. I don't like children who have so much to say. I don't want an orphan girl and if I did she isn't the style I'd

---

[1] Cf. Leviticus 20.3; Ezekiel 4.3; 13.17; 15.7.
[2] "An awkward state of affairs, a mess, a muddle" (*Brewer's*).

pick out. There's something I don't understand about her. No, she's got to be despatched straight-way back to where she came from."

"I could hire a French boy to help me," said Matthew, "and she'd be company for you."

"I'm not suffering for company," said Marilla shortly. "And I'm not going to keep her."

"Well now, it's just as you say, of course, Marilla," said Matthew rising and putting his pipe away. "I'm going to bed."

To bed went Matthew. And to bed, when she had put her dishes away, went Marilla, frowning most resolutely. And upstairs, in the east gable, a lonely, heart-hungry, friendless child cried herself to sleep.

CHAPTER IV

MORNING AT GREEN GABLES

IT was broad daylight when Anne awoke and sat up in bed, staring confusedly at the window through which a flood of cheery sunshine was pouring and outside of which something white and feathery waved across glimpses of blue sky.

For a moment she could not remember where she was. First came a delightful thrill, as of something very pleasant; then a horrible remembrance. This was Green Gables and they didn't want her because she wasn't a boy!

But it was morning and, yes, it was a cherry-tree in full bloom outside of her window. With a bound she was out of bed and across the floor. She pushed up the sash—it went up stiffly and creakily, as if it hadn't been opened for a long time, which was the case; and it stuck so tight that nothing was needed to hold it up.

Anne dropped on her knees and gazed out into the June morning, her eyes glistening with delight. Oh, wasn't it beautiful? Wasn't it a lovely place? Suppose she wasn't really going to stay here! She would imagine she was. There was scope for imagination here.

A huge cherry-tree grew outside, so close that its boughs tapped against the house, and it was so thick-set with blossoms that hardly a leaf was to be seen. On both sides of the house was a big orchard, one of apple-trees and one of cherry trees, also showered over with blossoms; and their grass was all sprinkled with dandelions. In the garden below were lilac-trees purple with flowers, and their dizzily sweet fragrance drifted up to the window on the morning wind.

Below the garden a green field lush with clover sloped down to the hollow where the brook ran and where scores of white birches grew, upspringing airily out of an undergrowth suggestive of delightful possibilities in ferns and mosses and woodsy things generally. Beyond it was a hill, green and feathery with spruce and fir; there was a gap in it where the gray gable end of the little house she had seen from the other side of the Lake of Shining Waters was visible.

Off to the left were the big barns and beyond them, away down over green, low-sloping fields, was a sparkling blue glimpse of sea.

Anne's beauty-loving eyes lingered on it all, taking everything greedily in; she had looked on so many unlovely places in her life, poor child; but this was as lovely as anything she had ever dreamed.

She knelt there, lost to everything but the loveliness around her, until she was startled by a hand on her shoulder. Marilla had come in unheard by the small dreamer.

"It's time you were dressed," she said curtly.

Marilla really did not know how to talk to the child, and her uncomfortable ignorance made her crisp and curt when she did not mean to be.

Anne stood up and drew a long breath.

"Oh, isn't it wonderful?" she said, waving her hand comprehensively at the good world outside.

"It's a big tree," said Marilla, "and it blooms great, but the fruit don't amount to much never—small and wormy."

"Oh, I don't mean just the tree; of course it's lovely—yes, it's *radiantly* lovely—it blooms as if it meant it—but I meant everything, the garden and the orchard and the brook and the woods, the whole big dear world.[1] Don't you feel as if you just loved the world on a morning like this? And I can hear the brook laughing

---

[1] Cf. *SJ* I 1.

all the way up here. Have you ever noticed what cheerful things brooks are? They're always laughing. Even in winter-time I've heard them under the ice. I'm so glad there's a brook near Green Gables. Perhaps you think it doesn't make any difference to me when you're not going to keep me, but it does. I shall always like to remember that there is a brook at Green Gables even if I never see it again. If there wasn't a brook I'd be *haunted* by the uncomfortable feeling that there ought to be one. I'm not in the depths of despair this morning. I never can be in the morning. Isn't it a splendid thing that there are mornings? But I feel very sad. I've just been imagining that it was really me you wanted after all and that I was to stay here for ever and ever. It was a great comfort while it lasted. But the worst of imagining things is that the time comes when you have to stop and that hurts."

"You'd better get dressed and come down-stairs and never mind your imaginings," said Marilla as soon as she could get a word in edgewise. "Breakfast is waiting. Wash your face and comb your hair. Leave the window up and turn your bedclothes back over the foot of the bed. Be as smart as you can."

Anne could evidently be smart to some purpose for she was down-stairs in ten minutes' time, with her clothes neatly on, her hair brushed and braided, her face washed, and a comfortable consciousness pervading her soul that she had fulfilled all Marilla's requirements. As a matter of fact, however, she had forgotten to turn back the bedclothes.

"I'm pretty hungry this morning," she announced, as she slipped into the chair Marilla placed for her. "The world doesn't seem such a howling wilderness[1] as it did last night. I'm so glad it's a sunshiny morning. But I like rainy mornings real well, too. All sorts of mornings are interesting, don't you think? You don't know what's going to happen through the day, and there's so much scope for imagination. But I'm glad it's not rainy to-day because it's easier to be cheerful and bear up under affliction on a sunshiny day. I feel that I have a good deal to bear up under. It's all very well to read about sorrows and imagine yourself living through them heroically, but it's not so nice when you really come to have them, is it?"

---

[1] Cf. Deuteronomy 32.10.

"For pity's sake hold your tongue," said Marilla. "You talk entirely too much for a little girl."

Thereupon Anne held her tongue so obediently and thoroughly that her continued silence made Marilla rather nervous, as if in the presence of something not exactly natural. Matthew also held his tongue,—but this at least was natural,—so that the meal was a very silent one.

As it progressed Anne became more and more abstracted, eating mechanically, with her big eyes fixed unswervingly and unseeingly on the sky outside the window. This made Marilla more nervous than ever; she had an uncomfortable feeling that while this odd child's body might be there at the table her spirit was far away in some remote airy cloudland, borne aloft on the wings of imagination. Who would want such a child about the place?

Yet Matthew wished to keep her, of all unaccountable things! Marilla felt that he wanted it just as much this morning as he had the night before, and that he would go on wanting it. That was Matthew's way—take a whim into his head and cling to it with the most amazing silent persistency—a persistency ten times more potent and effectual in its very silence than if he had talked it out.

When the meal was ended Anne came out of her reverie and offered to wash the dishes.

"Can you wash dishes right?" asked Marilla distrustfully.

"Pretty well. I'm better at looking after children, though. I've had so much experience at that. It's such a pity you haven't any here for me to look after."

"I don't feel as if I wanted any more children to look after than I've got at present. You're problem enough in all conscience. What's to be done with you I don't know. Matthew is a most ridiculous man."

"I think he's lovely," said Anne reproachfully. "He is so very sympathetic. He didn't mind how much I talked—he seemed to like it. I felt that he was a kindred spirit[1] as soon as ever I saw him."

---

[1] There is a range of possible sources for the term "kindred spirit," which is now associated primarily with *AGG*. Elizabeth Epperly notes in *The Fragrance of Sweet-Grass: L.M. Montgomery's Heroines and the Pursuit of Romance* (Toronto: U of Toronto P, 1992) that Montgomery may be referring to "Elegy Written in a Country Churchyard" (1751) by Thomas Gray (1716–61): "If chance, by lonely Contemplation led,/ Some kindred

"You're both queer enough, if that's what you mean by kindred spirits," said Marilla with a sniff. "Yes, you may wash the dishes. Take plenty of hot water, and be sure you dry them well. I've got enough to attend to this morning for I'll have to drive over to White Sands in the afternoon and see Mrs. Spencer. You'll come with me and we'll settle what's to be done with you. After you've finished the dishes go up-stairs and make your bed."

Anne washed the dishes deftly enough, as Marilla, who kept a sharp eye on the process, discerned. Later on she made her bed less successfully, for she had never learned the art of wrestling with a feather tick.[1] But it was done somehow and smoothed down; and then Marilla, to get rid of her, told her she might go out-of-doors and amuse herself until dinner-time.

Anne flew to the door, face alight, eyes glowing. On the very threshold she stopped short, wheeled about, came back and sat down by the table, light and glow as effectually blotted out as if someone had clapped an extinguisher on her.

"What's the matter now?" demanded Marilla.

"I don't dare go out," said Anne, in the tone of a martyr relinquishing all earthly joys. "If I can't stay here there is no use in my loving Green Gables. And if I go out there and get acquainted

---

spirit shall enquire thy fate" (95–6). This poem appeared in the *Fifth Royal Reader* (164–69), as well as in many anthologies and collections of the nineteenth century. Epperly also notes that the term occurs in *The Story of an African Farm* (1883) by South African writer Olive Schreiner (1855–1920). Montgomery had read and admired this novel (Schreiner 68; see also *SJ* I 197, 248). The term also appears in a novel of 1898, *Elizabeth and Her German Garden*, by New Zealand writer Elizabeth von Arnim (1866–1941). Montgomery notes in her journal she had read this book in May 1905, or just before she began writing *AGG* (Epperly n.3, 252; see also *SJ* I 307): "... I long more and more for a kindred spirit—it seems so greedy to have so much loveliness to oneself—but kindred spirits are so very, very rare" (von Arnim 36). Montgomery wrote that she found Elizabeth "delightful [....] My 'twin soul' must live in *Elizabeth*, as far as gardening is concerned" (*SJ* I 307). Another possible reference is Felicia Hemans, "The Song of a Seraph" (1808): "Kindred spirit! Rise with me,/ Thine the meed of victory." Montgomery makes several references to the poetry of Hemans in *AGG*. Cf. also John Keats, "O Solitude! If I must with thee dwell" (1817): "... and it sure must be/ Almost the highest bliss of human-kind,/ When to the haunts two kindred spirits flee." The phrase also occurs in at least one of the "Pansy" novels by Isabella Macdonald Alden, books to which Montgomery refers in *AGG*. See, for example, *Ruth Erskine's Crosses* (London: Routledge, n.d.) (30).

1   Refers to a case or cover containing feathers, forming a mattress.

with all those trees and flowers and the orchard and the brook I'll not be able to help loving it. It's hard enough now, so I won't make it any harder. I want to go out so much—everything seems to be calling to me, 'Anne, Anne, come out to us. Anne, Anne, we want a playmate'—but it's better not. There is no use in loving things if you have to be torn from them, is there? And it's *so* hard to keep from loving things, isn't it? That was why I was so glad when I thought I was going to live here. I thought I'd have so many things to love and nothing to hinder me. But that brief dream is over. I am resigned to my fate now, so I don't think I'll go out for fear I'll get unresigned again. What is the name of that geranium on the window-sill, please?"

"That's the apple-scented geranium."

"Oh, I don't mean that sort of a name. I mean just a name you gave it yourself. Didn't you give it a name? May I give it one then? May I call it—let me see—Bonny would do—may I call it Bonny while I'm here? Oh, do let me!"

"Goodness, I don't care. But where on earth is the sense of naming a geranium?"

"Oh, I like things to have handles even if they are only geraniums. It makes them seem more like people. How do you know but that it hurts a geranium's feelings just to be called a geranium and nothing else? You wouldn't like to be called nothing but a woman all the time. Yes, I shall call it Bonny.[1] I named that cherry-tree outside my bedroom window this morning. I called it Snow Queen because it was so white. Of course, it won't always be in blossom, but one can imagine that it is, can't one?"

"I never in all my life saw or heard anything to equal her," muttered Marilla, beating a retreat down cellar after potatoes. "She *is* kind of interesting, as Matthew says. I can feel already that I'm wondering what on earth she'll say next. She'll be casting a spell over me, too. She's cast it over Matthew. That look he gave me when he went out said everything he said or hinted last night over again. I wish he was like other men and would talk things out. A body could answer back then and argue him into reason. But what's to be done with a man who just *looks*?"

---

[1] Cf. *SJ* I 1.

Anne had relapsed into reverie, with her chin in her hands and her eyes on the sky, when Marilla returned from her cellar pilgrimage. There Marilla left her until the early dinner was on the table.

"I suppose I can have the mare and buggy this afternoon, Matthew?" said Marilla.

Matthew nodded and looked wistfully at Anne. Marilla intercepted the look and said grimly:

"I'm going to drive over to White Sands and settle this thing. I'll take Anne with me and Mrs. Spencer will probably make arrangements to send her back to Nova Scotia at once. I'll set your tea out for you and I'll be home in time to milk the cows."

Still Matthew said nothing and Marilla had a sense of having wasted words and breath. There is nothing more aggravating than a man who won't talk back—unless it is a woman who won't.

Matthew hitched the sorrel into the buggy in due time and Marilla and Anne set off. Matthew opened the yard gate for them, and as they drove slowly through, he said, to nobody in particular as it seemed:

"Little Jerry Buote from the Creek was here this morning, and I told him I guessed I'd hire him for the summer."

Marilla made no reply, but she hit the unlucky sorrel such a vicious clip with the whip that the fat mare, unused to such treatment, whizzed indignantly down the lane at an alarming pace. Marilla looked back once as the buggy bounced along and saw that aggravating Matthew leaning over the gate, looking wistfully after them.

CHAPTER V

ANNE'S HISTORY

"DO you know," said Anne confidentially, "I've made up my mind to enjoy this drive. It's been my experience that you can nearly always enjoy things if you make up your mind firmly that you will. Of course, you must make it up *firmly*. I am not going to think about going back to the asylum while we're having our drive. I'm just going to think about the drive. Oh, look, there's one little early wild rose out! Isn't it lovely? Don't you think it must be glad to be a rose? Wouldn't it be nice if roses could talk? I'm sure they could tell us such lovely things. And isn't pink the most bewitching colour in the world? I love it, but I can't wear it. Redheaded people can't wear pink, not even in imagination. Did you ever know of anybody whose hair was red when she was young, but got to be another colour when she grew up?"

"No, I don't know as I ever did," said Marilla mercilessly, "and I shouldn't think it likely to happen in your case, either."

Anne sighed.

"Well, that is another hope gone. My life is a perfect grave-yard of buried hopes.[1] That's a sentence I read in a book once, and I say it over to comfort myself whenever I'm disappointed in anything."

"I don't see where the comforting comes in myself," said Marilla.

"Why, because it sounds so nice and romantic, just as if I were a heroine in a book, you know. I am so fond of romantic things, and a graveyard full of buried hopes is about as romantic a thing as one can imagine, isn't it? I'm rather glad I have one. Are we going across the Lake of Shining Waters to-day?"

"We're not going over Barry's pond, if that's what you mean by your Lake of Shining Waters. We're going by the shore road."

"Shore road sounds nice," said Anne dreamily. "Is it as nice as it sounds? Just when you said 'shore road' I saw it in a picture in my mind, as quick as that! And White Sands is a pretty name, too; but I don't like it as well as Avonlea. Avonlea is a lovely name. It just sounds like music. How far is it to White Sands?"

"It's five miles; and as you're evidently bent on talking you might as well talk to some purpose by telling me what you know about yourself."

"Oh, what I *know* about myself isn't really worth telling," said Anne eagerly. "If you'll only let me tell you what I *imagine* about myself you'll think it ever so much more interesting."

---

[1]   Like "depths of despair," a sentimental cliché. Cf. "God Bless You, Dear, To-Day!" by American poet John Bennett (b. 1865), in *An American Anthology, 1787–1900* (712).

"No, I don't want any of your imaginings. Just you stick to bald facts. Begin at the beginning. Where were you born and how old are you?"

"I was eleven last March," said Anne, resigning herself to bald facts with a little sigh. "And I was born in Bolingbroke, Nova Scotia. My father's name was Walter Shirley, and he was a teacher in the Bolingbroke High School. My mother's name was Bertha Shirley. Aren't Walter and Bertha lovely names? I'm so glad my parents had nice names. It would be a real disgrace to have a father named—well, say Jedediah, wouldn't it?"

"I guess it doesn't matter what a person's name is as long as he behaves himself," said Marilla, feeling herself called upon to inculcate a good and useful moral.

"Well, I don't know." Anne looked thoughtful. "I read in a book once that a rose by any other name would smell as sweet,[1] but I've never been able to believe it. I don't believe a rose *would* be as nice if it was called a thistle or a skunk cabbage. I suppose my father could have been a good man even if he had been called Jedediah; but I'm sure it would have been a cross. Well, my mother was a teacher in the High School, too, but when she married father she gave up teaching, of course. A husband was enough responsibility.[2] Mrs. Thomas said that they were a pair of babies and as poor as church mice. They went to live in a weeny-teeny little yellow house in Bolingbroke. I've never seen that house, but I've imagined it thousands of times. I think it must have had honeysuckle over the parlour window and lilacs in the front yard and lilies of the valley just inside the gate. Yes, and muslin curtains in all the windows. Muslin curtains give a house such an air. I was born in that house. Mrs. Thomas said I was the homeliest baby she ever saw, I was so scrawny and tiny and nothing but eyes, but that mother thought I was perfectly beautiful. I should think a mother would be a better judge than a poor woman who came in to scrub, wouldn't you? I'm glad she was satisfied with me anyhow; I would feel so sad if I thought I was a disappointment to her— because she didn't live very long after that, you see. She died of

---

1   See Shakespeare, *Romeo and Juliet* 2.2.43–44.
2   Cf. Appendix C, "Famous Author and Simple Mother."

fever when I was just three months old. I do wish she'd lived long enough for me to remember calling her mother. I think it would be so sweet to say 'mother,' don't you? And father died four days afterwards from fever, too. That left me an orphan and folks were at their wits' end, so Mrs. Thomas said, what to do with me. You see, nobody wanted me even then. It seems to be my fate. Father and mother had both come from places far away and it was well known they hadn't any relatives living. Finally Mrs. Thomas said she'd take me, though she was poor and had a drunken husband. She brought me up by hand. Do you know if there is anything in being brought up by hand that ought to make people who are brought up that way better than other people? Because whenever I was naughty Mrs. Thomas would ask me how I could be such a bad girl when she had brought me up by hand—reproachful-like.

"Mr. and Mrs. Thomas moved away from Bolingbroke to Marysville, and I lived with them until I was eight years old. I helped look after the Thomas children—there were four of them younger than me—and I can tell you they took a lot of looking after. Then Mr. Thomas was killed falling under a train and his mother offered to take Mrs. Thomas and the children, but she didn't want me. Mrs. Thomas was at *her* wits' end, so she said, what to do with me. Then Mrs. Hammond from up the river came down and said she'd take me, seeing I was handy with children, and I went up the river to live with her in a little clearing among the stumps. It was a very lonesome place. I'm sure I could never have lived there if I hadn't had an imagination. Mr. Hammond worked a little saw-mill up there, and Mrs. Hammond had eight children. She had twins three times. I like babies in moderation, but twins three times in succession is *too much*. I told Mrs. Hammond so firmly, when the last pair came. I used to get so dreadfully tired carrying them about.

"I lived up river with Mrs. Hammond over two years, and then Mr. Hammond died and Mrs. Hammond broke up housekeeping. She divided her children among her relatives and went to the States. I had to go to the asylum at Hopetown, because nobody would take me. They didn't want me at the asylum, either; they said they were overcrowded as it was. But they had to take me and I was there four months until Mrs. Spencer came."

Anne finished up with another sigh, of relief this time.

Evidently she did not like talking about her experiences in a world that had not wanted her.

"Did you ever go to school?" demanded Marilla, turning the sorrel mare down the shore road.

"Not a great deal. I went a little the last year I stayed with Mrs. Thomas. When I went up river we were so far from a school that I couldn't walk it in winter and there was vacation in summer, so I could only go in the spring and fall. But of course I went while I was at the asylum. I can read pretty well and I know ever so many pieces of poetry off by heart—'The Battle of Hohenlinden'[1] and 'Edinburgh after Flodden,'[2] and 'Bingen on the Rhine,'[3] and lots of 'The Lady of The Lake'[4] and most of 'The Seasons,' by James Thompson.[5] Don't you just love poetry that gives you a crinkly feeling up and down your back? There is a piece in the Fifth Reader—'The Downfall of Poland'—that is just full of thrills.[6] Of

---

[1] A poem by Scottish poet Thomas Campbell (1777–1814). This poem appears in many readers and anthologies of the late nineteenth century; Francis Palgrave, for instance, includes it (as "Hohenlinden") in *The Golden Treasury* (London: Oxford UP, 1861, 1912) in 1875 (212–13).

[2] A poem by William Edmonstoune Aytoun (1818–1865), published in 1849 in *Lays of the Scottish Cavaliers* (Edinburgh: Blackwood, 1883) and, like most of the other poems cited in *AGG*, included in many anthologies and readers of the late nineteenth century: it is included in the *Sixth Royal Reader* (59–62).

[3] A poem by Caroline Sheridan Norton (1808–1877). This poem was included in the *Sixth Royal Reader* (26–7), and, like "The Battle of Hohenlinden," regularly figured in many elocutionary and other readers of the nineteenth century: Edward Hartley Dewart's *Canadian Speaker and Elocutionary Reader* (Toronto: Adam Miller, 1868), for instance, contains both poems. Also like "Hohenlinden," "Bingen on the Rhine" was regarded as a poem which addressed primarily English readers, despite its non-English national specificity: the note in the *Royal Reader* suggests that "[T]he spirit of the poem is independent of place or time. It gives expression, in a very touching way, to the dying thoughts of a soldier stricken down in a foreign land, far away from friends and home" (n.2, 27). The poem is quoted later in *AGG*. See 193, note 5 and 194, note 1.

[4] A poem by Sir Walter Scott, published in 1810. Like *Marmion*, it is a poem in six cantos. As Montgomery notes in her journal (*SJ* I 247), the whole of the poem was included in the *Sixth Royal Reader* (149–167). It is cited again in *AGG*: see 277, note 1.

[5] Properly, James Thomson (1700–1748). The name is spelled incorrectly in 1908, as well as in the MS. *The Seasons* was originally published as a series of poems between 1726 and 1730, and collected in 1730.

[6] Another poem by Thomas Campbell. *AA* suggests that the title is properly "On the Downfall of Poland" and notes this text as an excerpt from Campbell's 1799 poem "The Pleasures of Hope." This poem, like the others Anne cites, was much anthologized in the nineteenth and early twentieth centuries; it appears in the *Fifth Royal Reader* (471–72). See *AA* (226–28).

course, I wasn't in the Fifth Reader—I was only in the Fourth—but the big girls used to lend me theirs to read."

"Were those women—Mrs. Thomas and Mrs. Hammond—good to you?" asked Marilla, looking at Anne out of the corner of her eye.

"O-o-o-h," faltered Anne. Her sensitive little face suddenly flushed scarlet and embarrassment sat on her brow. "Oh, they *meant* to be—I know they meant to be just as good and kind as possible. And when people mean to be good to you, you don't mind very much when they're not quite—always. They had a good deal to worry them, you know. It's very trying to have a drunken husband, you see; and it must be very trying to have twins three times in succession, don't you think? But I feel sure they meant to be good to me."

Marilla asked no more questions. Anne gave herself up to a silent rapture over the shore road and Marilla guided the sorrel abstractedly while she pondered deeply. Pity was suddenly stirring in her heart for the child. What a starved, unloved life she had had—a life of drudgery and poverty and neglect; for Marilla was shrewd enough to read between the lines of Anne's history and divine the truth. No wonder she had been so delighted at the prospect of a real home. It was a pity she had to be sent back. What if she, Marilla, should indulge Matthew's unaccountable whim and let her stay? He was set on it; and the child seemed a nice, teachable little thing.

"She's got too much to say," thought Marilla, "but she might be trained out of that. And there's nothing rude or slangy in what she does say. She's ladylike. It's likely her people were nice folks."

The shore road was "woodsy and wild and lonesome."[1] On the right hand, scrub firs, their spirits quite unbroken by long years of tussle with the gulf winds, grew thickly. On the left were the steep red sandstone cliffs, so near the track in places that a mare of less steadiness than the sorrel might have tried the nerves of the people

---

[1]   See John Greenleaf Whittier, "Cobbler Keezar's Vision" (1861, 1864). The phrase "woodsy and wild and lonesome" occurs twice in the poem (21, 29). This is a settler narrative: it is noted at the beginning of the poem in the Cambridge edition (cited here) that "Cobbler Keezar was a noted character among the first settlers in the valley of the Merrimac" (76).

behind her. Down at the base of the cliffs were heaps of surf-worn rocks or little sandy coves inlaid with pebbles as with ocean jewels; beyond lay the sea, shimmering and blue, and over it soared the gulls, their pinions flashing silvery in the sunlight.

"Isn't the sea wonderful?" said Anne, rousing from a long, wide-eyed silence. "Once, when I lived in Marysville, Mr. Thomas hired an express-wagon and took us all to spend the day at the shore ten miles away. I enjoyed every moment of that day, even if I had to look after the children all the time. I lived it over in happy dreams for years. But this shore is nicer than the Marysville shore. Aren't those gulls splendid? Would you like to be a gull? I think I would—that is, if I couldn't be a human girl. Don't you think it would be nice to wake up at sunrise and swoop down over the water and away out over that lovely blue all day; and then at night to fly back to one's nest? Oh, I can just imagine myself doing it. What big house is that just ahead, please?"

"That's the White Sands Hotel. Mr. Kirke runs it, but the season hasn't begun yet. There are heaps of Americans come there for the summer. They think this shore is just about right."

"I was afraid it might be Mrs. Spencer's place," said Anne mournfully. "I don't want to get there. Somehow, it will seem like the end of everything."

CHAPTER VI

MARILLA MAKES UP HER MIND

GET there they did, however, in due season. Mrs. Spencer lived in a big yellow house at White Sands Cove, and she came to the door with surprise and welcome mingled on her benevolent face.

"Dear, dear," she exclaimed, "you're the last folks I was looking for to-day, but I'm real glad to see you. You'll put your horse in? And how are you, Anne?"

"I'm as well as can be expected, thank you," said Anne smilelessly. A blight seemed to have descended on her.

"I suppose we'll stay a little while to rest the mare," said Marilla, "but I promised Matthew I'd be home early. The fact is, Mrs. Spencer, there's been a queer mistake somewhere, and I've come over to see where it is. We sent word, Matthew and I, for you to bring us a boy from the asylum. We told your brother Robert to tell you we wanted a boy ten or eleven years old."

"Marilla Cuthbert, you don't say so!" said Mrs. Spencer in distress. "Why, Robert sent the word down by his daughter Nancy and she said you wanted a girl—didn't she, Flora Jane?" appealing to her daughter who had come out to the steps.

"She certainly did, Miss Cuthbert," corroborated Flora Jane earnestly.

"I'm dreadful sorry," said Mrs. Spencer. "It is too bad; but it certainly wasn't my fault, you see, Miss Cuthbert. I did the best I could and I thought I was following your instructions. Nancy is a terrible flighty thing. I've often had to scold her well for her heedlessness."

"It was our own fault," said Marilla resignedly. "We should have come to you ourselves and not left an important message to be passed along by word of mouth in that fashion. Anyhow, the mistake has been made and the only thing to do now is to set it right. Can we send the child back to the asylum? I suppose they'll take her back, won't they?"

"I suppose so," said Mrs. Spencer thoughtfully, "but I don't think it will be necessary to send her back. Mrs. Peter Blewett was up here yesterday, and she was saying to me how much she wished she'd sent by me for a little girl to help her. Mrs. Peter has a large family, you know, and she finds it hard to get help. Anne will be the very girl for her. I call it positively providential."

Marilla did not look as if she thought Providence had much to do with the matter. Here was an unexpectedly good chance to get this unwelcome orphan off her hands, and she did not even feel grateful for it.

She knew Mrs. Peter Blewett only by sight as a small, shrewish-faced woman without an ounce of superfluous flesh on her bones. But she had heard of her. "A terrible worker and driver," Mrs. Peter was said to be; and discharged servant girls told fearsome tales of her temper and stinginess, and her family of pert, quarrelsome children. Marilla felt a qualm of conscience at the thought of handing Anne over to her tender mercies.[1]

"Well, I'll go in and we'll talk the matter over," she said.

"And if there isn't Mrs. Peter coming up the lane this blessed minute!" exclaimed Mrs. Spencer, bustling her guests through the hall into the parlour, where a deadly chill struck on them as if the air had been strained so long through dark green, closely drawn blinds that it had lost every particle of warmth it had ever possessed. "That is real lucky, for we can settle the matter right away. Take the armchair, Miss Cuthbert. Anne, you sit here on the ottoman and don't wriggle. Let me take your hats. Flora Jane, go out and put the kettle on. Good afternoon, Mrs. Blewett. We were just saying how fortunate it was you happened along. Let me introduce you two ladies. Mrs. Blewett, Miss Cuthbert. Please excuse me for just a moment. I forgot to tell Flora Jane to take the buns out of the oven."

Mrs. Spencer whisked away, after pulling up the blinds. Anne, sitting mutely on the ottoman, with her hands clasped tightly in her lap, stared at Mrs. Blewett as one fascinated. Was she to be given into the keeping of this sharp-faced, sharp-eyed woman? She felt a lump coming up in her throat and her eyes smarted painfully. She was beginning to be afraid she couldn't keep the tears back when Mrs. Spencer returned, flushed and beaming, quite capable of taking any and every difficulty, physical, mental or spiritual, into consideration and settling it out of hand.

"It seems there's been a mistake about this little girl, Mrs. Blewett," she said. "I was under the impression that Mr. and Miss Cuthbert wanted a little girl to adopt. I was certainly told so. But it seems it was a boy they wanted. So if you're still of the same mind you were yesterday, I think she'll be just the thing for you."

Mrs. Blewett darted her eyes over Anne from head to foot.

"How old are you and what's your name?" she demanded.

"Anne Shirley," faltered the shrinking child, not daring to make any stipulations regarding the spelling thereof, "and I'm eleven years old."

"Humph! You don't look as if there was much to you. But

---

[1]   There are many biblical occurrences, especially in Psalms. Cf. Proverbs 12.10.

you're wiry. I don't know but the wiry ones are the best after all. Well, if I take you you'll have to be a good girl, you know—good and smart and respectful. I'll expect you to earn your keep, and no mistake about that. Yes, I suppose I might as well take her off your hands, Miss Cuthbert. The baby's awful fractious,[1] and I'm clean worn out attending to him. If you like I can take her right home now."

Marilla looked at Anne and softened at the sight of the child's pale face with its look of mute misery—the misery of a helpless little creature who finds itself once more caught in the trap from which it had escaped. Marilla felt an uncomfortable conviction that, if she denied the appeal of that look, it would haunt her to her dying day. Moreover, she did not fancy Mrs. Blewett. To hand a sensitive, "high-strung" child over to such a woman! No, she could not take the responsibility of doing that!

"Well, I don't know," she said slowly. "I didn't say that Matthew and I had absolutely decided that we wouldn't keep her. In fact, I may say that Matthew is disposed to keep her. I just came over to find out how the mistake had occurred. I think I'd better take her home again and talk it over with Matthew. I feel that I oughtn't to decide on anything without consulting him. If we make up our mind not to keep her we'll bring or send her over to you to-morrow night. If we don't you may know that she is going to stay with us. Will that suit you, Mrs. Blewett?"

"I suppose it'll have to," said Mrs. Blewett ungraciously.

During Marilla's speech a sunrise had been dawning on Anne's face. First the look of despair faded out; then came a faint flush of hope; her eyes grew deep and bright as morning stars. The child was quite transfigured; and, a moment later, when Mrs. Spencer and Mrs. Blewett went out in quest of a recipe the latter had come to borrow, she sprang up and flew across the room to Marilla.

"Oh, Miss Cuthbert, did you really say that perhaps you would let me stay at Green Gables?" she said in a breathless whisper, as if speaking aloud might shatter the glorious possibility. "Did you really say it? Or did I only imagine that you did?"

"I think you'd better learn to control that imagination of

---

[1] "Refractory, unruly; now chiefly cross, fretful, peevish; *esp.* of children" (*OED*).

yours, Anne, if you can't distinguish between what is real and what isn't," said Marilla crossly. "Yes, you did hear me say just that and no more. It isn't decided yet and perhaps we will conclude to let Mrs. Blewett take you after all. She certainly needs you much more than I do."

"I'd rather go back to the asylum than go to live with her," said Anne passionately. "She looks exactly like a—like a gimlet."[1]

Marilla smothered a smile under the conviction that Anne must be reproved for such a speech.

"A little girl like you should be ashamed of talking so about a lady and a stranger," she said severely. "Go back and sit down quietly and hold your tongue and behave as a good girl should."

"I'll try to do and be anything you want me, if you'll only keep me," said Anne, returning meekly to her ottoman.

When they arrived back at Green Gables that evening Matthew met them in the lane. Marilla from afar had noted him prowling along it and guessed his motive. She was prepared for the relief she read in his face when he saw that she had at least brought Anne back with her. But she said nothing to him, relative to the affair, until they were both out in the yard behind the barn milking the cows. Then she briefly told him Anne's history and the result of the interview with Mrs. Spencer.

"I wouldn't give a dog I liked to that Blewett woman," said Matthew with unusual vim.

"I don't fancy her style myself," admitted Marilla, "but it's that or keeping her ourselves, Matthew. And, since you seem to want her, I suppose I'm willing—or have to be. I've been thinking over the idea until I've got kind of used to it. It seems a sort of duty. I've never brought up a child, especially a girl, and I dare say I'll make a terrible mess of it. But I'll do my best. So far as I'm concerned, Matthew, she may stay."

Matthew's shy face was a glow of delight.

"Well now, I reckoned you'd come to see it in that light, Marilla," he said. "She's such an interesting little thing."

"It'd be more to the point if you could say she was a useful

---

[1]   A gimlet is "A kind of boring tool" (OED). Anne seems to mean that Mrs. Blewett appears to her to be sharp and angular.

little thing," retorted Marilla, "but I'll make it my business to see she's trained to be that. And mind, Matthew, you're not to go interfering with my methods. Perhaps an old maid doesn't know much about bringing up a child, but I guess she knows more than an old bachelor. So you just leave me to manage her. When I fail it'll be time enough to put your oar in."

"There, there, Marilla, you can have your own way," said Matthew reassuringly. "Only be as good and kind to her as you can be without spoiling her. I kind of think she's one of the sort you can do anything with if you only get her to love you."

Marilla sniffed, to express her contempt for Matthew's opinions concerning anything feminine, and walked off to the dairy with the pails.

"I won't tell her to-night that she can stay," she reflected, as she strained the milk into the creamers. "She'd be so excited that she wouldn't sleep a wink. Marilla Cuthbert, you're fairly in for it. Did you ever suppose you'd see the day when you'd be adopting an orphan girl? It's surprising enough; but not so surprising as that Matthew should be at the bottom of it, him that always seemed to have such a moral dread of little girls. Anyhow, we've decided on the experiment and goodness only knows what will come of it."

CHAPTER VII

ANNE SAYS HER PRAYERS

WHEN Marilla took Anne up to bed that night she said stiffly:

"Now, Anne, I noticed last night that you threw your clothes all about the floor when you took them off. That is a very untidy habit, and I can't allow it at all. As soon as you take off any article of clothing fold it neatly and place it on the chair. I haven't any use at all for little girls who aren't neat."

"I was so harrowed up in my mind last night that I didn't think about my clothes at all," said Anne. "I'll fold them nicely to-night. They always made us do that at the asylum. Half the time, though, I'd forget, I'd be in such a hurry to get into bed nice and quiet and imagine things."

"You'll have to remember a little better if you stay here," admonished Marilla. "There, that looks something like. Say your prayers now and get into bed."

"I never say any prayers," announced Anne.

Marilla looked horrified astonishment.

"Why, Anne, what do you mean? Were you never taught to say your prayers? God always wants little girls to say their prayers. Don't you know who God is, Anne?"

"'God is a spirit, infinite, eternal and unchangeable, in His being, wisdom, power, holiness, justice, goodness, and truth,'" responded Anne promptly and glibly.[1]

Marilla looked rather relieved.

"So you do know something then, thank goodness! You're not quite a heathen. Where did you learn that?"

"Oh, at the asylum Sunday-school. They made us learn the whole catechism. I liked it pretty well. There's something splendid about some of the words. 'Infinite, eternal and unchangeable.' Isn't that grand? It has such a roll to it—just like a big organ playing. You couldn't quite call it poetry, I suppose, but it sounds a lot like it, doesn't it?"

"We're not talking about poetry, Anne—we are talking about saying your prayers. Don't you know it's a terrible wicked thing not to say your prayers every night? I'm afraid you are a very bad little girl."

"You'd find it easier to be bad than good if you had red hair," said Anne reproachfully. "People who haven't red hair don't know what trouble is. Mrs. Thomas told me that God made my hair red *on purpose*, and I've never cared about Him since. And

---

[1] See *The Shorter Catechism of the Assembly of Divines with the Proofs Thereof Out of the Scriptures. In Words at Length, for the Benefit of Christians in General, and of Youth and Children in Particular* (Toronto: Copp Clark, n.d.). *The Shorter Catechism* dates from 1643–52, following the Westminster Assembly's meetings between July 1643 and November 1647. It is described thus in this Canadian edition: "It is more than a mere string of questions and answers, it is a system of Bible divinity" (n.p.). Anne clearly admires the language of the Catechism, but deplores Sunday-school teachers who only ask the questions without requiring students to think about the answers. Cf. 126, note 1.

anyhow I'd always be too tired at night to bother saying prayers. People who have to look after twins can't be expected to say their prayers. Now, do you honestly think they can?"

Marilla decided that Anne's religious training must be begun at once. Plainly there was no time to be lost.

"You must say your prayers while you are under my roof, Anne."

"Why, of course, if you want me to," assented Anne cheerfully. "I'd do anything to oblige you. But you'll have to tell me what to say for this once. After I get into bed I'll imagine out a real nice prayer to say always. I believe that it will be quite interesting, now that I come to think of it."

"You must kneel down," said Marilla in embarrassment.

Anne knelt at Marilla's knee and looked up gravely.

"Why must people kneel down to pray? If I really wanted to pray I'll tell you what I'd do. I'd go out into a great big field all alone or into the deep, deep woods, and I'd look up into the sky—up—up—up—into that lovely blue sky that looks as if there was no end to its blueness. And then I'd just *feel* a prayer. Well, I'm ready. What am I to say?"

Marilla felt more embarrassed than ever. She had intended to teach Anne the childish classic, "Now I lay me down to sleep."[1] But she had, as I have told you, the glimmerings of a sense of humour—which is simply another name for a sense of the fitness of things; and it suddenly occurred to her that that simple little prayer, sacred to white-robed childhood lisping at motherly knees, was entirely unsuited to this freckled witch of a girl who knew and cared nothing about God's love, since she had never had it translated to her through the medium of human love.

"You're old enough to pray for yourself, Anne," she said finally. "Just thank God for your blessings and ask Him humbly for the things you want."

"Well, I'll do my best," promised Anne, burying her face in Marilla's lap. "Gracious heavenly Father—that's the way the

---

[1]   *Bartlett's Familiar Quotations*, 15th ed. (Boston: Little, Brown, 1980) notes that "[t]he first record of this prayer is found in the *Enchiridion Leonis* (1160)." The early editions of the [*New England*] *Primer*, a popular book of prayers and early learning for children which was first printed in the U.S. in the 1690s, give various versions of the first and second lines.

ministers say it in church, so I suppose it's all right in a private prayer, isn't it?" she interjected, lifting her head for a moment. "Gracious heavenly Father, I thank Thee for the White Way of Delight and the Lake of Shining Waters and Bonny and the Snow Queen. I'm really extremely grateful for them. And that's all the blessings I can think of just now to thank Thee for. As for the things I want, they're so numerous that it would take a great deal of time to name them all, so I will only mention the two most important. Please let me stay at Green Gables; and please let me be good-looking when I grow up. I remain,

"Yours respectfully,

"ANNE SHIRLEY.

"There, did I do it all right?" she asked eagerly, getting up. "I could have made it much more flowery if I'd had a little more time to think it over."

Poor Marilla was only preserved from complete collapse by remembering that it was not irreverence, but simply spiritual ignorance on the part of Anne that was responsible for this extraordinary petition. She tucked the child up in bed, mentally vowing that she should be taught a prayer the very next day, and was leaving the room with the light when Anne called her back.

"I've just thought of it now. I should have said 'Amen' in place of 'yours respectfully,' shouldn't I?—the way the ministers do. I'd forgotten it, but I felt a prayer should be finished off in some way, so I put in the other. Do you suppose it will make any difference?"

"I—I don't suppose it will," said Marilla. "Go to sleep now like a good child. Good night."

"I can say good night to-night with a clear conscience," said Anne, cuddling luxuriously down among her pillows.

Marilla retreated to the kitchen, set the candle firmly on the table, and glared at Matthew.

"Matthew Cuthbert, it's about time somebody adopted that child and taught her something. She's next door to a perfect heathen. Will you believe that she never said a prayer in her life till to-night? I'll send to the manse[1] to-morrow and borrow the

---

[1]   A minister's residence.

Peep of Day series, that's what I'll do.[1] And she shall go to Sunday-school just as soon as I can get some suitable clothes made for her. I foresee that I shall have my hands full. Well, well, we can't get through this world without our share of trouble. I've had a pretty easy life of it so far, but my time has come at last and I suppose I'll just have to make the best of it."

CHAPTER VIII

ANNE'S BRINGING-UP IS BEGUN

FOR reasons best known to herself, Marilla did not tell Anne that she was to stay at Green Gables until the next afternoon. During the forenoon she kept the child busy with various tasks and watched over her with a keen eye while she did them. By noon she had concluded that Anne was smart and obedient, willing to work and quick to learn; her most serious shortcoming seemed to be a tendency to fall into daydreams in the middle of a task and forget all about it until such time as she was sharply recalled to earth by a reprimand or a catastrophe.

When Anne had finished washing the dinner dishes she suddenly confronted Marilla with the air and expression of one desperately determined to learn the worst. Her thin little body trembled from head to foot; her face flushed and her eyes dilated until they were almost black; she clasped her hands tightly and said in an imploring voice:

"Oh, please, Miss Cuthbert, won't you tell me if you are going to send me away or not? I've tried to be patient all the morning, but I really feel that I cannot bear not knowing any longer. It's a dreadful feeling. Please tell me."

"You haven't scalded the dish-cloth in clean hot water as I

---

[1] *Peep of Day series:* Tracts written by Mrs. Favell Lee Bevan Mortimer (1802–1878) and published in the U.S. The series was recommended for inexperienced teachers of "the infant poor," as a "reward-book for poor children," as an aid to mothers, and as a book of Sunday reading for young children (3rd ed., 1883, iii).

told you to do," said Marilla immovably. "Just go and do it before you ask any more questions, Anne."

Anne went and attended to the dish-cloth. Then she returned to Marilla and fastened imploring eyes on the latter's face.

"Well," said Marilla, unable to find any excuse for deferring her explanation longer, "I suppose I might as well tell you. Matthew and I have decided to keep you—that is, if you will try to be a good little girl and show yourself grateful. Why, child, whatever is the matter?"

"I'm crying," said Anne in a tone of bewilderment. "I can't think why. I'm glad as glad can be. Oh, *glad* doesn't seem the right word at all. I was glad about the White Way and the cherry blossoms—but this! Oh, it's something more than glad. I'm so happy. I'll try to be so good. It will be up-hill work, I expect, for Mrs. Thomas often told me I was desperately wicked.[1] However, I'll do my very best. But can you tell me why I'm crying?"

"I suppose it's because you're all excited and worked up," said Marilla disapprovingly. "Sit down on that chair and try to calm yourself. I'm afraid you both cry and laugh far too easily. Yes, you can stay here and we will try to do right by you. You must go to school; but it's only a fortnight till vacation so it isn't worth while for you to start before it opens again in September."

"What am I to call you?" asked Anne. "Shall I always say Miss Cuthbert? Can I call you Aunt Marilla?"

"No; you'll call me just plain Marilla. I'm not used to being called Miss Cuthbert and it would make me nervous."

"It sounds awfully disrespectful to say just Marilla," protested Anne.

"I guess there'll be nothing disrespectful in it if you're careful to speak respectfully. Everybody, young and old, in Avonlea calls me Marilla except the minister. He says Miss Cuthbert—when he thinks of it."

"I'd love to call you Aunt Marilla," said Anne wistfully. "I've never had an aunt or any relation at all—not even a grand-mother. It would make me feel as if I really belonged to you. Can't I call you Aunt Marilla?"

---

1   Cf. Jeremiah 17.9.

"No. I'm not your aunt and I don't believe in calling people names that don't belong to them."

"But we could imagine you were my aunt."

"I couldn't," said Marilla grimly.

"Do you never imagine things different from what they really are?" asked Anne wide-eyed.

"No."

"Oh!" Anne drew a long breath. "Oh, Miss—Marilla, how much you miss!"

"I don't believe in imagining things different from what they really are," retorted Marilla. "When the Lord puts us in certain circumstances He doesn't mean for us to imagine them away. And that reminds me. Go into the sitting-room, Anne—be sure your feet are clean and don't let any flies in—and bring me out the illustrated card that's on the mantelpiece. The Lord's Prayer is on it and you'll devote your spare time this afternoon to learning it off by heart.[1] There's to be no more of such praying as I heard last night."

"I suppose I was very awkward," said Anne apologetically, "but then, you see, I'd never had any practice. You couldn't really expect a person to pray very well the first time she tried, could you? I thought out a splendid prayer after I went to bed, just as I promised you I would. It was nearly as long as a minister's and so poetical. But would you believe it? I couldn't remember one word when I woke up this morning. And I'm afraid I'll never be able to think out another one as good. Somehow, things never are so good when they're thought out a second time. Have you ever noticed that?"

"Here is something for you to notice, Anne. When I tell you to do a thing I want you to obey me at once and not stand stock-still and discourse about it. Just you go and do as I bid you."

Anne promptly departed for the sitting-room across the hall; she failed to return; after waiting ten minutes Marilla laid down her knitting and marched after her with a grim expression. She found Anne standing motionless before a picture hanging on the wall between the two windows, with her hands clasped behind her, her

---

[1] "The Lord's Prayer" is a well-known Christian prayer. See Matthew 6.9–13.

face uplifted, and her eyes astar with dreams. The white and green light strained through apple-trees and clustering vines outside fell over the rapt little figure with a half-unearthly radiance.

"Anne, whatever are you thinking of?" demanded Marilla sharply.

Anne came back to earth with a start.

"That," she said, pointing to the picture—a rather vivid chromo[1] entitled, "Christ Blessing Little Children"—"and I was just imagining I was one of them—that I was the little girl in the blue dress, standing off by herself in the corner as if she didn't belong to anybody, like me. She looks lonely and sad, don't you think? I guess she hadn't any father or mother of her own. But she wanted to be blessed, too, so she just crept shyly up on the outside of the crowd, hoping nobody would notice her—except Him. I'm sure I know just how she felt. Her heart must have beat and her hands must have got cold, like mine did when I asked you if I could stay. She was afraid He mightn't notice her. But it's likely He did, don't you think? I've been trying to imagine it all out—her edging a little nearer all the time until she was quite close to Him; and then He would look at her and put His hand on her hair and oh, such a thrill of joy as would run over her! But I wish the artist hadn't painted Him so sorrowful-looking. All His pictures are like that, if you've noticed. But I don't believe He could really have looked so sad or the children would have been afraid of Him."

"Anne," said Marilla, wondering why she had not broken into this speech long before, "you shouldn't talk that way. It's irreverent—positively irreverent."

Anne's eyes marvelled.

"Why, I felt just as reverent as could be. I'm sure I didn't mean to be irreverent."

"Well, I don't suppose you did—but it doesn't sound right to talk so familiarly about such things. And another thing, Anne, when I send you after something you're to bring it at once and not fall into mooning and imagining before pictures. Remember

---

1 "Colloquial shortening of chromolithograph. A picture printed in colours from stone" (OED).

that. Take that card and come right to the kitchen. Now, sit down in the corner and learn that prayer off by heart."

Anne set the card up against the jugful of apple blossoms she had brought in to decorate the dinner-table—Marilla had eyed that decoration askance, but had said nothing—propped her chin on her hands, and fell to studying it intently for several minutes.

"I like this," she announced at length. "It's beautiful. I've heard it before—I heard the superintendent of the asylum Sunday-school say it over once. But I didn't like it then. He had such a cracked voice and he prayed it so mournfully. I really felt sure he thought praying was a disagreeable duty. This isn't poetry, but it makes me feel just the same way poetry does. 'Our Father who art in heaven, hallowed be Thy name.'[1] That is just like a line of music. Oh, I'm so glad you thought of making me learn this, Miss—Marilla."

"Well, learn it and hold your tongue," said Marilla shortly.

Anne tipped the vase of apple blossoms near enough to bestow a soft kiss on a pink-cupped bud, and then studied diligently for some moments longer.

"Marilla," she demanded presently, "do you think that I shall ever have a bosom friend[2] in Avonlea?"

"A—a what kind of a friend?"

"A bosom friend—an intimate friend, you know—a really kindred spirit to whom I can confide my inmost soul. I've dreamed of meeting her all my life. I never really supposed I would, but so many of my loveliest dreams have come true all at once that perhaps this one will, too. Do you think it's possible?"

"Diana Barry lives over at Orchard Slope and she's about your age. She's a very nice little girl, and perhaps she will be a play-mate for you when she comes home. She's visiting her aunt over at Carmody just now. You'll have to be careful how you behave yourself, though. Mrs. Barry is a very particular woman. She won't let Diana play with any little girl who isn't nice and good."

Anne looked at Marilla through the apple blossoms, her eyes aglow with interest.

---

[1]   First line of "The Lord's Prayer." See 104, note 1.
[2]   A very dear friend. Cf. Felicia Hemans, "To Hope" (1808), lines 25–26, and John Keats, "To Autumn" (1819), lines 1–2.

"What is Diana like? Her hair isn't red, is it? Oh, I hope not. It's bad enough to have red hair myself, but I positively couldn't endure it in a bosom friend."

"Diana is a very pretty little girl. She has black eyes and hair and rosy cheeks. And she is good and smart, which is better than being pretty."

Marilla was as fond of morals as the Duchess in Wonderland,[1] and was firmly convinced that one should be tacked on to every remark made to a child who was being brought up.

But Anne waved the moral inconsequently aside and seized only on the delightful possibilities before it.

"Oh, I'm so glad she's pretty. Next to being beautiful oneself—and that's impossible in my case—it would be best to have a beautiful bosom friend. When I lived with Mrs. Thomas she had a bookcase in her sitting-room with glass doors. There weren't any books in it; Mrs. Thomas kept her best china and her preserves there—when she had any preserves to keep. One of the doors was broken. Mr. Thomas smashed it one night when he was slightly intoxicated. But the other was whole and I used to pretend that my reflection in it was another little girl who lived in it. I called her Katie Maurice, and we were very intimate. I used to talk to her by the hour, especially on Sunday, and tell her everything. Katie was the comfort and consolation of my life. We used to pretend that the bookcase was enchanted and that if I only knew the spell I could open the door and step right into the room where Katie Maurice lived, instead of into Mrs. Thomas' shelves of preserves and china. And then Katie Maurice would have taken me by the hand and led me out into a wonderful place, all flowers and sunshine and fairies, and we would have lived there happy for ever after. When I went to live with Mrs. Hammond it just broke my heart to leave Katie Maurice. She felt it dreadfully, too, I know she did, for she was crying when she kissed me good-bye through the bookcase door. There was no bookcase at Mrs. Hammond's. But just up the river a little way from the house there was a long green little valley, and the

---

1   Reference to Lewis Carroll's *Alice's Adventures in Wonderland* (1865). See Chapter IX, "The Mock-Turtle's Story": "Everything's got a moral, if only you can find it." Lewis Carroll, *The Annotated Alice*, ed. Martin Gardner (New York, NY: Bramhall House, 1960) 120–21.

loveliest echo lived there. It echoed back every word you said, even if you didn't talk a bit loud. So I imagined that it was a little girl called Violetta and we were great friends and I loved her almost as well as I loved Katie Maurice—not quite, but almost, you know. The night before I went to the asylum I said good-bye to Violetta, and oh, her good-bye came back to me in such sad, sad tones. I had become so attached to her that I hadn't the heart to imagine a bosom friend at the asylum, even if there had been any scope for imagination there."

"I think it's just as well there wasn't," said Marilla drily. "I don't approve of such goings-on. You seem to half believe your own imaginations. It will be well for you to have a real live friend to put such nonsense out of your head. But don't let Mrs. Barry hear you talking about your Katie Maurices and your Violettas or she'll think you tell stories."

"Oh, I won't. I couldn't talk of them to everybody—their memories are too sacred for that. But I thought I'd like to have you know about them. Oh, look, here's a big bee just tumbled out of an apple blossom. Just think what a lovely place to live—in an apple blossom! Fancy going to sleep in it when the wind was rocking it. If I wasn't a human girl I think I'd like to be a bee and live among the flowers."

"Yesterday you wanted to be a sea-gull," sniffed Marilla. "I think you are very fickle-minded. I told you to learn that prayer and not talk. But it seems impossible for you to stop talking if you've got anybody that will listen to you. So go up to your room and learn it."

"Oh, I know it pretty nearly all now—all but just the last line."

"Well, never mind, do as I tell you. Go to your room and finish learning it well, and stay there until I call you down to help me get tea."

"Can I take the apple blossoms with me for company?" pleaded Anne.

"No; you don't want your room cluttered up with flowers. You should have left them on the tree in the first place."

"I did feel a little that way, too," said Anne. "I kind of felt I shouldn't shorten their lovely lives by picking them—I wouldn't want to be picked if I were an apple blossom. But the temptation was *irresistible*. What do you do when you meet with an irresistible temptation?"

"Anne, did you hear me tell you to go to your room?"

Anne sighed, retreated to the east gable, and sat down in a chair by the window.

"There—I know this prayer. I learned that last sentence coming up-stairs. Now I'm going to imagine things into this room so that they'll always stay imagined. The floor is covered with a white velvet carpet with pink roses all over it and there are pink silk curtains at the windows. The walls are hung with gold and silver brocade tapestry. The furniture is mahogany. I never saw any mahogany, but it does sound *so* luxurious. This is a couch all heaped with gorgeous silken cushions, pink and blue and crimson and gold, and I am reclining gracefully on it. I can see my reflection in that splendid big mirror hanging on the wall. I am tall and regal, clad in a gown of trailing white lace, with a pearl cross on my breast and pearls in my hair. My hair is of midnight darkness and my skin is a clear ivory pallor. My name is the Lady Cordelia Fitzgerald. No, it isn't—I can't make *that* seem real."

She danced up to the little looking-glass and peered into it. Her pointed freckled face and solemn gray eyes peered back at her.

"You're only Anne of Green Gables," she said earnestly, "and I see you, just as you are looking now, whenever I try to imagine I'm the Lady Cordelia. But it's a million times nicer to be Anne of Green Gables than Anne of nowhere in particular, isn't it?"

She bent forward, kissed her reflection affectionately, and betook herself to the open window.

"Dear Snow Queen, good afternoon. And good afternoon, dear birches down in the hollow. And good afternoon, dear gray house up on the hill. I wonder if Diana is to be my bosom friend. I hope she will, and I shall love her very much. But I must never quite forget Katie Maurice and Violetta. They would feel so hurt if I did and I'd hate to hurt anybody's feelings, even a little book-case girl's or a little echo girl's. I must be careful to remember them and send them a kiss every day."

Anne blew a couple of airy kisses from her finger-tips past the cherry blossoms and then, with her chin in her hands, drifted luxuriously out on a sea of day-dreams.

CHAPTER IX

MRS. RACHEL LYNDE
IS PROPERLY HORRIFIED

ANNE had been a fortnight at Green Gables before Mrs. Lynde arrived to inspect her. Mrs. Rachel, to do her justice, was not to blame for this. A severe and unseasonable attack of grippe[1] had confined that good lady to her house ever since the occasion of her last visit to Green Gables. Mrs. Rachel was not often sick and had a well-defined contempt for people who were; but grippe, she asserted, was like no other illness on earth and could only be interpreted as one of the special visitations of Providence. As soon as her doctor allowed her to put her foot out-of-doors she hurried up to Green Gables, bursting with curiosity to see Matthew's and Marilla's orphan, concerning whom all sorts of stories and suppositions had gone abroad in Avonlea.

Anne had made good use of every waking moment of that fortnight. Already she was acquainted with every tree and shrub about the place. She had discovered that a lane opened out below the apple orchard and ran up through a belt of woodland; and she had explored it to its furthest end in all its delicious vagaries of brook and bridge, fir coppice and wild cherry arch, corners thick with fern, and branching byways of maple and mountain ash.

She had made friends with the spring down in the hollow— that wonderful deep, clear icy-cold spring; it was set about with smooth red sandstones and rimmed in by great palm-like clumps of water fern; and beyond it was a log bridge over the brook.

That bridge led Anne's dancing feet up over a wooded hill beyond, where perpetual twilight reigned under the straight, thick-growing firs and spruces; the only flowers there were myriads of delicate "June bells," those shyest and sweetest of woodland blooms, and a few pale, aerial starflowers, like the spirits of last year's blossoms. Gossamers glimmered like threads of silver among the trees and the fir boughs and tassels seemed to utter friendly speech.

---

[1] Influenza.

All these raptured voyages of exploration were made in the odd half-hours which she was allowed for play, and Anne talked Matthew and Marilla half-deaf over her discoveries. Not that Matthew complained, to be sure; he listened to it all with a wordless smile of enjoyment on his face; Marilla permitted the "chatter" until she found herself becoming too interested in it, whereupon she always promptly quenched Anne by a curt command to hold her tongue.

Anne was out in the orchard when Mrs. Rachel came, wandering at her own sweet will through the lush, tremulous grasses splashed with ruddy evening sunshine; so that good lady had an excellent chance to talk her illness fully over, describing every ache and pulse-beat with such evident enjoyment that Marilla thought even grippe must bring its compensations. When details were exhausted Mrs. Rachel introduced the real reason of her call.

"I've been hearing some surprising things about you and Matthew."

"I don't suppose you are any more surprised than I am myself," said Marilla. "I'm getting over my surprise now."

"It was too bad there was such a mistake," said Mrs. Rachel sympathetically. "Couldn't you have sent her back?"

"I suppose we could, but we decided not to. Matthew took a fancy to her. And I must say I like her myself—although I admit she has her faults. The house seems a different place already. She's a real bright little thing."

Marilla said more than she had intended to say when she began, for she read disapproval in Mrs. Rachel's expression.

"It's a great responsibility you've taken on yourself," said that lady gloomily, "especially when you've never had any experience with children. You don't know much about her or her real disposition, I suppose, and there's no guessing how a child like that will turn out. But I don't want to discourage you I'm sure, Marilla."

"I'm not feeling discouraged," was Marilla's dry response. "When I make up my mind to do a thing it stays made up. I suppose you'd like to see Anne. I'll call her in."

Anne came running in presently, her face sparkling with the delight of her orchard rovings; but, abashed at finding herself in the unexpected presence of a stranger, she halted confusedly inside the door. She certainly was an odd-looking little creature in the short tight wincey dress she had worn from the asylum, below which her thin legs seemed ungracefully long. Her freckles were more numerous and obtrusive than ever; the wind had ruffled her hatless hair into over-brilliant disorder; it had never looked redder than at that moment.

"Well, they didn't pick you for your looks, that's sure and certain," was Mrs. Rachel Lynde's emphatic comment. Mrs. Rachel was one of those delightful and popular people who pride themselves on speaking their mind without fear or favour. "She's terrible skinny and homely, Marilla. Come here, child, and let me have a look at you. Lawful heart, did anyone ever see such freckles? And hair as red as carrots! Come here, child, I say."

Anne "came there," but not exactly as Mrs. Rachel expected. With one bound she crossed the kitchen floor and stood before Mrs. Rachel, her face scarlet with anger, her lips quivering, and her whole slender form trembling from head to foot.

"I hate you," she cried in a choked voice, stamping her foot on the floor. "I hate you—I hate you—I hate you—" a louder stamp with each assertion of hatred. "How dare you call me skinny and ugly? How dare you say I'm freckled and red-headed? You are a rude, impolite, unfeeling woman."

"Anne!" exclaimed Marilla in consternation.

But Anne continued to face Mrs. Rachel undauntedly, head up, eyes blazing, hands clenched, passionate indignation exhaling from her like an atmosphere.

"How dare you say such things about me?" she repeated vehemently. "How would you like to have such things said about you? How would you like to be told that you are fat and clumsy and probably hadn't a spark of imagination in you? I don't care if I do hurt your feelings by saying so! I hope I hurt them. You have hurt mine worse than they were ever hurt before even by Mrs. Thomas' intoxicated husband. And I'll *never* forgive you for it, never, never!"

Stamp! Stamp!

"Did anybody ever see such a temper!" exclaimed the horrified Mrs. Rachel.

"'I HATE YOU,' SHE CRIED IN A CHOKED VOICE, STAMPING HER FOOT ON THE FLOOR."

"Anne, go to your room and stay there until I come up," said Marilla, recovering her powers of speech with difficulty.

Anne, bursting into tears, rushed to the hall door, slammed it until the tins on the porch wall outside rattled in sympathy, and fled through the hall and up the stairs like a whirlwind. A subdued slam above told that the door of the east gable had been shut with equal vehemence.

"Well, I don't envy you your job bringing *that* up, Marilla," said Mrs. Rachel with unspeakable solemnity.

Marilla opened her lips to say she knew not what of apology or deprecation. What she did say was a surprise to herself then and ever afterwards.

"You shouldn't have twitted her about her looks, Rachel."

"Marilla Cuthbert, you don't mean to say that you are upholding her in such a terrible display of temper as we've just seen?" demanded Mrs. Rachel indignantly.

"No," said Marilla slowly, "I'm not trying to excuse her. She's been very naughty and I'll have to give her a talking to about it. But we must make allowances for her. She's never been taught what is right. And you *were* too hard on her, Rachel."

Marilla could not help tacking on that last sentence, although she was again surprised at herself for doing it. Mrs. Rachel got up with an air of offended dignity.

"Well, I see that I'll have to be very careful what I say after this, Marilla, since the fine feelings of orphans, brought from goodness knows where, have to be considered before anything else. Oh, no, I'm not vexed—don't worry yourself. I'm too sorry for you to leave any room for anger in my mind. You'll have your own troubles with that child. But if you'll take my advice— which I suppose you won't do, although I've brought up ten children and buried two—you'll do that 'talking to' you mention with a fair-sized birch switch. I should think *that* would be the most effective language for that kind of a child. Her temper matches her hair I guess. Well, good evening, Marilla. I hope you'll come down to see me often as usual. But you can't expect me to visit here again in a hurry, if I'm liable to be flown at and insulted in such a fashion. It's something new in *my* experience."

Whereat Mrs. Rachel swept out and away—if a fat woman

who always waddled *could* be said to sweep away—and Marilla with a very solemn face betook herself to the east gable.

On the way up-stairs she pondered uneasily as to what she ought to do. She felt no little dismay over the scene that had just been enacted. How unfortunate that Anne should have displayed such temper before Mrs. Rachel Lynde, of all people! Then Marilla suddenly became aware of an uncomfortable and rebuking consciousness that she felt more humiliation over this than sorrow over the discovery of such a serious defect in Anne's disposition. And how was she to punish her? The amiable suggestion of the birch switch—to the efficiency of which all of Mrs. Rachel's own children could have borne smarting testimony—did not appeal to Marilla. She did not believe she could whip a child. No, some other method of punishment must be found to bring Anne to a proper realization of the enormity of her offence.

Marilla found Anne face downward on her bed, crying bitterly, quite oblivious of muddy boots on a clean counterpane.

"Anne," she said, not ungently.

No answer.

"Anne," with greater severity, "get off that bed this minute and listen to what I have to say to you."

Anne squirmed off the bed and sat rigidly on a chair beside it, her face swollen and tear-stained and her eyes fixed stubbornly on the floor.

"This is a nice way for you to behave, Anne! Aren't you ashamed of yourself?"

"She hadn't any right to call me ugly and red-headed," retorted Anne, evasive and defiant.

"You hadn't any right to fly into such a fury and talk the way you did to her, Anne. I was ashamed of you—thoroughly ashamed of you. I wanted you to behave nicely to Mrs. Lynde, and instead of that you have disgraced me. I'm sure I don't know why you should lose your temper like that just because Mrs. Lynde said you were red-haired and homely. You say it yourself often enough."

"Oh, but there's such a difference between saying a thing yourself and hearing other people say it," wailed Anne. "You may know a thing is so, but you can't help hoping other people don't quite think it is. I suppose you think I have an awful temper, but I couldn't help it. When she said those things something just rose right up in me and choked me. I *had* to fly out at her."

"Well, you made a fine exhibition of yourself I must say. Mrs. Lynde will have a nice story to tell about you everywhere—and she'll tell it, too. It was a dreadful thing for you to lose your temper like that, Anne."

"Just imagine how you would feel if somebody told you to your face that you were skinny and ugly," pleaded Anne tearfully.

An old remembrance suddenly rose up before Marilla. She had been a very small child when she had heard one aunt say of her to another, "What a pity she is such a dark, homely little thing." Marilla was every day of fifty before the sting had gone out of that memory.

"I don't say that I think Mrs. Lynde was exactly right in saying what she did to you, Anne," she admitted in a softer tone. "Rachel is too outspoken. But that is no excuse for such behaviour on your part. She was a stranger and an elderly person and my visitor—all three very good reasons why you should have been respectful to her. You were rude and saucy and"—Marilla had a saving inspiration of punishment—"you must go to her and tell her you are very sorry for your bad temper and ask her to forgive you."

"I can never do that," said Anne determinedly and darkly. "You can punish me in any way you like, Marilla. You can shut me up in a dark, damp dungeon inhabited by snakes and toads and feed me only on bread and water and I shall not complain. But I cannot ask Mrs. Lynde to forgive me."

"We're not in the habit of shutting people up in dark, damp dungeons," said Marilla drily, "especially as they're rather scarce in Avonlea. But apologize to Mrs. Lynde you must and shall and you'll stay here in your room until you can tell me you're willing to do it."

"I shall have to stay here for ever then," said Anne mournfully, "because I can't tell Mrs. Lynde I'm sorry I said those things to her. How can I? I'm *not* sorry. I'm sorry I've vexed you; but I'm *glad* I told her just what I did. It was a great satisfaction. I can't say I'm sorry when I'm not, can I? I can't even *imagine* I'm sorry."

"Perhaps your imagination will be in better working order by the morning," said Marilla, rising to depart. "You'll have the night to think over your conduct in and come to a better frame of mind. You said you would try to be a very good girl if we kept you at Green Gables, but I must say it hasn't seemed very much like it this evening."

Leaving this Parthian shaft[1] to rankle in Anne's stormy bosom, Marilla descended to the kitchen, grievously troubled in mind and vexed in soul. She was as angry with herself as with Anne, because, whenever she recalled Mrs. Rachel's dumfounded countenance her lips twitched with amusement and she felt a most reprehensible desire to laugh.

CHAPTER X

ANNE'S APOLOGY

MARILLA said nothing to Matthew about the affair that evening; but when Anne proved still refractory the next morning an explanation had to be made to account for her absence from the breakfast-table. Marilla told Matthew the whole story, taking pains to impress him with a due sense of the enormity of Anne's behaviour.

"It's a good thing Rachel Lynde got a calling down; she's a meddlesome old gossip," was Matthew's consolatory rejoinder.

"Matthew Cuthbert, I'm astonished at you. You know that Anne's behaviour was dreadful, and yet you take her part! I suppose you'll be saying next thing that she oughtn't to be punished at all."

"Well now—no—not exactly," said Matthew uneasily. "I reckon she ought to be punished a little. But don't be too hard on her, Marilla. Recollect she hasn't ever had any one to teach her right. You're—you're going to give her something to eat, aren't you?"

---

[1]   A parting shot. According to *Brewer's*, an "allusion to the ancient practice of Parthian horsemen turning in flight to discharge arrows and missiles at their pursuers." *Parthia*: ancient western Asian kingdom.

"When did you ever hear of me starving people into good behaviour?" demanded Marilla indignantly. "She'll have her meals regular, and I'll carry them up to her myself. But she'll stay up there until she's willing to apologize to Mrs. Lynde, and that's final, Matthew."

Breakfast, dinner, and supper were very silent meals—for Anne still remained obdurate. After each meal Marilla carried a well-filled tray to the east gable and brought it down later on not noticeably depleted. Matthew eyed its last descent with a troubled eye. Had Anne eaten anything at all?

When Marilla went out that evening to bring the cows from the back pasture, Matthew, who had been hanging about the barns and watching, slipped into the house with the air of a burglar and crept up-stairs. As a general thing Matthew gravitated between the kitchen and the little bedroom off the hall where he slept; once in a while he ventured uncomfortably into the parlour or sitting-room when the minister came to tea. But he had never been up-stairs in his own house since the spring he helped Marilla paper the spare bedroom, and that was four years ago.

He tiptoed along the hall and stood for several minutes outside the door of the east gable before he summoned courage to tap on it with his fingers and then open the door to peep in.

Anne was sitting on the yellow chair by the window, gazing mournfully out into the garden. Very small and unhappy she looked, and Matthew's heart smote him. He softly closed the door and tiptoed over to her.

"Anne," he whispered, as if afraid of being overheard, "how are you making it, Anne?"

Anne smiled wanly.

"Pretty well. I imagine a good deal, and that helps to pass the time. Of course, it's rather lonesome. But then, I may as well get used to that."

Anne smiled again, bravely facing the long years of solitary imprisonment before her.

Matthew recollected that he must say what he had come to say without loss of time, lest Marilla return prematurely.

"Well now, Anne, don't you think you'd better do it and have it over with?" he whispered. "It'll have to be done sooner or later, you know, for Marilla's a dreadful determined woman—dreadful determined, Anne. Do it right off, I say, and have it over."

"Do you mean apologize to Mrs. Lynde?"

"Yes—apologize—that's the very word," said Matthew eagerly. "Just smooth it over so to speak. That's what I was trying to get at."

"I suppose I could do it to oblige you," said Anne thoughtfully. "It would be true enough to say I am sorry, because I *am* sorry now. I wasn't a bit sorry last night. I was mad clear through, and I stayed mad all night. I know I did because I woke up three times and I was just furious every time. But this morning it was all over. I wasn't in a temper any more—and it left a dreadful sort of goneness, too. I felt so ashamed of myself. But I just couldn't think of going and telling Mrs. Lynde so. It would be so humiliating. I made up my mind I'd stay shut up here for ever rather than do that. But still— I'd do anything for you—if you really want me to—"

"Well now, of course I do. It's terrible lonesome down-stairs without you. Just go and smooth it over—that's a good girl."

"Very well," said Anne resignedly. "I'll tell Marilla as soon as she comes in that I've repented."

"That's right—that's right, Anne. But don't tell Marilla I said anything about it. She might think I was putting my oar in and I promised not to do that."

"Wild horses won't drag the secret from me," promised Anne solemnly. "How would wild horses drag a secret from a person anyhow?"

But Matthew was gone, scared at his own success. He fled hastily to the remotest corner of the horse pasture lest Marilla should suspect what he had been up to. Marilla herself, upon her return to the house, was agreeably surprised to hear a plaintive voice calling, "Marilla," over the banisters.

"Well?" she said, going into the hall.

"I'm sorry I lost my temper and said rude things, and I'm willing to go and tell Mrs. Lynde so."

"Very well." Marilla's crispness gave no sign of her relief. She had been wondering what under the canopy[1] she should do if Anne did not give in. "I'll take you down after milking."

---

[1] Sky, heavens.

Accordingly, after milking, behold Marilla and Anne walking down the lane, the former erect and triumphant, the latter drooping and dejected. But half-way down Anne's dejection vanished as if by enchantment. She lifted her head and stepped lightly along, her eyes fixed on the sunset sky and an air of subdued exhilaration about her. Marilla beheld the change disapprovingly. This was no meek penitent such as it behooved her to take into the presence of the offended Mrs. Lynde.

"What are you thinking of, Anne?" she asked sharply.

"I'm imagining out what I must say to Mrs. Lynde," answered Anne dreamily.

This was satisfactory—or should have been so. But Marilla could not rid herself of the notion that something in her scheme of punishment was going askew. Anne had no business to look so rapt and radiant.

Rapt and radiant Anne continued until they were in the very presence of Mrs. Lynde, who was sitting knitting by her kitchen window. Then the radiance vanished. Mournful penitence appeared on every feature. Before a word was spoken Anne suddenly went down on her knees before the astonished Mrs. Rachel and held out her hands beseechingly.

"Oh, Mrs. Lynde, I am so extremely sorry," she said with a quiver in her voice. "I could never express all my sorrow, no, not if I used up a whole dictionary. You must just imagine it. I behaved terribly to you—and I've disgraced the dear friends, Matthew and Marilla, who have let me stay at Green Gables although I'm not a boy. I'm a dreadfully wicked and ungrateful girl, and I deserve to be punished and cast out by respectable people for ever. It was very wicked of me to fly into a temper because you told me the truth. It *was* the truth; every word you said was true. My hair is red and I'm freckled and skinny and ugly. What I said to you was true, too, but I shouldn't have said it. Oh, Mrs. Lynde, please, please forgive me. If you refuse it will be a lifelong sorrow to me. You wouldn't like to inflict a lifelong sorrow on a poor little orphan girl, would you, even if she had a dreadful temper? Oh, I am sure you wouldn't. Please say you forgive me, Mrs. Lynde."

Anne clasped her hands together, bowed her head, and waited for the word of judgment.

There was no mistaking her sincerity—it breathed in every tone of her voice. Both Marilla and Mrs. Lynde recognized its unmistakable ring. But the former understood in dismay that Anne was actually enjoying her valley of humiliation—was revelling in the thoroughness of her abasement. Where was the wholesome punishment upon which she, Marilla, had plumed herself? Anne had turned it into a species of positive pleasure.

Good Mrs. Lynde, not being overburdened with perception, did not see this. She only perceived that Anne had made a very thorough apology and all resentment vanished from her kindly, if somewhat officious, heart.

"There, there, get up, child," she said heartily. "Of course I forgive you. I guess I was a little too hard on you, anyway. But I'm such an outspoken person. You just mustn't mind me, that's what. It can't be denied your hair is terrible red; but I knew a girl once—went to school with her, in fact—whose hair was every mite as red as yours when she was young, but when she grew up it darkened to a real handsome auburn. I wouldn't be a mite surprised if yours did, too—not a mite."

"Oh, Mrs. Lynde!" Anne drew a long breath as she rose to her feet. "You have given me a hope. I shall always feel that you are a benefactor. Oh, I could endure anything if I only thought my hair would be a handsome auburn when I grew up. It would be so much easier to be good if one's hair was a handsome auburn, don't you think? And now may I go out into your garden and sit on that bench under the apple-trees while you and Marilla are talking? There is so much more scope for imagination out there."

"Laws, yes, run along, child. And you can pick a bouquet of them white June lilies over in the corner if you like."

As the door closed behind Anne Mrs. Lynde got briskly up to light a lamp.

"She's a real odd little thing. Take this chair, Marilla; it's easier than the one you've got; I just keep that for the hired boy to sit on. Yes, she certainly is an odd child, but there is something kind of taking about her after all. I don't feel so surprised at you and Matthew keeping her as I did—nor so sorry for you, either. She may turn out all right. Of course, she has a queer way of expressing herself—a little too—well, too kind of forcible, you know; but she'll likely get over that now that she's come to live among civilized folks. And then, her temper's pretty quick, I guess; but there's one comfort, a child that has a quick temper, just blaze up and cool down, ain't never likely to be sly or deceitful. Preserve me from a sly child, that's what. On the whole, Marilla, I kind of like her."

When Marilla went home Anne came out of the fragrant twilight of the orchard with a sheaf of white narcissi in her hands.

"I apologized pretty well, didn't I?" she said proudly as they went down the lane. "I thought since I had to do it I might as well do it thoroughly."

"You did it thoroughly, all right enough," was Marilla's comment. Marilla was dismayed at finding herself inclined to laugh over the recollection. She had also an uneasy feeling that she ought to scold Anne for apologizing so well; but then, that was ridiculous! She compromised with her conscience by saying severely:

"I hope you won't have occasion to make many more such apologies. I hope you'll try to control your temper now, Anne."

"That wouldn't be so hard if people wouldn't twit me about my looks," said Anne with a sigh. "I don't get cross about other things; but I'm *so* tired of being twitted about my hair and it just makes me boil right over. Do you suppose my hair will really be a handsome auburn when I grow up?"

"You shouldn't think so much about your looks, Anne. I'm afraid you are a very vain little girl."

"How can I be vain when I know I'm homely?" protested Anne. "I love pretty things; and I hate to look in the glass and see something that isn't pretty. It makes me feel so sorrowful— just as I feel when I look at any ugly thing. I pity it because it isn't beautiful."

"Handsome is as handsome does,"[1] quoted Marilla.

"I've had that said to me before, but I have my doubts about it," remarked sceptical Anne, sniffing at her narcissi. "Oh, aren't

---

[1] Roughly, beauty is in good conduct. *The Oxford Dictionary of American Proverbs* cites several occurrences, from 1580, Munday, *Sunday Examples* (see also *Oxford Dictionary of Proverbs*: "But as the ancient adage is, goodly is he that goodly dooth"). *ODP* also cites Oliver Goldsmith (1728–1774), *The Vicar of Wakefield* (1766), ch. 1: "They are as heaven made them, handsome enough if they be good enough; for handsome is that handsome does."

these flowers sweet! It was lovely of Mrs. Lynde to give them to me. I have no hard feelings against Mrs. Lynde now. It gives you a lovely, comfortable feeling to apologize and be forgiven, doesn't it? Aren't the stars bright to-night? If you could live in a star, which one would you pick? I'd like that lovely clear big one away over there above that dark hill."

"Anne, do hold your tongue," said Marilla, thoroughly worn out trying to follow the gyrations of Anne's thoughts.

Anne said no more until they turned into their own lane. A little gypsy wind came down it to meet them, laden with the spicy perfume of young dew-wet ferns. Far up in the shadows a cheerful light gleamed out through the trees from the kitchen at Green Gables. Anne suddenly came close to Marilla and slipped her hand into the older woman's hard palm.

"It's lovely to be going home and know it's home," she said. "I love Green Gables already, and I never loved any place before. No place ever seemed like home. Oh, Marilla, I'm so happy. I could pray right now and not find it a bit hard."

Something warm and pleasant welled up in Marilla's heart at touch of that thin little hand in her own—a throb of the maternity she had missed, perhaps. Its very unaccustomedness and sweetness disturbed her. She hastened to restore her sensations to their normal calm by inculcating a moral.

"If you'll be a good girl you'll always be happy, Anne. And you should never find it hard to say your prayers."

"Saying one's prayers isn't exactly the same thing as praying," said Anne meditatively. "But I'm going to imagine that I'm the wind that is blowing up there in those tree-tops. When I get tired of the trees I'll imagine I'm gently waving down here in the ferns—and then I'll fly over to Mrs. Lynde's garden and set the flowers dancing—and then I'll go with one great swoop over the clover field—and then I'll blow over the Lake of Shining Waters and ripple it all up into little sparkling waves. Oh, there's so much scope for imagination in a wind! So I'll not talk any more just now, Marilla."

"Thanks be to goodness for that," breathed Marilla in devout relief.

CHAPTER XI

ANNE'S IMPRESSIONS OF SUNDAY-SCHOOL

"WELL, how do you like them?" said Marilla.

Anne was standing in the gable-room, looking solemnly at three new dresses spread out on the bed. One was of snuffy coloured[1] gingham[2] which Marilla had been tempted to buy from a pedlar the preceding summer because it looked so serviceable; one was of black-and-white checked sateen[3] which she had picked up at a bargain counter in the winter; and one was a stiff print of an ugly blue shade which she had purchased that week at a Carmody store.

She had made them up herself, and they were all made alike—plain skirts fulled tightly to plain waists, with sleeves as plain as waist and skirt and tight as sleeves could be.

"I'll imagine that I like them," said Anne soberly.

"I don't want you to imagine it," said Marilla, offended. "Oh, I can see you don't like the dresses! What is the matter with them? Aren't they neat and clean and new?"

"Yes."

"Then why don't you like them?"

"They're—they're not—pretty," said Anne reluctantly.

"Pretty!" Marilla sniffed. "I didn't trouble my head about getting pretty dresses for you. I don't believe in pampering vanity, Anne, I'll tell you that right off. Those dresses are good, sensible, serviceable dresses, without any frills or furbelows about them, and they're all you'll get this summer. The brown gingham and the blue print will do you for school when you begin to go. The

---

[1] Yellowish or brownish in colour, like snuff or tobacco.

[2] "A medium or lightweight cotton fabric, plain weave and yarn dyed, made with carded or combed yarns. [...] Gingham in which two colours are used is generally called *check*, and that in which three of more colours are used are referred to as *plaid"* (*Fairchild's Dictionary of Textiles*).

[3] "A strong, lustrous cotton or cotton blend fabric. [...] The term is used to distinguish between the cotton-system spun yarn fabric and satin fabric made of silk or manufactured fibre filament yarns" (*Fairchild's Dictionary of Textiles*).

sateen is for church and Sunday-school. I'll expect you to keep them neat and clean and not to tear them. I should think you'd be grateful to get most anything after those skimpy wincey things you've been wearing."

"Oh, I *am* grateful," protested Anne. "But I'd be ever so much gratefuller if—if you'd made just one of them with puffed sleeves. Puffed sleeves are so fashionable now. It would give me such a thrill, Marilla, just to wear a dress with puffed sleeves."

"Well, you'll have to do without your thrill. I hadn't any material to waste on puffed sleeves. I think they are ridiculous-looking things anyhow. I prefer the plain, sensible ones."

"But I'd rather look ridiculous when everybody else does than plain and sensible all by myself," persisted Anne mournfully.

"Trust you for that! Well, hang those dresses carefully up in your closet, and then sit down and learn the Sunday-school lesson. I got a quarterly[1] from Mr. Bell for you and you'll go to Sunday-school to-morrow," said Marilla, disappearing downstairs in high dudgeon.

Anne clasped her hands and looked at the dresses.

"I did hope there would be a white one with puffed sleeves," she whispered disconsolately. "I prayed for one, but I didn't much expect it on that account. I didn't suppose God would have time to bother about a little orphan girl's dress. I knew I'd just have to depend on Marilla for it. Well, fortunately I can imagine that one of them is of snow-white muslin with lovely lace frills and three-puffed sleeves." The next morning warnings of a sick headache prevented Marilla from going to Sunday-school with Anne.

"You'll have to go down and call for Mrs. Lynde, Anne," she said. "She'll see that you get into the right class. Now, mind you behave yourself properly. Stay to preaching afterwards and ask Mrs. Lynde to show you our pew. Here's a cent for collection. Don't stare at people and don't fidget. I shall expect you to tell me the text when you come home."

Anne started off irreproachably, arrayed in the stiff black-and-white sateen, which, while decent as regards length, and certainly

---

[1]   Publication produced four times a year; in this case, a reference to a publication
    containing Sunday-school lessons for a quarter of the year.

not open to the charge of skimpiness, contrived to emphasize every corner and angle of her thin figure. Her hat was a little flat, glossy, new sailor, the extreme plainness of which had likewise much disappointed Anne, who had permitted herself secret visions of ribbon and flowers. The latter, however, were supplied before Anne reached the main road, for, being confronted half-way down the lane with a golden frenzy of wind-stirred butter-cups and a glory of wild roses, Anne promptly and liberally garlanded her hat with a heavy wreath of them. Whatever other people might have thought of the result it satisfied Anne, and she tripped gaily down the road, holding her ruddy head with its decoration of pink and yellow very proudly.

When she reached Mrs. Lynde's house she found that lady gone. Nothing daunted Anne proceeded onward to the church alone. In the porch she found a crowd of little girls, all more or less gaily attired in whites and blues and pinks, and all staring with curious eyes at this stranger in their midst, with her extraordinary head adornment. Avonlea little girls had already heard queer stories about Anne; Mrs. Lynde said she had an awful temper; Jerry Buote, the hired boy at Green Gables, said she talked all the time to herself or to the trees and flowers like a crazy girl. They looked at her and whispered to each other behind their quarterlies. Nobody made any friendly advances, then or later on when the opening exercises were over and Anne found herself in Miss Rogerson's class.

Miss Rogerson was a middle-aged lady who had taught a Sunday-school class for twenty years. Her method of teaching was to ask the printed questions from the quarterly and look sternly over its edge at the particular little girl she thought ought to answer the question.[1] She looked very often at Anne, and Anne, thanks to Marilla's drilling, answered promptly; but it may be questioned if she understood very much about either question or answer.

She did not think she liked Miss Rogerson, and she felt very miserable; every other little girl in the class had puffed sleeves.

---

[1] Criticism such as is implicit here is a standard element of the *Pansy* didacticism, in the novels by Isabella Macdonald Alden. See for instance *Links in Rebecca's Life* (London: Ward Lock, n.d.) (77) or *The Man of the House* (London: Ward Lock, n.d.) (183–84). On the *Pansy* books see 160, note 2. See also Introduction 18–19, and 19, note 1.

"THEY LOOKED AT HER AND WHISPERED TO EACH OTHER."

Anne felt that life was really not worth living without puffed sleeves.

"Well, how did you like Sunday-school?" Marilla wanted to know when Anne came home. Her wreath having faded, Anne had discarded it in the lane, so Marilla was spared the knowledge of that for a time.

"I didn't like it a bit. It was horrid."

"Anne Shirley!" said Marilla rebukingly.

Anne sat down on the rocker with a long sigh, kissed one of Bonny's leaves, and waved her hand to a blossoming fuchsia.

"They might have been lonesome while I was away," she explained. "And now about the Sunday-school. I behaved well, just as you told me. Mrs. Lynde was gone, but I went right on myself. I went into the church, with a lot of other little girls, and I sat in the corner of a pew by the window while the opening exercises went on. Mr. Bell made an awfully long prayer. I would have been dreadfully tired before he got through if I hadn't been sitting by that window. But it looked right out on the Lake of Shining Waters, so I just gazed at that and imagined all sorts of splendid things."

"You shouldn't have done anything of the sort. You should have listened to Mr. Bell."

"But he wasn't talking to me," protested Anne. "He was talking to God and he didn't seem to be very much interested in it, either. I think he thought God was too far off to make it worth while. I said a little prayer myself, though. There was a long row of white birches hanging over the lake and the sunshine fell down through them, 'way, 'way down, deep into the water. Oh, Marilla, it was like a beautiful dream! It gave me a thrill and I just said, 'Thank you for it, God,' two or three times."

"Not out loud, I hope," said Marilla anxiously.

"Oh, no, just under my breath. Well, Mr. Bell did get through at last and they told me to go into the class-room with Miss Rogerson's class. There were nine other girls in it. They all had puffed sleeves. I tried to imagine mine were puffed, too, but I couldn't. Why couldn't I? It was as easy as could be to imagine they were puffed when I was alone in the east gable, but it was awfully hard there among the others who had really truly puffs."

"You shouldn't have been thinking about your sleeves in

Sunday-school. You should have been attending to the lesson. I hope you knew it."

"Oh, yes; and I answered a lot of questions. Miss Rogerson asked ever so many. I don't think it was fair for her to do all the asking. There were lots I wanted to ask her, but I didn't like to because I didn't think she was a kindred spirit. Then all the other little girls recited a paraphrase.[1] She asked me if I knew any. I told her I didn't, but I could recite 'The Dog at His Master's Grave' if she liked.[2] That's in the Third Royal Reader. It isn't a really truly religious piece of poetry, but it's so sad and melancholy that it might as well be. She said it wouldn't do and she told me to learn the nineteenth paraphrase for next Sunday. I read it over in church afterwards and it's splendid. There are two lines in particular that just thrill me.

'Quick as the slaughtered squadrons fell
In Midian's evil day.'[3]

I don't know what 'squadrons' means nor 'Midian,' either, but it sounds *so* tragical. I can hardly wait until next Sunday to recite it. I'll practise it all the week. After Sunday-school I asked Miss Rogerson—because Mrs. Lynde was too far away—to show me your pew. I sat just as still as I could and the text was Revelations, third chapter, second and third verses.[4] It was a very long text. If I was a minister I'd pick the short, snappy ones. The sermon was awfully long, too. I suppose the minister had to match it to the text. I didn't think he was a bit interesting. The trouble with him

---

1 See *Translations and Paraphrases, in Verse, of Several Passages of Sacred Scripture. Collected and Prepared by a Committee of the General Assembly of the Church of Scotland, in Order to be Sung in Churches* (Halifax, 1790). OED notes that the first edition was "printed and issued for consideration in 1745. That finally adopted was published in 1781."

2 A poem by American poet Lydia Howard Huntley Sigourney (1791–1865).

3 See *Translations and Paraphrases XIX*, Isaiah 9.2–8 (18). See also in *The Presbyterian Book of Praise, Approved and Commended by the General Assembly of the Presbyterian Church in Canada* (1904), Hymn 27, "The race that long in darkness pined" by John Morison. *Midian.* "In the Bible, one of the peoples of North Arabia whom the Hebrews recognized as distant kinsmen, representing them as sons of Abraham's wife Keturah [....] A place, Midian, is mentioned in I Kings xi.18, apparently between Edom and Paran, and in later times the name lingered in the district east of the Gulf of Akaba" (*Encyclopaedia Britannica,* 11th ed. vol 18, 418–19).

4 Properly, Revelation (The Revelation of St. John the Divine), last book of the New Testament.

seems to be that he hasn't enough imagination. I didn't listen to him very much. I just let my thoughts run and I thought of the most surprising things."

Marilla felt helplessly that all this should be sternly reproved, but she was hampered by the undeniable fact that some of the things Anne had said, especially about the minister's sermons and Mr. Bell's prayers, were what she herself had really thought deep down in her heart for years, but had never given expression to. It almost seemed to her that those secret, unuttered, critical thoughts had suddenly taken visible and accusing shape and form in the person of this outspoken morsel of neglected humanity.

CHAPTER XII

A SOLEMN VOW AND PROMISE

IT was not until the next Friday that Marilla heard the story of the flower-wreathed hat. She came home from Mrs. Lynde's and called Anne to account.

"Anne, Mrs. Rachel says you went to church last Sunday with your hat rigged out ridiculous with roses and buttercups. What on earth put you up to such a caper? A pretty-looking object you must have been!"

"Oh, I know pink and yellow aren't becoming to me," began Anne.

"Becoming fiddlesticks! It was putting flowers on your hat at all, no matter what colour they were, that was ridiculous. You are the most aggravating child!"

"I don't see why it's any more ridiculous to wear flowers on your hat than on your dress," protested Anne. "Lots of little girls there had bouquets pinned on their dresses. What was the difference?"

Marilla was not to be drawn from the safe concrete into dubious paths of the abstract.

"Don't answer me back like that, Anne. It was very silly of you to do such a thing. Never let me catch you at such a trick again. Mrs. Rachel says she thought she would sink through the floor when she saw you come in all rigged out like that. She couldn't get near enough to tell you to take them off till it was too late. She says people talked about it something dreadful. Of course they would think I had no better sense than to let you go decked out like that."

"Oh, I'm so sorry," said Anne, tears welling into her eyes. "I never thought you'd mind. The roses and buttercups were so sweet and pretty I thought they'd look lovely on my hat. Lots of the little girls had artificial flowers on their hats. I'm afraid I'm going to be a dreadful trial to you. Maybe you'd better send me back to the asylum. That would be terrible; I don't think I could endure it; most likely I would go into consumption;[1] I'm so thin as it is, you see. But that would be better than being a trial to you."

"Nonsense," said Marilla, vexed at herself for having made the child cry. "I don't want to send you back to the asylum, I'm sure. All I want is that you should behave like other little girls and not make yourself ridiculous. Don't cry any more. I've got some news for you. Diana Barry came home this afternoon. I'm going up to see if I can borrow a skirt pattern from Mrs. Barry, and if you like you can come with me and get acquainted with Diana."

Anne rose to her feet, with clasped hands, the tears still glistening on her cheeks; the dish-towel she had been hemming slipped unheeded to the floor.

"Oh, Marilla, I'm frightened—now that it has come I'm actually frightened. What if she shouldn't like me! It would be the most tragical disappointment of my life."

"Now, don't get into a fluster. And I do wish you wouldn't use such long words. It sounds so funny in a little girl. I guess Diana'll like you well enough. It's her mother you've got to reckon with. If she doesn't like you it won't matter how much Diana does. If she has heard about your outburst to Mrs. Lynde and going to church with buttercups round your hat I don't know what she'll think of you. You must be polite and well-behaved, and don't make any of your startling speeches. For pity's sake, if the child isn't actually trembling!"

---

[1] Term used throughout the nineteenth century and into the twentieth to refer to pulmonary tuberculosis or phthisis. Later in *AGG* Marilla will fear Anne's death by consumption, when the Spencervale doctor warns her to ensure that Anne gets enough fresh air. See 281, note 2.

Anne *was* trembling. Her face was pale and tense.

"Oh, Marilla, you be excited, too, if you were going to meet a little girl you hoped to be your bosom friend and whose mother mightn't like you," she said as she hastened to get her hat.

They went over to Orchard Slope by the short cut across the brook and up the firry hill grove. Mrs. Barry came to the kitchen door in answer to Marilla's knock. She was a tall, black-eyed, black-haired woman, with a very resolute mouth. She had the reputation of being very strict with her children.

"How do you do, Marilla?" she said cordially. "Come in. And this is the little girl you have adopted, I suppose."

"Yes, this is Anne Shirley," said Marilla.

"Spelled with an *e*," gasped Anne, who, tremulous and excited as she was, was determined there should be no misunderstanding on that important point.

Mrs. Barry, not hearing or not comprehending, merely shook hands and said kindly:

"How are you?"

"I am well in body although considerably rumpled up in spirit, thank you, ma'am," said Anne gravely. Then aside to Marilla in an audible whisper, "There wasn't anything startling in that, was there, Marilla?"

Diana was sitting on the sofa, reading a book which she dropped when the callers entered. She was a very pretty little girl, with her mother's black eyes and hair, and rosy cheeks, and the merry expression which was her inheritance from her father.

"This is my little girl, Diana," said Mrs. Barry. "Diana, you might take Anne out into the garden and show her your flowers. It will be better for you than straining your eyes over that book. She reads entirely too much—" this to Marilla as the little girls went out— "and I can't prevent her, for her father aids and abets her. She's always poring over a book. I'm glad she has the prospect of a play-mate—perhaps it will take her more out-of-doors."

Outside in the garden, which was full of mellow sunset light streaming through the dark old firs to the west of it, stood Anne and Diana, gazing bashfully at one another over a clump of gorgeous tiger lilies.

The Barry garden was a bowery wilderness of flowers which

would have delighted Anne's heart at any time less fraught with destiny. It was encircled by huge old willows and tall firs, beneath which flourished flowers that loved the shade. Prim, right-angled paths, neatly bordered with clam-shells, intersected it like moist red ribbons and in the beds between old-fashioned flowers ran riot. There were rosy bleeding-hearts and great splendid crimson peonies; white, fragrant narcissi and thorny, sweet Scotch roses; pink and blue and white columbines and lilac-tinted Bouncing Bets; clumps of southernwood and ribbon grass and mint; purple Adam-and-Eve, daffodils, and masses of sweet clover white with its delicate, fragrant, feathery sprays; scarlet lightning that shot its fiery lances over prim white musk-flowers; a garden it was where sunshine lingered and bees hummed, and winds, beguiled into loitering, purred and rustled.

"Oh, Diana," said Anne at last, clasping her hands and speaking almost in a whisper, "do you think—oh, do you think you can like me a little—enough to be my bosom friend?"

Diana laughed. Diana always laughed before she spoke.

"Why, I guess so," she said frankly. "I'm awfully glad you've come to live at Green Gables. It will be jolly to have somebody to play with. There isn't any other girl who lives near enough to play with, and I've no sisters big enough."

"Will you swear to be my friend for ever and ever?" demanded Anne eagerly.

Diana looked shocked.

"Why, it's dreadfully wicked to swear," she said rebukingly.

"Oh, no, not my kind of swearing. There are two kinds, you know."

"I never heard of but one kind," said Diana doubtfully.

"There really is another. Oh, it isn't wicked at all. It just means vowing and promising solemnly."

"Well, I don't mind doing that," agreed Diana, relieved. "How do you do it?"

"We must join hands—so," said Anne gravely. "It ought to be over running water. We'll just imagine this path is running water. I'll repeat the oath first. I solemnly swear to be faithful to my bosom friend, Diana Barry, as long as the sun and moon shall endure. Now you say it and put my name in."

Diana repeated the "oath" with a laugh fore and aft. Then she said:

"You're a queer girl, Anne. I heard before that you were queer. But I believe I'm going to like you real well."

When Marilla and Anne went home Diana went with them as far as the log bridge. The two little girls walked with their arms about each other. At the brook they parted with many promises to spend the next afternoon together.

"Well, did you find Diana a kindred spirit?" asked Marilla as they went up through the garden of Green Gables.

"Oh, yes," sighed Anne, blissfully unconscious of any sarcasm on Marilla's part. "Oh, Marilla, I'm the happiest girl on Prince Edward Island this very moment. I assure you I'll say my prayers with a right good-will to-night. Diana and I are going to build a playhouse in Mr. William Bell's birch grove to-morrow. Can I have those broken pieces of china that are out in the wood-shed? Diana's birthday is in February and mine is in March. Don't you think that is a very strange coincidence? Diana is going to lend me a book to read. She says it's perfectly splendid and tremenjusly exciting. She's going to show me a place back in the woods where rice lilies grow. Don't you think Diana has got very soulful eyes? I wish I had soulful eyes. Diana is going to teach me to sing a song called 'Nelly in the Hazel Dell.'[1] She's going to give me a picture to put up in my room; it's a perfectly beautiful picture, she says— a lovely lady in a pale blue silk dress. A sewing-machine agent gave it to her. I wish I had something to give Diana. I'm an inch taller than Diana, but she is ever so much fatter; she says she'd like to be thin because it's so much more graceful, but I'm afraid she only said it to soothe my feelings. We're going to the shore some day to gather shells. We have agreed to call the spring down by the log bridge the Dryad's Bubble. Isn't that a perfectly elegant name? I read a story once about a spring called that. A dryad[2] is a sort of grown-up fairy, I think."

"Well, all I hope is you won't talk Diana to death," said Marilla. "But remember this in all your planning, Anne. You're

---

[1] Properly, "The Hazel Dell," a song of the mid-nineteenth century by George Frederick Root. Reproduced in *AA* (464).

[2] A wood-nymph.

not going to play all the time nor most of it. You'll have your work to do and it'll have to be done first."

Anne's cup of happiness was full, and Matthew caused it to overflow. He had just got home from a trip to the store at Carmody, and he sheepishly produced a small parcel from his pocket and handed it to Anne, with a deprecatory look at Marilla.

"I heard you say you liked chocolate sweeties, so I got you some," he said.

"Humph," sniffed Marilla. "It'll ruin her teeth and stomach. There, there, child, don't look so dismal. You can eat those, since Matthew has gone and got them. He'd better have brought you peppermints. They're wholesomer. Don't sicken yourself eating them all at once now."

"Oh, no, indeed I won't," said Anne eagerly. "I'll eat just one to-night, Marilla. And I can give Diana half of them, can't I? The other half will taste twice as sweet to me if I give some to her. It's delightful to think I have something to give her."

"I will say it for the child," said Marilla when Anne had gone to her gable, "she isn't stingy. I'm glad, for of all faults I detest stinginess in a child. Dear me, it's only three weeks since she came and it seems as if she'd been here always. I can't imagine the place without her. Now, don't be looking I-told-you-so, Matthew. That's bad enough in a woman, but it isn't to be endured in a man. I'm perfectly willing to own up that I'm glad I consented to keep the child and that I'm getting fond of her, but don't you rub it in, Matthew Cuthbert."

CHAPTER XIII

THE DELIGHTS OF ANTICIPATION

"IT'S time Anne was in to do her sewing," said Marilla, glancing at the clock and then out into the yellow August afternoon where everything drowsed in the heat. "She stayed playing with Diana more than half an hour more'n I gave her leave to; and now she's perched out there on the woodpile talking to

Matthew, nineteen to the dozen,[1] when she knows perfectly well that she ought to be at her work. And of course he's listening to her like a perfect ninny. I never saw such an infatuated man. The more she talks and the odder the things she says, the more he's delighted evidently. Anne Shirley, you come right in here this minute, do you hear me!"

A series of staccato taps on the west window brought Anne flying in from the yard, eyes shining, cheeks faintly flushed with pink, unbraided hair streaming behind her in a torrent of brightness.

"Oh, Marilla," she exclaimed breathlessly, "there's going to be a Sunday-school picnic next week—in Mr. Harmon Andrews' field, right near the Lake of Shining Waters. And Mrs. Superintendent Bell and Mrs. Rachel Lynde are going to make ice-cream—think of it, Marilla—*ice-cream*! And oh, Marilla, can I go to it?"

"Just look at the clock, if you please, Anne. What time did I tell you to come in?"

"Two o'clock—but isn't it splendid about the picnic, Marilla? Please can I go? Oh, I've never been to a picnic—I've dreamed of picnics, but I've never—"

"Yes, I told you to come at two o'clock. And it's a quarter to three. I'd like to know why you didn't obey me, Anne."

"Why, I meant to, Marilla, as much as could be. But you have no idea how fascinating Idlewild is. And then, of course, I had to tell Matthew about the picnic. Matthew is such a sympathetic listener. Please can I go?"

"You'll have to learn to resist the fascination of Idle-what-ever-you-call it. When I tell you to come in at a certain time I mean that time and not half an hour later. And you needn't stop to discourse with sympathetic listeners on your way, either. As for the picnic, of course you can go. You're a Sunday-school scholar, and it's not likely I'd refuse to let you go when all the other little girls are going."

"But—but," faltered Anne, "Diana says that everybody must take a basket of things to eat. I can't cook, as you know, Marilla, and—and—I don't mind going to a picnic without puffed sleeves so much, but I'd feel terribly humiliated if I had to go

---

[1] To talk very quickly.

without a basket. It's been preying on my mind ever since Diana told me."

"Well, it needn't prey any longer. I'll bake you a basket."

"Oh, you dear good Marilla. Oh, you are so kind to me. Oh, I'm so much obliged to you."

Getting through with her "oh's" Anne cast herself into Marilla's arms and rapturously kissed her sallow cheek. It was the first time in her whole life that childish lips had voluntarily touched Marilla's face. Again that sudden sensation of startling sweetness thrilled her. She was secretly vastly pleased at Anne's impulsive caress, which was probably the reason why she said brusquely:

"There, there, never mind your kissing nonsense. I'd sooner see you doing strictly as you're told. As for cooking, I mean to begin giving you lessons in that some of these days. But you're so feather-brained, Anne, I've been waiting to see if you'd sober down a little and learn to be steady before I begin. You've got to keep your wits about you in cooking and not stop in the middle of things to let your thoughts rove over all creation. Now, get out your patchwork and have your square done before tea-time."

"I do *not* like patchwork," said Anne dolefully, hunting out her workbasket and sitting down before a little heap of red and white diamonds with a sigh. "I think some kinds of sewing would be nice; but there's no scope for imagination in patchwork. It's just one little seam after another and you never seem to be getting anywhere. But of course I'd rather be Anne of Green Gables sewing patchwork than Anne of any other place with nothing to do but play. I wish time went as quick sewing patches as it does when I'm playing with Diana, though. Oh, we do have such elegant times, Marilla. I have to furnish most of the imagination, but I'm well able to do that. Diana is simply perfect in every other way. You know that little piece of land across the brook that runs up between our farm and Mr. Barry's. It belongs to Mr. William Bell, and right in the corner there is a little ring of white birch trees—the most romantic spot, Marilla. Diana and I have our play-house there. We call it Idlewild. Isn't that a poetical name? I assure you it took me some time to think it out. I stayed awake nearly a whole night before I invented it. Then, just as I was dropping off to sleep, it came like an inspiration. Diana was *enraptured* when she heard it. We have got our house fixed up elegantly. You must come and see it, Marilla—won't you? We have great big stones, all covered with moss, for seats, and boards from tree to tree for shelves. And we have all our dishes on them. Of course, they're all broken but it's the easiest thing in the world to imagine that they are whole. There's a piece of a plate with a spray of red and yellow ivy on it that is especially beautiful. We keep it in the parlour and we have the fairy glass there, too. The fairy glass is as lovely as a dream. Diana found it out in the woods behind their chicken house. It's all full of rainbows—just little young rainbows that haven't grown big yet—and Diana's mother told her it was broken off a hanging lamp they once had. But it's nicer to imagine the fairies lost it one night when they had a ball, so we call it the fairy glass. Matthew is going to make us a table. Oh, we have named that little round pool over in Mr. Barry's field Willowmere. I got that name out of the book Diana lent me. That was a thrilling book, Marilla. The heroine had five lovers. I'd be satisfied with one, wouldn't you? She was very handsome and she went through great tribulations. She could faint as easy as anything. I'd love to be able to faint, wouldn't you, Marilla? It's so romantic. But I'm really very healthy for all I'm so thin. I believe I'm getting fatter, though. Don't you think I am? I look at my elbows every morning when I get up to see if any dimples are coming. Diana is having a new dress made with elbow sleeves. She is going to wear it to the picnic. Oh, I do hope it will be fine next Wednesday. I don't feel I could endure the disappointment if anything happened to prevent me from getting to the picnic. I suppose I'd live through it, but I'm certain it would be a lifelong sorrow. It wouldn't matter if I got to a hundred picnics in after years; they wouldn't make up for missing this one. They're going to have boats on the Lake of Shining Waters—and ice-cream as I told you. I have never tasted ice-cream. Diana tried to explain what it was like, but I guess ice-cream is one of those things that are beyond imagination."

"Anne, you have talked even on for ten minutes by the clock," said Marilla. "Now, just for curiosity's sake, see if you can hold your tongue for the same length of time."

Anne held her tongue as desired. But for the rest of the week she talked picnic and thought picnic and dreamed picnic. On

Saturday it rained and she worked herself up into such a frantic state lest it should keep on raining until and over Wednesday, that Marilla made her sew an extra patchwork square by way of steadying her nerves.

On Sunday Anne confided to Marilla on the way home from church that she grew actually cold all over with excitement when the minister announced the picnic from the pulpit.

"Such a thrill as went up and down my back, Marilla! I don't think I'd ever really believed until then that there was honestly going to be a picnic. I couldn't help fearing I'd only imagined it. But when a minister says a thing in the pulpit you just have to believe it."

"You set your heart too much on things, Anne," said Marilla with a sigh. "I'm afraid there'll be a great many disappointments in store for you through life."

"Oh, Marilla, looking forward to things is half the pleasure of them," exclaimed Anne. "You mayn't get the things themselves; but nothing can prevent you from having the fun of looking forward to them. Mrs. Lynde says, 'Blessed are they who expect nothing for they shall not be disappointed.'[1] But I think it would be worse to expect nothing than to be disappointed."

Marilla wore her amethyst brooch to church that day as usual. Marilla always wore her amethyst brooch to church. She would have thought it rather sacrilegious to leave it off—as bad as forgetting her Bible or her collection dime.[2] That amethyst brooch was Marilla's most treasured possession. A sea-faring uncle had given it to her mother who in turn had bequeathed it to Marilla. It was an old-fashioned oval, containing a braid of her mother's hair, surrounded by a border of very fine amethysts. Marilla knew too little about precious stones to realize how fine the amethysts actually were; but she thought them very beautiful and was always pleasantly conscious of their violet shimmer

---

[1] This phrase is attributed to Alexander Pope (1688–1744). *Bartlett's* cites his letter to Fortescue (23 Sep. 1725) ("'Blessed is the man who expects nothing, for he shall never be disappointed' was the ninth beatitude"); *Oxford Dictionary of English Proverbs* cites a letter from Pope to John Gay in 1727, with similar phrasing. *The Beatitudes* or blessings: see Matthew 5.3–11.

[2] Money collected at a church service.

at her throat, above her good brown satin dress, even although she could not see it.

Anne had been smitten with delighted admiration when she first saw that brooch.

"Oh, Marilla, it's a perfectly elegant brooch. I don't know how you can pay attention to the sermon or the prayers when you have it on. *I* couldn't, I know. I think amethysts are just sweet. They are what I used to think diamonds were like. Long ago, before I had ever seen a diamond, I read about them and I tried to imagine what they would be like. I thought they would be lovely glimmering purple stones. When I saw a real diamond in a lady's ring one day I was so disappointed I cried. Of course, it was very lovely but it wasn't my idea of a diamond. Will you let me hold the brooch for one minute, Marilla? Do you think amethysts can be the souls of good violets?"

CHAPTER XIV

ANNE'S CONFESSION

ON the Monday evening before the picnic Marilla came down from her room with a troubled face.

"Anne," she said to that small personage, who was shelling peas by the spotless table and singing "Nelly of the Hazel Dell" with a vigour and expression that did credit to Diana's teaching, "did you see anything of my amethyst brooch? I thought I stuck it in my pincushion when I came home from church yesterday evening, but I can't find it anywhere."

"I—I saw it this afternoon when you were away at the Aid Society," said Anne, a little slowly. "I was passing your door when I saw it on the cushion, so I went in to look at it."

"Did you touch it?" said Marilla sternly.

"Y-e-e-s," admitted Anne, "I took it up and I pinned it on my breast just to see how it would look."

"You had no business to do anything of the sort. It's very wrong in a little girl to meddle. You shouldn't have gone into my room in the first place and you shouldn't have touched a brooch that didn't belong to you in the second. Where did you put it?"

"Oh, I put it back on the bureau. I hadn't it on a minute. Truly, I didn't mean to meddle, Marilla. I didn't think about its being wrong to go in and try on the brooch; but I see now that it was and I'll never do it again. That's one good thing about me. I never do the same naughty thing twice."

"You didn't put it back," said Marilla. "That brooch isn't anywhere on the bureau. You've taken it out or something, Anne."

"I *did* put it back," said Anne quickly—pertly, Marilla thought. "I don't just remember whether I stuck it on the pincushion or laid it in the china tray. But I'm perfectly certain I put it back."

"I'll go and have another look," said Marilla, determining to be just. "If you put that brooch back it's there still. If it isn't I'll know you didn't, that's all!"

Marilla went to her room and made a thorough search, not only over the bureau but in every other place she thought the brooch might possibly be. It was not to be found and she returned to the kitchen.

"Anne, the brooch is gone. By your own admission you were the last person to handle it. Now, what have you done with it? Tell me the truth at once. Did you take it out and lose it?"

"No, I didn't," said Anne solemnly, meeting Marilla's angry gaze squarely. "I never took the brooch out of your room and that is the truth, if I was to be led to the block for it—although I'm not very certain what a block is.[1] So there, Marilla."

Anne's "so there" was only intended to emphasize her assertion, but Marilla took it as a display of defiance.

"I believe you are telling me a falsehood, Anne," she said sharply. "I know you are. There now, don't say anything more unless you are prepared to tell the whole truth. Go to your room and stay there until you are ready to confess."

"Will I take the peas with me?" said Anne meekly.

"No, I'll finish shelling them myself. Do as I bid you."

When Anne had gone Marilla went about her evening tasks

---

[1]   "The piece of wood on which the condemned were beheaded or mutilated" (*OED*). Later, Anne will recite Henry Glassford Bell's poem "Mary Queen of Scots" in which Mary is led to a block for execution. See 227, notes 1 and 2.

in a very disturbed state of mind. She was worried about her valuable brooch. What if Anne had lost it? And how wicked of the child to deny having taken it, when anybody could see she must have! With such an innocent face, too!

"I don't know what I wouldn't sooner have had happen," thought Marilla, as she nervously shelled the peas. "Of course, I don't suppose she meant to steal it or anything like that. She's just taken it to play with or help along that imagination of hers. She must have taken it, that's clear, for there hasn't been a soul in that room since she was in it, by her own story, until I went up to-night. And the brooch is gone, there's nothing surer. I suppose she has lost it and is afraid to own up for fear she'll be punished. It's a dreadful thing to think she tells falsehoods. It's a far worse thing than her fit of temper. It's a fearful responsibility to have a child in your house you can't trust. Slyness and untruthfulness—that's what she has displayed. I declare I feel worse about that than about the brooch. If she'd only have told the truth about it I wouldn't mind so much."

Marilla went to her room at intervals all through the evening and searched for the brooch, without finding it. A bed-time visit to the east gable produced no result. Anne persisted in denying that she knew anything about the brooch but Marilla was only the more firmly convinced that she did.

She told Matthew the story the next morning. Matthew was confounded and puzzled; he could not so quickly lose faith in Anne but he had to admit that circumstances were against her.

"You're sure it hasn't fell down behind the bureau?" was the only suggestion he could offer.

"I've moved the bureau and I've taken out the drawers and I've looked in every crack and cranny," was Marilla's positive answer. "The brooch is gone and that child has taken it and lied about it. That's the plain, ugly truth, Matthew Cuthbert, and we might as well look it in the face."

"Well now, what are you going to do about it?" Matthew asked forlornly, feeling secretly thankful that Marilla and not he had to deal with the situation. He felt no desire to put his oar in this time.

"She'll stay in her room until she confesses," said Marilla grimly, remembering the success of this method in the former case. "Then we'll see. Perhaps we'll be able to find the brooch if she'll only tell where she took it; but in any case she'll have to be severely punished, Matthew."

"Well now, you'll have to punish her," said Matthew, reaching for his hat. "I've nothing to do with it, remember. You warned me off yourself."

Marilla felt deserted by everyone. She could not even go to Mrs. Lynde for advice. She went up to the east gable with a very serious face and left it with a face more serious still. Anne steadfastly refused to confess. She persisted in asserting that she had not taken the brooch. The child had evidently been crying and Marilla felt a pang of pity which she sternly repressed. By night she was, as she expressed it, "beat out."

"You'll stay in this room until you confess, Anne. You can make up your mind to that," she said firmly.

"But the picnic is to-morrow, Marilla," cried Anne. "You won't keep me from going to that, will you? You'll just let me out for the afternoon, won't you? Then I'll stay here as long as you like afterwards, *cheerfully*. But I *must* go to the picnic."

"You'll not go to picnics nor anywhere else until you've confessed, Anne."

"Oh, Marilla," gasped Anne.

But Marilla had gone out and shut the door.

Wednesday morning dawned as bright and fair as if expressly made to order for the picnic. Birds sang around Green Gables; the Madonna lilies in the garden sent out whiffs of perfume that entered in on viewless winds[1] at every door and window, and wandered through halls and rooms like spirits of benediction. The birches in the hollow waved joyful hands as if watching for Anne's usual morning greeting from the east gable. But Anne was not at her window. When Marilla took her breakfast up to her she found the child sitting primly on her bed, pale and resolute, with tight-shut lips and gleaming eyes.

"Marilla, I'm ready to confess."

"Ah!" Marilla laid down her tray. Once again her method had succeeded; but her success was very bitter to her. "Let me hear what you have to say then, Anne."

---

1   Cf. Shakespeare, *Measure for Measure* (3.1.124).

"I took the amethyst brooch," said Anne, as if repeating a lesson she had learned. "I took it just as you said. I didn't mean to take it when I went in. But it did look so beautiful, Marilla, when I pinned it on my breast that I was overcome by an irresistible temptation. I imagined how perfectly thrilling it would be to take it to Idlewild and play I was the Lady Cordelia Fitzgerald. It would be so much easier to imagine I was the Lady Cordelia if I had a real amethyst brooch on. Diana and I made necklaces of roseberries but what are roseberries compared to amethysts? So I took the brooch. I thought I could put it back before you came home. I went all the way around by the road to lengthen out the time. When I was going over the bridge across the Lake of Shining Waters I took the brooch off to have another look at it. Oh, how it did shine in the sunlight! And then, when I was leaning over the bridge, it just slipped through my fingers—so—and went down—down—down, all purply-sparkling, and sank forevermore beneath the Lake of Shining Waters. And that's the best I can do at confessing, Marilla."

Marilla felt hot anger surge up into her heart again. This child had taken and lost her treasured amethyst brooch and now sat there calmly reciting the details thereof without the least apparent compunction or repentance.

"Anne, this is terrible," she said, trying to speak calmly. "You are the very wickedest girl I ever heard of."

"Yes, I suppose I am," agreed Anne tranquilly. "And I know I'll have to be punished. It'll be your duty to punish me, Marilla. Won't you please get it over right off because I'd like to go to the picnic with nothing on my mind."

"Picnic, indeed! You'll go to no picnic to-day, Anne Shirley. That shall be your punishment. And it isn't half severe enough either for what you've done!"

"Not go to the picnic!" Anne sprang to her feet and clutched Marilla's hand. "But you *promised* me I might! Oh, Marilla, I must go to the picnic. That was why I confessed. Punish me any way you like but that. Oh, Marilla, please, please, let me go to the picnic! Think of the ice-cream! For anything you know I may never have a chance to taste ice-cream again."

Marilla disengaged Anne's clinging hands stonily.

"You needn't plead, Anne. You are not going to the picnic and that's final. No, not a word."

Anne realized that Marilla was not to be moved. She clasped her hands together, gave a piercing shriek, and then flung herself face downwards on the bed, crying and writhing in an utter abandonment of disappointment and despair.

"For the land's sake!" gasped Marilla, hastening from the room. "I believe the child is crazy. No child in her senses would behave as she does. If she isn't she's utterly bad. Oh dear, I'm afraid Rachel was right from the first. But I've put my hand to the plough[1] and I won't look back."

That was a dismal morning. Marilla worked fiercely and scrubbed the porch floor and the dairy shelves when she could find nothing else to do. Neither the shelves nor the porch needed it—but Marilla did. Then she went out and raked the yard.

When dinner was ready she went to the stairs and called Anne. A tear-stained face appeared, looking tragically over the banisters.

"Come down to your dinner, Anne."

"I don't want any dinner, Marilla," said Anne sobbingly. "I couldn't eat anything. My heart is broken. You'll feel remorse of conscience some day, I expect, for breaking it, Marilla, but I forgive you. Remember when the time comes that I forgive you. But please don't ask me to eat anything, especially boiled pork and greens. Boiled pork and greens are so unromantic when one is in affliction."

Exasperated Marilla returned to the kitchen and poured out her tale of woe to Matthew, who, between his sense of justice and his unlawful sympathy with Anne, was a miserable man.

"Well now, she shouldn't have taken the brooch, Marilla, or told stories about it," he admitted, mournfully surveying his plateful of unromantic pork and greens as if he, like Anne, thought it a food unsuited to crises of feeling, "but she's such a little thing—such an interesting little thing, Marilla. Don't you think it's pretty rough not to let her go to the picnic when she's so set on it?"

---

1 Cf. Luke 9.62.

"Matthew Cuthbert, I'm amazed at you. I think I've let her off entirely too easy. And she doesn't appear to realize how wicked she's been at all—that's what worries me most. If she'd really felt sorry it wouldn't be so bad. And you don't seem to realize it, neither; you're making excuses for her all the time to yourself—I can see that."

"Well now, she's such a little thing," feebly reiterated Matthew. "And there should be allowances made, Marilla. You know she's never had any bringing up."

"Well, she's having it now," retorted Marilla.

The retort silenced Matthew if it did not convince him. That dinner was a very dismal meal. The only cheerful thing about it was Jerry Buote, the hired boy, and Marilla resented his cheerfulness as a personal insult.

When her dishes were washed and her bread sponge set[1] and her hens fed Marilla remembered that she had noticed a small rent in her best black lace shawl when she had taken it off on Monday afternoon on returning from the Ladies' Aid. She would go and mend it.

The shawl was in a box in her trunk. As Marilla lifted it out, the sunlight, falling through the vines that clustered thickly about the window, struck upon something caught in the shawl—something that glittered and sparkled in facets of violet light. Marilla snatched at it with a gasp. It was the amethyst brooch, hanging to a thread of the lace by its catch.

"Dear life and heart," said Marilla blankly, "what does this mean? Here's my brooch safe and sound that I thought was at the bottom of Barry's pond. Whatever did that girl mean by saying she took it and lost it? I declare I believe Green Gables is bewitched. I remember now that when I took off my shawl Monday afternoon I laid it on the bureau for a minute. I suppose the brooch got caught in it somehow. Well!"

Marilla betook herself to the east gable, brooch in hand. Anne had cried herself out and was sitting dejectedly by the window.

---

[1] According to Fannie Farmer's *Boston Cooking School Cook Book* (1896; 1941), sponge "is a batter to which yeast is added" (68); the sponge is left to rise for several hours. Sometimes called a "sponge starter," it is the basis for many bread recipes.

"Anne Shirley," said Marilla solemnly, "I've just found my brooch hanging to my black lace shawl. Now I want to know what that rigamarole you told me this morning meant."

"Why, you said you'd keep me here until I confessed," returned Anne wearily, "and so I decided to confess because I was bound to get to the picnic. I thought out a confession last night after I went to bed and made it as interesting as I could. And I said it over and over so that I wouldn't forget it. But you wouldn't let me go to the picnic after all, so all my trouble was wasted."

Marilla had to laugh in spite of herself. But her conscience pricked her.

"Anne, you do beat all! But I was wrong—I see that now. I shouldn't have doubted your word when I'd never known you to tell a story. Of course, it wasn't right for you to confess to a thing you hadn't done—it was very wrong to do so. But I drove you to it. So if you'll forgive me, Anne, I'll forgive you and we'll start square again. And now get yourself ready for the picnic."

Anne flew up like a rocket.

"Oh, Marilla, isn't it too late?"

"No, it's only two o'clock. They won't be more than well gathered yet and it'll be an hour before they have tea. Wash your face and comb your hair and put on your gingham. I'll fill a basket for you. There's plenty of stuff baked in the house. And I'll get Jerry to hitch up the sorrel and drive you down to the picnic ground."

"Oh, Marilla," exclaimed Anne, flying to the washstand. "Five minutes ago I was so miserable I was wishing I'd never been born and now I wouldn't change places with an angel!"

That night a thoroughly happy, completely tired out Anne returned to Green Gables in a state of beatification impossible to describe.

"Oh, Marilla, I've had a perfectly scrumptious time. Scrumptious is a new word I learned to-day. I heard Mary Alice Bell use it. Isn't it very expressive? Everything was lovely. We had a splendid tea and then Mr. Harmon Andrews took us all for a row on the Lake of Shining Waters—six of us at a time. And Jane Andrews nearly fell overboard. She was leaning out to pick water lilies and if Mr. Andrews hadn't caught her by her sash just in the nick of time she'd have fallen in and prob'ly been drowned. I wish it had been me. It would have been such a romantic experience to have been nearly drowned. It would be such a thrilling tale to tell. And we had the ice-cream. Words fail me to describe that ice-cream. Marilla, I assure you it was sublime."

That evening Marilla told the whole story to Matthew over her stocking basket.

"I'm willing to own up that I made a mistake," she concluded candidly, "but I've learned a lesson. I have to laugh when I think of Anne's 'confession,' although I suppose I shouldn't for it really was a falsehood. But it doesn't seem as bad as the other would have been, somehow, and anyhow I'm responsible for it. That child is hard to understand in some respects. But I believe she'll turn out all right yet. And there's one thing certain, no house will ever be dull that she's in."

CHAPTER XV

A TEMPEST IN THE SCHOOL TEAPOT [1]

"WHAT a splendid day!" said Anne, drawing a long breath. "Isn't it good just to be alive on a day like this? I pity the people who aren't born yet for missing it. They may have good days, of course, but they can never have this one. And it's splendider still to have such a lovely way to go to school by, isn't it?"

"It's a lot nicer than going round by the road; that is so dusty and hot," said Diana practically, peeping into her dinner basket and mentally calculating if the three juicy, toothsome, raspberry tarts reposing there were divided among ten girls how many bites each girl would have.

The little girls of Avonlea school always pooled their lunches, and to eat three raspberry tarts all alone or even to share them only with one's best chum would have forever and ever branded as "awful mean" the girl who did it. And yet, when the tarts were

---

[1] A play on the expression "*A storm in a teacup*," meaning "making a fuss about nothing."

divided among ten girls you just got enough to tantalize you.

The way Anne and Diana went to school *was* a pretty one. Anne thought those walks to and from school with Diana couldn't be improved upon even by imagination. Going around by the main road would have been so unromantic; but to go by Lovers' Lane and Willowmere and Violet Vale and the Birch Path was romantic, if ever anything was.

Lovers' Lane opened out below the orchard at Green Gables and stretched far up into the woods to the end of the Cuthbert farm. It was the way by which the cows were taken to the back pasture and the wood hauled home in winter. Anne had named it Lovers' Lane before she had been a month at Green Gables.

"Not that lovers ever really walk there," she explained to Marilla, "but Diana and I are reading a perfectly magnificent book and there's a Lovers' Lane in it. So we want to have one, too. And it's a very pretty name, don't you think? So romantic! We can imagine the lovers into it, you know. I like that lane because you can think out loud there without people calling you crazy."

Anne, starting out alone in the morning, went down Lovers' Lane as far as the brook. Here Diana met her, and the two little girls went on up the lane under the leafy arch of maples—"maples are such sociable trees," said Anne; "they're always rustling and whispering to you,"—until they came to a rustic bridge. Then they left the lane and walked through Mr. Barry's back field and past Willowmere. Beyond Willowmere came Violet Vale—a little green dimple in the shadow of Mr. Andrew Bell's big woods. "Of course there are no violets there now," Anne told Marilla, "but Diana says there are millions of them in spring. Oh, Marilla, can't you just imagine you see them? It actually takes away my breath. I named it Violet Vale. Diana says she never saw the beat of me for hitting on fancy names for places. It's nice to be clever at something, isn't it? But Diana named the Birch Path. She wanted to, so I let her; but I'm sure I could have found something more poetical than plain Birch Path. Anybody can think of a name like that. But the Birch Path is one of the prettiest places in the world, Marilla."

It was. Other people besides Anne thought so when they stumbled on it. It was a little narrow, twisting path, winding down over a long hill straight through Mr. Bell's woods, where the light came down sifted through so many emerald screens that it was as flawless as the heart of a diamond. It was fringed in all its length with slim young birches, white-stemmed and lissom boughed; ferns and starflowers and wild lilies-of-the-valley and scarlet tufts of pigeon berries grew thickly along it; and always there was a delightful spiciness in the air and music of bird calls and the murmur and laugh of wood winds in the trees overhead. Now and then you might see a rabbit skipping across the road if you were quiet—which, with Anne and Diana, happened about once in a blue moon.[1] Down in the valley the path came out to the main road and then it was just up the spruce hill to the school.

The Avonlea school was a whitewashed building, low in the eaves and wide in the windows, furnished inside with comfortable substantial old-fashioned desks that opened and shut, and were carved all over their lids with the initials and hieroglyphics of three generations of school-children. The schoolhouse was set back from the road and behind it was a dusky fir wood and a brook where all the children put their bottles of milk in the morning to keep cool and sweet until dinner hour.

Marilla had seen Anne start off to school on the first day of September with many secret misgivings. Anne was such an odd girl. How would she get on with the other children? And how on earth would she ever manage to hold her tongue during school hours?

Things went better than Marilla feared, however. Anne came home that evening in high spirits.

"I think I'm going to like school here," she announced. "I don't think much of the master, though. He's all the time curling his moustache and making eyes at Prissy Andrews. Prissy is grown-up, you know. She's sixteen and she's studying for the entrance examination into Queen's Academy at Charlottetown next year. Tillie Boulter says the master is *dead gone* on her. She's got a beautiful complexion and curly brown hair and she does it up so elegantly. She sits in the long seat at the back and he sits there, too, most of the time—to explain her lessons, he says. But Ruby Gillis

---

[1] Happening rarely. The term "blue moon" originally referred to an absurdity. (See *OED* which cites Roy, *Rede Me* from 1528: "Yf they saye the mone is belewe, We must beleve that it is true.")

says she saw him writing something on her slate and when Prissy read it she blushed as red as a beet and giggled; and Ruby Gillis says she doesn't believe it had anything to do with the lesson."

"Anne Shirley, don't let me hear you talking about your teacher in that way again," said Marilla sharply. "You don't go to school to criticize the master. I guess he can teach *you* something and it's your business to learn. And I want you to understand right off that you are not to come home telling tales about him. That is something I won't encourage. I hope you were a good girl."

"Indeed I was," said Anne comfortably. "It wasn't so hard as you might imagine, either. I sit with Diana. Our seat is right by the window and we can look down to the Lake of Shining Waters. There are a lot of nice girls in school and we had scrumptious fun playing at dinner time. It's so nice to have a lot of little girls to play with. But of course I like Diana best and always will. I *adore* Diana. I'm dreadfully far behind the others. They're all in the fifth book and I'm only in the fourth. I feel that it's kind of a disgrace. But there's not one of them has such an imagination as I have and I soon found that out. We had reading and geography and Canadian History and dictation to-day. Mr. Phillips said my spelling was disgraceful and he held up my slate so that everybody could see it, all marked over. I felt so mortified, Marilla; he might have been politer to a stranger, I think. Ruby Gillis gave me an apple and Sophia Sloane lent me a lovely pink card with 'May I see you home?' on it. I'm to give it back to her to-morrow. And Tillie Boulter let me wear her bead ring all the afternoon. Can I have some of those pearl beads off the old pincushion in the garret to make myself a ring? And oh Marilla, Jane Andrews told me that Minnie MacPherson told her that she heard Prissy Andrews tell Sara Gillis that I had a very pretty nose. Marilla, that is the first compliment I have ever had in my life and you can't imagine what a strange feeling it gave me. Marilla, have I really a pretty nose? I know you'll tell me the truth."

"Your nose is well enough," said Marilla shortly. Secretly she thought Anne's nose was a remarkably pretty one; but she had no intention of telling her so.

That was three weeks ago and all had gone smoothly so far. And now, this crisp September morning, Anne and Diana were tripping blithely down the Birch Path, two of the happiest little girls in Avonlea.

"I guess Gilbert Blythe will be in school to-day," said Diana. "He's been visiting his cousins over in New Brunswick all summer and he only came home Saturday night. He's *aw'fly* handsome, Anne. And he teases the girls something terrible. He just torments our lives out."

Diana's voice indicated that she rather liked having her life tormented out than not.

"Gilbert Blythe?" said Anne, "Isn't it his name that's written up on the porch wall with Julia Bell's and a big 'Take Notice' over them?"

"Yes," said Diana, tossing her head, "but I'm sure he doesn't like Julia Bell so very much. I've heard him say he studied the multiplication table by her freckles."

"Oh, don't speak about freckles to me," implored Anne. "It isn't delicate when I've got so many. But I do think that writing take-notices up on the wall about the boys and girls is the silliest ever. I should just like to see anybody dare to write my name up with a boy's. Not, of course," she hastened to add, "that anybody would."

Anne sighed. She didn't want her name written up. But it was a little humiliating to know that there was no danger of it.

"Nonsense," said Diana, whose black eyes and glossy tresses had played such havoc with the hearts of Avonlea schoolboys that her name figured on the porch walls in half a dozen take-notices. "It's only meant as a joke. And don't you be too sure your name won't ever be written up. Charlie Sloane is *dead gone* on you. He told his mother—his *mother*, mind you—that you were the smartest girl in school. That's better than being good-looking."

"No, it isn't," said Anne, feminine to the core. "I'd rather be pretty than clever. And I hate Charlie Sloane. I can't bear a boy with goggle eyes. If any one wrote my name up with his I'd *never* get over it, Diana Barry. But it *is* nice to keep head of your class."

"You'll have Gilbert in your class after this," said Diana, "and he's used to being head of his class, I can tell you. He's only in the fourth book although he's nearly fourteen. Four years ago his father was sick and had to go out to Alberta for his health and Gilbert went with him. They were there three years and Gil didn't go to school hardly any until they came back. You won't find it so easy to keep head after this, Anne."

"I'm glad," said Anne quickly. "I couldn't really feel proud of keeping head of little boys and girls of just nine or ten. I got up yesterday spelling 'ebullition.' Josie Pye was head and, mind you, she peeped in her book. Mr. Phillips didn't see her—he was looking at Prissy Andrews—but I did. I just swept her a look of freezing scorn and she got as red as a beet and spelled it wrong after all."

"Those Pye girls are cheats all round," said Diana indignantly, as they climbed the fence of the main road. "Gertie Pye actually went and put her milk bottle in my place in the brook yesterday. Did you ever? I don't speak to her now."

When Mr. Phillips was in the back of the room hearing Prissy Andrews' Latin Diana whispered to Anne, "That's Gilbert Blythe sitting right across the aisle from you, Anne. Just look at him and see if you don't think he's handsome."

Anne looked accordingly. She had a good chance to do so, for the said Gilbert Blythe was absorbed in stealthily pinning the long yellow braid of Ruby Gillis, who sat in front of him, to the back of her seat. He was a tall boy, with curly brown hair, roguish hazel eyes and a mouth twisted into a teasing smile. Presently Ruby Gillis started up to take a sum to the master; she fell back into her seat with a little shriek, believing that her hair was pulled out by the roots. Everybody looked at her and Mr. Phillips glared so sternly that Ruby began to cry. Gilbert had whisked the pin out of sight and was studying his history with the soberest face in the world; but when the commotion subsided he looked at Anne and winked with inexpressible drollery.

"I think your Gilbert Blythe *is* handsome," confided Anne to Diana, "but I think he's very bold. It isn't good manners to wink at a strange girl."

But it was not until the afternoon that things really began to happen.

Mr. Phillips was back in the corner explaining a problem to Prissy Andrews and the rest of the scholars were doing pretty much as they pleased, eating green apples, whispering, drawing pictures on their slates, and driving crickets, harnessed to strings, up and down the aisle. Gilbert Blythe was trying to make Anne Shirley look at him and failing utterly, because Anne was at that moment totally oblivious, not only of the very existence of Gilbert Blythe, but of every other scholar in Avonlea School and of Avonlea school itself. With her chin propped on her hands and her eyes fixed on the blue glimpse of the Lake of Shining Waters that the west window afforded, she was far away in a gorgeous dreamland, hearing and seeing nothing save her own wonderful visions.

Gilbert Blythe wasn't used to putting himself out to make a girl look at him and meeting with failure. She *should* look at him, that red-haired Shirley girl with the little pointed chin and the big eyes that weren't like the eyes of any other girl in Avonlea school.

Gilbert reached across the aisle, picked up the end of Anne's long red braid, held it out at arm's length and said in a piercing whisper,

"Carrots! Carrots!"

Then Anne looked at him with a vengeance!

She did more than look. She sprang to her feet, her bright fancies fallen into cureless ruin. She flashed one indignant glance at Gilbert from eyes whose angry sparkle was swiftly quenched in equally angry tears.

"You mean, hateful boy!" she exclaimed passionately. "How dare you!"

And then—Thwack! Anne had brought her slate down on Gilbert's head and cracked it—slate, not head—clear across.

Avonlea school always enjoyed a scene. This was an especially enjoyable one. Everybody said, "Oh" in horrified delight. Diana gasped. Ruby Gillis, who was inclined to be hysterical, began to cry. Tommy Sloane let his team of crickets escape him altogether while he stared open-mouthed at the tableau.

Mr. Phillips stalked down the aisle and laid his hand heavily on Anne's shoulder.

"Anne Shirley, what does this mean?" he said angrily.

Anne returned no answer. It was asking too much of flesh and blood to expect her to tell before the whole school that she had been called "carrots." Gilbert it was who spoke up stoutly.

"It was my fault, Mr. Phillips. I teased her."

Mr. Phillips paid no heed to Gilbert.

"THWACK! ANNE HAD BROUGHT HER SLATE DOWN ON GIL-
BERT'S HEAD."

"I am sorry to see a pupil of mine displaying such a temper and such a vindictive spirit," he said in a solemn tone, as if the mere fact of being a pupil of his ought to root out all evil passions from the hearts of small imperfect mortals. "Anne, go and stand on the platform in front of the blackboard for the rest of the afternoon."

Anne would have infinitely preferred a whipping to this punishment, under which her sensitive spirit quivered as from a whiplash. With a white, set face she obeyed. Mr. Phillips took a chalk crayon and wrote on the blackboard above her head,

"Ann Shirley has a very bad temper. Ann Shirley must learn to control her temper," and then read it out loud so that even the primer class,[1] who couldn't read writing, should understand it.

Anne stood there the rest of the afternoon with that legend above her. She did not cry or hang her head.[2] Anger was still too hot in her heart for that and it sustained her amid all her agony of humiliation. With resentful eyes and passion-red cheeks she confronted alike Diana's sympathetic gaze and Charlie Sloane's indignant nods and Josie Pye's malicious smiles. As for Gilbert Blythe, she would not even look at him. She would *never* look at him again! She would never speak to him!!

When school was dismissed Anne marched out with her red head held high. Gilbert Blythe tried to intercept her at the porch door.

"I'm awful sorry I made fun of your hair, Anne," he whispered contritely. "Honest I am. Don't be mad for keeps, now."

Anne swept by disdainfully, without look or sign of hearing. "Oh, how could you, Anne?" breathed Diana as they went down the road, half reproachfully, half admiringly. Diana felt that *she* could never have resisted Gilbert's plea.

---

1   A reference to the youngest class in the school. A *primer* is "an elementary school book for teaching children to read" (*OED*).

2   This scene is evocative of Jane Eyre's punishment at Lowood school in Charlotte Brontë's 1847 novel. Jane, similarly, especially dislikes this punishment, and describes her feelings thus: "I, who had said I could not bear the shame of standing on my natural feet in the middle of the room, was now exposed to general view on a pedestal of infamy" (*Jane Eyre*, 1847. Ed. Richard Nemsevari [Peterborough, ON: Broadview, 1999] 130). See also 210, note 2.

"I shall never forgive Gilbert Blythe," said Anne firmly. "And Mr. Phillips spelled my name without an *e*, too. The iron has entered into my soul,[1] Diana."

Diana hadn't the least idea what Anne meant but she understood it was something terrible.

"You mustn't mind Gilbert making fun of your hair," she said soothingly. "Why, he makes fun of all the girls. He laughs at mine because it's so black. He's called me a crow a dozen times; and I never heard him apologize for anything before, either."

"There's a great deal of difference between being called a crow and being called carrots," said Anne with dignity. "Gilbert Blythe has hurt my feelings *excruciatingly*, Diana."

It is possible the matter might have blown over without more excruciation if nothing else had happened. But when things begin to happen they are apt to keep on.

Avonlea scholars often spent noon hour picking gum[2] in Mr. Bell's spruce grove over the hill and across his big pasture field. From there they could keep an eye on Eben Wright's house, where the master boarded. When they saw Mr. Phillips emerging therefrom they ran for the schoolhouse; but the distance being about three times longer than Mr. Wright's lane they were very apt to arrive there, breathless and gasping, some three minutes too late.

On the following day Mr. Phillips was seized with one of his spasmodic fits of reform and announced, before going home to dinner, that he should expect to find all the scholars in their seats when he returned. Any one who came in late would be punished.

All the boys and some of the girls went to Mr. Bell's spruce grove as usual, fully intending to stay only long enough to "pick a chew." But spruce groves are seductive and yellow nuts of gum beguiling; they picked and loitered and strayed; and as usual the first thing that recalled them to a sense of the flight of time was Jimmy Glover shouting from the top of a patriarchal old spruce, "Master's coming."

The girls, who were on the ground, started first and managed to reach the schoolhouse in time but without a second to spare.

---

[1] A phrase that conveys an increased determination to resist or oppose oppression or to counter insult or injury. Cf. *The Book of Common Prayer*, Psalm 105.18.

[2] I.e., gum of a spruce tree.

The boys, who had to wriggle hastily down from the trees, were later; and Anne, who had not been picking gum at all but was wandering happily in the far end of the grove, waist deep among the bracken, singing softly to herself, with a wreath of rice lilies on her hair as if she were some wild divinity of the shadowy places, was latest of all. Anne could run like a deer, however; run she did with the impish result that she overtook the boys at the door and was swept into the schoolhouse among them just as Mr. Phillips was in the act of hanging up his hat.

Mr. Phillips' brief reforming energy was over; he didn't want the bother of punishing a dozen pupils; but it was necessary to do something to save his word, so he looked about for a scapegoat and found it in Anne, who had dropped into her seat, gasping for breath, with her forgotten lily wreath hanging askew over one ear and giving her a particularly rakish and dishevelled appearance.

"Anne Shirley, since you seem to be so fond of the boys' company we shall indulge your taste for it this afternoon," he said sarcastically. "Take those flowers out of your hair and sit with Gilbert Blythe."

The other boys snickered. Diana, turning pale with pity, plucked the wreath from Anne's hair and squeezed her hand. Anne stared at the master as if turned to stone.

"Did you hear what I said, Anne?" queried Mr. Phillips sternly.

"Yes, sir," said Anne slowly, "but I didn't suppose you really meant it."

"I assure you I did,"—still with the sarcastic inflection which all the children, and Anne especially, hated. It flicked on the raw. "Obey me at once."

For a moment Anne looked as if she meant to disobey. Then, realizing that there was no help for it, she rose haughtily, stepped across the aisle, sat down beside Gilbert Blythe, and buried her face in her arms on the desk. Ruby Gillis, who got a glimpse of it as it went down, told the others going home from school that she'd "acksually never seen anything like it—it was so white, with awful little red spots in it."

To Anne, this was as the end of all things. It was bad enough to be singled out for punishment from among a dozen equally guilty ones; it was worse still to be sent to sit with a boy; but that

that boy should be Gilbert Blythe was heaping insult on injury to a degree utterly unbearable. Anne felt that she could *not* bear it and it would be of no use to try. Her whole being seethed with shame and anger and humiliation.

At first the other scholars looked and whispered and giggled and nudged. But as Anne never lifted her head and as Gilbert worked fractions as if his whole soul was absorbed in them and them only, they soon returned to their own tasks and Anne was forgotten. When Mr. Phillips called the history class out Anne should have gone; but Anne did not move, and Mr. Phillips, who had been writing some verses "To Priscilla" before he called the class, was thinking about an obstinate rhyme still and never missed her. Once, when nobody was looking, Gilbert took from his desk a little pink candy heart with a gold motto on it, "You are sweet," and slipped it under the curve of Anne's arm. Whereupon Anne arose, took the pink heart gingerly between the tips of her fingers, dropped it on the floor, ground it to powder beneath her heel, and resumed her position without deigning to bestow a glance on Gilbert.

When school went out Anne marched to her desk, ostentatiously took out everything therein, books and writing tablet, pen and ink, testament and arithmetic, and piled them neatly on her cracked slate.

"What are you taking all those things home for, Anne?" Diana wanted to know, as soon as they were out on the road. She had not dared to ask the question before.

"I am not coming back to school any more," said Anne.

Diana gasped and stared at Anne to see if she meant it.

"Will Marilla let you stay home?" she asked.

"She'll have to," said Anne. "I'll *never* go to school to that man again."

"Oh, Anne!" Diana looked as if she were ready to cry. "I do think you're mean. What shall I do? Mr. Phillips will make me sit with that horrid Gertie Pye—I know he will because she is sitting alone. Do come back, Anne."

"I'd do almost anything in the world for you, Diana," said Anne sadly. "I'd let myself be torn limb from limb if it would do you any good. But I can't do this, so please don't ask it. You harrow up my very soul."

"Just think of all the fun you will miss," mourned Diana. "We are going to build the loveliest new house down by the brook; and we'll be playing ball[1] next week and you've never played ball, Anne. It's tremenjusly exciting. And we're going to learn a new song—Jane Andrews is practising it up now; and Alice Andrews is going to bring a new Pansy[2] book next week and we're all going to read it out loud, chapter about, down by the brook. And you know you are so fond of reading out loud, Anne."

Nothing moved Anne in the least. Her mind was made up. She would not go to school to Mr. Phillips again; she told Marilla so when she got home.

"Nonsense," said Marilla.

"It isn't nonsense at all," said Anne, gazing at Marilla with solemn, reproachful eyes. "Don't you understand, Marilla? I've been insulted."

"Insulted fiddlesticks! You'll go to school to-morrow as usual."

"Oh, no." Anne shook her head gently. "I'm not going back, Marilla. I'll learn my lessons at home and I'll be as good as I can be and hold my tongue all the time if it's possible at all. But I will not go back to school I assure you."

Marilla saw something remarkably like unyielding stubbornness looking out of Anne's small face. She understood that she would have trouble in overcoming it; but she resolved wisely to say nothing more just then.

"I'll run down and see Rachel about it this evening," she thought. "There's no use reasoning with Anne now. She's too worked up and I've an idea she can be awful stubborn if she takes the notion. Far as I can make out from her story, Mr. Phillips has been carrying matters with a rather high hand. But it would never do to say so to her. I'll just talk it over with Rachel. She's sent ten children to school and she ought to know

---

[1]   Probably baseball or some variant.
[2]   Pen-name of American novelist Isabella Macdonald Alden (1841–1930). According to *The Feminist Companion to Literature in English* (New Haven: Yale UP, 1990), Alden wrote over 120 books, mostly for children, largely for a Sunday School readership; she also edited a Sunday School magazine called *Pansy*. Her novels, which Montgomery had read as a child (see *SJ* I 37, 253), often present "believable female characters, not afraid to stand up for their principles of Christian love in action," as the *FCLE* suggests of her 1870 work, *Ester Reid* (14). See 126, note 1.

something about it. She'll have heard the whole story, too, by this time."

Marilla found Mrs. Lynde knitting quilts as industriously and cheerfully as usual.

"I suppose you know what I've come about," she said, a little shamefacedly.

Mrs. Rachel nodded.

"About Anne's fuss in school, I reckon," she said. "Tillie Boulter was in on her way from school and told me about it."

"I don't know what to do with her," said Marilla. "She declares she won't go back to school. I never saw a child so worked up. I've been expecting trouble ever since she started to school. I knew things were going too smooth to last. She's so high-strung. What would you advise, Rachel?"

"Well, since you've asked my advice, Marilla," said Mrs. Lynde amiably—Mrs. Lynde dearly loved to be asked for advice—"I'd just humour her a little at first, that's what I'd do. It's my belief that Mr. Phillips was in the wrong. Of course, it doesn't do to say so to the children, you know. And of course he did right to punish her yesterday for giving way to temper. But to-day it was different. The others who were late should have been punished as well as Anne, that's what. And I don't believe in making the girls sit with the boys for punishment. It isn't modest. Tillie Boulter was real indignant. She took Anne's part right through and said all the scholars did, too. Anne seems real popular among them, somehow. I never thought she'd take with them so well."

"Then you really think I'd better let her stay home," said Marilla in amazement.

"Yes. That is, I wouldn't say school to her again until she said it herself. Depend upon it, Marilla, she'll cool off in a week or so and be ready enough to go back of her own accord, that's what, while, if you were to make her go back right off, dear knows what freak or tantrum she'd take next and make more trouble than ever. The less fuss made the better, in my opinion. She won't miss much by not going to school, as far as *that* goes. Mr. Phillips isn't any good at all as a teacher. The order he keeps is scandalous, that's what, and he neglects the young fry and puts all his time on those big scholars he's getting ready for Queens.

He'd never have got the school for another year if his uncle hadn't been a trustee—*the* trustee, for he just leads the other two around by the nose, that's what. I declare, I don't know what education in this Island is coming to."

Mrs. Rachel shook her head, as much as to say if she were only at the head of the educational system of the Province things would be much better managed.

Marilla took Mrs. Rachel's advice and not another word was said to Anne about going back to school. She learned her lessons at home, did her chores, and played with Diana in the chilly purple autumn twilights; but when she met Gilbert Blythe on the road or encountered him in Sunday-school she passed him by with an icy contempt that was no whit thawed by his evident desire to appease her. Even Diana's efforts as a peacemaker were of no avail. Anne had evidently made up her mind to hate Gilbert Blythe to the end of life.

As much as she hated Gilbert however, did she love Diana, with all the love of her passionate little heart, equally intense in its likes and dislikes. One evening Marilla, coming in from the orchard with a basket of apples, found Anne sitting alone by the east window in the twilight, crying bitterly.

"Whatever's the matter now, Anne?" she asked.

"It's about Diana," sobbed Anne luxuriously. "I love Diana so, Marilla. I cannot ever live without her. But I know very well when we grow up that Diana will get married and go away and leave me. And oh, what shall I do? I hate her husband—I just hate him furiously. I've been imagining it all out—the wedding and everything—Diana dressed in snowy garments, with a veil, and looking as beautiful and regal as a queen; and me the brides-maid, with a lovely dress, too, and puffed sleeves, but with a breaking heart hid beneath my smiling face. And then bidding Diana good-bye-e-e—" Here Anne broke down entirely and wept with increasing bitterness.

Marilla turned quickly away to hide her twitching face; but it was no use; she collapsed on the nearest chair and burst into such a hearty and unusual peal of laughter that Matthew, crossing the yard outside, halted in amazement. When had he heard Marilla laugh like that before?

"Well, Anne Shirley," said Marilla, as soon as she could speak, "if you must borrow trouble, for pity's sake borrow it handier home. I should think you had an imagination, sure enough."

CHAPTER XVI

DIANA IS INVITED TO TEA WITH TRAGIC RESULTS

OCTOBER was a beautiful month at Green Gables, when the birches in the hollow turned as golden as sunshine and the maples behind the orchard were royal crimson and the wild cherry-trees along the lane put on the loveliest shades of dark red and bronzy green, while the fields sunned themselves in aftermaths.

Anne revelled in the world of colour about her.

"Oh, Marilla," she exclaimed one Saturday morning, coming dancing in with her arms full of gorgeous boughs, "I'm so glad I live in a world where there are Octobers. It would be terrible if we just skipped from September to November, wouldn't it? Look at these maple branches. Don't they give you a thrill—several thrills? I'm going to decorate my room with them."

"Messy things," said Marilla, whose aesthetic sense was not noticeably developed. "You clutter up your room entirely too much with out-of-doors stuff, Anne. Bedrooms were made to sleep in."

"Oh, and dream in too, Marilla. And you know one can dream so much better in a room where there are pretty things. I'm going to put these boughs in the old blue jug and set them on my table."

"Mind you don't drop leaves all over the stairs then. I'm going to a meeting of the Aid Society[1] at Carmody this afternoon, Anne, and I won't likely be home before dark. You'll have to get Matthew and Jerry their supper, so mind you don't forget

---

[1]   A reference to the Ladies' Aids, church-based organizations of women for charitable and, often, church and municipal work.

to put the tea to draw until you sit down at the table as you did last time."

"It was dreadful of me to forget," said Anne apologetically, "but that was the afternoon I was trying to think of a name for Violet Vale and it crowded other things out. Matthew was so good. He never scolded a bit. He put the tea down himself and said we could wait awhile as well as not. And I told him a lovely fairy story while we were waiting, so he didn't find the time long at all. It was a beautiful fairy story, Marilla. I forgot the end of it, so I made up an end for it myself and Matthew said he couldn't tell where the join came in."

"Matthew would think it all right, Anne, if you took a notion to get up and have dinner in the middle of the night. But you keep your wits about you this time. And—I don't really know if I'm doing right—it may make you more addle-pated than ever—but you can ask Diana to come over and spend the afternoon with you and have tea here."

"Oh, Marilla!" Anne clasped her hands. "How perfectly lovely! You *are* able to imagine things after all or else you'd never have understood how I've longed for that very thing. It will seem so nice and grown-uppish. No fear of my forgetting to put the tea to draw when I have company. Oh, Marilla, can I use the rosebud spray tea-set?"

"No, indeed! The rosebud tea-set! Well, what next? You know I never use that except for the minister or the Aids. You'll put down the old brown tea-set. But you can open the little yellow crock of cherry preserves. It's time it was being used anyhow—I believe it's beginning to work. And you can cut some fruit-cake and have some of the cookies and snaps."

"I can just imagine myself sitting down at the head of the table and pouring out the tea," said Anne, shutting her eyes ecstatically. "And asking Diana if she takes sugar! I know she doesn't but of course I'll ask her just as if I didn't know. And then pressing her to take another piece of fruit-cake and another helping of preserves. Oh, Marilla, it's a wonderful sensation just to think of it. Can I take her into the spare room to lay off her hat when she comes? And then into the parlour to sit?"

"No. The sitting-room will do for you and your company.

But there's a bottle half full of raspberry cordial[1] that was left over from the church social the other night. It's on the second shelf of the sitting-room closet and you and Diana can have it if you like, and a cooky to eat with it along in the afternoon, for I daresay Matthew'll be late coming in to tea since he's hauling potatoes to the vessel."

Anne flew down to the hollow, past the Dryad's Bubble and up the spruce path to Orchard Slope, to ask Diana to tea. As a result, just after Marilla had driven off to Carmody, Diana came over, dressed in her second best dress and looking exactly as it is proper to look when asked out to tea. At other times she was wont to run into the kitchen without knocking; but now she knocked primly at the front door. And when Anne, dressed in *her* second best, as primly opened it, both little girls shook hands as gravely as if they had never met before. This unnatural solemnity lasted until after Diana had been taken to the east gable to lay off her hat and then had sat for ten minutes in the sitting-room, toes in position.

"How is your mother?" inquired Anne politely, just as if she had not seen Mrs. Barry picking apples that morning in excellent health and spirits.

"She is very well, thank you. I suppose Mr. Cuthbert is hauling potatoes to the *Lily Sands* this afternoon, is he?" said Diana, who had ridden down to Mr. Harmon Andrews' that morning in Matthew's cart.

"Yes. Our potato crop is very good this year. I hope your father's potato crop is good, too."

"It is fairly good, thank you. Have you picked many of your apples yet?"

"Oh, ever so many," said Anne, forgetting to be dignified and jumping up quickly. "Let's go out to the orchard and get some of the Red Sweetings, Diana. Marilla says we can have all that are left on the tree. Marilla is a very generous woman. She said we could have fruit-cake and cherry preserves for tea. But it isn't good manners to tell your company what you are going to give them to eat, so I won't tell you what she said we could have to drink. Only it begins with an *r* and a *c* and it's a bright red colour.

---

[1]   A sweet drink.

I love bright red drinks, don't you? They taste twice as good as any other colour."

The orchard, with its great sweeping boughs that bent to the ground with fruit, proved so delightful that the little girls spent most of the afternoon in it, sitting in a grassy corner where the frost had spared the green and the mellow autumn sunshine lingered warmly, eating apples and talking as hard as they could. Diana had much to tell Anne of what went on in school. She had to sit with Gertie Pye and she hated it; Gertie squeaked her pencil all the time and it just made her—Diana's—blood run cold; Ruby Gillis had charmed all her warts away, true's you live, with a magic pebble that old Mary Joe from the Creek gave her. You had to rub the warts with the pebble and then throw it away over your left shoulder at the time of the new moon and the warts would all go. Charlie Sloane's name was written up with Em White's on the porch wall and Em White was *awful mad* about it; Sam Boulter had "sassed" Mr. Phillips in class and Mr. Phillips whipped him and Sam's father came down to the school and dared Mr. Phillips to lay a hand on one of his children again; and Mattie Andrews had a new red hood and a blue crossover[1] with tassels on it and the airs she put on about it were perfectly sickening; and Lizzie Wright didn't speak to Mamie Wilson because Mamie Wilson's grown-up sister had cut out Lizzie Wright's grown-up sister with her beau; and everybody missed Anne so and wished she'd come to school again; and Gilbert Blythe—

But Anne didn't want to hear about Gilbert Blythe. She jumped up hurriedly and said suppose they go in and have some raspberry cordial.

Anne looked on the second shelf of the room pantry but there was no bottle of raspberry cordial there. Search revealed it away back on the top shelf. Anne put it on a tray and set it on the table with a tumbler.

"Now, please help yourself, Diana," she said politely. "I don't believe I'll have any just now. I don't feel as if I wanted any after all those apples."

---

[1] "A woman's wrap (usually knitted, or of crochet-work) worn round the shoulders and crossed upon the breast" (*OED*).

Diana poured herself out a tumblerful, looked at its bright red hue admiringly, and then sipped it daintily.

"That's awfully nice raspberry cordial, Anne," she said. "I didn't know raspberry cordial was so nice."

"I'm real glad you like it. Take as much as you want. I'm going to run out and stir the fire up. There are so many responsibilities on a person's mind when they're keeping house, isn't there?"

When Anne came back from the kitchen Diana was drinking her second glassful of cordial; and, being entreated thereto by Anne, she offered no particular objection to the drinking of a third. The tumblerfuls were generous ones and the raspberry cordial was certainly very nice.

"The nicest I ever drank," said Diana. "It's ever so much nicer than Mrs. Lynde's although she brags of hers so much. It doesn't taste a bit like hers."

"I should think Marilla's raspberry cordial would prob'ly be much nicer than Mrs. Lynde's," said Anne loyally. "Marilla is a famous cook. She is trying to teach me to cook but I assure you, Diana, it is uphill work. There's so little scope for imagination in cookery. You just have to go by rules. The last time I made a cake I forgot to put the flour in. I was thinking the loveliest story about you and me, Diana. I thought you were desperately ill with smallpox and everybody deserted you, but I went boldly to your bedside and nursed you back to life; and then I took the smallpox and died and I was buried under those poplar trees in the graveyard and you planted a rosebush by my grave and watered it with your tears; and you never, never forgot the friend of your youth who sacrificed her life for you. Oh, it was such a pathetic tale, Diana. The tears just rained down over my cheeks while I mixed the cake. But I forgot the flour and the cake was a dismal failure. Flour is so essential to cakes, you know. Marilla was very cross and I don't wonder. I'm a great trial to her. She was terribly mortified about the pudding sauce last week. We had a plum pudding for dinner on Tuesday and there was half the pudding and a pitcherful of sauce left over. Marilla said there was enough for another dinner and told me to set it on the pantry shelf and cover it. I meant to cover it just as much as could be, Diana, but when I carried it in I was imagining I was a nun—of course I'm a Protestant but I imagined I was a Catholic—taking the veil to bury a broken heart in cloistered seclusion; and I forgot all about covering the pudding sauce. I thought of it next morning and ran to the pantry. Diana, fancy if you can my extreme horror at finding a mouse drowned in that pudding sauce! I lifted the mouse out with a spoon and threw it out in the yard and then I washed the spoon in three waters. Marilla was out milking and I fully intended to ask her when she came in if I'd give the sauce to the pigs; but when she did come in I was imagining that I was a frost fairy[1] going through the woods turning the trees red and yellow, whichever they wanted to be, so I never thought about the pudding sauce again and Marilla sent me out to pick apples. Well, Mr. and Mrs. Chester Ross from Spencervale came here that morning. You know they are very stylish people, especially Mrs. Chester Ross. When Marilla called me in dinner was all ready and everybody was at the table. I tried to be as polite and dignified as I could be, for I wanted Mrs. Chester Ross to think I was a ladylike little girl even if I wasn't pretty. Everything went right until I saw Marilla coming with the plum pudding in one hand and the pitcher of pudding sauce, *warmed up*, in the other. Diana, that was a terrible moment. I remembered everything and I just stood up in my place and shrieked out, 'Marilla, you mustn't use that pudding sauce. There was a mouse drowned in it. I forgot to tell you before.' Oh, Diana, I shall never forget that awful moment if I live to be a hundred. Mrs. Chester Ross just *looked* at me and I thought I would sink through the floor with mortification. She is such a perfect housekeeper and fancy what she must have thought of us. Marilla turned red as fire but she never said a word—then. She just carried that sauce and pudding out and brought in some strawberry preserves. She even offered me some, but I couldn't swallow a mouthful. It was like heaping coals of fire on my head.[2] After Mrs. Chester Ross went away Marilla gave me a dreadful scolding. Why, Diana what is the matter?"

---

[1]   Cf. James Russell Lowell's "The Vision of Sir Launfall," quoted in *AGG* at the beginning of Chapter II (see 61, note 1); here from Prelude to Part Second, 32.37.

[2]   Making someone feel remorseful by responding to unkindness with generosity. Cf. Romans 12.20 and Proverbs 25.21–22.

Diana had stood up very unsteadily; then she sat down again, putting her hands to her head.

"I'm—I'm awful sick," she said, a little thickly. "I—I—must go right home."

"Oh, you mustn't dream of going home without your tea," cried Anne in distress. "I'll get it right off—I'll go and put the tea down this very minute."

"I must go home," repeated Diana, stupidly but determinedly.

"Let me get you a lunch[1] anyhow," implored Anne. "Let me give you a bit of fruit-cake and some of the cherry preserves. Lie down on the sofa for a little while and you'll be better. Where do you feel bad?"

"I must go home," said Diana, and that was all she would say. In vain Anne pleaded.

"I never heard of company going home without tea," she mourned. "Oh, Diana, do you suppose that it's possible you're really taking the smallpox? If you are I'll go and nurse you, you can depend on that. I'll never forsake you. But I do wish you'd stay till after tea. Where do you feel bad?"

"I'm awful dizzy," said Diana.

And indeed, she walked very dizzily. Anne, with tears of disappointment in her eyes, got Diana's hat and went with her as far as the Barry yard fence. Then she wept all the way back to Green Gables, where she sorrowfully put the remainder of the raspberry cordial back into the pantry and got tea ready for Matthew and Jerry, with all the zest gone out of the performance.

The next day was Sunday and as the rain poured down in torrents from dawn till dusk Anne did not stir abroad from Green Gables. Monday afternoon Marilla sent her down to Mrs. Lynde's on an errand. In a very short space of time Anne came flying back up the lane, with tears rolling down her cheeks. Into the kitchen she dashed and flung herself face downward on the sofa in an agony.

"Whatever has gone wrong now, Anne?" queried Marilla in doubt and dismay. "I do hope you haven't gone and been saucy to Mrs. Lynde again."

---

[1] A snack.

No answer from Anne save more tears and stormier sobs!

"Anne Shirley, when I ask you a question I want to be answered. Sit right up this very minute and tell me what you are crying about."

Anne sat up, tragedy personified.

"Mrs. Lynde was up to see Mrs. Barry to-day and Mrs. Barry was in an awful state," she wailed. "She says that I set Diana *drunk* Saturday and sent her home in a disgraceful condition. And she says I must be a thoroughly bad, wicked little girl and she's never, never going to let Diana play with me again. Oh, Marilla, I'm just overcome with woe."

Marilla stared in blank amazement.

"Set Diana drunk!" she said when she found her voice. "Anne, are you or Mrs. Barry crazy? What on earth did you give her?"

"Not a thing but raspberry cordial," sobbed Anne. "I never thought raspberry cordial would set people drunk, Marilla,—not even if they drank three big tumblerfuls as Diana did. Oh, it sounds so—so—like Mrs. Thomas' husband! But I didn't mean to set her drunk."

"Drunk fiddlesticks!" said Marilla, marching to the sitting-room pantry. There on the shelf was a bottle which she at once recognized as one containing some of her three year old home-made currant wine for which she was celebrated in Avonlea, although certain of the stricter sort, Mrs. Barry among them, disapproved strongly of it. And at the same time Marilla recollected that she had put the bottle of raspberry cordial down in the cellar instead of in the pantry as she had told Anne.

She went back to the kitchen with the wine bottle in her hand. Her face was twitching in spite of herself.

"Anne, you certainly have a genius for getting into trouble. You went and gave Diana currant wine instead of raspberry cordial. Didn't you know the difference yourself?"

"I never tasted it," said Anne. "I thought it was the cordial. I meant to be so—so—hospitable. Diana got awfully sick and had to go home. Mrs. Barry told Mrs. Lynde she was simply dead drunk. She just laughed silly like when her mother asked her what was the matter and went to sleep and slept for hours. Her mother smelled her breath and knew she was drunk. She had a fearful headache all day yesterday. Mrs. Barry is so indignant. She will never believe but what I did it on purpose."

"I should think she would better punish Diana for being so greedy as to drink three glassfuls of anything," said Marilla shortly. "Why, three of those big glasses would have made her sick even if it had only been cordial. Well, this story will be a nice handle for those folks who are so down on me for making currant wine, although I haven't made any for three years ever since I found out that the minister didn't approve. I just kept that bottle for sickness. There, there, child, don't cry. I can't see as you were to blame although I'm sorry it happened so."

"I must cry," said Anne. "My heart is broken. The stars in their courses[1] fight against me, Marilla. Diana and I are parted forever. Oh, Marilla, I little dreamed of this when first we swore our vows of friendship."

"Don't be foolish, Anne. Mrs. Barry will think better of it when she finds you're not really to blame. I suppose she thinks you've done it for a silly joke or something of that sort. You'd best go up this evening and tell her how it was."

"My courage fails me at the thought of facing Diana's injured mother," sighed Anne. "I wish you'd go, Marilla. You're so much more dignified than I am. Likely she'd listen to you quicker than to me."

"Well, I will," said Marilla, reflecting that it would probably be the wiser course. "Don't cry any more, Anne. It will be all right."

Marilla had changed her mind about its being all right by the time she got back from Orchard Slope. Anne was watching for her coming and flew to the porch door to meet her.

"Oh, Marilla, I know by your face that it's been no use," she said sorrowfully. "Mrs. Barry won't forgive me?"

"Mrs. Barry, indeed!" snapped Marilla. "Of all the unreasonable women I ever saw she's the worst. I told her it was all a mistake and you weren't to blame, but she just simply didn't believe me. And she rubbed it well in about my currant wine and how I'd always said it couldn't have the least effect on anybody. I just told her plainly that currant wine wasn't meant to be drunk

---

[1] Cf. Judges 5.20.

three tumblerfuls at a time and that if a child I had to do with was so greedy I'd sober her up with a right good spanking."

Marilla whisked into the kitchen, grievously disturbed, leaving a very much distracted little soul in the porch behind her. Presently Anne stepped out bare-headed into the chill autumn dusk; very determinedly and steadily she took her way down through the sere clover field over the log bridge and up through the spruce grove, lighted by a pale little moon hanging low over the western woods. Mrs. Barry, coming to the door in answer to a timid knock, found a white-lipped, eager-eyed suppliant on the doorstep.

Her face hardened. Mrs. Barry was a woman of strong preju- dices and dislikes, and her anger was of the cold, sullen sort which is always hardest to overcome. To do her justice, she really believed Anne had made Diana drunk out of sheer malice prepense,[1] and she was honestly anxious to preserve her little daughter from the contamination of further intimacy with such a child.

"What do you want?" she said stiffly.

Anne clasped her hands.

"Oh, Mrs. Barry, please forgive me. I did not mean to—to— intoxicate Diana. How could I? Just imagine if you were a poor little orphan girl that kind people had adopted and you had just one bosom friend in all the world. Do you think you would intoxicate her on purpose? I thought it was only raspberry cordial. I was firmly convinced it was raspberry cordial. Oh, please don't say that you won't let Diana play with me any more. If you do you will cover my life with a dark cloud of woe."

This speech, which would have softened good Mrs. Lynde's heart in a twinkling, had no effect on Mrs. Barry except to irri- tate her still more. She was suspicious of Anne's big words and dramatic gestures and imagined that the child was making fun of her. So she said, coldly and cruelly:

"I don't think you are a fit little girl for Diana to associate with. You'd better go home and behave yourself."

Anne's lip quivered.

---

[1] "A legal term indicating malice premeditated or planned beforehand; wrong or injury purposely done" (*OED*).

"Won't you let me see Diana just once to say farewell?" she implored.

"Diana has gone over to Carmody with her father," said Mrs. Barry, going in and shutting the door.

Anne went back to Green Gables calm with despair.

"My last hope is gone," she told Marilla. "I went up and saw Mrs. Barry myself and she treated me very insultingly. Marilla, I do *not* think she is a well-bred woman. There is nothing more to do except to pray and I haven't much hope that that'll do much good because, Marilla, I do not believe that God Himself can do very much with such an obstinate person as Mrs. Barry."

"Anne, you shouldn't say such things," rebuked Marilla, striving to overcome that unholy tendency to laughter which she was dismayed to find growing upon her. And, indeed, when she told the whole story to Matthew that night, she did laugh heartily over Anne's tribulations.

But when she slipped into the east gable before going to bed and found that Anne had cried herself to sleep an unaccustomed softness crept into her face.

"Poor little soul," she murmured, lifting a loose curl of hair from the child's tear-stained face. Then she bent down and kissed the flushed cheek on the pillow.

CHAPTER XVII

A NEW INTEREST IN LIFE

THE next afternoon Anne, bending over her patchwork at the kitchen window, happened to glance out and beheld Diana down by the Dryad's Bubble beckoning mysteriously. In a trice Anne was out of the house and flying down to the hollow, astonishment and hope struggling in her expressive eyes. But the hope faded when she saw Diana's dejected countenance.

"Your mother hasn't relented?" she gasped.

Diana shook her head mournfully.

"No; and oh, Anne, she says I'm never to play with you again.

I've cried and cried and I told her it wasn't your fault, but it wasn't any use. I had ever such a time coaxing her to let me come down and say good-bye to you. She said I was only to stay ten minutes and she's timing me by the clock."

"Ten minutes isn't very long to say an eternal farewell in," said Anne tearfully. "Oh, Diana, will you promise faithfully never to forget me, the friend of your youth, no matter what dearer friends may caress thee?"

"Indeed I will," sobbed Diana, "And I'll never have another bosom friend—I don't want to have. I couldn't love anybody as I love you."

"Oh, Diana," cried Anne, clasping her hands, "do you *love* me?"

"Why, of course I do. Didn't you know that?"

"No." Anne drew a long breath. "I thought you *liked* me of course, but I never hoped you *loved* me. Why, Diana, I didn't think anybody could love me. Nobody ever has loved me since I can remember. Oh, this is wonderful! It's a ray of light which will forever shine on the darkness of a path severed from thee, Diana. Oh, just say it once again."

"I love you devotedly, Anne," said Diana staunchly, "and I always will, you may be sure of that."

"And I will always love thee, Diana," said Anne, solemnly extending her hand. "In the years to come thy memory will shine like a star over my lonely life, as that last story we read together says. Diana, wilt thou give me a lock of thy jet-black tresses in parting to treasure forevermore?"

"Have you got anything to cut it with?" queried Diana, wiping away the tears which Anne's affecting accents had caused to flow afresh, and returning to practicalities.

"Yes. I've got my patchwork scissors in my apron pocket fortunately," said Anne. She solemnly clipped one of Diana's curls. "Fare thee well, my beloved friend. Henceforth we must be as strangers though living side by side. But my heart will ever be faithful to thee."

Anne stood and watched Diana out of sight, mournfully waving her hand to the latter whenever she turned to look back. Then she returned to the house, not a little consoled for the time being by this romantic parting.

"It is all over," she informed Marilla. "I shall never have another friend. I'm really worse off than before, for I haven't Katie Maurice and Violetta now. And even if I had it wouldn't be the same. Somehow, little dream girls are not satisfying after a real friend. Diana and I had such an affecting farewell down by the spring. It will be sacred in my memory forever. I used the most pathetic language I could think of and said 'thou' and 'thee.' 'Thou' and 'thee' seem so much more romantic than 'you.' Diana gave me a lock of her hair and I'm going to sew it up in a little bag and wear it around my neck all my life. Please see that it is buried with me, for I don't believe I'll live very long. Perhaps when she sees me lying cold and dead before her Mrs. Barry may feel remorse for what she has done and will let Diana come to my funeral."

"I don't think there is much fear of your dying of grief as long as you can talk, Anne," said Marilla unsympathetically.

The following Monday Anne surprised Marilla by coming down from her room with her basket of books on her arm and her lips primmed up into a line of determination.

"I'm going back to school," she announced. "That is all there is left in life for me, now that my friend has been ruthlessly torn from me. In school I can look at her and muse over days departed."

"You'd better muse over your lessons and sums," said Marilla, concealing her delight at this development of the situation. "If you're going back to school I hope we'll hear no more of breaking slates over people's heads and such carryings-on. Behave yourself and do just what your teacher tells you."

"I'll try to be a model pupil," agreed Anne dolefully. "There won't be much fun in it, I expect. Mr. Phillips said Minnie Andrews was a model pupil and there isn't a spark of imagination or life in her. She is just dull and poky and never seems to have a good time. But I feel so depressed that perhaps it will come easy to me now. I'm going round by the road. I couldn't bear to go by the Birch Path all alone. I should weep bitter tears if I did."

Anne was welcomed back to school with open arms. Her imagination had been sorely missed in games, her voice in the singing, and her dramatic ability in the perusal aloud of books at dinner hour. Ruby Gillis smuggled three blue plums over to her during testament reading; Ella May Macpherson gave her an enormous yellow pansy cut from the covers of a floral catalogue—a species of desk decoration much prized in Avonlea school. Sophia Sloane offered to teach her a perfectly elegant new pattern of knit lace, *so nice for trimming aprons.* Katie Boulter gave her a perfume bottle to keep slate-water in and Julia Bell copied carefully on a piece of pale pink paper, scalloped on the edges, the following effusion:

"TO ANNE
"When twilight drops her curtain down
And pins it with a star
Remember that you have a friend
Though she may wander far."

"It's so nice to be appreciated," sighed Anne rapturously to Marilla that night.

The girls were not the only scholars who "appreciated" her. When Anne went to her seat after dinner hour—she had been told by Mr. Phillips to sit with the model Minnie Andrews—she found on her desk a big luscious "strawberry apple." Anne caught it up all ready to take a bite, when she remembered that the only place in Avonlea where strawberry apples grew was in the old Blythe orchard on the other side of the Lake of Shining Waters. Anne dropped the apple as if it were a red-hot coal and ostentatiously wiped her fingers on her handkerchief. The apple lay untouched on her desk until the next morning, when little Timothy Andrews, who swept the school and kindled the fire, annexed it as one of his perquisites. Charlie Sloane's slate pencil, gorgeously bedizened[1] with striped red and yellow paper, costing two cents where ordinary pencils cost only one, which he sent up to her after dinner hour, met with a more favourable reception. Anne was graciously pleased to accept it and rewarded the donor with a smile which exalted that infatuated youth straightway into the seventh heaven of delight[2] and caused him to make such fearful errors in his dictation that Mr. Phillips kept him in after school to rewrite it.

But as,

---

[1]   Gaudily decorated.
[2]   Supremely happy.

"The Caesar's pageant shorn of Brutus' bust
Did but of Rome's best son remind her more,"[1]

so the marked absence of any tribute or recognition from Diana
Barry, who was sitting with Gertie Pye, embittered Anne's little
triumph.

"Diana might just have smiled at me once, I think," she
mourned to Marilla that night. But the next morning a note,
most fearfully and wonderfully[2] twisted and folded, and a small
parcel, were passed across to Anne.

"Dear Anne," ran the former, "Mother says I'm not to play with
you or talk to you even in school. It isn't my fault and don't be
cross at me, because I love you as much as ever. I miss you awfully
to tell all my secrets to and I don't like Gertie Pye one bit. I made
you one of the new bookmarkers out of red tissue paper. They are
awfully fashionable now and only three girls in school know how
to make them. When you look at it remember
            "Your true friend,
                "DIANA BARRY."

Anne read the note, kissed the bookmark, and despatched a
prompt reply back to the other side of the school.

    "MY OWN DARLING DIANA:—

"Of course I am not cross at you because you have to obey your
mother. Our spirits can comune. I shall keep your lovely present
forever. Minnie Andrews is a very nice little girl—although she
has no imagination—but after having been Diana's busum friend
I cannot be Minnie's. Please excuse mistakes because my spelling
isn't very good yet, although much improoved.

        "Yours until death us do part,
            "ANNE or CORDELIA SHIRLEY.

    "P.S. I shall sleep with your letter under my pillow to-night.
                "A. or C.S."

Marilla pessimistically expected more trouble since Anne had
again begun to go to school. But none developed. Perhaps Anne
caught something of the "model" spirit from Minnie Andrews; at

---

1   George Gordon, Lord Byron (1788–1824), *Childe Harold's Pilgrimage* 4.59.2–3. See
    also 212, note 3.
2   Cf. Psalm 139.14.

least she got on very well with Mr. Phillips thenceforth. She flung herself into her studies heart and soul, determined not to be outdone in any class by Gilbert Blythe. The rivalry between them was soon apparent; it was entirely good-natured on Gilbert's side; but it is much to be feared that the same thing cannot be said of Anne, who had certainly an unpraiseworthy tenacity for holding grudges. She was as intense in her hatreds as in her loves. She would not stoop to admit that she meant to rival Gilbert in school work, because that would have been to acknowledge his existence which Anne persistently ignored; but the rivalry was there and honours fluctuated between them. Now Gilbert was head of the spelling class; now Anne, with a toss of her long red braids, spelled him down. One morning Gilbert had all his sums done correctly and had his name written on the blackboard on the roll of honour; the next morning Anne, having wrestled wildly with decimals the entire evening before, would be first. One awful day they were ties and their names were written up together. It was almost as bad as a "take notice" and Anne's mortification was as evident as Gilbert's satisfaction. When the written examinations at the end of each month were held the suspense was terrible. The first month Gilbert came out three marks ahead. The second Anne beat him by five. But her triumph was marred by the fact that Gilbert congratulated her heartily before the whole school. It would have been ever so much sweeter to her if he had felt the sting of his defeat.

Mr. Phillips might not be a very good teacher; but a pupil so inflexibly determined on learning as Anne was could hardly escape making progress under any kind of a teacher. By the end of the term Anne and Gilbert were both promoted into the fifth class and allowed to begin studying the elements of "the branches"—by which Latin, geometry, French and algebra were meant. In geometry Anne met her Waterloo.[1]

"It's perfectly awful stuff, Marilla," she groaned. "I'm sure I'll never be able to make head or tail of it. There is no scope for imagination in it at all. Mr. Phillips says I'm the worst dunce he ever saw at it. And Gil—I mean some of the others are so smart at it. It is

---

[1] To suffer defeat. The reference is to the defeat of Napoleon by Wellington and Blücher at Waterloo in 1815.

extremely mortifying, Marilla. Even Diana gets along better than I do. But I don't mind being beaten by Diana. Even although we meet as strangers now I still love her with an *inextinguishable* love. It makes me very sad at times to think about her. But really, Marilla, one can't stay sad very long in such an interesting world, can one?"

CHAPTER XVIII

ANNE TO THE RESCUE

ALL things great are wound up with all things little. At first glance it might not seem that the decision of a certain Canadian Premier[1] to include Prince Edward Island in a political tour could have much or anything to do with the fortunes of little Anne Shirley at Green Gables. But it had.

It was in January the Premier came, to address his loyal supporters and such of his non-supporters as chose to be present at the monster mass meeting held in Charlottetown. Most of the Avonlea people were on the Premier's side of politics; hence, on the night of the meeting nearly all the men and a goodly proportion of the women had gone to town, thirty miles away. Mrs. Rachel Lynde had gone too. Mrs. Rachel Lynde was a red-hot politician and couldn't have believed that the political rally could be carried through without her, although she was on the opposite side of politics.[2] So she went to town and took her husband—Thomas would be useful in looking after the horse— and Marilla Cuthbert with her. Marilla had a sneaking interest in politics herself, and as she thought it might be her only chance to see a real live Premier, she promptly took it, leaving Anne and Matthew to keep house until her return the following day.

Hence, while Marilla and Mrs. Rachel were enjoying themselves hugely at the mass meeting, Anne and Matthew had the

---

[1]   The first minister or Prime Minister of Canada.

[2]   The implication is that Mrs. Lynde is on the "opposite side" of the Premier's politics, or Liberal rather than Conservative (the two political parties operating at this time in Canada).

cheerful kitchen at Green Gables all to themselves. A bright fire was glowing in the old-fashioned Waterloo stove[1] and blue-white frost crystals were shining on the window-panes. Matthew nodded over a *Farmers' Advocate*[2] on the sofa and Anne at the table studied her lessons with grim determination, despite sundry wistful glances at the clock shelf, where lay a new book that Jane Andrews had lent her that day. Jane had assured her that it was warranted to produce any number of thrills, or words to that effect, and Anne's fingers tingled to reach out for it. But that would mean Gilbert Blythe's triumph on the morrow. Anne turned her back on the clock shelf and tried to imagine it wasn't there.

"Matthew, did you ever study geometry when you went to school?"

"Well now, no, I didn't," said Matthew, coming out of his doze with a start.

"I wish you had," sighed Anne, "because then you'd be able to sympathize with me. You can't sympathize properly if you've never studied it. It is casting a cloud over my whole life. I'm such a dunce at it, Matthew."

"Well now, I dunno," said Matthew soothingly. "I guess you're all right at anything. Mr. Phillips told me last week in Blair's store at Carmody that you was the smartest scholar in school and was making rapid progress. 'Rapid progress' was his very words. There's them as runs down Teddy Phillips and says he ain't much of a teacher; but I guess he's all right."

Matthew would have thought any one who praised Anne was "all right."

"I'm sure I'd get on better with geometry if only he wouldn't change the letters," complained Anne. "I learn the proposition off by heart, and then he draws it on the blackboard and puts differ-ent letters from what are in the book and I get all mixed up. I don't think a teacher should take such a mean advantage, do you?

---

[1]   Possibly a reference to a kind of stove of the "Step-Top" style, made from the 1820s to the later nineteenth century. The suggestion that the stove is "old-fashioned" seems to be foregrounded here.

[2]   Magazine published in London, Ontario between 1866 and 1965, and, after 1890, in Winnipeg in a "Manitoba and Western edition." Sometimes *The Farmers' Advocate and Home Magazine*.

We're studying agriculture now and I've found out at last what makes the roads red.[1] It's a great comfort. I wonder how Marilla and Mrs. Lynde are enjoying themselves. Mrs. Lynde says Canada is going to the dogs the way things are being run at Ottawa,[2] and that it's an awful warning to the electors. She says if women were allowed to vote we would soon see a blessed change.[3] What way do you vote, Matthew?"

"Conservative," said Matthew promptly. To vote Conservative was part of Matthew's religion.

"Then I'm Conservative too," said Anne decidedly. "I'm glad, because Gil—because some of the boys in school are Grits.[4] I guess Mr. Phillips is a Grit too, because Prissy Andrews' father is one, and Ruby Gillis says that when a man is courting he always has to agree with the girl's mother in religion and her father in politics. Is that true, Matthew?"

"Well now, I dunno," said Matthew.

"Did you ever go courting, Matthew?"

"Well now, no, I dunno's I ever did," said Matthew, who had certainly never thought of such a thing in his whole existence.

Anne reflected with her chin in her hands.

"It must be rather interesting, don't you think, Matthew? Ruby Gillis says when she grows up she's going to have ever so many beaus[5] on the string and have them all crazy about her; but I think that would be too exciting. I'd rather have just one in his

---

1   See 67, note 1.
2   The capital of Canada and the location of the Canadian Parliament.
3   Women were federally enfranchised in Canada on May 24, 1918; suffrage was reaffirmed in the Dominion Elections Act, 1920. See Catherine Cleverdon, *The Woman Suffrage Movement in Canada* (Toronto: U of Toronto P, 1950, 1974) 2. Mrs. Lynde's position on woman suffrage might appear to be somewhat at odds with her view of women and education, but it is not unusual in the context of first-wave feminism for such a view to be held—that women should have the vote precisely because their "feminine" characteristics would influence politics and the state beneficially. Mrs. Lynde's "red-hot" position is also somewhat at odds with her views on women and education and women as ministers. Cf. English-Canadian suffragist Nellie L. McClung: "Women have cleaned up things since time began; and if women ever get into politics there will be a cleaning-out of pigeon-holes and forgotten corners, on which the dust of years has fallen, and the sound of the political carpet-beater will be heard in the land" (*In Times Like These* [Toronto: McLeod and Allen, 1915] 66).
4   Liberals. See 179, note 2.
5   Often, *beaux*. Sweethearts, suitors.

right mind. But Ruby Gillis knows a great deal about such matters because she has so many big sisters, and Mrs. Lynde says the Gillis girls have gone off like hot cakes. Mr. Phillips goes up to see Prissy Andrews nearly every evening. He says it is to help her with her lessons, but Miranda Sloane is studying for Queen's, too, and I should think she needed help a lot more than Prissy because she's ever so much stupider, but he never goes to help her in the evenings at all. There are a great many things in this world that I can't understand very well, Matthew."

"Well now, I dunno as I comprehend them all myself," acknowledged Matthew.

"Well, I suppose I must finish up my lessons. I won't allow myself to open that new book Jane lent me until I'm through. But it's a terrible temptation, Matthew. Even when I turn my back on it I can see it there just as plain. Jane said she cried herself sick over it. I love a book that makes me cry. But I think I'll carry that book into the sitting-room and lock it in the jam closet and give you the key. And you must *not* give it to me, Matthew, until my lessons are done, not even if I implore you on my bended knees. It's all very well to say resist temptation, but it's ever so much easier to resist it if you can't get the key. And then shall I run down the cellar and get some russets, Matthew? Wouldn't you like some russets?"

"Well now, I dunno but what I would," said Matthew, who never ate russets but knew Anne's weakness for them.

Just as Anne emerged triumphantly from the cellar with her plateful of russets came the sound of flying footsteps on the icy board walk outside and the next moment the kitchen door was flung open and in rushed Diana Barry, white-faced and breathless, with a shawl wrapped hastily around her head. Anne promptly let go of her candle and plate in her surprise, and plate, candle, and apples crashed together down the cellar ladder and were found at the bottom embedded in melted grease, the next day, by Marilla, who gathered them up and thanked mercy the house hadn't been set on fire.

"Whatever is the matter, Diana?" cried Anne. "Has your mother relented at last?"

"Oh, Anne, do come quick," implored Diana nervously. "Minnie May is awful sick—she's got croup, Young Mary Joe says—and father and mother are away to town and there's nobody to go for the doctor. Minnie May is awful bad and Young Mary Joe doesn't know what to do—and oh, Anne, I'm so scared!"

Matthew, without a word, reached out for cap and coat, slipped past Diana and away into the darkness of the yard.

"He's gone to harness the sorrel mare to go to Carmody for the doctor," said Anne, who was hurrying on hood and jacket. "I know it as well as if he'd said so. Matthew and I are such kindred spirits I can read his thoughts without words at all."

"I don't believe he'll find the doctor at Carmody," sobbed Diana. "I know that Doctor Blair went to town and I guess Doctor Spencer would go too, Young Mary Joe never saw anybody with croup and Mrs. Lynde is away. Oh, Anne!"

"Don't cry, Di," said Anne cheerily. "I know exactly what to do for croup. You forget that Mrs. Hammond had twins three times. When you look after three pairs of twins you naturally get a lot of experience. They all had croup regularly. Just wait till I get the ipecac[1] bottle—you mayn't have any at your house. Come on now."

The two little girls hastened out hand in hand and hurried through Lovers' Lane and across the crusted field beyond, for the snow was too deep to go by the shorter wood way. Anne, although sincerely sorry for Minnie May, was far from being insensible to the romance of the situation and to the sweetness of once more sharing that romance with a kindred spirit.

The night was clear and frosty, all ebony of shadow and silver of snowy slope; big stars were shining over the silent fields; here and there the dark pointed firs stood up with snow powdering their branches and the wind whistling through them. Anne thought it was truly delightful to go skimming through all this mystery and loveliness with your bosom friend who had been so long estranged.

Minnie May, aged three, was really very sick. She lay on the kitchen sofa, feverish and restless, while her hoarse breathing could be heard all over the house. Young Mary Joe, a buxom,

---

[1] Used to induce nausea, a substance derived from the root of a South American plant, *Cephaëlis Ipecacuanha.*

broad-faced French girl from the Creek, whom Mrs. Barry had engaged to stay with the children during her absence, was helpless and bewildered, quite incapable of thinking what to do, or doing it if she thought of it.

Anne went to work with skill and promptness.

"Minnie May has croup all right; she's pretty bad, but I've seen them worse. First we must have lots of hot water. I declare, Diana, there isn't more than a cupful in the kettle! There, I've filled it up, and, Mary Joe, you may put some wood in the stove. I don't want to hurt your feelings, but it seems to me you might have thought of this before if you'd any imagination. Now, I'll undress Minnie May and put her to bed, and you try to find some soft flannel cloths, Diana. I'm going to give her a dose of ipecac first of all."

Minnie May did not take kindly to the ipecac, but Anne had not brought up three pairs of twins for nothing. Down that ipecac went, not only once, but many times during the long, anxious night when the two little girls worked patiently over the suffering Minnie May, and Young Mary Joe, honestly anxious to do all she could, kept on a roaring fire and heated more water than would have been needed for a hospital of croupy babies.

It was three o'clock when Matthew came with the doctor, for he had been obliged to go all the way to Spencervale for one. But the pressing need for assistance was past. Minnie May was much better and was sleeping soundly.

"I was awfully near giving up in despair," explained Anne. "She got worse and worse until she was sicker than ever the Hammond twins were, even the last pair. I actually thought she was going to choke to death. I gave her every drop of ipecac in that bottle, and when the last dose went down I said to myself—not to Diana or Young Mary Joe, because I didn't want to worry them any more than they were worried, but I had to say it to myself just to relieve my feelings—'This is the last lingering hope and I fear 'tis a vain one.'[1] But in about three minutes she coughed up the phlegm and began to get better right away. You must just imagine my relief, doctor, because I can't express it in words. You know there

---

[1] Cf. Felicia Hemans (1793–1835), "The Siege of Valencia," a dramatic poem: "And my last lingering hope, that thou/ shouldst win" (185). There are several allusions in *AGG* to the popular and well-known poetry of Hemans.

are some things that cannot be expressed in words."

"Yes, I know," nodded the doctor. He looked at Anne as if he were thinking some things about her that couldn't be expressed in words. Later on, however, he expressed them to Mr. and Mrs. Barry.

"That little red-headed girl they have over at Cuthbert's is as smart as they make 'em. I tell you she saved that baby's life, for it would have been too late by the time I got here. She seems to have a skill and presence of mind perfectly wonderful in a child of her age. I never saw anything like the eyes of her when she was explaining the case out to me."

Anne had gone home in the wonderful, white-frosted winter morning, heavy-eyed from loss of sleep, but still talking unweariedly to Matthew as they crossed the long white field and walked under the glittering fairy arch of the Lovers' Lane maples

"Oh, Matthew, isn't it a wonderful morning? The world looks like something God had just imagined for His own pleasure, doesn't it? Those trees look as if I could blow them away with a breath—pouf! I'm so glad I live in a world where there are white frosts, aren't you? And I'm so glad Mrs. Hammond had three pairs of twins after all. If she hadn't I mightn't have known what to do for Minnie May. I'm real sorry I was ever cross with Mrs. Hammond for having twins. But, oh, Matthew, I'm so sleepy. I can't go to school. I just know I couldn't keep my eyes open and I'd be so stupid. But I hate to stay home for Gil—some of the others will get head of the class, and it's so hard to get up again—although of course the harder it is the more satisfaction you have when you do get up, haven't you?"

"Well now, I guess you'll manage all right," said Matthew, looking at Anne's white little face and the dark shadows under her eyes. "You just go right to bed and have a good sleep. I'll do all the chores."

Anne accordingly went to bed and slept so long and soundly that it was well on in the white and rosy winter afternoon when she awoke and descended to the kitchen where Marilla, who had arrived home in the meantime, was sitting knitting.

"Oh, did you see the Premier?" exclaimed Anne at once. "What did he look like, Marilla?"

"Well, he never got to be Premier on account of his looks," said Marilla. "Such a nose as that man had! But he can speak. I was proud of being a Conservative. Rachel Lynde, of course, being a

Liberal, had no use for him.Your dinner is in the oven, Anne; and you can get yourself some blue plum preserve out of the pantry. I guess you're hungry. Matthew has been telling me about last night. I must say it was fortunate you knew what to do. I wouldn't have had any idea myself, for I never saw a case of croup. There now, never mind talking till you've had your dinner. I can tell by the look of you that you're just full up with speeches, but they'll keep."

Marilla had something to tell Anne, but she did not tell it just then, for she knew if she did Anne's consequent excitement would lift her clear out of the region of such material matters as appetite or dinner. Not until Anne had finished her saucer of blue plums did Marilla say:

"Mrs. Barry was here this afternoon, Anne. She wanted to see you, but I wouldn't wake you up. She says you saved Minnie May's life, and she is very sorry she acted as she did in that affair of the currant wine. She says she knows now you didn't mean to set Diana drunk, and she hopes you'll forgive her and be good friends with Diana again.You're to go over this evening if you like, for Diana can't stir outside the door on account of a bad cold she caught last night. Now, Anne Shirley, for pity's sake don't fly clean up into the air."

The warning seemed not unnecessary, so uplifted and aerial was Anne's expression and attitude as she sprang to her feet, her face irradiated with the flame of her spirit.

"Oh, Marilla, can I go right now—without washing my dishes? I'll wash them when I come back, but I cannot tie myself down to anything so unromantic as dish-washing at this thrilling moment."

"Yes, yes, run along," said Marilla indulgently. "Anne Shirley— are you crazy? Come back this instant and put something on you. I might as well call to the wind. She's gone without a cap or wrap. Look at her tearing through the orchard with her hair streaming. It'll be a mercy if she doesn't catch her death of cold."

Anne came dancing home in the purple winter twilight across the snowy places. Afar in the southwest was the great shimmering, pearl-like sparkle of an evening star in a sky that was pale golden and ethereal rose over gleaming white spaces and dark glens of spruce. The tinkles of sleigh-bells among the snowy hills came like elfin chimes through the frosty air, but their music was not sweeter than the song in Anne's heart and on her lips.

"You see before you a perfectly happy person, Marilla," she announced. "I'm perfectly happy—yes, in spite of my red hair. Just at present I have a soul above red hair. Mrs. Barry kissed me and cried and said she was so sorry and she could never repay me. I felt fearfully embarrassed, Marilla, but I just said as politely as I could, 'I have no hard feelings for you, Mrs. Barry. I assure you once for all that I did not mean to intoxicate Diana and henceforth I shall cover the past with the mantle of oblivion.'[1] That was a pretty dignified way of speaking, wasn't it, Marilla? I felt that I was heaping coals of fire on Mrs. Barry's head. And Diana and I had a lovely afternoon. Diana showed me a new fancy crochet stitch her aunt over at Carmody taught her. Not a soul in Avonlea knows it but us, and we pledged a solemn vow never to reveal it to any one else. Diana gave me a beautiful card with a wreath of roses on it and a verse of poetry:
"'If you love me as I love you
"'Nothing but death can part us two.'"
"And that is true, Marilla. We're going to ask Mr. Phillips to let us sit together in school again, and Gertie Pye can go with Minnie Andrews. We had an elegant tea. Mrs. Barry had the very best china set out, Marilla, just as if I was real company. I can't tell you what a thrill it gave me. Nobody ever used their very best china on my account before. And we had fruit-cake and pound-cake and doughnuts and two kinds of preserves, Marilla. And Mrs. Barry asked me if I took tea and said, 'Pa, why don't you pass the biscuits to Anne?' It must be lovely to be grown up, Marilla, when just being treated as if you were is so nice."

"I don't know about that," said Marilla with a brief sigh.

"Well, anyway, when I am grown up," said Anne decidedly, "I'm always going to talk to little girls as if they were, too, and I'll never laugh when they use big words. I know from sorrowful experience how that hurts one's feelings. After tea Diana and I made taffy. The taffy wasn't very good, I suppose because neither Diana nor I had ever made any before. Diana left me to stir it while she buttered the plates and I forgot and let it burn; and then when we set it out on the platform to cool the cat walked over one plate and that had to be thrown away. But the making of it

---

1   Cf. Felicia Hemans, "Night Scene in Genoa," lines 78–83.

was splendid fun. Then when I came home Mrs. Barry asked me to come over as often as I could and Diana stood at the window and threw kisses to me all the way down to Lovers' Lane. I assure you, Marilla, that I feel like praying to-night and I'm going to think out a special brand-new prayer in honour of the occasion."

CHAPTER XIX

A CONCERT, A CATASTROPHE, AND A CONFESSION

"MARILLA, can I go over to see Diana just for a minute?" asked Anne, running breathlessly down from the east gable one February evening.

"I don't see what you want to be traipsing about after dark for," said Marilla shortly. "You and Diana walked home from school together and then stood down there in the snow for half an hour more, your tongues going the whole blessed time, clickety-clack. So I don't think you're very badly off to see her again."

"But she wants to see me," pleaded Anne. "She has something very important to tell me."

"How do you know she has?"

"Because she just signalled to me from her window. We have arranged a way to signal with our candles and cardboard. We set the candle on the window-sill and make flashes by passing the cardboard back and forth. So many flashes mean a certain thing. It was my idea, Marilla."

"I'll warrant you it was," said Marilla emphatically. "And the next thing you'll be setting fire to the curtains with your signalling nonsense."

"Oh, we're very careful, Marilla. And it's so interesting. Two flashes mean, 'Are you there?' Three mean 'yes' and four 'no.' Five mean, 'Come over as soon as possible, because I have something important to reveal.' Diana has just signalled five flashes, and I'm really suffering to know what it is."

"Well, you needn't suffer any longer," said Marilla sarcastically.

"You can go, but you're to be back here in just ten minutes, remember that."

Anne did remember it and was back in the stipulated time, although probably no mortal will ever know just what it cost her to confine the discussion of Diana's important communication within the limits of ten minutes. But at least she had made good use of them.

"Oh, Marilla, what do you think? You know to-morrow is Diana's birthday. Well, her mother told her she could ask me to go home with her from school and stay all night with her. And her cousins are coming over from Newbridge in a big pung sleigh[1] to go to the Debating Club concert at the hall to-morrow night. And they are going to take Diana and me to the concert—if you'll let me go, that is. You will, won't you, Marilla? Oh, I feel so excited."

"You can calm down then, because you're not going. You're better at home in your own bed, and as for that Club concert, it's all nonsense, and little girls should not be allowed to go out to such places at all."

"I'm sure the Debating Club is a most respectable affair," pleaded Anne.

"I'm not saying it isn't. But you're not going to begin gadding about[2] to concerts and staying out all hours of the night. Pretty doings for children. I'm surprised at Mrs. Barry's letting Diana go."

"But it's such a very special occasion," mourned Anne, on the verge of tears. "Diana has only one birthday in a year. It isn't as if birthdays were common things, Marilla. Prissy Andrews is going to recite 'Curfew Must Not Ring To-night.'[3] That is such a good moral piece, Marilla, I'm sure it would do me lots of good to hear

---

1   One- or two-horse sleigh.

2   A favourite term of Marilla's for social activities, it implies "constantly making visits, gossip[ing]" (Eric Partridge, *Dictionary of Slang and Unconventional English*, London: Routledge, 1970).

3   A poem by American writer Rose Thorpe (1850–1939). This poem figures in many elocution readers of the late nineteenth century. For instance, *The New Dramatic Reader* by John Andrew (Montreal: Dawson, 1876), includes it, although it indicates its author as "Anon." (136–39). Anne describes the poem as "moral," presumably because it presents a story of heroism for love: it is a narrative of a young girl who grasps the clapper of the church bell and clings to it while it is being rung in order to prevent it from making noise; she does this to save her lover from the death to which he is condemned at the tolling of the curfew. *AA* notes its first publication in 1867 and reproduces the poem (473–4). See 193, note 1.

it. And the choir are going to sing four lovely pathetic songs that are pretty near as good as hymns. And oh, Marilla, the minister is going to take part; yes, indeed, he is; he's going to give an address. That will be just about the same thing as a sermon. Please, mayn't I go, Marilla?"

"You heard what I said, Anne, didn't you? Take off your boots now and go to bed. It's past eight."

"There's just one more thing, Marilla," said Anne, with the air of producing the last shot in her locker.[1] "Mrs. Barry told Diana that we might sleep in the spare-room bed. Think of the honour of your little Anne being put in the spare-room bed."

"It's an honour you'll have to get along without. Go to bed, Anne, and don't let me hear another word out of you."

When, Anne, with tears rolling over her cheeks, had gone sorrowfully up-stairs, Matthew, who had been apparently sound asleep on the lounge during the whole dialogue, opened his eyes and said decidedly:

"Well now, Marilla, I think you ought to let Anne go."

"I don't then," retorted Marilla. "Who's bringing this child up, Matthew, you or me?"

"Well now, you," admitted Matthew.

"Don't interfere then."

"Well now, I ain't interfering. It ain't interfering to have your own opinion. And my opinion is that you ought to let Anne go."

"You'd think I ought to let Anne go to the moon if she took the notion, I've no doubt," was Marilla's amiable rejoinder. "I might have let her spend the night with Diana, if that was all. But I don't approve of this concert plan. She'd go there and catch cold like as not, and have her head filled up with nonsense and excitement. It would unsettle her for a week. I understand that child's disposition and what's good for it better than you, Matthew."

"I think you ought to let Anne go," repeated Matthew firmly. Argument was not his strong point, but holding fast to his opinion certainly was. Marilla gave a gasp of helplessness and took refuge in silence. The next morning, when Anne was washing the breakfast dishes in the pantry, Matthew paused on his way

---

[1]   I.e., the ammunition locker as on a warship.

out to the barn to say to Marilla again:

"I think you ought to let Anne go, Marilla."

For a moment Marilla looked things not lawful to be uttered. Then she yielded to the inevitable and said tartly:

"Very well, she can go, since nothing else'll please you."

Anne flew out of the pantry, dripping dish-cloth in hand.

"Oh, Marilla, Marilla, say those blessed words again."

"I guess once is enough to say them. This is Matthew's doings and I wash my hands of it. If you catch pneumonia sleeping in a strange bed or coming out of that hot hall in the middle of the night, don't blame me, blame Matthew. Anne Shirley, you're dripping greasy water all over the floor. I never saw such a careless child."

"Oh, I know I'm a great trial to you, Marilla," said Anne repentantly. "I make so many mistakes. But then just think of all the mistakes I don't make, although I might. I'll get some sand and scrub up the spots before I go to school. Oh, Marilla, my heart was just set on going to that concert. I never was to a concert in my life, and when the other girls talk about them in school I feel so out of it. You didn't know just how I felt about it, but you see Matthew did. Matthew understands me, and it's so nice to be understood, Marilla."

Anne was too excited to do herself justice as to lessons that morning in school. Gilbert Blythe spelled her down in class and left her clear out of sight in mental arithmetic. Anne's consequent humiliation was less than it might have been, however, in view of the concert and the spare-room bed. She and Diana talked so constantly about it all day that with a stricter teacher than Mr. Phillips dire disgrace must inevitably have been their portion.

Anne felt that she could not have borne it if she had not been going to the concert, for nothing else was discussed that day in school. The Avonlea Debating Club, which met fortnightly all winter, had had several smaller free entertainments; but this was to be a big affair, admission ten cents, in aid of the library. The Avonlea young people had been practising for weeks, and all the scholars were especially interested in it by reason of older brothers and sisters who were going to take part. Everybody in school over nine years of age expected to go, except Carrie Sloane, whose father shared Marilla's opinions about small girls going out to night concerts. Carrie Sloane cried into her grammar all the afternoon and felt that life was not worth living.

For Anne the real excitement began with the dismissal of school and increased therefrom in crescendo until it reached to a crash of positive ecstasy in the concert itself. They had a "perfectly elegant tea"; and then came the delicious occupation of dressing in Diana's little room up-stairs. Diana did Anne's front hair in the new pompadour style[1] and Anne tied Diana's bows with the especial knack she possessed; and they experimented with at least half a dozen different ways of arranging their back hair. At last they were ready, cheeks scarlet and eyes glowing with excitement.

True, Anne could not help a little pang when she contrasted her plain black tam and shapeless, tight-sleeved, home-made gray cloth coat with Diana's jaunty fur cap and smart little jacket. But she remembered in time that she had an imagination and could use it.

Then Diana's cousins, the Murrays from Newbridge, came; they all crowded into the big pung sleigh, among straw and furry robes. Anne revelled in the drive to the hall, slipping along over the satin-smooth roads with the snow crisping under the runners. There was a magnificent sunset, and the snowy hills and deep blue water of the St. Lawrence Gulf seemed to rim in the splendour like a huge bowl of pearl and sapphire brimmed with wine and fire. Tinkles of sleigh-bells and distant laughter, that seemed like the mirth of wood elves, came from every quarter.

"Oh, Diana," breathed Anne, squeezing Diana's mittened hand under the fur robe, "isn't it all like a beautiful dream? Do I really look the same as usual? I feel so different that it seems to me it must show in my looks."

"You look awfully nice," said Diana, who having just received a compliment from one of her cousins, felt that she ought to pass it on. "You've got the loveliest colour."

The programme that night was a series of "thrills" for at least one listener in the audience, and, as Anne assured Diana, every succeeding thrill was thrillier than the last. When Prissy Andrews, attired in a new pink silk waist[2] with a string of pearls about her

---

[1] "A style of arranging women's hair, in which it is turned back off the forehead in a roll, sometimes over a pad" (*OED*).

[2] Blouse.

smooth white throat and real carnations in her hair—rumour whispered that the master had sent all the way to town for them for her—"climbed the slimy ladder, dark without one ray of light,"[1] Anne shivered in luxurious sympathy; when the choir sang "Far Above the Gentle Daisies"[2] Anne gazed at the ceiling as if it were frescoed with angels; when Sam Sloane proceeded to explain and illustrate "How Sockery Set a Hen"[3] Anne laughed until people sitting near her laughed too, more out of sympathy with her than with amusement at a selection that was rather threadbare even in Avonlea; and when Mr. Phillips gave Mark Antony's oration over the dead body of Caesar[4] in the most heart-stirring tones—looking at Prissy Andrews at the end of every sentence—Anne felt that she could rise and mutiny on the spot if but one Roman citizen led the way.

Only one number on the programme failed to interest her. When Gilbert Blythe recited "Bingen on the Rhine"[5] Anne picked up Rhoda Murray's library book and read it until he had finished, when she sat rigidly stiff and motionless while Diana clapped her hands until they tingled.

It was eleven when they got home, sated with dissipation, but with the exceeding sweet pleasure of talking it all over still to come. Everybody seemed asleep and the house was dark and silent. Anne and Diana tiptoed into the parlour, a long narrow room out of which the spare room opened. It was pleasantly warm and dimly lighted by the embers of a fire in the grate.

"Let's undress here," said Diana. "It's so nice and warm."

"Hasn't it been a delightful time?" sighed Anne rapturously.

---

[1] A line from "Curfew Must Not Ring Tonight" by Rose Hartwick Thorpe; properly, "climbed the dusty ladder/ On which fell no ray of light." See 189, note 3.

[2] Song of 1869, lyrics by George Cooper, music by Harrison Millard; according to *AA*, properly, "Far Above the Daisies" (217, note 10). Reproduced in *AA* (465).

[3] Recitation piece of late nineteenth century. This and other "Sockery" pieces appear in many collections, such as *Dick's Recitations and Readings* 10 (1879): 117–18 and 16 (1879): 52–54 ("Sockery Kadahcut's Kat"); and the *Scrap-book Recitation Series* 1 (1879), pp. 54–4 (as "Sockery Setting a Hen").

[4] Shakespeare, *Julius Caesar* 3.2.73–230. This speech seems to have been a standard recitation piece: Dewart, for instance, includes it under the title "Mark Antony over the Dead Body of Caesar" (225–227). See *The Canadian Speaker and Elocutionary Reader* (Toronto: Adam Miller, 1868).

[5] See earlier reference to this poem by Caroline Sheridan Norton, 91, note 3.

"It must be splendid to get up and recite there. Do you suppose we will ever be asked to do it, Diana?"

"Yes, of course, some day. They're always wanting the big scholars to recite. Gilbert Blythe does often and he's only two years older than us. Oh, Anne, how could you pretend not to listen to him? When he came to the line,

"'There's another, *not* a sister,'[1]

he looked right down at you."

"Diana," said Anne with dignity, "you are my bosom friend, but I cannot allow even you to speak to me of that person. Are you ready for bed? Let's run a race and see who'll get to the bed first."

The suggestion appealed to Diana. The two little white-clad figures flew down the long room, through the spare room door, and bounded on the bed at the same moment. And then—something—moved beneath them, there was a gasp and a cry—and somebody said in muffled accents:[2]

"Merciful goodness!"

Anne and Diana were never able to tell just how they got off that bed and out of the room. They only knew that after one frantic rush they found themselves tiptoeing shiveringly up-stairs.

"Oh, who was it—*what* was it?" whispered Anne, her teeth chattering with cold and fright.

"It was Aunt Josephine," said Diana, gasping with laughter. "Oh, Anne, it was Aunt Josephine, however she came to be there. Oh, and I know she will be furious. It's dreadful—it's really dreadful—but did you ever know anything so funny, Anne?"

"Who is your Aunt Josephine?"

"She's father's aunt and she lives in Charlottetown. She's awfully old—seventy anyhow—and I don't believe she was *ever* a little girl. We were expecting her out for a visit, but not so soon. She's awfully prim and proper and she'll scold dreadfully about this, I know. Well, we'll have to sleep with Minnie May— and you can't think how she kicks."

---

[1]   A line from "Bingen on the Rhine" (33). Properly, "There's *another*—not a sister..." See 91, note 3.

[2]   This scene, in which Anne and Diana jump on Miss Josephine Barry in bed, had been developed in an earlier story by Mongomery. See Appendix A.

Miss Josephine Barry did not appear at the early breakfast the next morning. Mrs. Barry smiled kindly at the two little girls.

"Did you have a good time last night? I tried to stay awake until you came home, for I wanted to tell you Aunt Josephine had come and that you would have to go up-stairs after all, but I was so tired I fell asleep. I hope you didn't disturb your aunt, Diana."

Diana preserved a discreet silence, but she and Anne exchanged furtive smiles of guilty amusement across the table. Anne hurried home after breakfast and so remained in blissful ignorance of the disturbance which presently resulted in the Barry household until the late afternoon, when she went down to Mrs. Lynde's on an errand for Marilla.

"So you and Diana nearly frightened poor old Miss Barry to death last night?" said Mrs. Lynde severely, but with a twinkle in her eye. "Mrs. Barry was here a few minutes ago on her way to Carmody. She's feeling real worried over it. Old Miss Barry was in a terrible temper when she got up this morning—and Josephine Barry's temper is no joke, I can tell you that. She wouldn't speak to Diana at all."

"It wasn't Diana's fault," said Anne contritely. "It was mine. I suggested racing to see who would get into bed first."

"I knew it!" said Mrs. Lynde with the exultation of a correct guesser. "I knew that idea came out of your head. Well, it's made a nice lot of trouble, that's what. Old Miss Barry came out to stay for a month, but she declares she won't stay another day and is going right back to town to-morrow, Sunday and all as it is. She'd have gone to-day if they could have taken her. She had promised to pay for a quarter's music lessons for Diana, but now she is determined to do nothing at all for such a tomboy. Oh, I guess they had a lively time of it there this morning. The Barrys must feel cut up. Old Miss Barry is rich and they'd like to keep on the good side of her. Of course, Mrs. Barry didn't say just that to me, but I'm a pretty good judge of human nature, that's what."

"I'm such an unlucky girl," mourned Anne. "I'm always getting into scrapes myself and getting my best friends—people I'd shed my heart's blood for—into them, too. Can you tell me why it is so, Mrs. Lynde?"

"It's because you're too heedless and impulsive, child, that's what. You never stop to think—whatever comes into your head to say or do you say or do it without a moment's reflection."

"Oh, but that's the best of it," protested Anne. "Something just flashes into your mind, so exciting, and you must out with it. If you stop to think it over you spoil it all. Haven't you never felt that yourself, Mrs. Lynde?"

No, Mrs. Lynde had not. She shook her head sagely.

"You must learn to think a little, Anne, that's what. The proverb you need to go by is 'Look before you leap'[1] —especially into spare-room beds."

Mrs. Lynde laughed comfortably over her mild joke, but Anne remained pensive. She saw nothing to laugh at in the situation, which to her eyes appeared very serious. When she left Mrs. Lynde's she took her way across the crusted fields to Orchard Slope. Diana met her at the kitchen door.

"Your Aunt Josephine was very cross about it, wasn't she?" whispered Anne.

"Yes," answered Diana, stifling a giggle with an apprehensive glance over her shoulder at the closed sitting-room door. "She was fairly dancing with rage, Anne. Oh, how she scolded. She said I was the worst-behaved girl she ever saw and that my parents ought to be ashamed of the way they had brought me up. She says she won't stay and I'm sure I don't care. But father and mother do."

"Why didn't you tell them it was my fault?" demanded Anne.

"It's likely I'd do such a thing, isn't it?" said Diana with just scorn. "I'm no telltale, Anne Shirley, and anyhow I was just as much to blame as you."

"Well, I'm going to tell her myself," said Anne resolutely. Diana stared.

"Anne Shirley, you'd never! why—she'll eat you alive!"

"Don't frighten me any more than I am frightened," implored Anne. "I'd rather walk up to a cannon's mouth. But I've got to do it, Diana. It was my fault and I've got to confess. I've had practice in confessing fortunately."

---

[1] Think before you act. The origins of this proverb are obscure. *The Macmillan Book of Proverbs, Maxims, and Famous Phrases* (New York: Macmillan, 1948) cites Aesop's fable, "The Fox and the Goat," as well as noting occurrences in books of proverbs and advice from c.1350.

"Well, she's in the room," said Diana. "You can go in if you want to. I wouldn't dare. And I don't believe you'll do a bit of good."

With this encouragement Anne bearded the lion in its den[1]— that is to say, walked resolutely up to the sitting-room door and knocked faintly. A sharp "Come in" followed.

Miss Josephine Barry, thin, prim and rigid, was knitting fiercely by the fire, her wrath quite unappeased and her eyes snapping through her gold-rimmed glasses. She wheeled around in her chair, expecting to see Diana, and beheld a white-faced girl whose great eyes were brimmed up with a mixture of desperate courage and shrinking terror.

"Who are you?" demanded Miss Josephine Barry without ceremony.

"I'm Anne of Green Gables," said the small visitor tremulously, clasping her hands with her characteristic gesture, "and I've come to confess, if you please."

"Confess what?"

"That it was all my fault about jumping into bed on you last night. I suggested it. Diana would never have thought of such a thing, I am sure. Diana is a very lady-like girl, Miss Barry. So you must see how unjust it is to blame her."

"Oh, I must, hey? I rather think Diana did her share of the jumping at least. Such carryings-on in a respectable house!"

"But we were only in fun," persisted Anne. "I think you ought to forgive us, Miss Barry, now that we've apologized. And anyhow, please forgive Diana and let her have her music lessons. Diana's heart is set on her music lessons, Miss Barry, and I know too well what it is to set your heart on a thing and not get it. If you must be cross with any one, be cross with me. I've been so used in my early days to having people cross at me that I can endure it much better than Diana can."

Much of the snap had gone out of the old lady's eyes by this time and was replaced by a twinkle of amused interest. But she still said severely:

"I don't think it is any excuse for you that you were only in fun. Little girls never indulged in that kind of fun when I was

---

[1]   See 63, note 1.

young. You don't know what it is to be awakened out of a sound sleep, after a long and arduous journey, by two great girls coming bounce down on you."

"I don't *know*, but I can *imagine*," said Anne eagerly. "I'm sure it must have been very disturbing. But then, there is our side of it too. Have you any imagination, Miss Barry? If you have, just put yourself in our place. We didn't know there was anybody in that bed and you nearly scared us to death. It was simply awful the way we felt. And then we couldn't sleep in the spare room after being promised. I suppose you are used to sleeping in spare rooms. But just imagine what you would feel like if you were a little orphan girl who had never had such an honour."

All the snap had gone by this time. Miss Barry actually laughed—a sound which caused Diana, waiting in speechless anxiety in the kitchen outside, to give a great gasp of relief.

"I'm afraid my imagination is a little rusty—it's so long since I used it," she said. "I dare say your claim to sympathy is just as strong as mine. It all depends on the way we look at it. Sit down here and tell me about yourself."

"I am very sorry I can't," said Anne firmly. "I would like to, because you seem like an interesting lady, and you might even be a kindred spirit although you don't look very much like it. But it is my duty to go home to Miss Marilla Cuthbert. Miss Marilla Cuthbert is a very kind lady who has taken me to bring up properly. She is doing her best, but it is very discouraging work. You must not blame her because I jumped on the bed. But before I go I do wish you would tell me if you will forgive Diana and stay just as long as you meant to in Avonlea."

"I think perhaps I will if you will come over and talk to me occasionally," said Miss Barry.

That evening Miss Barry gave Diana a silver bangle bracelet and told the senior members of the household that she had unpacked her valise.

"I've made up my mind to stay simply for the sake of getting better acquainted with that Anne-girl," she said frankly. "She amuses me, and at my time of life an amusing person is a rarity."

Marilla's only comment when she heard the story was, "I told you so." This was for Matthew's benefit.

Miss Barry stayed her month out and over. She was a more agreeable guest than usual, for Anne kept her in good humour. They became firm friends.

When Miss Barry went away she said:

"Remember, you Anne-girl, when you come to town you're to visit me and I'll put you in my very sparest spare-room bed to sleep."

"Miss Barry was a kindred spirit, after all," Anne confided to Marilla. "You wouldn't think so to look at her, but she is. You don't find it right out at first, as in Matthew's case, but after awhile you come to see it. Kindred spirits are not so scarce as I used to think. It's splendid to find out there are so many of them in the world."

CHAPTER XX

A GOOD IMAGINATION GONE WRONG

SPRING had come once more to Green Gables—the beautiful, capricious, reluctant Canadian spring, lingering along through April and May in a succession of sweet, fresh, chilly days, with pink sunsets and miracles of resurrection and growth. The maples in Lovers' Lane were red-budded and little curly ferns pushed up around the Dryad's Bubble. Away up in the barrens, behind Mr. Silas Sloane's place, the Mayflowers blossomed out, pink and white stars of sweetness under their brown leaves. All the school girls and boys had one golden afternoon gathering them, coming home in the clear, echoing twilight with arms and baskets full of flowery spoil.

"I'm so sorry for people who live in lands where there are no Mayflowers," said Anne. "Diana says perhaps they have something better, but there couldn't be anything better than Mayflowers, could there, Marilla? And Diana says if they don't know what they are like they don't miss them. But I think that is the saddest thing of all. I think it would be *tragic*, Marilla, not to know what Mayflowers are like and *not* to miss them. Do you know what I think Mayflowers are, Marilla? I think they must be the souls of the flowers that died last summer and this is their heaven. But we had a splendid time to-day, Marilla. We had our lunch down in a big mossy hollow by an old well—such a *romantic* spot. Charlie Sloane dared Arty Gillis to jump over it, and Arty did because he wouldn't take a dare. Nobody would in school. It is very *fashionable* to dare. Mr. Phillips gave all the Mayflowers he found to Prissy Andrews and I heard him say 'sweets to the sweet.' He got that out of a book,[1] I know; but it shows he has some imagination. I was offered some Mayflowers too, but I rejected them with scorn. I can't tell you the person's name because I have vowed never to let it cross my lips. We made wreaths of the Mayflowers and put them on our hats; and when the time came to go home we marched in procession down the road, two by two, with our bouquets and wreaths, singing 'My Home On The Hill.'[2] Oh, it was so thrilling, Marilla. All Mr. Silas Sloane's folks rushed out to see us and everybody we met on the road stopped and stared after us. We made a real sensation."

"Not much wonder! Such silly doings!" was Marilla's response.

After the Mayflowers came the violets, and Violet Vale was empurpled with them. Anne walked through it on her way to school with reverent steps and worshipping eyes, as if she trod on holy ground.[3]

"Somehow," she told Diana, "when I'm going through here I don't really care whether Gil—whether anybody gets ahead of me in class or not. But when I'm up in school it's all different and I care as much as ever. There's such a lot of different Annes in me. I sometimes think that is why I'm such a troublesome person. If I was just the one Anne it would be ever so much more comfortable, but then it wouldn't be half so interesting."

One June evening, when the orchards were pink-blossomed again, when the frogs were singing silverly sweet in the marshes

---

1   The "book" in question is Shakespeare's *Hamlet* (5.1.243).
2   Song of 1866, lyrics and music by W.C. Baker. Reproduced in *AA* (466).
3   This is a phrase that occurs often in Wordsworth's poetry: see, for instance, "Taken during a pedestrian tour among the Alps" (1) and "A parsonage in Oxfordshire" (1). See also Felicia Hemans, "The Landing of the Pilgrim Fathers in New England" (1825), lines 37–38 and Longfellow, "The Spanish Student" (2.3).

about the head of the Lake of Shining Waters, and the air was full of the savour of clover fields and balsamic fir woods, Anne was sitting by her gable window. She had been studying her lessons, but it had grown too dark to see the book, so she had fallen into wide-eyed reverie, looking out past the boughs of the Snow Queen, once more bestarred with its tufts of blossom.

In all essential respects the little gable chamber was unchanged. The walls were as white, the pincushion as hard, the chairs as stiffly and yellowly upright as ever. Yet the whole character of the room was altered. It was full of a new vital, pulsing personality that seemed to pervade it and to be quite independent of schoolgirl books and dresses and ribbons, and even of the cracked blue jug full of apple blossoms on the table. It was as if all the dreams, sleeping and waking, of its vivid occupant had taken a visible although immaterial form and had tapestried the bare room with splendid filmy tissues of rainbow and moonshine. Presently Marilla came briskly in with some of Anne's freshly ironed school aprons. She hung them over a chair and sat down with a short sigh. She had had one of her headaches that afternoon, and although the pain had gone she felt weak and "tuckered out," as she expressed it. Anne looked at her with eyes limpid with sympathy.

"I do truly wish I could have had the headache in your place, Marilla. I would have endured it joyfully for your sake."

"I guess you did your part in attending to the work and letting me rest," said Marilla. "You seem to have got on fairly well and made fewer mistakes than usual. Of course it wasn't exactly necessary to starch Matthew's handkerchiefs! And most people when they put a pie in the oven to warm up for dinner take it out and eat it when it gets hot instead of leaving it to be burned to a crisp. But that doesn't seem to be your way evidently."

Headaches always left Marilla somewhat sarcastic.

"Oh, I'm so sorry," said Anne penitently. "I never thought about that pie from the moment I put it in the oven till now, although I felt *instinctively* that there was something missing on the dinner table. I was firmly resolved, when you left me in charge this morning, not to imagine anything, but keep my thoughts on facts. I did pretty well until I put the pie in, and then an irresistible temptation came to me to imagine I was an enchanted princess shut up in a lonely tower with a handsome knight riding to my rescue on a coal-black steed. So that is how I came to forget the pie. I didn't know I starched the handkerchiefs. All the time I was ironing I was trying to think of a name for a new island Diana and I have discovered up the brook. It's the most ravishing spot, Marilla. There are two maple-trees on it and the brook flows right around it. At last it struck me that it would be splendid to call it Victoria Island because we found it on the Queen's birthday.[1] Both Diana and I are very loyal. But I'm very sorry about that pie and the handkerchiefs. I wanted to be extra good to-day because it's an anniversary. Do you remember what happened this day last year, Marilla?"

"No, I can't think of anything special."

"Oh, Marilla, it was the day I came to Green Gables. I shall never forget it. It was the turning-point in my life. Of course it wouldn't seem so important to you. I've been here for a year and I've been so happy. Of course, I've had my troubles, but one can live down troubles. Are you sorry you kept me, Marilla?"

"No, I can't say I'm sorry," said Marilla, who sometimes wondered how she could have lived before Anne came to Green Gables, "no, not exactly sorry. If you've finished your lessons, Anne, I want you to run over and ask Mrs. Barry if she'll lend me Diana's apron pattern."

"Oh—it's—it's too dark," cried Anne.

"Too dark? Why, it's only twilight. And goodness knows you've gone over often enough after dark."

"I'll go over early in the morning," said Anne eagerly. "I'll get up at sunrise and go over, Marilla."

"What has got into your head now, Anne Shirley? I want that pattern to cut out your new apron this evening. Go at once and be smart, too."

"I'll have to go around by the road, then," said Anne, taking up her hat reluctantly.

"Go by the road and waste half an hour! I'd like to catch you!"

"I can't go through the Haunted Wood, Marilla," cried Anne desperately.

---

[1] Established as a holiday in Canada West in 1845, and as a national holiday in 1901, to be observed on the 24th of May; also known as Victoria Day.

Marilla stared.

"The Haunted Wood! Are you crazy? What under the canopy is the Haunted Wood?"

"The spruce wood over the brook," said Anne in a whisper.

"Fiddlesticks! There is no such thing as a haunted wood anywhere. Who has been telling you such stuff?"

"Nobody," confessed Anne. "Diana and I just imagined the wood was haunted. All the places around here are so—so—*commonplace*. We just got this up for our own amusement. We began it in April. A haunted wood is so very romantic, Marilla. We chose the spruce grove because it's so gloomy. Oh, we have imagined the most harrowing things. There's a white lady walks along the brook just about this time of the night and wrings her hands and utters wailing cries. She appears when there is to be a death in the family. And the ghost of a little murdered child haunts the corner up by Idlewild; it creeps up behind you and lays its cold fingers on your hand—so. Oh, Marilla, it gives me a shudder to think of it. And there's a headless man stalks up and down the path and skeletons glower at you between the boughs. Oh, Marilla, I wouldn't go through the Haunted Wood after dark now for anything. I'd be sure that white things would reach out from behind the trees and grab me."

"Did ever anyone hear the like!" ejaculated Marilla, who had listened in dumb amazement. "Anne Shirley, do you mean to tell me you believe all that wicked nonsense of your own imagination?"

"Not believe *exactly*," faltered Anne. "At least, I don't believe it in daylight. But after dark, Marilla, it's different. That is when ghosts walk."

"There are no such things as ghosts, Anne."

"Oh, but there are, Marilla," cried Anne eagerly. "I know people who have seen them. And they are respectable people. Charlie Sloane says that his grandmother saw his grandfather driving home the cows one night after he'd been buried for a year. You know Charlie Sloane's grandmother wouldn't tell a story for anything. She's a very religious woman. And Mrs. Thomas' father was pursued home one night by a lamb of fire with its head cut off hanging by a strip of skin. He said he knew it was the spirit of his brother and that it was a warning he would die within nine days. He didn't, but he died two years after, so you see it was really true. And Ruby Gillis says—"

"Anne Shirley," interrupted Marilla firmly, "I never want to hear you talking in this fashion again. I've had my doubts about that imagination of yours right along, and if this is going to be the outcome of it, I won't countenance any such doings. You'll go right over to Barry's, and you'll go through that spruce grove, just for a lesson and a warning to you. And never let me hear a word out of your head about haunted woods again."

Anne might plead and cry as she liked—and did, for her terror was very real. Her imagination had run away with her and she held the spruce grove in mortal dread after nightfall. But Marilla was inexorable. She marched the shrinking ghostseer down to the spring and ordered her to proceed straightway over the bridge and into the dusky retreats of wailing ladies and headless spectres beyond.

"Oh, Marilla, how can you be so cruel?" sobbed Anne. "What would you feel like if a white thing did snatch me up and carry me off?"

"I'll risk it," said Marilla unfeelingly. "You know I always mean what I say. I'll cure you of imagining ghosts into places. March, now."

Anne marched. That is, she stumbled over the bridge and went shuddering up the horrible dim path beyond. Anne never forgot that walk. Bitterly did she repent the license she had given to her imagination. The goblins of her fancy lurked in every shadow about her, reaching out their cold, fleshless hands to grasp the terrified small girl who had called them into being. A white strip of birch bark blowing up from the hollow over the brown floor of the grove made her heart stand still. The long-drawn wail of two old boughs rubbing against each other brought out the perspiration in beads on her forehead. The swoop of bats in the darkness over her was as the wings of unearthly creatures. When she reached Mr. William Bell's field she fled across it as if pursued by an army of white things, and arrived at the Barry kitchen door so out of breath that she could hardly gasp out her request for the apron pattern. Diana was away so that she had no excuse to linger. The dreadful return journey had to be faced.

Anne went back over it with shut eyes, preferring to take the risk of dashing her brains out among the boughs to that of seeing a white thing. When she finally stumbled over the log bridge she drew one long shivering breath of relief.

"Well, so nothing caught you?" said Marilla unsympathetically.

"Oh, Mar—Marilla," chattered Anne, "I'll b-b-be cont-t-tented with c-c-commonplace places after this."

CHAPTER XXI

A NEW DEPARTURE IN FLAVOURINGS[1]

"DEAR me, there is nothing but meetings and partings in this world, as Mrs. Lynde says," remarked Anne plaintively, putting her slate and books down on the kitchen table on the last day of June and wiping her red eyes with a very damp handkerchief. "Wasn't it fortunate, Marilla, that I took an extra handkerchief to school to-day? I had a presentiment that it would be needed."

"I never thought you were so fond of Mr. Phillips that you'd require two handkerchiefs to dry your tears just because he was going away," said Marilla.

"I don't think I was crying because I was really so very fond of him," reflected Anne. "I just cried because all the others did. It was Ruby Gillis started it. Ruby Gillis has always declared she hated Mr. Phillips, but just as soon as he got up to make his farewell speech she burst into tears. Then all the girls began to cry, one after the other. I tried to hold out, Marilla. I tried to remember the time Mr. Phillips made me sit with Gil—with a boy; and the time he spelled my name without an *e* on the black-board; and how he said I was the worst dunce he ever saw at geometry and laughed at my spelling; and all the times he had been so horrid and sarcastic; but somehow I couldn't, Marilla, and I just had to cry too. Jane Andrews has been talking for a month

---

[1] See Appendix A. Mongomery produced at least one version of this chapter as a story prior to the publication of *AGG*.

about how glad she'd be when Mr. Phillips went away and she declared she'd never shed a tear. Well, she was worse than any of us and had to borrow a handkerchief from her brother—of course the boys didn't cry—because she hadn't brought one of her own, not expecting to need it. Oh, Marilla, it was heartrending. Mr. Phillips made such a beautiful farewell speech beginning, 'The time has come for us to part.' It was very affecting. And he had tears in his eyes too, Marilla. Oh, I felt dreadfully sorry and remorseful for all the times I'd talked in school and drawn pictures of him on my slate and made fun of him and Prissy. I can tell you I wished I'd been a model pupil like Minnie Andrews. *She* hadn't anything on her conscience. The girls cried all the way home from school. Carrie Sloane kept saying every few minutes, 'The time has come for us to part,' and that would start us off again whenever we were in any danger of cheering up. I do feel dreadfully sad, Marilla. But one can't feel quite in the depths of despair with two months vacation before them, can they, Marilla? And besides, we met the new minister and his wife coming from the station. For all I was feeling so bad about Mr. Phillips going away I couldn't help taking a little interest in a new minister, could I? His wife is very pretty. Not exactly regally lovely, of course—it wouldn't do, I suppose, for a minister to have a regally lovely wife, because it might set a bad example. Mrs. Lynde says the minister's wife over at Newbridge sets a very bad example because she dresses so fashionably. Our new minister's wife was dressed in blue muslin with lovely puffed sleeves and a hat trimmed with roses. Jane Andrews said she thought puffed sleeves were too worldly for a minster's wife, but I didn't make any such uncharitable remark, Marilla, because I know what it is to long for puffed sleeves. Besides, she's only been a minister's wife for a little while, so one should make allowances, shouldn't they? They are going to board with Mrs. Lynde until the manse is ready."

If Marilla, in going down to Mrs. Lynde's that evening, was actuated by any motive save her avowed one of returning the quilting-frames she had borrowed the preceding winter, it was an amiable weakness[1] shared by most of the Avonlea people.

---

[1]   Cf. Henry Fielding (1707–54), *The History of Tom Jones, A Foundling* (1749) Bk. 10, Ch. 8.

Many a thing Mrs. Lynde had lent, sometimes never expecting to see it again, came home that night in charge of the borrowers thereof. A new minister, and moreover a minister with a wife, was a lawful object of curiosity in a quiet little country settlement where sensations were few and far between.

Old Mr. Bentley, the minister whom Anne had found lacking in imagination, had been pastor of Avonlea for eighteen years. He was a widower when he came, and a widower he remained, despite the fact that gossip regularly married him to this, that or the other one, every year of his sojourn. In the preceding February he had resigned his charge and departed amid the regrets of his people, most of whom had the affection born of long intercourse for their good old minister in spite of his shortcomings as an orator. Since then the Avonlea church had enjoyed a variety of religious dissipation in listening to the many and various candidates and "supplies" who came Sunday after Sunday to preach on trial. These stood or fell by the judgment of the fathers and mothers in Israel;[1] but a certain small, red-haired girl who sat meekly in the corner of the old Cuthbert pew also had her opinions about them and discussed the same in full with Matthew, Marilla always declining from principle to criticize ministers in any shape or form.

"I don't think Mr. Smith would have done, Matthew," was Anne's final summing up. "Mrs. Lynde says his delivery was so poor, but I think his worst fault was just like Mr. Bentley's—he had no imagination. And Mr. Terry had too much; he let it run away with him just as I did mine in the matter of the Haunted Wood. Besides, Mrs. Lynde says his theology wasn't sound. Mr. Gresham was a very good man and a very religious man, but he told too many funny stories and made the people laugh in church; he was undignified, and you must have some dignity about a minister, mustn't you, Matthew? I thought Mr. Marshall was decidedly attractive; but Mrs. Lynde says he isn't married, or even engaged, because she made special inquiries about him, and she says it would never do to have a young unmarried minister in Avonlea, because he might marry in the congregation and that

---

[1] Cf. 2 Samuel 20.19 and Judges 5.7.

would make trouble. Mrs. Lynde is a very far-seeing woman, isn't she, Matthew? I'm very glad they've called Mr. Allan. I liked him because his sermon was interesting and he prayed as if he meant it and not just as if he did it because he was in the habit of it. Mrs. Lynde says he isn't perfect, but she says she supposes we couldn't expect a perfect minister for seven hundred and fifty dollars a year, and anyhow his theology is sound because she questioned him thoroughly on all the points of doctrine. And she knows his wife's people and they are most respectable and the women are all good housekeepers. Mrs. Lynde says that sound doctrine in the man and good housekeeping in the woman make an ideal combination for a minister's family."

The new minister and his wife were a young, pleasant-faced couple, still in their honeymoon, and full of all good and beautiful enthusiasms for their chosen life-work. Avonlea opened its heart to them from the start. Old and young liked the frank, cheerful young man with his high ideals, and the bright, gentle little lady who assumed the mistress-ship of the manse. With Mrs. Allan Anne fell promptly and whole-heartedly in love. She had discovered another kindred spirit.

"Mrs. Allan is perfectly lovely," she announced one Sunday afternoon. "She's taken our class and she's a splendid teacher. She said right away she didn't think it was fair for the teacher to ask all the questions, and you know, Marilla, that is exactly what I've always thought. She said we could ask her any question we liked, and I asked ever so many. I'm good at asking questions, Marilla."

"I believe you," was Marilla's emphatic comment.

"Nobody else asked any except Ruby Gillis, and she asked if there was to be a Sunday-school picnic this summer. I didn't think that was a very proper question to ask because it hadn't any connection with the lesson—the lesson was about Daniel in the lions' den[1]—but Mrs. Allan just smiled and said she thought there would be. Mrs. Allan has a lovely smile; she has such *exquisite* dimples in her cheeks. I wish I had dimples in my cheeks, Marilla. I'm not half so skinny as I was when I came here, but I have no dimples yet. If I had perhaps I could influence people for good.

---

[1] See Daniel 6.16–23. See also 63, note 1.

Mrs. Allan said we ought always to try to influence other people for good. She talked so nice about everything. I never knew before that religion was such a cheerful thing. I always thought it was kind of melancholy, but Mrs. Allan's isn't, and I'd like to be a Christian if I could be one like her. I wouldn't want to be one like Mr. Superintendent Bell."

"It's very naughty of you to speak so about Mr. Bell," said Marilla severely. "Mr. Bell is a real good man."

"Oh, of course he's good," agreed Anne, "but he doesn't seem to get any comfort out of it. If I could be good I'd dance and sing all day because I was glad of it. I suppose Mrs. Allan is too old to dance and sing and of course it wouldn't be dignified in a minister's wife. But I can just feel she's glad she's a Christian and that she'd be one even if she could get to heaven without it."

"I suppose we must have Mr. and Mrs. Allan up to tea some day soon," said Marilla reflectively. "They've been most everywhere but here. Let me see. Next Wednesday would be a good time to have them. But don't say a word to Matthew about it, for if he knew they were coming he'd find some excuse to be away that day. He'd got so used to Mr. Bentley he didn't mind him, but he's going to find it hard to get acquainted with a new minister, and a new minister's wife will frighten him to death."

"I'll be as secret as the dead," assured Anne. "But oh, Marilla, will you let me make a cake for the occasion? I'd love to do something for Mrs. Allan, and you know I can make a pretty good cake by this time."

"You can make a layer cake," promised Marilla.

Monday and Tuesday great preparations went on at Green Gables. Having the minister and his wife to tea was a serious and important undertaking, and Marilla was determined not to be eclipsed by any of the Avonlea housekeepers. Anne was wild with excitement and delight. She talked it all over with Diana Tuesday night in the twilight, as they sat on the big red stones by the Dryad's Bubble and made rainbows in the water with little twigs dipped in fir balsam.

"Everything is ready, Diana, except my cake which I'm to make in the morning, and the baking-powder biscuits which Marilla will make just before tea-time. I assure you, Diana, that Marilla and

I have had a busy two days of it. It's such a responsibility having a minister's family to tea. I never went through such an experience before. You should just see our pantry. It's a sight to behold. We're going to have jellied chicken and cold tongue. We're to have two kinds of jelly, red and yellow, and whipped cream and lemon pie, and cherry pie, and three kinds of cookies, and fruit-cake, and Marilla's famous yellow plum preserves that she keeps especially for ministers, and pound cake and layer cake, and biscuits as aforesaid; and new bread and old both, in case the minister is dyspeptic[1] and can't eat new. Mrs. Lynde says ministers mostly are dyspeptic, but I don't think Mr. Allan has been a minister long enough for it to have had a bad effect on him. I just grow cold when I think of my layer cake. Oh, Diana, what if it should-n't be good! I dreamed last night that I was chased all around by a fearful goblin with a big layer cake for a head."

"It'll be good, all right," assured Diana, who was a very comfortable sort of friend. "I'm sure that piece of the one you made that we had for lunch in Idlewild two weeks ago was perfectly elegant."

"Yes; but cakes have such a terrible habit of turning out bad just when you especially want them to be good," sighed Anne, setting a particularly well-balsamed twig afloat. "However, I suppose I shall just have to trust to Providence and be careful to put in the flour. Oh, look, Diana, what a lovely rainbow! Do you suppose the dryad will come out after we go away and take it for a scarf?"[2]

"You know there is no such thing as a dryad," said Diana. Diana's mother had found out about the Haunted Wood and had been decidedly angry over it. As a result Diana had abstained from any further imitative flights of imagination and did not think it prudent to cultivate a spirit of belief even in harmless dryads.

"But it's so easy to imagine there is," said Anne. "Every night, before I go to bed, I look out of my window and wonder if the

---

[1] Subject to indigestion.
[2] Cf. Charlotte Brontë, *Jane Eyre* (1847): "How would a white or a pink cloud answer for a gown, do you think? And one could cut a pretty enough scarf out of a rain-bow" (1999 353). This echo of Brontë's text is not different from the other many allu-sions Mongomery makes to canonical English and American texts of the period, but it does reinforce the idea of a connection between Anne and Jane, already indicated in note regarding the school humiliation scenes (156, note 2).

dryad is really sitting here, combing her locks with the spring for a mirror. Sometimes I look for her footprints in the dew in the morning. Oh, Diana, don't give up your faith in the dryad!"

Wednesday morning came. Anne got up at sunrise because she was too excited to sleep. She had caught a severe cold in the head by reason of her dabbling in the spring on the preceding evening; but nothing short of absolute pneumonia could have quenched her interest in culinary matters that morning. After breakfast she proceeded to make her cake. When she finally shut the oven door upon it she drew a long breath.

"I'm sure I haven't forgotten anything this time, Marilla. But do you think it will rise? Just suppose perhaps the baking-powder isn't good? I used it out of the new can. And Mrs. Lynde says you can never be sure of getting good baking-powder nowadays when everything is so adulterated.[1] Mrs. Lynde says the Government ought to take the matter up, but she says we'll never see the day when a Tory[2] Government will do it. Marilla, what if that cake doesn't rise?"

"We'll have plenty without it," was Marilla's unimpassioned way of looking at the subject.

The cake did rise, however, and came out of the oven as light and feathery as golden foam. Anne, flushed with delight, clapped it together with layers of ruby jelly and, in imagination, saw Mrs. Allan eating it and possibly asking for another piece!

---

[1] Loraine Swainston Goodwin suggests in *The Pure Food, Drink, and Drug Crusaders, 1879–1914* (Jefferson, NC: McFarland, 1999) that adulteration of many foods was common. She notes that crusaders of the period focused on "incidental adulteration" which "occurred when zinc, copper, and other metals leached from containers in which foods were stored, or when pathogens contaminated food during careless food preparation or handling" (50); as well as on "intentional adulteration" which occurred when processors used other foods as fillers. She points out that

    Samples of flour contained ground rice, plaster of paris, grit, and sand. In addition to being made with adulterated flour, bread contained copper sulfate as a preservative and ashes from cooking ovens. Butter contained copper, excess water and salt, lard, vegetable fats, and curd. Cheese contained mercury salts. Lard contained caustic lime, alum, starch, cottonseed oil, and water. Canned foods were adulterated with copper, tin, chemical preservatives, and excess water. (42–43)

    On the question of baking powders, Goodwin also observes that most of the available products "left a residue that hygienists and physicians considered harmful" (50).

[2] Conservative.

"You'll be using the best tea-set, of course, Marilla," she said. "Can I fix up the table with ferns and wild roses?"

"I think that's all nonsense," sniffed Marilla. "In my opinion it's the eatables that matter and not flummery[1] decorations."

"Mrs. Barry had *her* table decorated," said Anne, who was not entirely guiltless of the wisdom of the serpent,[2] "and the minister paid her an elegant compliment. He said it was a feast for the eye as well as the palate."

"Well, do as you like," said Marilla, who was quite determined not to be surpassed by Mrs. Barry or anybody else. "Only mind you leave enough room for the dishes and the food."

Anne laid herself out to decorate in a manner and after a fashion that should leave Mrs. Barry's nowhere. Having abundance of roses and ferns and a very artistic taste of her own, she made that tea-table such a thing of beauty that when the minister and his wife sat down to it they exclaimed in chorus over its loveliness.

"It's Anne's doings," said Marilla, grimly just; and Anne felt that Mrs. Allan's approving smile was almost too much happiness for this world.

Matthew was there, having been inveigled into the party only goodness and Anne knew how. He had been in such a state of shyness and nervousness that Marilla had given him up in despair, but Anne took him in hand so successfully that he now sat at the table in his best clothes and white collar and talked to the minister not uninterestingly. He never said a word to Mrs. Allan, but that perhaps was not to be expected.

All went merry as a marriage bell[3] until Anne's layer cake was passed. Mrs. Allan, having already been helped to a bewildering variety, declined it. But Marilla, seeing the disappointment on Anne's face, said smilingly:

"Oh, you must take a piece of this, Mrs. Allan. Anne made it on purpose for you."

"In that case I must sample it," laughed Mrs. Allan, helping herself to a plump triangle, as did also the minister and Marilla.

---

1 Usually, flattery, polite nonsense. Marilla is implying unnecessary adornment.
2 Cf. Matthew 10.16.
3 See Byron, *Childe Harold's Pilgrimage*, 3.21.8–9. See 177, note 1.

Mrs. Allan took a mouthful of hers and a most peculiar expression crossed her face; not a word did she say, however, but steadily ate away at it. Marilla saw the expression and hastened to taste the cake.

"Anne Shirley!" she exclaimed, "what on earth did you put into that cake?"

"Nothing but what the recipe said, Marilla," cried Anne with a look of anguish. "Oh, isn't it all right?"

"All right! It's simply horrible. Mrs. Allan, don't try to eat it. Anne, taste it yourself. What flavouring did you use?"

"Vanilla," said Anne, her face scarlet with mortification after tasting the cake. "Only vanilla. Oh, Marilla, it must have been the baking-powder. I had my suspicions of that bak—"

"Baking-powder fiddlesticks! Go and bring me the bottle of vanilla you used."

Anne fled to the pantry and returned with a small bottle partially filled with a brown liquid and labelled yellowly, "Best Vanilla."

Marilla took it, uncorked it, smelled it.

"Mercy on us, Anne, you've flavoured that cake with *anodyne liniment*.[1] I broke the liniment bottle last week and poured what was left into an old empty vanilla bottle. I suppose it's partly my fault—I should have warned you—but for pity's sake why couldn't you have smelled it?"

Anne dissolved into tears under this double disgrace.

"I couldn't—I had such a cold!" and with this she fairly fled to the gable chamber, where she cast herself on the bed and wept as one who refuses to be comforted.

Presently a light step sounded on the stairs and somebody entered the room.

"Oh, Marilla," sobbed Anne without looking up. "I'm disgraced for ever. I shall never be able to live this down. It will get out—things always do get out in Avonlea. Diana will ask me how my cake turned out and I shall have to tell her the truth. I shall always be pointed at as the girl who flavoured a cake with anodyne liniment. Gil—the boys in school will never get over laughing at it. Oh, Marilla, if you have a spark of Christian pity

---

[1]   A topical medication to alleviate pain.

don't tell me that I must go down and wash the dishes after this. I'll wash them when the minister and his wife are gone, but I cannot ever look Mrs. Allan in the face again. Perhaps she'll think I tried to poison her. Mrs. Lynde says she knows an orphan girl who tried to poison her benefactor. But the liniment isn't poisonous. It's meant to be taken internally—although not in cakes. Won't you tell Mrs. Allan so, Marilla?"

"Suppose you jump up and tell her so yourself," said a merry voice.

Anne flew up, to find Mrs. Allan standing by her bed, surveying her with laughing eyes.

"My dear little girl, you mustn't cry like this," she said, genuinely disturbed by Anne's tragic face. "Why, it's all just a funny mistake that anybody might make."

"Oh, no, it takes me to make such a mistake," said Anne forlornly. "And I wanted to have that cake so nice for you, Mrs. Allan."

"Yes, I know, dear. And I assure you I appreciate your kindness and thoughtfulness just as much as if it had turned out all right. Now, you mustn't cry any more, but come down with me and show me your flower garden. Miss Cuthbert tells me you have a little flower plot all your own. I want to see it, for I'm very much interested in flowers."

Anne permitted herself to be led down and comforted, reflecting that it was really providential that Mrs. Allan was a kindred spirit. Nothing more was said about the liniment cake, and when the guests went away Anne found that she had enjoyed the evening more than could have been expected, considering that terrible incident. Nevertheless she sighed deeply.

"Marilla, isn't it nice to think that to-morrow is a new day with no mistakes in it yet?"

"I'll warrant you'll make plenty in it," said Marilla. "I never saw your beat for making mistakes, Anne."

"Yes and well I know it," admitted Anne mournfully. "But have you ever noticed one encouraging thing about me, Marilla? I never make the same mistake twice."

"I don't know as that's much benefit when you're always making new ones."

"Oh, don't you see, Marilla? There *must* be a limit to the

mistakes one person can make, and when I get to the end of them, then I'll be through with them. That's a very comforting thought."

"Well, you'd better go and give that cake to the pigs," said Marilla. "It isn't fit for any human to eat, not even Jerry Buote."

CHAPTER XXII

ANNE IS INVITED OUT TO TEA

"AND what are your eyes popping out of your head about now?" asked Marilla, when Anne had just come in from a run to the post-office. "Have you discovered another kindred spirit?"

Excitement hung around Anne like a garment, shone in her eyes, kindled in every feature. She had come dancing up the lane, like a wind-blown sprite, through the mellow sunshine and lazy shadows of the August evening.

"No, Marilla, but oh, what do you think? I am invited to tea at the manse to morrow afternoon! Mr. Allan left the letter for me at the post-office. Just look at it, Marilla. 'Miss Anne Shirley, Green Gables.' That is the first time I was ever called 'Miss.' Such a thrill as it gave me! I shall cherish it for ever among my choicest treasures."

"Mrs. Allan told me she meant to have all the members of her Sunday-school class to tea in turn," said Marilla, regarding the wonderful event very coolly. "You needn't get in such a fever over it. Do learn to take things calmly, child."

For Anne to take things calmly would have been to change her nature. All "spirit and fire and dew,"[1] as she was, the pleasures and pains of life came to her with trebled intensity. Marilla felt this and was vaguely troubled over it, realizing that the ups and downs of existence would probably bear hardly on this impulsive soul and not sufficiently understanding that the equally great capacity for delight might more than compensate. Therefore Marilla conceived it to be her duty to drill Anne into

---

[1] Cf. epigraph. See Robert Browning, "Evelyn Hope" (1855), line 20.

a tranquil uniformity of disposition as impossible and alien to her as to a dancing sunbeam in one of the brook shallows. She did not make much headway, as she sorrowfully admitted to herself. The downfall of some dear hope or plan plunged Anne into "deeps of affliction." The fulfilment thereof exalted her to dizzy realms of delight. Marilla had almost begun to despair of ever fashioning this waif of the world into her model little girl of demure manners and prim deportment. Neither would she have believed that she really liked Anne much better as she was.

Anne went to bed that night speechless with misery because Matthew had said the wind was round northeast and he feared it would be a rainy day to-morrow. The rustle of the poplar leaves about the house worried her, it sounded so like pattering rain-drops, and the dull, faraway roar of the gulf, to which she listened delightedly at other times, loving its strange, sonorous, haunting rhythm, now seemed like a prophecy of storm and disaster to a small maiden who particularly wanted a fine day. Anne thought that the morning would never come.

But all things have an end, even nights before the day on which you are invited to take tea at the manse. The morning, in spite of Matthew's predictions, was fine, and Anne's spirits soared to their highest.

"Oh, Marilla, there is something in me to-day that makes me just love everybody I see," she exclaimed as she washed the breakfast dishes. "You don't know how good I feel! Wouldn't it be nice if it could last? I believe I could be a model child if I were just invited out to tea every day. But oh, Marilla, it's a solemn occasion, too. I feel so anxious. What if I shouldn't behave properly? You know I never had tea at a manse before, and I'm not sure that I know all the rules of etiquette, although I've been studying the rules given in the Etiquette Department of the *Family Herald*[1] ever since I came here. I'm so afraid I'll do something silly or forget to do something I should do. Would it be good manners to take a second helping of anything if you wanted to *very* much?"

---

[1] "Canada's National Farm Magazine," published in Canada with varying titles from 1869–September 1968, and in an early version from 1859–60. After 1873, it appears as *Family Herald and Weekly Star.* Montgomery published some early stories in this magazine; see Russell/Wilmshurst especially pages 67–68.

"The trouble with you, Anne, is that you're thinking too much about yourself. You should just think of Mrs. Allan and what would be nicest and most agreeable for her," said Marilla, hitting for once in her life on a very sound and pithy piece of advice. Anne instantly realized this.

"You are right, Marilla. I'll try not to think about myself at all."

Anne evidently got through her visit without any serious breach of "etiquette" for she came home through the twilight, under a great, high-sprung sky gloried over with trails of saffron and rosy cloud, in a beatified state of mind and told Marilla all about it happily, sitting on the big red sandstone slab at the kitchen door with her tired curly head in Marilla's gingham lap.

A cool wind was blowing down over the long harvest fields from the rims of firry western hills and whistling through the poplars. One clear star hung above the orchard and the fireflies were flitting over in Lovers' Lane, in and out among the ferns and rustling boughs. Anne watched them as she talked and somehow felt that wind and stars and fireflies were all tangled up together into something unutterably sweet and enchanting.

"Oh, Marilla, I've had a most *fascinating* time. I feel that I have not lived in vain and I shall always feel like that even if I should never be invited to tea at a manse again. When I got there Mrs. Allan met me at the door. She was dressed in the sweetest dress of pale pink organdy,[1] with dozens of frills and elbow sleeves, and she looked just like a seraph.[2] I really think I'd like to be a minister's wife when I grow up, Marilla. A minister mightn't mind my red hair because he wouldn't be thinking of such worldly things. But then of course one would have to be naturally good and I'll never be that, so I suppose there's no use in thinking about it. Some people are naturally good, you know, and others are not. I'm one of the others. Mrs. Lynde says I'm full of original sin.[3] No matter how hard I try to be good I can never make such a

---

[1] "A fine cotton fabric, sheer and very lightweight. [...] It has a characteristic stiff, crisp, and clear finish" (*Fairchild's Dictionary of Textiles*).

[2] Here, an angel.

[3] In Christian theology, "[t]he corruption which is born with us, and is the inheritance of all the offspring of Adam. Theology teaches that as Adam was founder of his race, when Adam fell the taint and penalty of his disobedience passes to all posterity" (*Brewer's*).

success of it as those who are naturally good. It's a good deal like geometry, I expect. But don't you think the trying so hard ought to count for something? Mrs. Allan is one of the naturally good people. I love her passionately. You know there are some people, like Matthew and Mrs. Allan, that you can love right off without any trouble. And there are others, like Mrs. Lynde, that you have to try very hard to love. You know you *ought* to love them because they know so much and are such active workers in the church, but you have to keep reminding yourself of it all the time or else you forget. There was another little girl at the manse to tea, from the White Sands Sunday-school. Her name was Lauretta Bradley, and she was a very nice little girl. Not exactly a kindred spirit, you know, but still very nice. We had an elegant tea, and I think I kept all the rules of etiquette pretty well. After tea Mrs. Allan played and sang and she got Lauretta and me to sing, too. Mrs. Allan says I have a good voice and she says I must sing in the Sunday-school choir after this. You can't think how I was thrilled at the mere thought. I've longed so to sing in the Sunday-school choir, as Diana does, but I feared it was an honour I could never aspire to. Lauretta had to go home early because there is a big concert in the White Sands hotel to-night and her sister is to recite at it. Lauretta says that the Americans at the hotel give a concert every fortnight in aid of the Charlottetown hospital, and they ask lots of the White Sands people to recite. Lauretta said she expected to be asked herself some day. I just gazed at her in awe. After she had gone Mrs. Allan and I had a heart to heart talk. I told her everything—about Mrs. Thomas and the twins and Katie Maurice and Violetta and coming to Green Gables and my troubles over geometry. And would you believe it, Marilla? Mrs. Allan told me she was a dunce at geometry, too. You don't know how that encouraged me. Mrs. Lynde came to the manse just before I left, and what do you think, Marilla? The trustees have hired a new teacher and it's a lady. Her name is Miss Muriel Stacy. Isn't that a romantic name? Mrs. Lynde says they've never had a female teacher in Avonlea before and she thinks it is a dangerous innovation. But I think it will be splendid to have a lady teacher, and I really don't see how I'm going to live through the two weeks before school begins, I'm so impatient to see her."

CHAPTER XXIII

ANNE COMES TO GRIEF IN AN
AFFAIR OF HONOUR

ANNE had to live through more than two weeks, as it happened. Almost a month having elapsed since the liniment cake episode, it was high time for her to get into fresh trouble of some sort, little mistakes, such as absent-mindedly emptying a pan of skim milk into a basket of yarn balls in the pantry instead of into the pigs' bucket, and walking clean over the edge of the log bridge into the brook while wrapped in imaginative reverie, not really being worth counting.

A week after the tea at the manse, Diana Barry gave a party.

"Small and select," Anne assured Marilla. "Just the girls in our class."

They had a very good time and nothing untoward happened until after tea, when they found themselves in the Barry garden, a little tired of all their games and ripe for any enticing form of mischief which might present itself. This presently took the form of "daring."

Daring was the fashionable amusement among the Avonlea small fry just then. It had begun among the boys, but soon spread to the girls, and all the silly things that were done in Avonlea that summer because the doers thereof were "dared" to do them would fill a book by themselves.

First of all Carrie Sloane dared Ruby Gillis to climb to a certain point in the huge old willow-tree before the front door; which Ruby Gillis, albeit in mortal dread of the fat green caterpillars with which said tree was infested and with the fear of her mother before her eyes if she should tear her new muslin dress, nimbly did, to the discomfiture of the aforesaid Carrie Sloane.

Then Josie Pye dared Jane Andrews to hop on her left leg around the garden without stopping once or putting her right foot to the ground; which Jane Andrews gamely tried to do, but gave out at the third corner and had to confess herself defeated.

Josie's triumph being rather more pronounced than good taste permitted, Anne Shirley dared her to walk along the top of the wood fence which bounded the garden to the east. Now, to "walk" board fences requires more skill and steadiness of head and heel than one might suppose who has never tried it. But Josie Pye, if deficient in some qualities that make for popularity, had at least a natural and inborn gift, duly cultivated, for walking board fences. Josie walked the Barry fence with an airy unconcern which seemed to imply that a little thing like that wasn't worth a "dare." Reluctant admiration greeted her exploit, for most of the other girls could appreciate it, having suffered many things themselves in their efforts to walk fences. Josie descended from her perch, flushed with victory, and darted a defiant glance at Anne.

Anne tossed her red braids.

"I don't think it's such a very wonderful thing to walk a little, low, board fence," she said. "I knew a girl in Marysville who could walk the ridge-pole[1] of a roof."

"I don't believe it," said Josie flatly. "I don't believe anybody could walk a ridge-pole. *You* couldn't, anyhow."

"Couldn't I?" cried Anne rashly.

"Then I dare you to do it," said Josie defiantly. "I dare you to climb up there and walk the ridge-pole of Mr. Barry's kitchen roof."

Anne turned pale, but there was clearly only one thing to be done. She walked towards the house, where a ladder was leaning against the kitchen roof. All the fifth-class girls said, "Oh!" partly in excitement, partly in dismay.

"Don't you do it, Anne," entreated Diana. "You'll fall off and be killed. Never mind Josie Pye. It isn't fair to dare anybody to do anything so dangerous."

"I must do it. My honour is at stake," said Anne solemnly. "I shall walk that ridge-pole, Diana, or perish in the attempt. If I am killed you are to have my pearl bead ring."

Anne climbed the ladder amid breathless silence, gained the ridge-pole, balanced herself uprightly on that precarious footing, and started to walk along it, dizzily conscious that she was uncomfortably high up in the world and that walking ridge-poles was not

---

[1] Point at which two slopes of a roof meet.

"BALANCED HERSELF UPRIGHTLY ON THAT PRECARIOUS
FOOTING."

a thing in which your imagination helped you out much. Nevertheless, she managed to take several steps before the catastrophe came. Then she swayed, lost her balance, stumbled, staggered and fell, sliding down over the sun-baked roof and crashing off it through the tangle of Virginia creeper beneath—all before the dismayed circle below could give a simultaneous, terrified shriek.

If Anne had tumbled off the roof on the side up which she ascended Diana would probably have fallen heir to the pearl bead ring then and there. Fortunately she fell on the other side, where the roof extended down over the porch so nearly to the ground that a fall therefrom was a much less serious thing. Nevertheless, when Diana and the other girls had rushed frantically around the house—except Ruby Gillis, who remained as if rooted to the ground and went into hysterics—they found Anne lying all white and limp among the wreck and ruin of the Virginia creeper.

"Anne, are you killed?" shrieked Diana, throwing herself on her knees beside her friend. "Oh, Anne, dear Anne, speak just one word to me and tell me if you're killed."

To the immense relief of all the girls, and especially of Josie Pye, who, in spite of lack of imagination, had been seized with horrible visions of a future branded as the girl who was the cause of Anne Shirley's early and tragic death, Anne sat dizzily up and answered uncertainly:

"No, Diana, I am not killed, but I think I am rendered unconscious."

"Where?" sobbed Carrie Sloane. "Oh, where, Anne?"

Before Anne could answer Mrs. Barry appeared on the scene. At sight of her Anne tried to scramble to her feet, but sank back again with a sharp little cry of pain.

"What's the matter? Where have you hurt yourself?" demanded Mrs. Barry.

"My ankle," gasped Anne. "Oh, Diana, please find your father and ask him to take me home. I know I can never walk there. And I'm sure I couldn't hop so far on one foot when Jane couldn't even hop around the garden."

Marilla was out in the orchard picking a panful of summer apples when she saw Mr. Barry coming over the log bridge and up the slope, with Mrs. Barry beside him and a whole procession of little girls trailing after him. In his arms he carried Anne, whose head lay limply against his shoulder.

At that moment Marilla had a revelation. In the sudden stab of fear that pierced to her very heart she realized what Anne had come to mean to her. She would have admitted that she liked Anne—nay, that she was very fond of Anne. But now she knew as she hurried wildly down the slope that Anne was dearer to her than anything on earth.

"Mr. Barry, what has happened to her?" she gasped, more white and shaken than the self-contained, sensible Marilla had been for many years. Anne herself answered, lifting her head.

"Don't be very frightened, Marilla. I was walking the ridge-pole and I fell off. I expect I have sprained my ankle. But, Marilla, I might have broken my neck. Let us look on the bright side of things."

"I might have known you'd go and do something of the sort when I let you go to that party," said Marilla, sharp and shrewish in her very relief. "Bring her in here, Mr. Barry, and lay her on the sofa. Mercy me, the child has gone and fainted!"

It was quite true. Overcome by the pain of her injury, Anne had one more of her wishes granted to her. She had fainted dead away.

Matthew, hastily summoned from the harvest field, was straightway despatched for the doctor, who in due time came, to discover that the injury was more serious than they had supposed. Anne's ankle was broken.

That night, when Marilla went up to the east gable, where a white-faced girl was lying, a plaintive voice greeted her from the bed.

"Aren't you very sorry for me, Marilla?"

"It was your own fault," said Marilla, twitching down the blind and lighting a lamp.

"And that is just why you should be sorry for me," said Anne, "because the thought that it *is* all my own fault is what makes it so hard. If I could blame it on anybody I would feel so much better. But what would you have done, Marilla, if you had been dared to walk a ridge-pole?"

"I'd have stayed on good firm ground and let them dare away. Such absurdity!" said Marilla.

Anne sighed.

"But you have such strength of mind, Marilla. I haven't. I just felt that I couldn't bear Josie Pye's scorn. She would have crowed over me all my life. And I think I have been punished so much that you needn't be very cross with me, Marilla. It's not a bit nice to faint, after all. And the doctor hurt me dreadfully when he was setting my ankle. I won't be able to go around for six or seven weeks and I'll miss the new lady teacher. She won't be new any more by the time I'm able to go to school. And Gil—everybody will get ahead of me in class. Oh, I am an afflicted mortal. But I'll try to bear it all bravely if only you won't be cross with me, Marilla."

"There, there, I'm not cross," said Marilla. "You're an unlucky child, there's no doubt about that; but, as you say, you'll have the suffering of it. Here now, try and eat some supper."

"Isn't it fortunate I've got such an imagination?" said Anne. "It will help me through splendidly, I expect. What do people who haven't any imagination do when they break their bones, do you suppose, Marilla?"

Anne had good reason to bless her imagination many a time and oft during the tedious seven weeks that followed. But she was not solely dependent on it. She had many visitors and not a day passed without one or more of the schoolgirls dropping in to bring her flowers and books and tell her all the happenings in the juvenile world of Avonlea.

"Everybody has been so good and kind, Marilla," sighed Anne happily, on the day when she could first limp across the floor. "It isn't very pleasant to be laid up; but there *is* a bright side to it, Marilla. You find out how many friends you have. Why, even Superintendent Bell came to see me, and he's really a very fine man. Not a kindred spirit, of course; but still I like him and I'm awfully sorry I ever criticized his prayers. I believe now he really does mean them, only he has got into the habit of saying them as if he didn't. He could get over that if he'd take a little trouble. I gave him a good broad hint. I told him how hard I tried to make my own little private prayers interesting. He told me all about the time he broke his ankle when he was a boy. It does seem strange to think of Superintendent Bell ever being a boy. Even my imagination has its limits for I can't imagine *that*. When I try to imagine him as a boy I see him with gray whiskers and spectacles, just as he looks in Sunday-school, only small. Now, it's so easy to imagine Mrs. Allan as a little girl. Mrs. Allan has been to see me fourteen times. Isn't that something to be proud of, Marilla? When a minister's wife has so many claims on her time! She is such a cheerful person to have visit you, too. She never tells you it's your own fault and she hopes you'll be a better girl on account of it. Mrs. Lynde always told me that when she came to see me; and she said it in a kind of way that made me feel she might hope I'd be a better girl, but didn't really believe I would. Even Josie Pye came to see me. I received her as politely as I could, because I think she was sorry she dared me to walk a ridge-pole. If I had been killed she would have had to carry a dark burden of remorse all her life. Diana has been a faithful friend. She's been over every day to cheer my lonely pillow. But oh, I shall be so glad when I can go to school for I've heard such exciting things about the new teacher. The girls all think she is perfectly sweet. Diana says she has the loveliest fair curly hair and such fascinating eyes. She dresses beautifully, and her sleeve puffs are bigger than anybody else's in Avonlea. Every other Friday afternoon she has recitations and everybody has to say a piece or take part in a dialogue. Oh, it's just glorious to think of it. Josie Pye says she hates it, but that is just because Josie has so little imagination. Diana and Ruby Gillis and Jane Andrews are preparing a dialogue, called 'A Morning Visit,'[1] for next Friday. And the Friday afternoons they don't have recitations Miss Stacy takes them all to the woods for a 'field' day and they study ferns and flowers and birds. And they have physical culture exercises[2] every morning and evening. Mrs.

---

[1] *AA* suggests the dialogue named here may be a poem by American writer Oliver Wendell Holmes (1809–94). See *AA* n.7, 257.

[2] The term used at the end of the nineteenth century and into the twentieth for physical education. Physical culture was introduced in schools on the principle that, as it is articulated in a manual issued under the auspices of the Minister of Education for Ontario in 1886, "Body and mind ought to be cultivated in harmony and neither of them at the expense of the other. The development of the body will assist the manifestations of the mind, and a good mental education will contribute to bodily health" (E.B. Houghton, *Physical Culture. First Book of Exercises, Drill, Calisthenics, and Gymnastics* [Toronto: Warwick, 1886] 2). Miss Stacy's introduction of physical culture can be understood in these terms, as well as in the moral terms outlined in this manual, which notes that "Hygiene and Physical Culture are concurrent subjects, and that one is incomplete without the other. In fact the pupils taking an active inter-

Lynde says she never heard of such goings-on and it all comes of having a lady teacher. But I think it must be splendid and I believe I shall find that Miss Stacy is a kindred spirit."

"There's one plain thing to be seen, Anne," said Marilla, "and that is that your fall off the Barry roof hasn't injured your tongue at all."

CHAPTER XXIV

MISS STACY AND HER PUPILS
GET UP A CONCERT

IT was October again when Anne was ready to go back to school—a glorious October, all red and gold, with mellow mornings when the valleys were filled with delicate mists as if the spirit of autumn had poured them in for the sun to drain—amethyst, pearl, silver, rose, and smoke-blue.[1] The dews were so heavy that the fields glistened like cloth of silver and there were such heaps of rustling leaves in the hollows of many-stemmed woods to run crisply through. The Birch Path was a canopy of yellow and the ferns were sere and brown all along it. There was a tang in the very air that inspired the hearts of small maidens tripping, unlike snails, swiftly and willingly to school;[2] and it *was* jolly to be back again at the little brown desk beside Diana, with Ruby Gillis nodding across the aisle and Carrie Sloane sending up notes and Julia Bell passing a "chew" of gum down from the back seat. Anne drew a long breath of happiness as she sharpened her pencil and

---

in physical culture will become alive to the importance of developing all the faculties of the body and mind to the highest standard" (3). Physical culture is perhaps best understood in the context of late nineteenth-century ideas of imperial "race" regeneration, and, for girls in particular, in relation to the ideas of improving the "mothers of the race" for the purposes of "better babies." (The 1886 manual stresses the importance of physical education for girls.) This same principle seems to inform Miss Stacy's careful instruction of the teen-age girls later in the novel.

[1]   Cf. John Keats, "Ode to Autumn" (1819).

[2]   See Shakespeare, *As You Like It* 2.7.145–47, from the well-known "All the world's a stage" speech (139–66). This speech was included in the *Sixth Royal Reader*, as "The Seven Ages of Man" (296–97).

arranged her picture cards in her desk. Life was certainly very interesting.

In the new teacher she found another true and helpful friend. Miss Stacy was a bright, sympathetic young woman with the happy gift of winning and holding the affections of her pupils and bringing out the best that was in them mentally and morally. Anne expanded like a flower under this wholesome influence and carried home to the admiring Matthew and the critical Marilla glowing accounts of school work and aims.

"I love Miss Stacy with my whole heart, Marilla. She is so ladylike and she has such a sweet voice. When she pronounces my name I feel *instinctively* that she's spelling it with an *e*. We had recitations this afternoon. I just wish you could have been there to hear me recite 'Mary, Queen of Scots.'[1] I just put my whole soul into it. Ruby Gillis told me coming home that the way I said the line, 'Now for my father's arm, she said, my woman's heart farewell,' just made her blood run cold."[2]

"Well now, you might recite it for me some of these days, out in the barn," suggested Matthew.

"Of course I will," said Anne meditatively, "but I won't be able to do it so well, I know. It won't be so exciting as it is when you have a whole schoolful before you hanging breathlessly on your words. I know I won't be able to make your blood run cold."

"Mrs. Lynde says it made *her* blood run cold to see the boys climbing to the very tops of those big trees on Bell's hill after crows' nests last Friday," said Marilla. "I wonder at Miss Stacy for encouraging it."

"But we wanted a crow's nest for nature study," explained Anne. "That was on our field afternoon. Field afternoons are splendid, Marilla. And Miss Stacy explains everything so beautifully. We have to write compositions on our field afternoons and I write the best ones."

"It's very vain of you to say so then. You'd better let your teacher say it."

---

[1] A poem by Scottish poet Henry Glassford Bell (1803–1874), included in the *Fifth Royal Reader* (31–35). See 141, note 1. Reproduced in *AA* (475–77).
[2] See "Mary, Queen of Scots" line 64.

"But she *did* say it, Marilla. And indeed I'm not vain about it. How can I be, when I'm such a dunce at geometry? Although I'm really beginning to see through it a little, too. Miss Stacy makes it so clear. Still, I'll never be good at it and I assure you it is a humbling reflection. But I love writing compositions. Mostly Miss Stacy lets us choose our own subjects; but next week we are to write a composition on some remarkable person. It's hard to choose among so many remarkable people who have lived. Mustn't it be splendid to be remarkable and have compositions written about you after you're dead? Oh, I would dearly love to be remarkable. I think when I grow up I'll be a trained nurse and go with the Red Crosses to the field of battle as a messenger of mercy. That is, if I don't go out as a foreign missionary. That would be very romantic, but one would have to be very good to be a missionary, and that would be a stumbling-block.[1] We have physical culture exercises every day, too. They make you graceful and promote digestion."

"Promote fiddlesticks!" said Marilla, who honestly thought it was all nonsense.

But all the field afternoons and recitation Fridays and physical culture contortions paled before a project which Miss Stacy brought forward in November. This was that the scholars of Avonlea school should get up a concert and hold it in the hall on Christmas night, for the laudable purpose of helping to pay for a schoolhouse flag.[2] The pupils one and all taking graciously to this plan, the preparations for a programme were begun at once. And of all the excited performers-elect none was so excited as Anne Shirley, who threw herself into the undertaking heart and soul, hampered as she was by Marilla's disapproval. Marilla thought it all rank foolishness.

"It's just filling your heads up with nonsense and taking time that ought to be put on your lessons," she grumbled. "I don't approve of children's getting up concerts and racing about to

---

[1]   "An obstacle to belief or understanding; something repugnant to one's prejudices" (*OED*).

[2]   Most likely a red ensign, imperial flag for Canada in each of the provinces and federally with provincial emblems; or possibly a Union Jack. The current Canadian flag with a red maple leaf between two bars on a white field was instituted in 1965.

practices. It makes them vain and forward and fond of gadding."

"But think of the worthy object," pleaded Anne. "A flag will cultivate a spirit of patriotism, Marilla."

"Fudge! There's precious little patriotism in the thoughts of any of you. All you want is a good time."

"Well, when you can combine patriotism and fun, isn't it all right? Of course it's real nice to be getting up a concert. We're going to have six choruses and Diana is to sing a solo. I'm in two dialogues—'The Society for the Suppression of Gossip'[1] and 'The Fairy Queen.'[2] The boys are going to have a dialogue, too. And I'm to have two recitations, Marilla. I just tremble when I think of it, but it's a nice thrilly kind of tremble. And we're to have a tableau at the last—'Faith, Hope and Charity.' Diana and Ruby and I are to be in it, all draped in white with flowing hair. I'm to be Hope, with my hands clasped—so—and my eyes uplifted. I'm going to practise my recitations in the garret. Don't be alarmed if you hear me groaning. I have to groan heartrendingly in one of them, and it's really hard to get up a good artistic groan, Marilla. Josie Pye is sulky because she didn't get the part she wanted in the dialogue. She wanted to be the fairy queen. That would have been ridiculous, for who ever heard of a fairy queen as fat as Josie? Fairy queens must be slender. Jane Andrews is to be the queen and I am to be one of her maids of honour. Josie says she thinks a red-haired fairy is just as ridiculous as a fat one, but I do not let myself mind what Josie says. I'm to have a wreath of white roses on my hair and Ruby Gillis is going to lend me her slippers because I haven't any of my own. It's necessary for fairies to have slippers, you know. You couldn't imagine a fairy wearing boots, could you? Especially with copper toes? We are going to decorate the hall with creeping spruce and fir mottoes with pink tissue-paper roses in them. And we are all to march in two by two after the audience is seated, while Emma White plays a march on the organ. Oh, Marilla, I know you are

---

[1] See T.S. Denison, *Friday Afternoon Series of Dialogues: A Collection of Original Dialogues Suitable for Boys and Girls in School Entertainments* (1879, 1970).

[2] Possibly, a poem by Bishop Thomas Percy (1729–1811). See *AA* (480). The T.S. Denison collection which contains "The Society for the Suppression of Gossip" also has a dialogue entitled "The May Queen" (44–46).

not so enthusiastic about it as I am, but don't you hope your little Anne will distinguish herself?"

"All I hope is that you'll behave yourself. I'll be heartily glad when all this fuss is over and you'll be able to settle down. You are simply good for nothing just now with your head stuffed full of dialogues and groans and tableaus. As for your tongue, it's a marvel it's not clean worn out."

Anne sighed and betook herself to the back yard, over which a young new moon was shining through the leafless poplar boughs from an apple-green western sky, and where Matthew was splitting wood. Anne perched herself on a block and talked the concert over with him, sure of an appreciative and sympathetic listener in this instance at least.

"Well now, I reckon it's going to be a pretty good concert. And I expect you'll do your part fine," he said, smiling down into her eager, vivacious little face. Anne smiled back at him. Those two were the best of friends and Matthew thanked his stars many a time and oft that he had nothing to do with bringing her up. That was Marilla's exclusive duty; if it had been his he would have been worried over frequent conflicts between inclination and said duty. As it was, he was free to "spoil Anne"—Marilla's phrasing—as much as he liked. But it was not such a bad arrangement after all; a little "appreciation" sometimes does quite as much good as all the conscientious "bringing up" in the world.

CHAPTER XXV

MATTHEW INSISTS ON PUFFED SLEEVES

MATTHEW was having a bad ten minutes of it. He had come into the kitchen, in the twilight of a cold, gray December evening, and had sat down in the wood-box corner to take off his heavy boots, unconscious of the fact that Anne and a bevy of her schoolmates were having a practice of "The Fairy Queen" in the sitting-room. Presently they came trooping through the hall and out into the kitchen, laughing and chattering gaily. They did not see Matthew, who shrank bashfully back into the shadows beyond the wood-box with a boot in one hand and a bootjack in the other, and he watched them shyly for the aforesaid ten minutes as they put on caps and jackets and talked about the dialogue and the concert. Anne stood among them, bright-eyed and animated as they; but Matthew suddenly became conscious that there was something about her different from her mates. And what worried Matthew was that the difference impressed him as being something that should not exist. Anne had a brighter face, and bigger, starrier eyes, and more delicate features than the others; even shy, unobservant Matthew had learned to take note of these things; but the difference that disturbed him did not consist in any of these respects. Then in what did it consist?

Matthew was haunted by this question long after the girls had gone, arm in arm, down the long, hard-frozen lane and Anne had betaken herself to her books. He could not refer it to Marilla, who, he felt, would be quite sure to sniff scornfully and remark that the only difference she saw between Anne and the other girls was that they sometimes kept their tongues quiet while Anne never did. This, Matthew felt, would be no great help.

He had recourse to his pipe that evening to help him study it out, much to Marilla's disgust. After two hours of smoking and hard reflection Matthew arrived at a solution of his problem. Anne was not dressed like the other little girls!

The more Matthew thought about the matter the more he was convinced that Anne never had been dressed like the other girls—never since she had come to Green Gables. Marilla kept her clothed in plain, dark dresses, all made after the same unvarying pattern. If Matthew knew there was such a thing as fashion in dress it is as much as he did; but he was quite sure that Anne's sleeves did not look at all like the sleeves the other girls wore. He recalled the cluster of little girls he had seen around her that evening—all gay in waists of red and blue and pink and white—and he wondered why Marilla always kept her so plainly and soberly gowned.

Of course, it must be all right. Marilla knew best and Marilla was bringing her up. Probably some wise, inscrutable motive was to be served thereby. But surely it would no harm to let the child have one pretty dress—something like Diana Barry always wore.

Matthew decided that he would give her one; that surely could not be objected to as an unwarranted putting in of his oar. Christmas was only a fortnight off. A nice new dress would be the very thing for a present. Matthew, with a sigh of satisfaction, put away his pipe and went to bed, while Marilla opened all the doors and aired the house.

The very next evening Matthew betook himself to Carmody to buy the dress, determined to get the worst over and have done with it. It would be, he felt assured, no trifling ordeal. There were some things Matthew could buy and prove himself no mean bargainer; but he knew he would be at the mercy of shopkeepers when it came to buying a girl's dress.

After much cogitation Matthew resolved to go to Samuel Lawson's store instead of William Blair's. To be sure, the Cuthberts had always gone to William Blair's; it was almost as much a matter of conscience with them as to attend the Presbyterian church and vote Conservative. But William Blair's two daughters frequently waited on customers there and Matthew held them in absolute dread. He could contrive to deal with them when he knew exactly what he wanted and could point it out; but in such a matter as this, requiring explanation and consultation, Matthew felt that he must be sure of a man behind the counter. So he would go to Lawson's, where Samuel or his son would wait on him.

Alas! Matthew did not know that Samuel, in the recent expansion of his business, had set up a lady clerk also; she was a niece of his wife's and a very dashing young person indeed, with a huge, drooping pompadour, big, rolling brown eyes, and a most extensive and bewildering smile. She was dressed with exceeding smartness and wore several bangle bracelets that glittered and rattled and tinkled with every movement of her hands. Matthew was covered with confusion at finding her there at all; and those bangles completely wrecked his wits at one fell swoop.

"What can I do for you this evening, Mr. Cuthbert?" Miss Lucilla Harris inquired, briskly and ingratiatingly, tapping the counter with both hands.

"Have you any—any—any—well now, say any garden rakes?" stammered Matthew.

Miss Harris looked somewhat surprised, as well she might, to hear a man inquiring for garden rakes in the middle of December.

"I believe we have one or two left over," she said, "but they're up-stairs in the lumber-room. I'll go and see."

During her absence Matthew collected his scattered senses for another effort.

When Miss Harris returned with the rake and cheerfully inquired: "Anything else to-night, Mr. Cuthbert?" Matthew took his courage in both hands and replied: "Well now, since you suggest it, I might as well—take—that is—look at—buy some—some hayseed."

Miss Harris had heard Matthew Cuthbert called odd. She now concluded that he was entirely crazy.

"We only keep hayseed in the spring," she explained loftily. "We've none on hand just now."

"Oh, certainly—certainly—just as you say," stammered unhappy Matthew, seizing the rake and making for the door. At the threshold he recollected that he had not paid for it and he turned miserably back. While Miss Harris was counting out his change he rallied his powers for a final desperate attempt.

"Well now—if it isn't too much trouble—I might as well— that is—I'd like to look at—at—some sugar."

"White or brown?" queried Miss Harris patiently.

"Oh—well now—brown," said Matthew feebly.

"There's a barrel of it over there," said Miss Harris, shaking her bangles at it. "It's the only kind we have."

"I'll—I'll take twenty pounds of it," said Matthew, with beads of perspiration standing on his forehead.

Matthew had driven half-way home before he was his own man again. It had been a gruesome experience, but it served him right, he thought, for committing the heresy of going to a strange store. When he reached home he hid the rake in the tool-house, but the sugar he carried in to Marilla.

"Brown sugar!" exclaimed Marilla. "Whatever possessed you to get so much? You know I never use it except for the hired man's porridge or black fruit-cake. Jerry's gone and I've made my cake long ago. It's not good sugar either—it's coarse and dark—William Blair doesn't usually keep sugar like that."

"I—I thought it might come in handy sometime," said Matthew, making good his escape.

When Matthew came to think the matter over he decided that a woman was required to cope with the situation. Marilla was out of the question. Matthew felt sure she would throw cold water on his project at once. Remained only Mrs. Lynde; for of no other woman in Avonlea would Matthew have dared to ask advice. To Mrs. Lynde he went accordingly, and that good lady promptly took the matter out of the harassed man's hands.

"Pick out a dress for you to give Anne? To be sure I will. I'm going to Carmody to-morrow and I'll attend to it. Have you something particular in mind? No? Well, I'll just go by my own judgment then. I believe a nice rich brown would just suit Anne, and William Blair has some new gloria[1] in that's real pretty. Perhaps you'd like me to make it up for her, too, seeing that if Marilla was to make it Anne would probably get wind of it before the time and spoil the surprise? Well, I'll do it. No, it isn't a mite of trouble. I like sewing. I'll make it to fit my niece, Jenny Gillis, for she and Anne are as like as two peas as far as figure goes."

"Well now, I'm much obliged," said Matthew, "and—and—I dunno—but I'd like—I think they make the sleeves different nowadays to what they used to be. If it wouldn't be asking too much I—I'd like them made in the new way."

"Puffs? Of course. You needn't worry a speck more about it, Matthew. I'll make it up in the very latest fashion," said Mrs. Lynde. To herself she added when Matthew had gone:

"It'll be a real satisfaction to see that poor child wearing something decent for once. The way Marilla dresses her is positively ridiculous, that's what, and I've ached to tell her so plainly a dozen times. I've held my tongue though, for I can see Marilla doesn't want advice and she thinks she knows more about bringing children up than I do for all she's an old maid. But that's always the way. Folks that has brought up children know that there's no hard and fast method in the world that'll suit every

---

[1] A "lightweight, closely woven fabric generally in a plain weave, but sometimes in twill and satin weaves. Formerly made with silk warp and cotton or worsted filling" (*Fairchild's Dictionary of Textiles*).

child. But them as never have think it's all as plain and easy as Rule of Three[1]—just set your three terms down so fashion, and the sum'll work out correct. But flesh and blood don't come under the head of arithmetic and that's where Marilla Cuthbert makes her mistake. I suppose she's trying to cultivate a spirit of humility in Anne by dressing her as she does; but it's more likely to cultivate envy and discontent. I'm sure the child must feel the difference between her clothes and the other girls'. But to think of Matthew taking notice of it! That man is waking up after being asleep for over sixty years."

Marilla knew all the following fortnight that Matthew had something on his mind, but what it was she could not guess, until Christmas Eve, when Mrs. Lynde brought up the new dress. Marilla behaved pretty well on the whole, although it is very likely she distrusted Mrs. Lynde's diplomatic explanation that she had made the dress because Matthew was afraid Anne would find out about it too soon if Marilla made it.

"So this is what Matthew has been looking so mysterious over and grinning about to himself for two weeks, is it?" she said a little stiffly but tolerantly. "I knew he was up to some foolishness. Well, I must say I don't think Anne needed any more dresses. I made her three good, warm, serviceable ones this fall, and anything more is sheer extravagance. There's enough material in those sleeves alone to make a waist, I declare there is. You'll just pamper Anne's vanity, Matthew, and she's as vain as a peacock now. Well, I hope she'll be satisfied at last, for I know she's been hankering after those silly sleeves ever since they came in, although she never said a word after the first. The puffs have been getting bigger and more ridiculous right along; they're as big as balloons now. Next year anybody who wears them will have to go through a door sideways."

Christmas morning broke on a beautiful white world. It had been a very mild December and people had looked forward to a green

---

[1] "Method of finding a fourth number from three given numbers, of which the first is in the same proportion to the second as the third is to the unknown fourth" (*OED*). Also referred to as the rule of proportion or the golden rule. *Bartlett's* cites an anonymous manuscript of 1570: "Multiplication is vexation,/ Division is as bad./ The rule of three doth puzzle me,/ And practice drives me mad" (917).

Christmas; but just enough snow fell softly in the night to transfigure Avonlea. Anne peeped out from her frosted gable window with delighted eyes. The firs in the Haunted Wood were all feathery and wonderful; the birches and wild cherry-trees were outlined in pearl; the ploughed fields were stretches of snowy dimples; and there was a crisp tang in the air that was glorious. Anne ran down-stairs singing, until her voice re-echoed through Green Gables.

"Merry Christmas, Marilla! Merry Christmas, Matthew! Isn't it a lovely Christmas? I'm so glad it's white. Any other kind of Christmas doesn't seem real, does it? I don't like green Christmases. They're *not* green—they're just nasty faded browns and grays. What makes people call them green? Why—why— Matthew, is that for me? Oh, Matthew!"

Matthew had sheepishly unfolded the dress from its paper swathings and held it out with a deprecatory glance at Marilla, who feigned to be contemptuously filling the teapot, but nevertheless watched the scene out of the corner of her eye with a rather interested air.

Anne took the dress and looked at it in reverent silence. Oh, how pretty it was—a lovely soft brown gloria with all the gloss of silk; a skirt with dainty frills and shirrings; a waist elaborately pin-tucked[1] in the most fashionable way, with a little ruffle of filmy lace at the neck. But the sleeves—they were the crowning glory! Long elbow cuffs, and above them two beautiful puffs divided by rows of shirring[2] and bows of brown silk ribbon.

"That's a Christmas present for you, Anne," said Matthew, shyly. "Why—why—Anne, don't you like it? Well now—well now."

For Anne's eyes had suddenly filled with tears.

"*Like* it! Oh, Matthew!" Anne laid the dress over a chair and clasped her hands. "Matthew, it's perfectly exquisite. Oh, I can

---

[1] According to Agnes M. Miall, *Complete Needlecraft* (London: C. Arthur Pearson, n.d.), "Tucks are rather narrow pleats which are usually stitched along their whole length. Some are very narrow indeed, taking up only the smallest possible ridge of material, and these are known as pin-tucks. Pin-tucks often go both ways, giving a check effect" (176).

[2] Refers to fabric gathered up by means of parallel threads. OED cites Caulfield and Saward, *Dictionary of Needlework* (1882): "Shirrings are close Runnings, or cords inserted between two pieces of cloth, as the lines of indiarubber in Shirred Braces or Garters, or the drawing and puckering up any material."

never thank you enough. Look at those sleeves! Oh, it seems to me this must be a happy dream."

"Well, well, let us have breakfast," interrupted Marilla. "I must say, Anne, I don't think you needed the dress; but since Matthew has got it for you, see that you take good care of it. There's a hair ribbon Mrs. Lynde left for you. It's brown, to match the dress. Come now, sit in."

"I don't see how I'm going to eat breakfast," said Anne rapturously. "Breakfast seems so commonplace at such an exciting moment. I'd rather feast my eyes on that dress. I'm so glad that puffed sleeves are still fashionable. It did seem to me that I'd never get over it if they went out before I had a dress with them. I'd never have felt quite satisfied, you see. It was lovely of Mrs. Lynde to give me the ribbon, too. I feel that I ought to be a very good girl indeed. It's at times like this I'm sorry I'm not a model little girl; and I always resolve that I will be in future. But somehow it's hard to carry out your resolutions when irresistible temptations come. Still, I really will make an extra effort after this."

When the commonplace breakfast was over Diana appeared, crossing the white log bridge in the hollow, a gay little figure in her crimson ulster.[1] Anne flew down the slope to meet her.

"Merry Christmas, Diana! And oh, it's a wonderful Christmas. I've something splendid to show you. Matthew has given me the loveliest dress, with *such* sleeves. I couldn't even imagine any nicer."

"I've got something more for you," said Diana breathlessly. "Here—this box. Aunt Josephine sent us out a big box with ever so many things in it—and this is for you. I'd have brought it over last night, but it didn't come until after dark, and I never feel very comfortable coming through the Haunted Wood in the dark now."

Anne opened the box and peeped in. First a card with "For the Anne-girl and Merry Christmas," written on it; and then, a pair of the daintiest little kid slippers, with beaded toes and satin bows and glistening buckles.

"Oh," said Anne, "Diana, this is too much. I must be dreaming."

---

[1]   "A heavy overcoat originally worn by men and women in Ulster, northern Ireland. A long, loose-fitting coat, usually double-breasted, with a full- or half-belt" (R. Turner Wilcox, *The Dictionary of Costume* [New York: Scribners 1969]).

"*I* call it providential," said Diana. "You won't have to borrow Ruby's slippers now, and that's a blessing, for they're two sizes too big for you, and it would be awful to hear a fairy shuffling. Josie Pye would be delighted. Mind you, Rob Wright went home with Gertie Pye from the practice night before last. Did you ever hear anything equal to that?"

All the Avonlea scholars were in a fever of excitement that day, for the hall had to be decorated and a last grand rehearsal held.

The concert came off in the evening and was a pronounced success. The little hall was crowded; all the performers did excellently well, but Anne was the bright particular star[1] of the occasion, as even envy, in the shape of Josie Pye, dared not deny.

"Oh, hasn't it been a brilliant evening?" sighed Anne, when it was all over and she and Diana were walking home together under a dark, starry sky.

"Everything went off very well," said Diana practically. "I guess we must have made as much as ten dollars. Mind you, Mr. Allan is going to send an account of it to the Charlottetown papers."

"Oh, Diana, will we really see our names in print? It makes me thrill to think of it. Your solo was perfectly elegant, Diana. I felt prouder than you did when it was encored. I just said to myself, 'It is my dear bosom friend who is so honoured.'"

"Well, your recitations just brought down the house, Anne. That sad one was simply splendid."

"Oh, I was so nervous, Diana. When Mr. Allan called out my name I really cannot tell how I ever got up on that platform. I felt as if a million eyes were looking at me and through me, and for one dreadful moment I was sure I couldn't begin at all. Then I thought of my lovely puffed sleeves and took courage. I knew that I must live up to those sleeves, Diana. So I started in, and my voice seemed to be coming from ever so far away. I just felt like a parrot. It's providential that I practised those recitations so often up in the garret, or I'd never have been able to get through. Did I groan all right?"

"Yes, indeed, you groaned lovely," assured Diana.

---

[1]   Cf. Shakespeare, *All's Well That Ends Well* (1.1.97).

"I saw old Mrs. Sloane wiping away tears when I sat down. It was splendid to think I had touched somebody's heart. It's so romantic to take part in a concert, isn't it? Oh, it's been a very memorable occasion indeed."

"Wasn't the boys' dialogue fine?" said Diana. "Gilbert Blythe was just splendid. Anne, I do think it's awful mean the way you treat Gil. Wait till I tell you. When you ran off the platform after the fairy dialogue one of your roses fell out of your hair. I saw Gil pick it up and put it in his breast-pocket. There now. You're so romantic that I'm sure you ought to be pleased at that."

"It's nothing to me what that person does," said Anne loftily. "I simply never waste a thought on him, Diana."

That night Marilla and Matthew, who had been out to a concert for the first time in twenty years, sat for awhile by the kitchen fire after Anne had gone to bed.

"Well now, I guess our Anne did as well as any of them," said Matthew proudly.

"Yes, she did," admitted Marilla. "She's a bright child, Matthew. And she looked real nice, too. I've been kind of opposed to this concert scheme, but I suppose there's no real harm in it after all. Anyhow, I was proud of Anne to-night, although I'm not going to tell her so."

"Well now, I was proud of her and I did tell her so 'fore she went up-stairs," said Matthew. "We must see what we can do for her some of these days, Marilla. I guess she'll need something more than Avonlea school by and by."

"There's time enough to think of that," said Marilla. "She's only thirteen in March. Though to-night it struck me she was growing quite a big girl. Mrs. Lynde made that dress a mite too long, and it makes Anne look so tall. She's quick to learn and I guess the best thing we can do for her will be to send her to Queen's after a spell. But nothing need be said about that for a year or two yet."

"Well now, it'll do no harm to be thinking it over off and on," said Matthew. "Things like that are all the better for lots of thinking over."

CHAPTER XXVI

THE STORY CLUB IS FORMED

JUNIOR Avonlea found it hard to settle down to humdrum existence again. To Anne in particular things seemed fearfully flat, stale, and unprofitable[1] after the goblet of excitement she had been sipping for weeks. Could she go back to the former quiet pleasures of those far-away days before the concert? At first, as she told Diana, she did not really think she could.

"I'm positively certain, Diana, that life can never be quite the same again as it was in those olden days," she said mournfully, as if referring to a period of at least fifty years back. "Perhaps after awhile I'll get used to it, but I'm afraid concerts spoil people for every-day life. I suppose that is why Marilla disapproves of them. Marilla is such a sensible woman. It must be a great deal better to be sensible; but still, I don't believe I'd really want to be a sensible person, because they are so unromantic. Mrs. Lynde says there is no danger of my ever being one, but you can never tell. I feel just now that I may grow up to be sensible yet. But perhaps that is only because I'm tired. I simply couldn't sleep last night for ever so long. I just lay awake and imagined the concert over and over again. That's one splendid thing about such affairs—it's so lovely to look back to them."

Eventually, however, Avonlea school slipped back into its old groove and took up its old interests. To be sure, the concert left traces. Ruby Gillis and Emma White, who had quarrelled over a point of precedence in their platform seats, no longer sat at the same desk, and a promising friendship of three years was broken up. Josie Pye and Julia Bell did not "speak" for three months, because Josie Pye had told Bessie Wright that Julia Bell's bow when she got up to recite made her think of a chicken jerking its head, and Bessie told Julia. None of the Sloanes would have any dealings with the Bells, because the Bells had declared that the Sloanes had too much to do in the programme, and the Sloanes

---

[1] Cf. Shakespeare, *Hamlet* (1.2.129–34): there, "weary, stale, flat, and unprofitable" (133).

had retorted that the Bells were not capable of doing the little they had to do properly. Finally, Charlie Sloane fought Moody Spurgeon MacPherson,[1] because Moody Spurgeon had said that Anne Shirley put on airs about her recitations, and Moody Spurgeon was "licked"; consequently Moody Spurgeon's sister, Ella May, would not "speak" to Anne Shirley all the rest of the winter. With the exception of these trifling frictions, work in Miss Stacy's little kingdom went on with regularity and smoothness.

The winter weeks slipped by. It was an unusually mild winter, with so little snow that Anne and Diana could go to school nearly every day by way of the Birch Path. On Anne's birthday they were tripping lightly down it, keeping eyes and ears alert amid all their chatter, for Miss Stacy had told them that they must soon write a composition on "A Winter's Walk in The Woods," and it behooved them to be observant.

"Just think, Diana, I'm thirteen years old to-day," remarked Anne in an awed voice. "I can scarcely realize that I'm in my teens. When I woke this morning it seemed to me that everything must be different. You've been thirteen for a month, so I suppose it doesn't seem such a novelty to you as it does to me. It makes life seem so much more interesting. In two more years I'll be really grown up. It's a great comfort to think that I'll be able to use big words then without being laughed at."

"Ruby Gillis says she means to have a beau as soon as she's fifteen," said Diana.

"Ruby Gillis thinks of nothing but beaus," said Anne disdainfully. "She's actually delighted when any one writes her name up in a take-notice for all she pretends to be so mad. But I'm afraid that is an uncharitable speech. Mrs. Allan says we should never make uncharitable speeches; but they do slip out so often before you think, don't they? I simply can't talk about Josie Pye with-

---

[1] Moody Spurgeon MacPherson is named for two famous preachers. Dwight Lyman Moody (1837–1899) was an American evangelist and popular preacher. He is identified as the "pre-eminent figure in 19th cent[ury] revivalist history in the United States and Britain" (*Columbia Encyclopedia* 2001). Charles Haddon Spurgeon (1834–1892) was, the *DNB* notes, "[a]t twenty-two [...] the most popular preacher of his day" (841); from 1855, "a sermon by him was published every week" in London newspapers (842). See 276, note 2.

out making an uncharitable speech, so I never mention her at all. You may have noticed that. I'm trying to be as much like Mrs. Allan as I possibly can, for I think she's perfect. Mr. Allan thinks so too. Mrs. Lynde says he just worships the ground she treads on and she doesn't really think it right for a minister to set his affections so much on a mortal being. But then, Diana, even ministers are human and have their besetting sins[1] just like everybody else. I had such an interesting talk with Mrs. Allan about besetting sins last Sunday afternoon. There are just a few things it's proper to talk about on Sundays and that is one of them. My besetting sin is imagining too much and forgetting my duties. I'm striving very hard to overcome it and now that I'm really thirteen perhaps I'll get on better."

"In four more years we'll be able to put our hair up," said Diana. "Alice Bell is only sixteen and she is wearing hers up, but I think that's ridiculous. I shall wait until I'm seventeen."

"If I had Alice Bell's crooked nose," said Anne decidedly, "I wouldn't—but there! I won't say what I was going to because it was extremely uncharitable. Besides, I was comparing it with my own nose and that's vanity. I'm afraid I think too much about my nose ever since I heard that compliment about it long ago. It really is a great comfort to me. Oh, Diana, look, there's a rabbit. That's something to remember for our woods composition. I really think the woods are just as lovely in winter as in summer. They're so white and still, as if they were asleep and dreaming pretty dreams."

"I won't mind writing that composition when its time comes," sighed Diana. "I can manage to write about the woods, but the one we're to hand in Monday is terrible. The idea of Miss Stacy telling us to write a story out of our own heads!"

"Why, it's as easy as wink," said Anne.

"It's easy for you because you have an imagination," retorted Diana, "but what would you do if you had been born without one? I suppose you have your composition all done?"

Anne nodded, trying hard not to look virtuously complacent and failing miserably.

"I wrote it last Monday evening. It's called 'The Jealous Rival;

---

[1] See Hebrews 12.1.

or, in Death Not Divided.'[1] I read it to Marilla and she said it was stuff and nonsense. Then I read it to Matthew and he said it was fine. That is the kind of critic I like. It's a sad, sweet story. I just cried like a child while I was writing it. It's about two beautiful maidens called Cordelia Montmorency and Geraldine Seymour who lived in the same village and were devotedly attached to each other. Cordelia was a regal brunette with a coronet of midnight hair and duskly flashing eyes. Geraldine was a queenly blonde with hair like spun gold and velvety purple eyes."

"I never saw anybody with purple eyes," said Diana dubiously.

"Neither did I. I just imagined them. I wanted something out of the common. Geraldine had an alabaster brow, too. I've found out what an alabaster[2] brow is. That is one of the advantages of being thirteen. You know so much more than you did when you were only twelve."

"Well, what became of Cordelia and Geraldine?" asked Diana, who was beginning to feel rather interested in their fate.

"They grew in beauty side by side until they were sixteen. Then Bertram DeVere came to their native village and fell in love with the fair Geraldine. He saved her life when her horse ran away with her in a carriage, and she fainted in his arms and he carried her home three miles; because, you understand, the carriage was all smashed up. I found it rather hard to imagine the proposal because I had no experience to go by. I asked Ruby Gillis if she knew anything about how men proposed because I thought she'd likely be an authority on the subject, having so many sisters married. Ruby told me she was hid in the hall pantry when Malcolm Andrews proposed to her sister Susan. She said Malcolm told Susan that his dad had given him the farm in his own name and then said, 'What do you say, darling pet, if we get hitched this fall?' And Susan said, 'Yes—no—I don't know—let me see'—and there they were, engaged as quick as that. But I didn't think that sort of a proposal was a very romantic one, so in

---

[1]   Anne's story, which seems to have no specific antecedent, is connected with nineteenth-century works such as Elizabeth Barrett Browning's "Lady Geraldine's Courtship," which, while a different story, figures a Bertram and a Geraldine. See also *AA* n.6, 280. Cf. 1 Samuel 2.23.

[2]   Cf. earlier reference, 69, note 1.

the end I had to imagine it out as well as I could. I made it very flowery and poetical and Bertram went on his knees, although Ruby Gillis says it isn't done nowadays. Geraldine accepted him in a speech a page long. I can tell you I took a lot of trouble with that speech. I rewrote it five times and I look upon it as my masterpiece. Bertram gave her a diamond ring and a ruby necklace and told her they would go to Europe for a wedding tour, for he was immensely wealthy. But then, alas, shadows began to darken over their path. Cordelia was secretly in love with Bertram herself and when Geraldine told her about the engagement she was simply furious, especially when she saw the necklace and the diamond ring. All her affection for Geraldine turned to bitter hate and she vowed that she should never marry Bertram. But she pretended to be Geraldine's friend the same as ever. One evening they were standing on the bridge over a rushing turbulent stream and Cordelia, thinking they were alone, pushed Geraldine over the brink with a wild, mocking, 'Ha, ha, ha.' But Bertram saw it all and he at once plunged into the current, exclaiming, 'I will save thee, my peerless Geraldine.' But alas, he had forgotten he couldn't swim, and they were both drowned, clasped in each other's arms. Their bodies were washed ashore soon afterwards. They were buried in the one grave and their funeral was most imposing, Diana. It's so much more romantic to end a story up with a funeral than a wedding. As for Cordelia, she went insane with remorse and was shut up in a lunatic asylum. I thought that was a poetical retribution for her crime."

"How perfectly lovely!" sighed Diana, who belonged to Matthew's school of critics. "I don't see how you can make up such thrilling things out of your own head, Anne. I wish my imagination was as good as yours."

"It would be if you'd only cultivate it," said Anne cheeringly. "I've just thought of a plan, Diana. Let's you and I have a story club all our own and write stories for practice. I'll help you along until you can do them by yourself. You ought to cultivate your imagination, you know. Miss Stacy says so. Only we must take the right way. I told her about the Haunted Wood, but she said we went the wrong way about it in that."

This was how the story club came into existence. It was

limited to Diana and Anne at first, but soon it was extended to include Jane Andrews and Ruby Gillis and one or two others who felt that their imaginations needed cultivating. No boys were allowed in it—although Ruby Gillis opined that their admission would make it more exciting—and each member had to produce one story a week.

"It's extremely interesting," Anne told Marilla. "Each girl has to read her story out loud and then we talk it over. We are going to keep them all sacredly and have them to read to our descendants. We each write under a nom-de-plume. Mine is Rosamond Montmorency. All the girls do pretty well. Ruby Gillis is rather sentimental. She puts too much love-making into her stories and you know too much is worse than too little. Jane never puts any because she says it makes her feel so silly when she has to read it out loud. Jane's stories are extremely sensible. Then Diana puts too many murders into hers. She says most of the time she doesn't know what to do with the people so she kills them off to get rid of them. I mostly always have to tell them what to write about, but that isn't hard for I've millions of ideas."

"I think this story-writing business is the foolishest yet," scoffed Marilla. "You'll get a pack of nonsense into your heads and waste time that should be put on your lessons. Reading stories is bad enough but writing them is worse."

"But we're so careful to put a moral into them all, Marilla," explained Anne. "I insist upon that. All the good people are rewarded and all the bad ones are suitably punished. I'm sure that must have a wholesome effect. The moral is the great thing. Mr. Allan says so. I read one of my stories to him and Mrs. Allan and they both agreed that the moral was excellent. Only they laughed in the wrong places. I like it better when people cry. Jane and Ruby almost always cry when I come to the pathetic parts. Diana wrote her Aunt Josephine about our club and her Aunt Josephine wrote back that we were to send her some of our stories. So we copied out four of our very best and sent them. Miss Josephine Barry wrote back that she had never read anything so amusing in her life. That kind of puzzled us because the stories were all very pathetic and almost everybody died. But I'm glad Miss Barry liked them. It shows our club is doing some good in the world.

Mrs. Allan says that ought to be our object in everything. I do really try to make it my object but I forget so often when I'm having fun. I hope I shall be a little like Mrs. Allan when I grow up. Do you think there is any prospect of it, Marilla?"

"I shouldn't say there was great deal," was Marilla's encouraging answer. "I'm sure Mrs. Allan was never such a silly, forgetful little girl as you are."

"No; but she wasn't always so good as she is now," said Anne seriously. "She told me so herself—that is, she said she was a dreadful mischief when she was a girl and was always getting into scrapes. I felt so encouraged when I heard that. Is it very wicked of me, Marilla, to feel encouraged when I hear that other people have been bad and mischievous? Mrs. Lynde says it is. Mrs. Lynde says she always feels shocked when she hears of any one ever having been naughty, no matter how small they were. Mrs. Lynde says she once heard a minister confess that when he was a boy he stole a strawberry tart out of his aunt's pantry and she never had any respect for that minister again. Now, I wouldn't have felt that way. I'd have thought that it was real noble of him to confess it, and I'd have thought what an encouraging thing it would be for small boys nowadays who do naughty things and are sorry for them to know that perhaps they may grow up to be ministers in spite of it. That's how I'd feel, Marilla."

"The way I feel at present, Anne," said Marilla "is that it's high time you had those dishes washed. You've taken half an hour longer than you should with your chattering. Learn to work first and talk afterwards."

CHAPTER XXVII

VANITY AND VEXATION OF SPIRIT[1]

MARILLA, walking home one late April evening from an Aid meeting, realized that the winter was over and gone with the

---

[1]   Ecclesiastes 1.14–15.

thrill of delight that spring never fails to bring to the oldest and saddest as well as to the youngest and merriest. Marilla was not given to subjective analysis of her thoughts and feelings. She probably imagined that she was thinking about the Aids and their missionary box and the new carpet for the vestry-room,[1] but under these reflections was a harmonious consciousness of red fields smoking into pale-purply mists in the declining sun, of long, sharp-pointed fir shadows falling over the meadow beyond the brook, of still, crimson-budded maples around a mirror-like wood-pool, of a wakening in the world and a stir of hidden pulses under the gray sod. The spring was abroad in the land[2] and Marilla's sober, middle-aged step was lighter and swifter because of its deep, primal gladness.

Her eyes dwelt affectionately on Green Gables, peering through its network of trees and reflecting the sunlight back from its windows in several little coruscations[3] of glory. Marilla, as she picked her steps along the damp lane, thought that it was really a satisfaction to know that she was going home to a briskly snapping wood fire and a table nicely spread for tea, instead of to the cold comfort of old Aid meeting evenings before Anne had come to Green Gables.

Consequently, when Marilla entered her kitchen and found the fire black out, with no sign of Anne anywhere, she felt justly disappointed and irritated. She had told Anne to be sure and have tea ready at five o'clock, but now she must hurry to take off her second-best dress and prepare the meal herself against Matthew's return from ploughing.

"I'll settle Miss Anne when she comes home," said Marilla grimly, as she shaved up kindlings with a carving knife and more vim than was strictly necessary. Matthew had come in and was waiting patiently for his tea in his corner. "She's gadding off

---

1   The vestry is the room in which church vestments and robes are kept.
2   Cf. Felicia Hemans, "The Voice of Spring": "The young leaves are dancing in breezy mirth./ Their light stems thrill to the wild-wood strains,/ And youth is abroad in my green domains" (34–36). Cf. Song of Solomon 2:11–12: "For lo, the winter is past, the rain is over and gone, and the voice of the turtle is heard in the land."
3   "A vibratory or quivering flash of light, or a display of such flashes; in early use always of atmospheric phenomena" (OED).

somewhere with Diana, writing stories or practising dialogues or some such tomfoolery, and never thinking once about the time or her duties. She's just got to be pulled up short and sudden on this sort of thing. I don't care if Mrs. Allan does say she's the brightest and sweetest child she ever knew. She may be bright and sweet enough, but her head is full of nonsense and there's never any knowing what shape it'll break out in next. Just as soon as she grows out of one freak she takes up with another. But there! Here I am saying the very thing I was so riled with Rachel Lynde for saying at the Aid to-day. I was real glad when Mrs. Allan spoke up for Anne, for if she hadn't I know I'd have said something too sharp to Rachel before everybody. Anne's got plenty of faults, goodness knows, and far be it from me to deny it. But I'm bringing her up and not Rachel Lynde, who'd pick faults in the Angel Gabriel[1] himself if he lived in Avonlea. Just the same, Anne has no business to leave the house like this when I told her she was to stay home this afternoon and look after things. I must say, with all her faults, I never found her disobedient or untrustworthy before and I'm real sorry to find her so now."

"Well now, I dunno," said Matthew, who, being patient and wise and, above all, hungry, had deemed it best to let Marilla talk her wrath out unhindered, having learned by experience that she got through with whatever work was on hand much quicker if not delayed by untimely argument. "Perhaps you're judging her too hasty, Marilla. Don't call her untrustworthy until you're sure she has disobeyed you. Mebbe it can all be explained—Anne's a great hand at explaining."

"She's not here when I told her to stay," retorted Marilla. "I reckon she'll find it hard to explain *that* to my satisfaction. Of course I knew you'd take her part, Matthew. But I'm bringing her up, not you."

It was dark when supper was ready, and still no sign of Anne, coming hurriedly over the log bridge or up Lovers' Lane, breathless and repentant with a sense of neglected duties. Marilla washed and put away the dishes grimly. Then, wanting a candle to light her down cellar, she went up to the east gable for the one that gener-

---

[1]   An archangel, or angel of highest rank.

ally stood on Anne's table. Lighting it, she turned around to see Anne herself lying on the bed, face downward among the pillows.

"Mercy on us," said astonished Marilla, "have you been asleep, Anne?"

"No," was the muffled reply.

"Are you sick then?" demanded Marilla anxiously, going over to the bed.

Anne cowered deeper into her pillows as if desirous of hiding herself for ever from mortal eyes.

"No. But please, Marilla, go away and don't look at me. I'm in the depths of despair and I don't care who gets head in class or writes the best composition or sings in the Sunday-school choir any more. Little things like that are of no importance now because I don't suppose I'll ever be able to go anywhere again. My career is closed. Please, Marilla, go away and don't look at me."

"Did anyone ever hear the like?" the mystified Marilla wanted to know. "Anne Shirley, whatever is the matter with you? What have you done? Get right up this minute and tell me. This minute, I say. There now, what is it?"

Anne had slid to the floor in despairing obedience.

"Look at my hair, Marilla," she whispered.

Accordingly, Marilla lifted her candle and looked scrutinizingly at Anne's hair, flowing in heavy masses down her back. It certainly had a very strange appearance.

"Anne Shirley, what have you done to your hair? Why, it's *green!*"

Green it might be called, if it were any earthly colour—a queer, dull, bronzy green, with streaks here and there of the original red to heighten the ghastly effect. Never in all her life had Marilla seen anything so grotesque as Anne's hair at that moment.

"Yes, it's green," moaned Anne. "I thought nothing could be as bad as red hair. But now I know it's ten times worse to have green hair. Oh, Marilla, you little know how utterly wretched I am."

"I little know how you got into this fix, but I mean to find out," said Marilla. "Come right down to the kitchen—it's too cold up here—and tell me just what you've done. I've been expecting something queer for some time. You haven't got into any scrape for over two months, and I was sure another one was due. Now, then, what did you do to your hair?"

"I dyed it."

"Dyed it! Dyed your hair! Anne Shirley, didn't you know it was a wicked thing to do?"

"Yes, I knew it was a little wicked," admitted Anne. "But I thought it was worth while to be a little wicked to get rid of red hair. I counted the cost, Marilla. Besides, I meant to be extra good in other ways to make up for it."

"Well," said Marilla sarcastically, "if I'd decided it was worth while to dye my hair I'd have dyed it a decent colour at least. I wouldn't have dyed it green."

"But I didn't mean to dye it green, Marilla," protested Anne dejectedly. "If I was wicked I meant to be wicked to some purpose. He said it would turn my hair a beautiful raven black— he positively assured me that it would. How could I doubt his word, Marilla? I know what it feels like to have your word doubted. And Mrs. Allan says we should never suspect any one of not telling us the truth unless we have proof that they're not. I have proof now—green hair is proof enough for anybody. But I hadn't then and I believed every word he said *implicitly.*"

"Who said? Who are you talking about?"

"The pedlar that was here this afternoon. I bought the dye from him."

"Anne Shirley, how often have I told you never to let one of those Italians in the house! I don't believe in encouraging them to come around at all."

"Oh, I didn't let him in the house. I remembered what you told me, and I went out, carefully shut the door, and looked at his things on the step. Besides, he wasn't an Italian—he was a German Jew. He had a big box of very interesting things and he told me he was working hard to make enough money to bring his wife and children out from Germany. He spoke so feelingly about them that it touched my heart. I wanted to buy something from him to help him in such a worthy object. Then all at once I saw the bottle of hair dye. The pedlar said it was warranted to dye any hair a beautiful raven black and wouldn't wash off. In a trice I saw myself with beautiful raven black hair and the temptation was irresistible. But the price of the bottle was seventy-five cents and I had only fifty cents left out of my chicken money. I think the pedlar had a very kind heart, for he said that, seeing it was me, he'd sell it for fifty cents and that was just giving it away. So I bought it, and as soon as he had gone I came up here and applied it with an old hair-brush as the directions said. I used up the whole bottle, and oh, Marilla, when I saw the dreadful colour it turned my hair I repented of being wicked, I can tell you. And I've been repenting ever since."

"Well, I hope you'll repent to good purpose," said Marilla severely, "and that you've got your eyes opened to where your vanity has led you, Anne. Goodness knows what's to be done. I suppose the first thing is to give your hair a good washing and see if that will do any good."

Accordingly, Anne washed her hair, scrubbing it vigorously with soap and water, but for all the difference it made she might as well have been scouring its original red. The pedlar had certainly spoken the truth when he declared that the dye wouldn't wash off, however his veracity might be impeached in other respects.

"Oh, Marilla, what shall I do?" questioned Anne in tears. "I can never live this down. People have pretty well forgotten my other mistakes—the liniment cake and setting Diana drunk and flying into a temper with Mrs. Lynde. But they'll never forget this. They will think I am not respectable. Oh, Marilla, 'what a tangled web we weave when first we practise to deceive.'[1] That is poetry, but it is true. And oh, how Josie Pye will laugh! Marilla, I *cannot* face Josie Pye. I am the unhappiest girl in Prince Edward Island."

Anne's unhappiness continued for a week. During that time she went nowhere and shampooed her hair every day. Diana alone of outsiders knew the fatal secret, but she promised solemnly never to tell, and it may be stated here and now that she kept her word. At the end of the week Marilla said decidedly:

"It's no use, Anne. That is fast dye if ever there was any. Your hair must be cut off; there is no other way. You can't go out with it looking like that."

Anne's lips quivered, but she realized the bitter truth of Marilla's remarks. With a dismal sigh she went for the scissors.

"Please cut it off at once, Marilla, and have it over. Oh, I feel

---

[1] See Sir Walter Scott's *Marmion* 6.17. This is yet another reference to the "Battle" canto which Montgomery cites elsewhere in *AGG* and which appears in the *Fifth Royal Reader* as "The Parting of Marmion and Douglas" (64–65). See 63, note 1.

that my heart is broken. This is such an unromantic affliction. The girls in books lose their hair in fevers or sell it to get money for some good deed, and I'm sure I wouldn't mind losing my hair in some such fashion half so much. But there is nothing comforting in having your hair cut off because you've dyed it a dreadful colour, is there? I'm going to weep all the time you're cutting it off, if it won't interfere. It seems such a tragic thing."

Anne wept then, but later on, when she went up-stairs and looked in the glass, she was calm with despair. Marilla had done her work thoroughly and it had been necessary to shingle the hair as closely as possible. The result was not becoming, to state the case as mildly as may be. Anne promptly turned her glass to the wall.

"I'll never, never look at myself again until my hair grows," she exclaimed passionately.

Then she suddenly righted the glass.

"Yes, I will, too. I'll do penance for being wicked that way. I'll look at myself every time I come to my room and see how ugly I am. And I won't try to imagine it away, either. I never thought I was vain about my hair, of all things, but now I know I was, in spite of its being red, because it was so long and thick and curly. I expect something will happen to my nose, next."

Anne's clipped head made a sensation in school on the following Monday, but to her relief nobody guessed the real reason for it, not even Josie Pye, who, however, did not fail to inform Anne that she looked like a perfect scarecrow.

"I didn't say anything when Josie said that to me," Anne confided that evening to Marilla, who was lying on the sofa after one of her headaches, "because I thought it was part of my punishment and I ought to bear it patiently. It's hard to be told you look like a scarecrow and I wanted to say something back. But I didn't. I just swept her one scornful look and then I forgave her. It makes you feel very virtuous when you forgive people, doesn't it? I mean to devote all my energies to being good after this and I shall never try to be beautiful again. Of course it's better to be good. I know it is, but it's sometimes so hard to believe a thing even when you know it. I do really want to be good, Marilla, like you and Mrs. Allan and Miss Stacy, and grow up to be a credit to you. Diana says when my hair begins to grow to tie a black velvet ribbon around my head with a bow at one side. She says she thinks it will be very becoming. I will call it a snood[1]—that sounds so romantic. But am I talking too much, Marilla? Does it hurt your head?"

"My head is better now. It was terrible bad this afternoon, though. These headaches of mine are getting worse and worse. I'll have to see a doctor about them. As for your chatter, I don't know that I mind it—I've got so used to it."

Which was Marilla's way of saying that she liked to hear it.

CHAPTER XXVIII

AN UNFORTUNATE LILY MAID

"OF course you must be Elaine, Anne," said Diana. "I could never have the courage to float down there."[2]

"Nor I," said Ruby Gillis with a shiver. "I don't mind floating down when there's two or three of us in the flat and we can sit up. It's fun then. But to lie down and pretend I was dead—I just couldn't. I'd die really of fright."

"Of course it would be romantic," conceded Jane Andrews. "But I know I couldn't keep still. I'd be popping up every minute or so to see where I was and if I wasn't drifting too far out. And you know, Anne, that would spoil the effect."

"But it's so ridiculous to have a red-headed Elaine," mourned Anne. "I'm not afraid to float down and I'd *love* to be Elaine. But it's ridiculous just the same. Ruby ought to be Elaine because she is so fair and has such lovely long golden hair—Elaine had 'all her bright hair streaming down,' you know.[3] And Elaine was

---

[1]   A hair ribbon. Anne's use of the word is romantic and archaic. According to *Brewer's*, "The snood was a ribbon with which a Scots lass braided her hair, and was the emblem of her maiden character."

[2]   The girls are performing Tennyson's idyll, *Lancelot and Elaine*, included, according to *AGG*, in the P.E.I. English literature curriculum, see 254, note 2.) The idyll was first published as "Elaine" in 1859. Christopher Ricks identifies the source as Malory (*Le Morte D'Arthur* [c.1469–70]) xviii.9–20 (*Poems of Tennyson* v.3 422). In the poem, Elaine is identified as "the lily maid of Astolat" (2), hence the title of this chapter.

[3]   See *Lancelot and Elaine* 1149.

the lily maid. Now, a red-haired person cannot be a lily maid."

"Your complexion is just as fair as Ruby's," said Diana earnestly, "and your hair is ever so much darker than it used to be before you cut it."

"Oh, do you really think so?" exclaimed Anne, flushing sensitively with delight. "I've sometimes thought it was myself—but I never dared to ask any one for fear she would tell me it wasn't. Do you think it could be called auburn now, Diana?"

"Yes, and I think it is real pretty," said Diana, looking admiringly at the short, silky curls that clustered over Anne's head and were held in place by a very jaunty black velvet ribbon and bow.

They were standing on the bank of the pond, below Orchard Slope, where a little headland fringed with birches ran out from the bank; at its tip was a small wooden platform built out into the water for the convenience of fishermen and duck hunters. Ruby and Jane were spending the midsummer afternoon with Diana, and Anne had come over to play with them.

Anne and Diana had spent most of their playtime that summer on and about the pond. Idlewild was a thing of the past, Mr. Bell having ruthlessly cut down the little circle of trees in his back pasture in the spring. Anne had sat among the stumps and wept, not without an eye to the romance of it; but she was speedily consoled, for, after all, as she and Diana said, big girls of thirteen, going on fourteen, were too old for such childish amusements as play-houses, and there were more fascinating sports to be found about the pond. It was splendid to fish for trout over the bridge and the two girls learned to row themselves about in the little flat-bottomed dory[1] Mr. Barry kept for duck shooting.

It was Anne's idea that they dramatize Elaine. They had studied Tennyson's poem in school the preceding winter, the Superintendent of Education having prescribed it in the English course for the Prince Edward Island schools.[2] They had analyzed

---

[1]   A skiff: a small light boat (*OED*).
[2]   Tennyson had been "prescribed" in schools throughout Canada, as in other parts of the British Empire, since at least 1898. See *Tennyson: Select Poems containing the Literature Prescribed for the Junior Matriculation and Junior Leaving Examinations, 1901* (ed. W.J. Alexander. [Toronto: Copp Clark, 1900]). *Lancelot and Elaine* is included in this text, and there are lengthy notes on the idyll.

and parsed[1] it. and torn it to pieces in general until it was a wonder there was any meaning at all left in it for them, but at least the fair lily maid and Lancelot and Guinevere and King Arthur had become very real people to them, and Anne was devoured by secret regret that she had not been born in Camelot.[2] Those days, she said, were so much more romantic than the present.

Anne's plan was hailed with enthusiasm. The girls had discovered that if the flat were pushed off from the landing-place it would drift down with the current under the bridge and finally strand itself on another headland lower down which ran out at a curve in the pond. They had often gone down like this and nothing could be more convenient for playing Elaine.

"Well, I'll be Elaine," said Anne, yielding reluctantly, for, although she would have been delighted to play the principal character, yet her artistic sense demanded fitness for it and this, she felt, her limitations made impossible. "Ruby, you must be King Arthur and Jane will be Guinevere and Diana must be Lancelot. But first you must be the brothers and the father. We can't have the old dumb servitor[3] because there isn't room for two in the flat when one is lying down. We must pall the barge all its length in blackest samite.[4] That old black shawl of your mother's will be just the thing, Diana."

The black shawl having been procured, Anne spread it over the flat and then lay down on the bottom, with closed eyes and hands folded over her breast.

"Oh, she does look really dead," whispered Ruby Gillis nervously, watching the still, white little face under the flickering shadows of the birches. "It makes me feel frightened, girls. Do you suppose it's really right to act like this? Mrs. Lynde says that all play-acting is abominably wicked."

"Ruby, you shouldn't talk about Mrs. Lynde," said Anne severely. "It spoils the effect because this is hundreds of years

---

1   "To describe (a word in a sentence) grammatically, by stating the part of speech, inflexion, and relation to the rest of the sentence; to resolve (a sentence, etc.) into its component parts of speech and describe them grammatically" (*OED*).

2   Location of the court of King Arthur.

3   See *Lancelot and Elaine* 1137.

4   "A rich, heavy silk fabric popular during the Middle Ages, generally interwoven with gold or silver threads in brocade effects. Uses: ecclesiastical garments, robes of state" (*Fairchild's Dictionary of Textiles*). See *Lancelot and Elaine* 1135.

before Mrs. Lynde was born. Jane, you arrange this. It's silly for Elaine to be talking when she's dead."

Jane rose to the occasion. Cloth of gold for coverlet there was none,[1] but an old piano scarf[2] of yellow Japanese crêpe[3] was an excellent substitute. A white lily was not obtainable just then, but the effect of a tall blue iris placed in one of Anne's folded hands was all that could be desired.

"Now, she's all ready," said Jane. "We must kiss her quiet brows and, Diana, you say, 'Sister, farewell forever,' and Ruby, you say, 'Farewell, sweet sister,' both of you as sorrowfully as you possibly can.[4] Anne, for goodness sake smile a little. You know Elaine 'lay as though she smiled.'[5] That's better. Now push the flat off."

The flat was accordingly pushed off, scraping roughly over an old embedded stake in the process. Diana and Jane and Ruby only waited long enough to see it caught in the current and headed for the bridge before scampering up through the woods, across the road, and down to the lower headland where, as Lancelot and Guinevere and the King, they were to be in readiness to receive the lily maid.

For a few minutes Anne, drifting slowly down, enjoyed the romance of her situation to the full. Then something happened not at all romantic. The flat began to leak. In a very few moments, it was necessary for Elaine to scramble to her feet, pick up her cloth of gold coverlet and pall of blackest samite and gaze blankly at a big crack in the bottom of her barge through which the water was literally pouring. The sharp stake at the landing had torn off the strip of batting nailed on the flat. Anne did not know this, but it did not take her long to realize that she was in a dangerous plight. At this rate the flat would fill and sink long before it could drift to the lower headland. Where were the oars? Left behind at the landing!

---

[1] See *Lancelot and Elaine* 1150; properly, in the poem, "coverlid."
[2] I.e., a decorative cloth for the top of a piano.
[3] "A general classification of fabrics that may be made of silk, rayon, acetate, cotton, wool, manufactured fibers, or blends, characterized by a broad range of crinkled or grained surface effects" (*Fairchild's Dictionary of Textiles*).
[4] See *Lancelot and Elaine* 1145.
[5] See *Lancelot and Elaine* 1154.

Anne gave one gasping little scream which nobody ever heard; she was white to the lips, but she did not lose her self-possession. There was one chance—just one.

"I was horribly frightened," she told Mrs. Allan the next day, "and it seemed like years while the flat was drifting down to the bridge and the water rising in it every moment. I prayed, Mrs. Allan, most earnestly, but I didn't shut my eyes to pray, for I knew the only way God could save me was to let the flat float close enough to one of the bridge piles for me to climb up on it. You know the piles are just old tree trunks and there are lots of knots and old branch stubs on them. It was proper to pray, but I had to do my part by watching out and right well I knew it. I just said, 'Dear God, please take the flat close to a pile and I'll do the rest,' over and over again. Under such circumstances you don't think much about making a flowery prayer. But mine was answered, for the flat bumped right into a pile for a minute and I flung the scarf and the shawl over my shoulder and scrambled up on a big providential stub. And there I was, Mrs. Allan, clinging to that slippery old pile with no way of getting up or down. It was a very unromantic position, but I didn't think about that at the time. You don't think much about romance when you have just escaped from a watery grave. I said a grateful prayer at once and then I gave all my attention to holding on tight, for I knew I should probably have to depend on human aid to get back to dry land."

The flat drifted under the bridge and then promptly sank in midstream. Ruby, Jane, and Diana, already awaiting it on the lower headland, saw it disappear before their very eyes and had not a doubt but that Anne had gone down with it. For a moment they stood still, white as sheets, frozen with horror at the tragedy; then, shrieking at the tops of their voices, they started on a frantic run up through the woods, never pausing as they crossed the main road to glance the way of the bridge. Anne, clinging desperately to her precarious foothold, saw their flying forms and heard their shrieks. Help would soon come, but meanwhile her position was a very uncomfortable one.

The minutes passed by, each seeming an hour to the unfortunate lily maid. Why didn't somebody come? Where had the girls gone? Suppose they had fainted, one and all! Suppose nobody ever came! Suppose she grew so tired and cramped that she could hold on no longer! Anne looked at the wicked green depths below her, wavering with long, oily shadows, and shivered. Her imagination began to suggest all manner of gruesome possibilities to her.

Then, just as she thought she really could not endure the ache in her arms and wrists another moment, Gilbert Blythe came rowing under the bridge in Harmon Andrews' dory!

Gilbert glanced up and, much to his amazement, beheld a little white scornful face looking down upon him with big, frightened but also scornful gray eyes.

"Anne Shirley! How on earth did you get there?" he exclaimed.

Without waiting for an answer he pulled close to the pile and extended his hand. There was no help for it; Anne, clinging to Gilbert Blythe's hand, scrambled down into the dory, where she sat, drabbled and furious, in the stern with her arms full of dripping shawl and wet crêpe. It was certainly extremely difficult to be dignified under the circumstances!

"What has happened, Anne?" asked Gilbert, taking up his oars.

"We were playing Elaine," explained Anne frigidly, without even looking at her rescuer, "and I had to drift down to Camelot in the barge—I mean the flat. The flat began to leak and I climbed out on the pile. The girls went for help. Will you be kind enough to row me to the landing?"

Gilbert obligingly rowed to the landing and Anne, disdaining assistance, sprang nimbly on shore.

"I'm very much obliged to you," she said haughtily as she turned away. But Gilbert had also sprung from the boat and now laid a detaining hand on her arm.

"Anne," he said hurriedly, "look here. Can't we be good friends? I'm awfully sorry I made fun of your hair that time. I didn't mean to vex you and I only meant it for a joke. Besides, it's so long ago. I think your hair is awfully pretty now—honest I do. Let's be friends."

For a moment Anne hesitated. She had an odd, newly awakened consciousness under all her outraged dignity that the half-shy, half-eager expression in Gilbert's hazel eyes was something that was very good to see. Her heart gave a quick, queer little

"HE PULLED CLOSE TO THE PILE AND EXTENDED HIS HAND."

beat. But the bitterness of her old grievance promptly stiffened up her wavering determination. That scene of two years before flashed back into her recollection as vividly as if it had taken place yesterday. Gilbert had called her "carrots" and had brought about her disgrace before the whole school. Her resentment, which to other and older people might be as laughable as its cause, was in no whit allayed and softened by time seemingly. She hated Gilbert Blythe! She would never forgive him!

"No," she said coldly, "I shall never be friends with you, Gilbert Blythe; and I don't want to be!"

"All right!" Gilbert sprang into his skiff with an angry colour in his cheeks. "I'll never ask you to be friends again, Anne Shirley. And I don't care either!"

He pulled away with swift defiant strokes, and Anne went up the steep, ferny little path under the maples. She held her head very high, but she was conscious of an odd feeling of regret. She almost wished she had answered Gilbert differently. Of course, he had insulted her terribly, but still—! Altogether, Anne rather thought it would be a relief to sit down and have a good cry. She was really quite unstrung, for the reaction from her fright and cramped clinging was making itself felt.

Half-way up the path she met Jane and Diana rushing back to the pond in a state narrowly removed from positive frenzy. They had found nobody at Orchard Slope, both Mr. and Mrs. Barry being away. Here Ruby Gillis had succumbed to hysterics, and was left to recover from them as best she might, while Jane and Diana flew through the Haunted Wood and across the brook to Green Gables. There they had found nobody either, for Marilla had gone to Carmody and Matthew was making hay in the back field.

"Oh, Anne," gasped Diana, fairly falling on the former's neck and weeping with relief and delight, "Oh, Anne—we thought— you were—drowned—and we felt like murderers—because we had made—you be—Elaine. And Ruby is in hysterics—oh, Anne, how did you escape?"

"I climbed up on one of the piles," explained Anne wearily, "and Gilbert Blythe came along in Mr. Andrews' dory and brought me to land."

"Oh, Anne, how splendid of him! Why, it's so romantic!" said Jane, finding breath enough for utterance at last. "Of course you'll speak to him after this."

"Of course I won't," flashed Anne with a momentary return of her old spirit. "And I don't want ever to hear the word romantic again, Jane Andrews. I'm awfully sorry you were so frightened, girls. It is all my fault. I feel sure I was born under an unlucky star. Everything I do gets me or my dearest friends into a scrape. We've gone and lost your father's flat, Diana, and I have a presentiment that we'll not be allowed to row on the pond any more."

Anne's presentiment proved more trustworthy than presentiments are apt to do. Great was the consternation in the Barry and Cuthbert households when the events of the afternoon became known.

"Will you *ever* have any sense, Anne?" groaned Marilla.

"Oh, yes, I think I will, Marilla," returned Anne optimistically. A good cry, indulged in the grateful solitude of the east gable, had soothed her nerves and restored her to her wonted cheerfulness. "I think my prospects of becoming sensible are brighter now than ever."

"I don't see how," said Marilla.

"Well," explained Anne, "I've learned a new and valuable lesson to-day. Ever since I came to Green Gables I've been making mistakes, and each mistake has helped to cure me of some great shortcoming. The affair of the amethyst brooch cured me of meddling with things that didn't belong to me. The Haunted Wood mistake cured me of letting my imagination run away with me. The liniment cake mistake cured me of carelessness in cooking. Dyeing my hair cured me of vanity. I never think about my hair and nose now—at least, very seldom. And to-day's mistake is going to cure me of being too romantic. I have come to the conclusion that it is no use trying to be romantic in Avonlea. It was probably easy enough in towered Camelot[1] but romance is not appreciated now. I feel quite sure that you will soon see a great improvement in me in this respect, Marilla."

"I'm sure I hope so," said Marilla skeptically.

---

[1]   Cf. Tennyson, "The Lady of Shalott" (1832), lines 122 and 149.

But Matthew, who had been sitting mutely in his corner, laid a hand on Anne's shoulder when Marilla had gone out.

"Don't give up all your romance, Anne," he whispered shyly, "a little of it is a good thing—not too much, of course—but keep a little of it, Anne, keep a little of it."

CHAPTER XXIX

AN EPOCH IN ANNE'S LIFE

ANNE was bringing the cows home from the back pasture by way of Lovers' Lane. It was a September evening and all the gaps and clearings in the woods were brimmed up with ruby sunset light. Here and there the lane was splashed with it, but for the most part it was already quite shadowy beneath the maples, and the spaces under the firs were filled with a clear violet dusk like airy wine. The winds were out in their tops, and there is no sweeter music on earth than that which the wind makes in the fir-trees at evening.

The cows swung placidly down the lane, and Anne followed them dreamily, repeating aloud the battle canto from "Marmion"[1]—which had also been part of their English course the preceding winter and which Miss Stacy had made them learn off by heart—and exulting in its rushing lines and the clash of spears in its imagery. When she came to the lines:

"The stubborn spearsmen[2] still made good
Their dark impenetrable wood,"

she stopped in ecstasy to shut her eyes that she might the better fancy herself one of that heroic ring. When she opened them again it was to behold Diana coming through the gate that led into the Barry field and looking so important that Anne instantly divined there was news to be told. But betray too eager curiosity she would not.

---

[1] Another reference to the excerpt from Scott's *Marmion* that appeared in the *Fifth Royal Reader*. See 251, note 1.

[2] Properly, *spearmen*. See *Marmion* 6.34.12–13.

"Isn't this evening just like a purple dream, Diana? It makes me so glad to be alive. In the mornings I always think the mornings are best; but when evening comes I think it's lovelier still."

"It's a very fine evening," said Diana, "but oh, I have such news, Anne. Guess. You can have three guesses."

"Charlotte Gillis is going to be married in the church after all and Mrs. Allan wants us to decorate it," cried Anne.

"No. Charlotte's beau won't agree to that, because nobody ever has been married in the church yet, and he thinks it would seem too much like a funeral. It's too mean, because it would be such fun. Guess again."

"Jane's mother is going to let her have a birthday party?"

Diana shook her head, her black eyes dancing with merriment.

"I can't think what it can be," said Anne in despair, "unless it's that Moody Spurgeon MacPherson saw you home from prayer-meeting last night. Did he?"

"I should think not," exclaimed Diana indignantly. "I wouldn't be likely to boast of it if he did, the horrid creature! I knew you couldn't guess it. Mother had a letter from Aunt Josephine to-day, and Aunt Josephine wants you and me to go to town next Tuesday and stop with her for the Exhibition.[1] There!"

"Oh, Diana," whispered Anne, finding it necessary to lean up against a maple-tree for support, "do you really mean it? But I'm afraid Marilla won't let me go. She will say that she can't encourage gadding about. That was what she said last week when Jane invited me to go with them in their double-seated buggy to the American concert at the White Sands Hotel. I wanted to go, but Marilla said I'd be better at home learning my lessons and so would Jane. I was bitterly disappointed, Diana. I felt so heart-broken that I wouldn't say my prayers when I went to bed. But I repented of that and got up in the middle of the night and said them."

"I'll tell you," said Diana, "we'll get mother to ask Marilla. She'll be more likely to let you go then; and if she does we'll have the time of our lives, Anne. I've never been to an Exhibition, and it's so aggravating to hear the other girls talking

---

[1] Provincial agricultural exhibition: according to *The Canadian Encyclopedia*, agricultural exhibitions became "primarily competitive showplaces for livestock and produce and settings for the display of new agricultural technology, as well as social events."

about their trips. Jane and Ruby have been twice, and they're going this year again."

"I'm not going to think about it at all until I know whether I can go or not," said Anne resolutely. "If I did and then was disappointed, it would be more than I could bear. But in case I do go I'm very glad my new coat will be ready by that time. Marilla didn't think I needed a new coat. She said my old one would do very well for another winter and that I ought to be satisfied with having a new dress. The dress is very pretty, Diana—navy blue and made so fashionably. Marilla always makes my dresses fashionably now, because she says she doesn't intend to have Matthew going to Mrs. Lynde to make them. I'm so glad. It is ever so much easier to be good if your clothes are fashionable. At least, it is easier for me. I suppose it doesn't make such a difference to naturally good people. But Matthew said I must have a new coat, so Marilla bought a lovely piece of blue broadcloth, and it's being made by a real dressmaker over at Carmody. It's to be done Saturday night, and I'm trying not to imagine myself walking up the church aisle on Sunday in my new suit and cap, because I'm afraid it isn't right to imagine such things. But it just slips into my mind in spite of me. My cap is so pretty. Matthew bought it for me the day we were over at Carmody. It is one of those little blue velvet ones that are all the rage, with gold cord and tassels. Your new hat is elegant, Diana, and so becoming. When I saw you come into church last Sunday my heart swelled with pride to think you were my dearest friend. Do you suppose it's wrong for us to think so much about our clothes? Marilla says it is very sinful. But it *is* such an interesting subject, isn't it?"

Marilla agreed to let Anne go to town, and it was arranged that Mr. Barry should take the girls in on the following Tuesday. As Charlottetown was thirty miles away and Mr. Barry wished to go and return the same day, it was necessary to make a very early start. But Anne counted it all joy, and was up before sunrise on Tuesday morning. A glance from her window assured her that the day would be fine, for the eastern sky behind the firs of the Haunted Wood was all silvery and cloudless. Through the gap in the trees a light was shining in the western gable of Orchard

Slope, a token that Diana was also up.

Anne was dressed by the time Matthew had the fire on and had the breakfast ready when Marilla came down, but for her own part was much too excited to eat. After breakfast the jaunty new cap and jacket were donned, and Anne hastened over the brook and up through the firs to Orchard Slope. Mr. Barry and Diana were waiting for her, and they were soon on the road.

It was a long drive, but Anne and Diana enjoyed every minute of it. It was delightful to rattle along over the moist roads in the early red sunlight that was creeping across the shorn harvest fields. The air was fresh and crisp, and little smoke-blue mists curled through the valleys and floated off from the hills. Sometimes the road went through woods where maples were beginning to hang out scarlet banners; sometimes it crossed rivers on bridges that made Anne's flesh cringe with the old, half-delightful fear; sometimes it wound along a harbour shore and passed by a little cluster of weather-gray fishing huts; again it mounted to hills whence a far sweep of curving upland or misty blue sky could be seen; but wherever it went there was much of interest to discuss. It was almost noon when they reached town and found their way to "Beechwood." It was quite a fine old mansion, set back from the street in a seclusion of green elms and branching beeches. Miss Barry met them at the door with a twinkle in her sharp black eyes.

"So you've come to see me at last, you Anne-girl," she said. "Mercy, child, how you have grown! You're taller than I am, I declare. And you're ever so much better-looking than you used to be, too. But I dare say you know that without being told."

"Indeed I didn't," said Anne radiantly. "I know I'm not so freckled as I used to be, so I've much to be thankful for, but I really hadn't dared to hope there was any other improvement. I'm so glad you think there is, Miss Barry."

Miss Barry's house was furnished with "great magnificence," as Anne told Marilla afterwards. The two little country girls were rather abashed by the splendour of the parlour where Miss Barry left them when she went to see about dinner.

"Isn't it just like a palace?" whispered Diana. "I never was in Aunt Josephine's house before, and I'd no idea it was so grand. I just wish Julia Bell could see this—she puts on such airs about her mother's parlour."

"Velvet carpet," sighed Anne luxuriously, "*and* silk curtains! I've dreamed of such things, Diana. But do you know I don't believe I feel very comfortable with them after all. There are so many things in this room and all so splendid that there is no scope for imagination. That is one consolation when you are poor—there are so many more things you can imagine about."

Their sojourn in town was something Anne and Diana dated from for years. From first to last it was crowded with delights.

On Wednesday Miss Barry took them to the Exhibition grounds and kept them there all day.

"It was splendid," Anne related to Marilla later on. "I never imagined anything so interesting. I don't really know which department was the most interesting. I think I liked the horses and the flowers and the fancy work[1] best. Josie Pye took first prize for knitted lace. I was real glad she did. And I was glad that I felt glad, for it shows I'm improving, don't you think, Marilla, when I can rejoice in Josie's success? Mr. Harmon Andrews took second prize for Gravenstein apples and Mr. Bell took first prize for a pig. Diana said she thought it was ridiculous for a Sunday-school superintendent to take a prize in pigs, but I don't see why. Do you? She said she would always think of it after this when he was praying so solemnly. Clara Louise Macpherson took a prize for painting, and Mrs. Lynde got first prize for home-made butter and cheese. So Avonlea was pretty well represented, wasn't it? Mrs. Lynde was there that day, and I never knew how much I really liked her until I saw her familiar face among all those strangers. There were thousands of people there, Marilla. It made me feel dreadfully insignificant. And Miss Barry took us up to the grand stand to see the horse-races. Mrs. Lynde wouldn't go; she said horse-racing was an abomination, and she, being a church-member, thought it her bounden duty to set a good example by staying away. But there were so many there I don't believe Mrs. Lynde's absence would ever be noticed. I don't think, though, that I ought to go very often to horse-races, because they *are* awfully

---

[1] Fine needlework. Cf. 330.

fascinating. Diana got so excited that she offered to bet me ten cents that the red horse would win. I didn't believe he would, but I refused to bet, because I wanted to tell Mrs. Allan all about everything, and I felt sure it wouldn't do to tell her that. It's always wrong to do anything you can't tell the minister's wife. It's as good as an extra conscience to have a minister's wife for your friend. And I was very glad I didn't bet, because the red horse *did* win, and I would have lost ten cents. So you see that virtue was its own reward.[1] We saw a man go up in a balloon. I'd love to go up in a balloon, Marilla; it would be simply thrilling; and we saw a man selling fortunes. You paid him ten cents and a little bird picked out your fortune for you. Miss Barry gave Diana and me ten cents each to have our fortunes told. Mine was that I would marry a dark-complected man who was very wealthy, and I would go across water to live. I looked carefully at all the dark men I saw after that, but I didn't care much for any of them, and anyhow I suppose it's too early to be looking out for him yet. Oh, it was a never-to-be forgotten day, Marilla. I was so tired I couldn't sleep at night. Miss Barry put us in the spare room, according to promise. It was an elegant room, Marilla, but somehow sleeping in a spare room isn't what I used to think it was. That's the worst of growing up, and I'm beginning to realize it. The things you wanted so much when you were a child don't seem half so wonderful to you when you get them."

Thursday the girls had a drive in the park, and in the evening Miss Barry took them to a concert in the Academy of Music, where a noted prima donna was to sing. To Anne the evening was a glittering vision of delight.

"Oh, Marilla, it was beyond description. I was so excited I couldn't even talk, so you may know what it was like. I just sat in enraptured silence. Madame Selitsky was perfectly beautiful, and wore white satin and diamonds. But when she began to sing I never thought about anything else. Oh, I can't tell you how I felt.

---

[1] *Bartlett's* cites several occurrences, dating from the first century: *Ipsa quidem virtus sibimet pulcherrima merces* [Virtue herself is her own fairest reward] (Silius Italicus, c. AD 25–99). Cf. also Scottish playwright John Home (1722–1808), from the popular tragedy *Douglas* (1756) (3.355), and Charles Dickens (1812–70), from *Martin Chuzzlewit* (1841): "The only reward of virtue is virtue" (Ch. 15).

But it seemed to me that it could never be hard to be good any more.[1] I felt like I do when I look up to the stars. Tears came into my eyes, but, oh, they were such happy tears. I was so sorry when it was all over, and I told Miss Barry I didn't see how I was ever to return to common life again. She said she thought if we went over to the restaurant across the street and had an ice-cream it might help me. That sounded so prosaic; but to my surprise I found it true. The ice-cream was delicious, Marilla, and it was so lovely and dissipated to be sitting there eating it at eleven o'clock at night. Diana said she believed she was born for city life. Miss Barry asked me what my opinion was, but I said I would have to think it over very seriously before I could tell her what I really thought. So I thought it over after I went to bed. That is the best time to think things out. And I came to the conclusion, Marilla, that I wasn't born for city life and that I was glad of it. It's nice to be eating ice-cream at brilliant restaurants at eleven o'clock at night once in awhile; but as a regular thing I'd rather be in the east gable at eleven, sound asleep, but kind of knowing even in my sleep that the stars were shining outside and that the wind was blowing in the fir trees across the brook. I told Miss Barry so at breakfast the next morning and she laughed. Miss Barry generally laughed at anything I said, even when I said the most solemn things. I don't think I liked it, Marilla, because I wasn't trying to be funny. But she is a most hospitable lady and treated us royally."

Friday brought going-home time, and Mr. Barry drove in for the girls.

"Well, I hope you've enjoyed yourselves," said Miss Barry, as she bade them good-bye.

"Indeed we have," said Diana.

"And you, Anne-girl?"

"I've enjoyed every minute of the time," said Anne, throwing her arms impulsively about the old woman's neck and kissing her wrinkled cheek. Diana would never have dared to do such a thing, and felt rather aghast at Anne's freedom. But Miss Barry was

---

[1]   This is a clear articulation of Montgomery's view of art as a moral vehicle, able to transform not through didacticism necessarily but through a process of spiritual uplifting.

pleased, and she stood on her veranda and watched the buggy out of sight. Then she went back into her big house with a sigh. It seemed very lonely, lacking those fresh young lives. Miss Barry was a rather selfish old lady, if the truth must be told, and had never cared much for anybody but herself. She valued people only as they were of service to her or amused her. Anne had amused her, and consequently stood high in the old lady's good graces. But Miss Barry found herself thinking less about Anne's quaint speeches than of her fresh enthusiasms, her transparent emotions, her little winning ways, and the sweetness of her eyes and lips.

"I thought Marilla Cuthbert was an old fool when I heard she'd adopted a girl out of an orphan asylum," she said to herself, "but I guess she didn't make much of a mistake after all. If I'd a child like Anne in the house all the time I'd be a better and happier woman."

Anne and Diana found the drive home as pleasant as the drive in—pleasanter, indeed, since there was the delightful consciousness of home waiting at the end of it. It was sunset when they passed through White Sands and turned into the shore road. Beyond, the Avonlea hills came out darkly against the saffron sky. Behind them the moon was rising out of the sea that grew all radiant and transfigured in her light. Every little cove along the curving road was a marvel of dancing ripples. The waves broke with a soft swish on the rocks below them, and the tang of the sea was in the strong, fresh air.

"Oh, but it's good to be alive and to be going home," breathed Anne.

When she crossed the log bridge over the brook the kitchen light of Green Gables winked her a friendly welcome back, and through the open door shone the hearth fire, sending out its warm red glow athwart the chilly autumn night. Anne ran blithely up the hill and into the kitchen, where a hot supper was waiting on the table.

"So you've got back?" said Marilla, folding up her knitting.

"Yes, and, oh, it's so good to be back," said Anne joyously. "I could kiss everything, even to the clock. Marilla, a broiled chicken! You don't mean to say you cooked that for me!"

"Yes, I did," said Marilla. "I thought you'd be hungry after such a drive and need something real appetizing. Hurry and take off your things, and we'll have supper as soon as Matthew comes in. I'm glad you've got back, I must say. It's been fearful lonesome here without you, and I never put in four longer days."

After supper Anne sat before the fire between Matthew and Marilla, and gave them a full account of her visit.

"I've had a splendid time," she concluded happily, "and I feel that it marks an epoch in my life. But the best of it all was the coming home."

CHAPTER XXX

THE QUEEN'S CLASS IS ORGANIZED

MARILLA laid her knitting in her lap and leaned back in her chair. Her eyes were tired, and she thought vaguely that she must see about having her glasses changed the next time she went to town, for her eyes had grown tired very often of late.

It was nearly dark, for the dull November twilight had fallen around Green Gables, and the only light in the kitchen came from the dancing red flames in the stove.

Anne was curled up Turk-fashion[1] on the hearth-rug, gazing into that joyous glow where the sunshine of a hundred summers was being distilled from the maple cord-wood. She had been reading, but her book had slipped to the floor, and now she was dreaming, with a smile on her parted lips. Glittering castles in Spain[2] were shaping themselves out of the mists and rainbows of her lively fancy; adventures wonderful and enthralling were happening to her in cloudland—adventures that always turned out triumphantly and never involved her in scrapes like those of actual life.

---

[1] Cross-legged.
[2] "A visionary day-dream, splendid imagining which has no real existence" (*Brewer's*). Cf. popular nineteenth-century American poet William Cullen Bryant (1794-1878), two blank verse fragments: "A Tale of Cloudland" and "Castles in the Air"; Longfellow, "The Castle-Builder" (1848); and Chaucer, translation of Jean de Meun, *Roman de la Rose:* "Thou shalt make castels thanne in Spain,/ And dreme of joy, all but in vayne."

Marilla looked at her with a tenderness that would never have been suffered to reveal itself in any clearer light than that soft mingling of fireshine and shadow. The lesson of a love that should display itself easily in spoken word and open look was one Marilla could never learn. But she had learned to love this slim, gray-eyed girl with an affection all the deeper and stronger from its very undemonstrativeness. Her love made her afraid of being unduly indulgent, indeed. She had an uneasy feeling that it was rather sinful to set one's heart so intensely on any human creature as she had set hers on Anne, and perhaps she performed a sort of unconscious penance for this by being stricter and more critical than if the girl had been less dear to her. Certainly, Anne herself had no idea how Marilla loved her. She sometimes thought wistfully that Marilla was very hard to please and distinctly lacking in sympathy and understanding. But she always checked the thought reproachfully, remembering what she owed to Marilla.

"Anne," said Marilla abruptly, "Miss Stacy was here this afternoon when you were out with Diana."

Anne came back from her other world with a start and a sigh.

"Was she? Oh, I'm so sorry I wasn't in. Why didn't you call me, Marilla? Diana and I were only over in the Haunted Wood. It's lovely in the woods now. All the little wood things—the ferns and the satin leaves and the crackerberries—have gone to sleep, just as if somebody had tucked them away until spring under a blanket of leaves. I think it was a little gray fairy with a rainbow scarf[1] that came tiptoeing along the last moonlight night and did it. Diana wouldn't say much about that, though. Diana has never forgotten the scolding her mother gave her about imagining ghosts into the Haunted Wood. It had a very bad effect on Diana's imagination. It blighted it. Mrs. Lynde says Myrtle Bell is a blighted being. I asked Ruby Gillis why Myrtle was blighted, and Ruby said she guessed it was because her young man had gone back on her. Ruby Gillis thinks of nothing but young men, and the older she gets the worse she is. Young men are all very well in their place, but it doesn't do to drag them into everything, does it? Diana and I are thinking seriously of promising

---

[1]   Another reference to the image in Brontë's *Jane Eyre*. See 210, note 2.

each other that we will never marry but be nice old maids and live together for ever. Diana hasn't quite made up her mind though, because she thinks perhaps it would be nobler to marry some wild, dashing, wicked young man and reform him. Diana and I talk a great deal about serious subjects now, you know. We feel that we are so much older than we used to be that it isn't becoming to talk of childish matters. It's such a solemn thing to be almost fourteen, Marilla. Miss Stacy took all us girls who are in our teens down to the brook last Wednesday, and talked to us about it. She said we couldn't be too careful what habits we formed and what ideals we acquired in our teens, because by the time we were twenty our characters would be developed and the foundation laid for our whole future life. And she said if the foundation was shaky we could never build anything really worth while on it. Diana and I talked the matter over coming home from school. We felt extremely solemn, Marilla. And we decided that we would try to be very careful indeed and form respectable habits and learn all we could and be as sensible as possible, so that by the time we were twenty our characters would be properly developed. It's perfectly appalling to think of being twenty, Marilla. It sounds so fearfully old and grown up. But why was Miss Stacy here this afternoon?"

"That is what I want to tell you, Anne, if you'll ever give me a chance to get a word in edgewise. She was talking about you."

"About me?" Anne looked rather scared. Then she flushed and exclaimed:

"Oh, I know what she was saying. I meant to tell you, Marilla, honestly I did, but I forgot. Miss Stacy caught me reading 'Ben Hur'[1] in school yesterday afternoon when I should have been studying my Canadian history. Jane Andrews lent it to me. I was reading it at dinner-hour, and I had just got to the chariot-race when school went in. I was simply wild to know how it turned out—although I felt sure 'Ben Hur' must win, because it would-n't be poetical justice if he didn't—so I spread the history open on my desk-lid and then tucked 'Ben Hur' between the desk and

---

[1] *Ben Hur: A Tale of the Christ* (1880), a popular novel by American writer Lew Wallace (1827–1905).

my knee. It just looked as if I were studying Canadian history, you know, while all the while I was revelling in 'Ben Hur.' I was so interested in it that I never noticed Miss Stacy coming down the aisle until all at once I just looked up and there she was looking down at me, so reproachful like. I can't tell you how ashamed I felt, Marilla, especially when I heard Josie Pye giggling. Miss Stacy took 'Ben Hur' away, but she never said a word then. She kept me in at recess and talked to me. She said I had done very wrong in two respects. First, I was wasting the time I ought to have put on my studies; and secondly I was deceiving my teacher in trying to make it appear I was reading a history when it was a story-book instead. I had never realized until that moment, Marilla, that what I was doing was deceitful. I was shocked. I cried bitterly, and asked Miss Stacy to forgive me and I'd never do such a thing again; and I offered to do penance by never so much as looking at 'Ben Hur' for a whole week, not even to see how the chariot-race turned out. But Miss Stacy said she wouldn't require that, and she forgave me freely. So I think it wasn't very kind of her to come up here to you about it after all."

"Miss Stacy never mentioned such a thing to me, Anne, and it's only your guilty conscience that's the matter with you. You have no business to be taking story-books to school. You read too many novels anyhow. When I was a girl I wasn't so much as allowed to look at a novel."

"Oh, how can you call 'Ben Hur' a novel when it's really such a religious book?" protested Anne. "Of course it's a little too exciting to be proper reading for Sunday, and I only read it on week-days. And I never read *any* book now unless either Miss Stacy or Mrs. Allan thinks it is a proper book for a girl thirteen and three-quarters to read. Miss Stacy made me promise that. She found me reading a book one day called 'The Lurid Mystery of the Haunted Hall.'[1] It was one Ruby Gillis had lent me, and, oh, Marilla, it was so fascinating and creepy. It just curdled the blood in my veins. But Miss Stacy said it was a very silly, unwholesome book, and she asked me not to read any more of

---

[1]   Appears to be an invented title; Montgomery is referring to a popular genre of sensational novels.

it or any like it. I didn't mind promising not to read any more like it, but it was *agonizing* to give back that book without knowing how it turned out. But my love for Miss Stacy stood the test and I did. It's really wonderful, Marilla, what you can do when you're truly anxious to please a certain person."

"Well, I guess I'll light the lamp and get to work," said Marilla. "I see plainly that you don't want to hear what Miss Stacy had to say. You're more interested in the sound of your own tongue than in anything else."

"Oh, indeed, Marilla, I do want to hear it," cried Anne contritely. "I won't say another word—not one. I know I talk too much, but I am really trying to overcome it, and although I say far too much, yet if you only knew how many things I want to say and don't, you'd give me some credit for it. Please tell me, Marilla."

"Well, Miss Stacy wants to organize a class among her advanced students who mean to study for the entrance examination into Queen's. She intends to give them extra lessons for an hour after school. And she came to ask Matthew and me if we would like to have you join it. What do you think about it yourself, Anne? Would you like to go to Queen's and pass for a teacher?"

"Oh, Marilla!" Anne straightened to her knees and clasped her hands. "It's been the dream of my life—that is, for the last six months, ever since Ruby and Jane began to talk of studying for the entrance. But I didn't say anything about it, because I supposed it would be perfectly useless. I'd love to be a teacher. But won't it be dreadfully expensive? Mr. Andrews says it cost him one hundred and fifty dollars to put Prissy through, and Prissy wasn't a dunce in geometry."

"I guess you needn't worry about that part of it. When Matthew and I took you to bring up we resolved we would do the best we could for you and give you a good education. I believe in a girl being fitted to earn her own living whether she ever has to or not. You'll always have a home at Green Gables as long as Matthew and I are here, but nobody knows what is going to happen in this uncertain world, and it's just as well to be prepared. So you can join the Queen's class if you like, Anne."

"Oh, Marilla, thank you." Anne flung her arms about Marilla's waist and looked up earnestly into her face. "I'm extremely grateful to you and Matthew. And I'll study as hard as I can and do my very best to be a credit to you. I warn you not to expect much in geometry, but I think I can hold my own in anything else if I work hard."

"I dare say you'll get along well enough. Miss Stacy says you are bright and diligent." Not for worlds would Marilla have told Anne just what Miss Stacy had said about her; that would have been to pamper vanity. "You needn't rush to any extreme of killing yourself over your books. There is no hurry. You won't be ready to try the entrance for a year and a half yet. But it's well to begin in time and be thoroughly grounded, Miss Stacy says."

"I shall take more interest than ever in my studies now," said Anne blissfully, "because I have a purpose in life. Mr. Allan says everybody should have a purpose in life and pursue it faithfully. Only he says we must first make sure that it is a worthy purpose. I would call it a worthy purpose to want to be a teacher like Miss Stacy, wouldn't you, Marilla? I think it's a very noble profession."

The Queen's class was organized in due time. Gilbert Blythe, Anne Shirley, Ruby Gillis, Jane Andrews, Josie Pye, Charlie Sloane, and Moody Spurgeon MacPherson joined it. Diana Barry did not, as her parents did not intend to send her to Queen's. This seemed nothing short of a calamity to Anne. Never, since the night on which Minnie May had had the croup, had she and Diana been separated in anything. On the evening when the Queen's class first remained in school for the extra lessons and Anne saw Diana go slowly out with the others, to walk home alone through the Birch Path and Violet Vale, it was all the former could do to keep her seat and refrain from rushing impulsively after her chum. A lump came into her throat, and she hastily retired behind the pages of her uplifted Latin grammar to hide the tears in her eyes. Not for worlds would Anne have had Gilbert Blythe or Josie Pye see those tears.

"But, oh, Marilla, I really felt that I had tasted the bitterness of death,[1] as Mr. Allan said in his sermon last Sunday, when I saw Diana go out alone," she said mournfully that night. "I thought how splendid it would have been if Diana had only been going

---

[1] Cf. 1 Samuel 15.32.

to study for the Entrance, too. But we can't have things perfect in this imperfect world, as Mrs. Lynde says. Mrs. Lynde isn't exactly a comforting person sometimes, but there's no doubt she says a great many very true things. And I think the Queen's class is going to be extremely interesting. Jane and Ruby are just going to study to be teachers. That is the height of their ambition. Ruby says she will only teach for two years after she gets through, and then she intends to be married. Jane says she will devote her whole life to teaching, and never, never marry, because you are paid a salary for teaching, but a husband won't pay you anything, and growls if you ask for a share in the egg and butter money. I expect Jane speaks from mournful experience, for Mrs. Lynde says that her father is a perfect old crank, and meaner than second skimmings.[1] Josie Pye says she is just going to college for education's sake, because she won't have to earn her own living; she says of course it is different with orphans who are living on charity—*they* have to hustle. Moody Spurgeon is going to be a minister. Mrs. Lynde says he couldn't be anything else with a name like that to live up to.[2] I hope it isn't wicked of me, Marilla, but really the thought of Moody Spurgeon being a minister makes me laugh. He's such a funny-looking boy with that big fat face, and his little blue eyes, and his ears sticking out like flaps. But perhaps he will be more intellectual-looking when he grows up. Charlie Sloane says he's going to go into politics and be a member of Parliament, but Mrs. Lynde says he'll never succeed at that, because the Sloanes are all honest people, and it's only rascals that get on in politics nowadays."

"What is Gilbert Blythe going to be?" queried Marilla, seeing that Anne was opening her Caesar.[3]

"I don't happen to know what Gilbert Blythe's ambition in life is—if he has any," said Anne scornfully.

There was open rivalry between Gilbert and Anne now. Previously the rivalry had been rather one-sided, but there was no longer any doubt that Gilbert was as determined to be first

---

[1] Stingy, miserly. A reference to the process of skimming cream from milk, normally done once.

[2] See note on Spurgeon and Moody, 241, note 1.

[3] Latin textbook.

in class as Anne was. He was a foeman worthy of her steel.[1] The other members of the class tacitly acknowledged their superiority, and never dreamed of trying to compete with them.

Since the day by the pond when she had refused to listen to his plea for forgiveness, Gilbert, save for the aforesaid rivalry, had evinced no recognition whatever of the existence of Anne Shirley. He talked and jested with the other girls, exchanged books and puzzles with them, discussed lessons and plans, sometimes walked home with one or the other of them from prayer-meeting or Debating Club. But Anne Shirley he simply ignored, and Anne found out that it is not pleasant to be ignored. It was in vain that she told herself with a toss of her head that she did not care. Deep down in her wayward, feminine little heart she knew that she did care, and that if she had that chance of the Lake of Shining Waters again she would answer very differently. All at once, as it seemed, and to her secret dismay, she found that the old resentment she had cherished against him was gone—gone just when she most needed its sustaining power. It was in vain that she recalled every incident and emotion of that memorable occasion and tried to feel the old satisfying anger. That day by the pond had witnessed its last spasmodic flicker. Anne realized that she had forgiven and forgotten without knowing it. But it was too late.

And at least neither Gilbert nor anybody else, not even Diana, should ever suspect how sorry she was and how much she wished she hadn't been so proud and horrid! She determined to "shroud her feelings in deepest oblivion,"[2] and it may be stated here and now that she did it, so successfully that Gilbert, who possibly was not quite so indifferent as he seemed, could not console himself with any belief that Anne felt his retaliatory scorn. The only poor comfort he had was that she snubbed Charlie Sloane, unmercifully, continually and undeservedly.

Otherwise the winter passed away in a round of pleasant duties and studies. For Anne the days slipped by like golden beads

---

[1] A well-matched opponent. See Sir Walter Scott, *The Lady of the Lake* 5.10.237–39. This poem appeared in the *Sixth Royal Reader* 149–67. See 91, note 4 and 312, note 1

[2] The reference is obscure; cf. Felicia Hemans, "Night Scene in Genoa," cited earlier (187, note 1).

on the necklace of the year. She was happy, eager, interested; there were lessons to be learned and honours to be won; delightful books to read; new pieces to be practised for the Sunday-school choir; pleasant Saturday afternoons at the manse with Mrs. Allan; and then, almost before Anne realized it, spring had come again to Green Gables and all the world was abloom once more.

Studies palled just a wee bit then; the Queen's class, left behind in school while the others scattered to green lanes and leafy wood-cuts and meadow by-ways, looked wistfully out of the windows and discovered that Latin verbs and French exercises had somehow lost the tang and zest they had possessed in the crisp winter months. Even Anne and Gilbert lagged and grew indifferent. Teacher and taught were alike glad when the term was ended and the glad vacation days stretched rosily before them.

"But you've done good work this past year," Miss Stacy told them on the last evening, "and you deserve a good, jolly vacation. Have the best time you can in the out-of-door world and lay in a good stock of health and vitality and ambition to carry you through next year. It will be the tug of war,[1] you know—the last year before the Entrance."

"Are you going to be back next year, Miss Stacy?" asked Josie Pye.

Josie Pye never scrupled to ask questions; in this instance the rest of the class felt grateful to her; none of them would have dared to ask it of Miss Stacy, but all wanted to, for there had been alarming rumours running at large through the school for some time that Miss Stacy was not coming back the next year—that she had been offered a position in the graded school[2] of her own home district and meant to accept. The Queen's class listened in breathless suspense for her answer.

"Yes, I think I will," said Miss Stacy. "I thought of taking another school, but I have decided to come back to Avonlea. To

---

[1]   "When Greek meets Greek, then comes the tug of war." I.e., "The light skirmishing betwixt the parties was ended, and the serious battle commenced" (*The Oxford Dictionary of English Proverbs*, 3rd ed., Oxford: Clarendon, 1970). *ODEP* cites the earliest occurrence in 1677, and notes that the phrase is used throughout the nineteenth century.

[2]   A school divided into grades rather than, as the Avonlea school, having all grades in one room.

tell the truth, I've grown so interested in my pupils here that I found I couldn't leave them. So I'll stay and see you through."

"Hurrah!" said Moody Spurgeon. Moody Spurgeon had never been so carried away by his feelings before, and he blushed uncomfortably every time he thought about it for a week.

"Oh, I'm so glad," said Anne with shining eyes. "Dear Miss Stacy, it would be perfectly dreadful if you didn't come back. I don't believe I could have the heart to go on with my studies at all if another teacher came here."

When Anne got home that night she stacked all her text-books away in an old trunk in the attic, locked it, and threw the key into the blanket box.

"I'm not even going to look at a school book in vacation," she told Marilla. "I've studied as hard all the term as I possibly could and I've pored over that geometry until I know every proposition in the first book off by heart, even when the letters *are* changed. I just feel tired of everything sensible and I'm going to let my imagination run riot for the summer. Oh, you needn't be alarmed, Marilla. I'll only let it run riot within reasonable limits. But I want to have a real good jolly time this summer, for maybe it's the last summer I'll be a little girl. Mrs. Lynde says that if I keep on stretching out next year as I've done this I'll have to put on longer skirts. She says I'm all running to legs and eyes. And when I put on longer skirts I shall feel that I have to live up to them and be very dignified. It won't even do to believe in fairies then, I'm afraid; so I'm going to believe in them with my whole heart this summer. I think we're going to have a very gay vacation. Ruby Gillis is going to have a birthday party soon and there's the Sunday-school picnic and the missionary concert next month. And Mr. Barry says that some evening he'll take Diana and me over to the White Sands Hotel and have dinner there. They have dinner there in the evening, you know. Jane Andrews was over once last summer and she says it was a dazzling sight to see the electric lights and the flowers and all the lady guests in such beautiful dresses. Jane says it was her first glimpse into high life and she'll never forget it to her dying day."

Mrs. Lynde came up the next afternoon to find out why Marilla had not been at the Aid meeting on Thursday. When

Marilla was not at Aid meeting people knew there was something wrong at Green Gables.

"Matthew had a bad spell with his heart Thursday," Marilla explained, "and I didn't feel like leaving him. Oh yes, he's all right again now, but he takes them spells oftener than he used to and I'm anxious about him. The doctor says he must be careful to avoid excitement. That's easy enough, for Matthew doesn't go about looking for excitement by any means and never did, but he's not to do any very heavy work either and you might as well tell Matthew not to breathe as not to work. Come and lay off your things, Rachel. You'll stay to tea?"

"Well, seeing you're so pressing, perhaps I might as well stay," said Mrs. Rachel, who had not the slightest intention of doing anything else.

Mrs. Rachel and Marilla sat comfortably in the parlour while Anne got the tea and made hot biscuits that were light and white enough to defy even Mrs. Rachel's criticism.

"I must say Anne has turned out a real smart girl," admitted Mrs. Rachel, as Marilla accompanied her to the end of the lane at sunset. "She must be a great help to you."

"She is," said Marilla, "and she's real steady and reliable now. I used to be afraid she'd never get over her feather-brained ways, but she has and I wouldn't be afraid to trust her in anything now."

"I never would have thought she'd have turned out so well that first day I was here three years ago," said Mrs. Rachel. "Lawful heart, shall I ever forget that tantrum of hers! When I went home that night I says to Thomas, says I, 'Mark my words, Thomas, Marilla Cuthbert'll live to rue the step she's took.' But I was mistaken and I'm real glad of it. I ain't one of those kind of people, Marilla, as can never be brought to own up that they've made a mistake. No, that never was my way, thank goodness. I did make a mistake in judging Anne, but it weren't no wonder, for an odder, unexpecteder witch of a child there never was in this world, that's what. There was no ciphering her out by the rules that worked with other children. It's nothing short of wonderful how she's improved these three years, but especially in her looks. She's a real pretty girl got to be, though I can't say I'm overly partial to that pale, big-eyed style myself. I like more

snap and colour, like Diana Barry has or Ruby Gillis. Ruby
Gillis' looks are real showy. But somehow—I don't know how it
is but when Anne and them are together, though she ain't half
as handsome, she makes them look kind of common and overdone—something like them white June lilies she calls narcissus
alongside of the big, red peonies, that's what."

CHAPTER XXXI

WHERE THE BROOK AND RIVER MEET[1]

ANNE had her "good" summer and enjoyed it whole-heartedly.
She and Diana fairly lived outdoors, revelling in all the delights
that Lovers' Lane and the Dryad's Bubble and Willowmere and
Victoria Island afforded. Marilla offered no objections to Anne's
gypsyings. The Spencervale doctor who had come the night
Minnie May had the croup met Anne at the house of a patient
one afternoon early in vacation, looked her over sharply, screwed
up his mouth, shook his head, and sent a message to Marilla
Cuthbert by another person. It was:
  "Keep that red-headed girl of yours in the open air all
summer and don't let her read books until she gets more spring
into her step."
  This message frightened Marilla wholesomely. She read Anne's
death-warrant by consumption in it unless it was scrupulously
obeyed.[2] As a result, Anne had the golden summer of her life as far
as freedom and frolic went. She walked, rowed, berried and
dreamed to her heart's content; and when September came she was
bright-eyed and alert, with a step that would have satisfied the
Spencervale doctor and a heart full of ambition and zest once more.
  "I feel just like studying with might and main," she declared as
she brought her books down from the attic. "Oh, you good old

---

1   See Longfellow, "Maidenhood" (1841): "Standing, with reluctant feet,/ Where the
     brook and river meet,/ Womanhood and childhood fleet!" (7–9). There is another
     echo of this poem later in the novel. See 326, note 1.
2   See earlier reference to consumption (131, note 1).

friends, I'm glad to see your honest faces once more—yes, even you, geometry. I've had a perfectly beautiful summer, Marilla, and now I'm rejoicing as a strong man to run a race,[1] as Mr. Allan said last Sunday. Doesn't Mr. Allan preach magnificent sermons? Mrs. Lynde says he is improving every day and the first thing we know some city church will gobble him up and then we'll be left and have to turn to and break in another green preacher. But I don't see the use of meeting trouble half-way, do you, Marilla? I think it would be better just to enjoy Mr. Allan while we have him. If I were a man I think I'd be a minister. They can have such an influence for good, if their theology is sound; and it must be thrilling to preach splendid sermons and stir your hearers' hearts. Why can't women be ministers, Marilla? I asked Mrs. Lynde that and she was shocked and said it would be a scandalous thing. She said there might be female ministers in the States and she believed there was, but thank goodness we hadn't got to that stage in Canada yet and she hoped we never would.[2] But I don't see why. I think women would make splendid ministers. When there is a social to be got up or a church tea or anything else to raise money the women have to turn to and do the work. I'm sure Mrs. Lynde can pray every bit as well as Superintendent Bell and I've no doubt she could preach too with a little practice."

"Yes, I believe she could," said Marilla drily. "She does plenty of unofficial preaching as it is. Nobody has much of a chance to go wrong in Avonlea with Rachel to oversee them."

"Marilla," said Anne in a burst of confidence, "I want to tell you something and ask you what you think about it. It has worried me terribly—on Sunday afternoons, that is, when I think specially about such matters. I do really want to be good; and when I'm with you or Mrs. Allan or Miss Stacy I want it more than ever and I want to do just what would please you and what you would approve of. But mostly when I'm with Mrs. Lynde I

---

[1] See Psalm 19.5.

[2] Again, Mrs. Lynde shows her conflicted position with regard to contemporary feminism in English Canada: she supports woman suffrage but not higher education for women or women as ministers. See 317, note 1 and 329, note 1. The Presbyterian church in Canada admitted women as deaconesses from the 1890s, but not as ministers. See Alison Prentice et al, *Canadian Women: A History* (315) on the "separate sphere" of deaconesses.

feel desperately wicked and as if I wanted to go and do the very thing she tells me I oughtn't to do. I feel irresistibly tempted to do it. Now, what do you think is the reason I feel like that? Do you think it's because I'm really bad and unregenerate?"

Marilla looked dubious for a moment. Then she laughed.

"If you are I guess I am too, Anne, for Rachel often has that very effect on me. I sometimes think she'd have more of an influence for good, as you say yourself, if she didn't keep nagging people to do right. There should have been a special commandment against nagging. But there, I shouldn't talk so. Rachel is a good Christian woman and she means well. There isn't a kinder soul in Avonlea and she never shirks her share of work."

"I'm very glad you feel the same," said Anne decidedly. "It's so encouraging. I sha'n't worry so much over that after this. But I dare say there'll be other things to worry me. They keep coming up new all the time—things to perplex you, you know. You settle one question and there's another right after. There are so many things to be thought over and decided when you're beginning to grow up. It keeps me busy all the time thinking them over and deciding what is right. It's a serious thing to grow up, isn't it, Marilla? But when I have such good friends as you and Matthew and Mrs. Allan and Miss Stacy I ought to grow up successfully, and I'm sure it will be my own fault if I don't. I feel it's a great responsibility because I have only the one chance. If I don't grow up right I can't go back and begin over again. I've grown two inches this summer, Marilla. Mr. Gillis measured me at Ruby's party. I'm so glad you made my new dresses longer. That dark green one is so pretty and it was sweet of you to put on the flounce. Of course I know it wasn't really necessary, but flounces are so stylish this fall and Josie Pye has flounces on all her dresses. I know I'll be able to study better because of mine. I shall have such a comfortable feeling deep down in my mind about that flounce."

"It's worth something to have that," admitted Marilla.

Miss Stacy came back to Avonlea School and found all her pupils eager for work once more. Especially did the Queen's class gird up their loins[1] for the fray, for at the end of the coming year,

---

[1]   Cf. Job 38.3.

dimly shadowing their pathway already, loomed up that fateful thing known as "the Entrance," at the thought of which one and all felt their hearts sink into their very shoes. Suppose they did not pass! That thought was doomed to haunt Anne through the waking hours of that winter, Sunday afternoons inclusive, to the almost entire exclusion of moral and theological problems. When Anne had bad dreams she found herself staring miserably at pass lists of the Entrance exams, where Gilbert Blythe's name was blazoned at the top and in which hers did not appear at all.

But it was a jolly, busy, happy swift-flying winter. School work was as interesting, class rivalry as absorbing, as of yore. New worlds of thought, feeling and ambition, fresh, fascinating fields of unexplored knowledge seemed to be opening out before Anne's eager eyes.

"Hills peeped o'er hill and Alps on Alps arose."[1]

Much of all this was due to Miss Stacy's tactful, careful, broad-minded guidance. She led her class to think and explore and discover for themselves and encouraged straying from the old beaten paths to a degree that quite shocked Mrs. Lynde and the school trustees, who viewed all innovations on established methods rather dubiously.

Apart from her studies Anne expanded socially, for Marilla, mindful of the Spencervale doctor's dictum, no longer vetoed occasional outings. The Debating Club flourished and gave several concerts; there were one or two parties almost verging on grown-up affairs; there were sleigh drives and skating frolics galore.

Between times Anne grew, shooting up so rapidly that Marilla was astonished one day, when they were standing side by side, to find the girl was taller than herself.

"Why, Anne, how you've grown!" she said, almost unbeliev-ingly. A sigh followed on the words. Marilla felt a queer regret over Anne's inches. The child she had learned to love had vanished somehow and here was this tall, serious-eyed girl of fifteen, with the thoughtful brows and the proudly poised little head, in her place. Marilla loved the girl as much as she had loved

---

[1] See Alexander Pope (1688-1744), *An Essay on Criticism* (1711) line 232; properly, "Hills peep o'er hills, and Alps on Alps arise!" I.e., new challenges appear.

the child, but she was conscious of a queer sorrowful sense of loss. And that night when Anne had gone to prayer-meeting with Diana Marilla sat alone in the wintry twilight and indulged in the weakness of a cry. Matthew, coming in with a lantern, caught her at it and gazed at her in such consternation that Marilla had to laugh through her tears.

"I was thinking about Anne," she explained. "She's got to be such a big girl—and she'll probably be away from us next winter. I'll miss her terrible."

"She'll be able to come home often," comforted Matthew, to whom Anne was as yet and always would be the little, eager girl he had brought home from Bright River on that June evening four years before. "The branch railroad will be built to Carmody by that time."

"It won't be the same thing as having her here all the time," sighed Marilla gloomily, determined to enjoy her luxury of grief uncomforted. "But there—men can't understand these things!"

There were other changes in Anne no less real than the physical change. For one thing, she became much quieter. Perhaps she thought all the more and dreamed as much as ever, but she certainly talked less. Marilla noticed and commented on this also.

"You don't chatter half as much as you used to, Anne, nor use half as many big words. What has come over you?"

Anne coloured and laughed a little, as she dropped her book and looked dreamily out of the window, where the big fat red buds were bursting out on the creeper in response to the lure of the spring sunshine.

"I don't know—I don't want to talk as much," she said, denting her chin thoughtfully with her forefinger. "It's nicer to think dear, pretty thoughts and keep them in one's heart, like treasures. I don't like to have them laughed at or wondered over. And somehow I don't want to use big words any more. It's almost a pity, isn't it, now that I'm really growing big enough to say them if I did want to. It's fun to be almost grown up in some ways, but it's not the kind of fun I expected, Marilla. There's so much to learn and do and think that there isn't time for big words. Besides, Miss Stacy says the short ones are much stronger and better. She makes us write all our essays as simply as possible. It was hard at first. I was so used to crowding in all the fine big words I could think of—and I thought of any number of them. But I've got used to it now and I see it's so much better."

"What has become of your story club? I haven't heard you speak of it for a long time."

"The story club isn't in existence any longer. We hadn't time for it—and anyhow I think we had got tired of it. It was silly to be writing about love and murder and elopements and mysteries. Miss Stacy sometimes has us write a story for training in composition, but she won't let us write anything but what might happen in Avonlea in our own lives, and she criticizes it very sharply and makes us criticize our own too. I never thought my compositions had so many faults until I began to look for them myself. I felt so ashamed I wanted to give up altogether, but Miss Stacy said I could learn to write well if I only trained myself to be my own severest critic. And so I am trying to."

"You've only two months more before the Entrance," said Marilla. "Do you think you'll be able to get through?"

Anne shivered.

"I don't know. Sometimes I think I'll be all right—and then I get horribly afraid. We've studied hard and Miss Stacy has drilled us thoroughly, but we mayn't get through for all that. We've each got a stumbling-block. Mine is geometry of course, and Jane's is Latin and Ruby's and Charlie's is algebra and Josie's is arithmetic. Moody Spurgeon says he feels it in his bones that he is going to fail in English history. Miss Stacy is going to give us examinations in June just as hard as we'll have at the Entrance and mark us just as strictly, so we'll have some idea. I wish it was all over, Marilla. It haunts me. Sometimes I wake up in the night and wonder what I'll do if I don't pass."

"Why, go to school next year and try again," said Marilla unconcernedly.

"Oh, I don't believe I'd have the heart for it. It would be such a disgrace to fail, especially if Gil—if the others passed. And I get so nervous in an examination that I'm likely to make a mess of it. I wish I had nerves like Jane Andrews. Nothing rattles her."

Anne sighed and, dragging her eyes from the witcheries of the spring world, the beckoning day of breeze and blue, and the green things upspringing in the garden, buried herself resolutely in her book. There would be other springs, but if she did not succeed in passing the Entrance Anne felt convinced that she would never recover sufficiently to enjoy them.

CHAPTER XXXII

THE PASS LIST IS OUT

WITH the end of June came the close of the term and the close of Miss Stacy's rule in Avonlea School. Anne and Diana walked home that evening feeling very sober indeed. Red eyes and damp handkerchiefs bore convincing testimony to the fact that Miss Stacy's farewell words must have been quite as touching as Mr. Phillips' had been under similar circumstances three years before. Diana looked back at the school-house from the foot of the spruce hill and sighed deeply.

"It does seem as if it was the end of everything, doesn't it?" she said dismally.

"You oughtn't to feel half as badly as I do," said Anne, hunting vainly for a dry spot on her handkerchief. "You'll be back again next winter, but I suppose I've left the dear old school for ever—if I have good luck, that is."

"It won't be a bit the same. Miss Stacy won't be there, nor you nor Jane nor Ruby probably. I shall have to sit all alone, for I couldn't bear to have another deskmate after you. Oh, we have had jolly times, haven't we, Anne? It's dreadful to think they're all over."

Two big tears rolled down by Diana's nose.

"If you would stop crying I could," said Anne imploringly. "Just as soon as I put away my hanky I see you brimming up and that starts me off again. As Mrs. Lynde says, 'If you can't be cheerful, be as cheerful as you can.' After all, I dare say I'll be back next year. This is one of the times I *know* I'm not going to pass. They're getting alarmingly frequent."

"Why, you came out splendidly in the exams Miss Stacy gave."

"Yes, but those exams didn't make me nervous. When I think

of the real thing you can't imagine what a horrid cold fluttery feeling comes round my heart. And then my number is thirteen and Josie Pye says it's so unlucky. I am *not* superstitious and I know it can make no difference. But still I wish it wasn't thirteen."

"I do wish I were going in with you," said Diana. "Wouldn't we have a perfectly elegant time? But I suppose you'll have to cram in the evenings."

"No; Miss Stacy has made us promise not to open a book at all. She says it would only tire and confuse us and we are to go out walking and not think about the exams at all and go to bed early. It's good advice, but I expect it will be hard to follow; good advice is apt to be, I think. Prissy Andrews told me that she sat up half the night every night of her Entrance week and crammed for dear life; and I had determined to sit up *at least* as long as she did. It was so kind of your Aunt Josephine to ask me to stay at Beechwood while I'm in town."

"You'll write to me while you're in, won't you?"

"I'll write Tuesday night and tell you how the first day goes," promised Anne.

"I'll be haunting the post-office Wednesday," vowed Diana.

Anne went to town the following Monday and on Wednesday Diana haunted the post-office, as agreed, and got her letter.

"Dearest Diana," wrote Anne, "here it is Tuesday night and I'm writing this in the library at Beechwood. Last night I was horribly lonesome all alone in my room and wished so much you were with me. I couldn't 'cram' because I'd promised Miss Stacy not to, but it was as hard to keep from opening my history as it used to be to keep from reading a story before my lessons were learned.

"This morning Miss Stacy came for me and we went to the Academy, calling for Jane and Ruby and Josie on our way. Ruby asked me to feel her hands and they were as cold as ice. Josie said I looked as if I hadn't slept a wink and she didn't believe I was strong enough to stand the grind of the teacher's course even if I did get through. There are times and seasons even yet when I don't feel that I've made any great headway in learning to like Josie Pye!

"When we reached the Academy there were scores of students there from all over the Island. The first person we saw was Moody Spurgeon sitting on the steps and muttering away to himself. Jane asked him what on earth he was doing and he said he was repeating the multiplication table over and over to steady his nerves and for pity's sake not to interrupt him, because if he stopped for a moment he got frightened and forgot everything he ever knew, but the multiplication table kept all his facts firmly in their proper place!

"When we were assigned to our rooms Miss Stacy had to leave us. Jane and I sat together and Jane was so composed that I envied her. No need of the multiplication table for good, steady, sensible Jane! I wondered if I looked as I felt and if they could hear my heart thumping clear across the room. Then a man came in and began distributing the English examination sheets. My hands grew cold then and my head fairly whirled around as I picked it up. Just one awful moment,—Diana, I felt exactly as I did four years ago when I asked Marilla if I might stay at Green Gables—and then everything cleared up in my mind and my heart began beating again—I forgot to say that it had stopped altogether!—for I knew I could do something with *that* paper anyhow.

"At noon we went home for dinner and then back again for history in the afternoon. The history was a pretty hard paper and I got dreadfully mixed up in the dates. Still, I think I did fairly well to-day. But oh, Diana, to-morrow the geometry exam comes off and when I think of it it takes every bit of determination I possess to keep from opening my Euclid.[1] If I thought the multiplication table would help me any I would recite it from now till to-morrow morning.

"I went down to see the other girls this evening. On my way I met Moody Spurgeon wandering distractedly around. He said he knew he had failed in history and he was born to be a disappointment to his parents and he was going home on the morning train; and it would be easier to be a carpenter than a minister, anyhow. I cheered him up and persuaded him to stay to the end because it would be unfair to Miss Stacy if he didn't. Sometimes I have wished I was born a boy, but when I see Moody Spurgeon I'm always glad I'm a girl and not his sister.

"Ruby was in hysterics when I reached their boarding-house;

---

[1] Geometry text book.

she had just discovered a fearful mistake she had made in her English paper. When she recovered we went up-town and had an ice-cream. How we wished you had been with us.

"Oh, Diana, if only the geometry examination were over! But then, as Mrs. Lynde would say, the sun will go on rising and setting whether I fail in geometry or not. That is true but not especially comforting. I think I'd rather it *didn't* go on if I failed!

"Yours devotedly,

"ANNE."

The geometry examination and all the others were over in due time and Anne arrived home on Friday evening, rather tired but with an air of chastened triumph about her. Diana was over at Green Gables when she arrived and they met as if they had been parted for years.

"You old darling, it's perfectly splendid to see you back again. It seems like an age since you went to town and oh, Anne, how did you get along?"

"Pretty well, I think, in everything but the geometry. I don't know whether I passed in it or not and I have a creepy, crawly presentiment that I didn't. Oh, how good it is to be back! Green Gables is the dearest, loveliest spot in the world."

"How did the others do?"

"The girls say they know they didn't pass, but I think they did pretty well. Josie says the geometry was so easy a child of ten could do it! Moody Spurgeon still thinks he failed in history and Charlie says he failed in algebra. But we don't really know anything about it and won't until the pass list is out. That won't be for a fortnight. Fancy living a fortnight in such suspense! I wish I could go to sleep and never wake up until it is over."

Diana knew it would be useless to ask how Gilbert Blythe had fared, so she merely said:

"Oh, you'll pass all right. Don't worry."

"I'd rather not pass at all than not come out pretty well up on the list," flashed Anne, by which she meant—and Diana knew she meant—that success would be incomplete and bitter if she did not come out ahead of Gilbert Blythe.

With this end in view Anne had strained every nerve during the examinations. So had Gilbert. They had met and passed each other on the street a dozen times without any sign of recognition and every time Anne had held her head a little higher and wished a little more earnestly that she had made friends with Gilbert when he asked her, and vowed a little more determinedly to surpass him in the examination. She knew that all Avonlea junior was wondering which would come out first; she even knew that Jimmy Glover and Ned Wright had a bet on the question and that Josie Pye had said there was no doubt in the world that Gilbert would be first; and she felt that her humiliation would be unbearable if she failed.

But she had another and nobler motive for wishing to do well. She wanted to "pass high" for the sake of Matthew and Marilla— especially Matthew. Matthew had declared to her his conviction that she "would beat the whole Island." That, Anne felt, was something it would be foolish to hope for even in the wildest dreams. But she did hope fervently that she would be among the first ten at least, so that she might see Matthew's kindly brown eyes gleam with pride in her achievement. That, she felt, would be a sweet reward indeed for all her hard work and patient grubbing among unimaginative equations and conjugations.

At the end of the fortnight Anne took to "haunting" the post-office also, in the distracted company of Jane, Ruby and Josie, opening the Charlottetown dailies with shaking hands and cold, sinkaway feelings, as bad as any experienced during the Entrance week. Charlie and Gilbert were not above doing this too, but Moody Spurgeon stayed resolutely away.

"I haven't got the grit to go there and look at a paper in cold blood," he told Anne. "I'm just going to wait until somebody comes and tells me suddenly whether I've passed or not."

When three weeks had gone by without the pass list appearing Anne began to feel that she really couldn't stand the strain much longer. Her appetite failed and her interest in Avonlea doings languished. Mrs. Lynde wanted to know what else you could expect with a Tory superintendent of education at the head of affairs, and Matthew, noting Anne's paleness and indifference and the lagging steps that bore her home from the post-office every afternoon, began seriously to wonder if he hadn't better vote Grit at the next election.

But one evening the news came. Anne was sitting at her open

window, for the time forgetful of the woes of examinations and the cares of the world, as she drank in the beauty of the summer dusk, sweet-scented with flower-breaths from the garden below and sibilant and rustling from the stir of poplars. The eastern sky above the firs was flushed faintly pink from the reflection of the west, and Anne was wondering dreamily if the spirit of colour looked like that, when she saw Diana come flying down through the firs, over the log bridge, and up the slope, with a fluttering newspaper in her hand.

Anne sprang to her feet, knowing at once what that paper contained. The pass list was out! Her head whirled and her heart beat until it hurt her. She could not move a step. It seemed an hour to her before Diana came rushing along the hall and burst into the room without even knocking, so great was her excitement.

"Anne, you've passed," she cried, "passed the *very first*—you and Gilbert both—you're ties—but your name is first. Oh, I'm so proud!"

Diana flung the paper on the table and herself on Anne's bed, utterly breathless and incapable of further speech. Anne lighted the lamp, oversetting the match-safe and using up half a dozen matches before her shaking hands could accomplish the task. Then she snatched up the paper. Yes, she had passed—there was her name at the very top of a list of two hundred! That moment was worth living for.

"You did just splendidly, Anne," puffed Diana, recovering sufficiently to sit up and speak, for Anne, starry-eyed and rapt, had not uttered a word. "Father brought the paper home from Bright River not ten minutes ago—it came out on the afternoon train, you know, and won't be here till to-morrow by mail—and when I saw the pass list I just rushed over like a wild thing. You've all passed, every one of you, Moody Spurgeon and all, although he's conditioned in history. Jane and Ruby did pretty well—they're half-way up—and so did Charlie. Josie just scraped through with three marks to spare, but you'll see she'll put on as many airs as if she'd led. Won't Miss Stacy be delighted? Oh, Anne, what does it feel like to see your name at the head of a pass list like that? If it were me I know I'd go crazy with joy. I am pretty near crazy as it is, but you're as calm and cool as a spring evening."

"I'm just dazzled inside," said Anne. "I want to say a hundred things, and I can't find words to say them in. I never dreamed of this—yes, I did, too, just once! I let myself think *once*, 'What if I should come out first?' quakingly, you know, for it seemed so vain and presumptuous to think I could lead the Island. Excuse me a minute, Diana. I must run right out to the field to tell Matthew. Then we'll go up the road and tell the good news to the others."

They hurried to the hayfield below the barn where Matthew was coiling hay, and, as luck would have it, Mrs. Lynde was talking to Marilla at the lane fence.

"Oh, Matthew," exclaimed Anne, "I've passed and I'm first— or one of the first! I'm not vain, but I'm thankful."

"Well now, I always said it," said Matthew, gazing at the pass list delightedly. "I knew you could beat them all easy."

"You've done pretty well, I must say, Anne," said Marilla, trying to hide her extreme pride in Anne from Mrs. Rachel's critical eye. But that good soul said heartily:

"I just guess she has done well, and far be it from me to be backward in saying it. You're a credit to your friends, Anne, that's what, and we're all proud of you."

That night Anne, who had wound up a delightful evening by a serious little talk with Mrs. Allan at the manse, knelt sweetly by her open window in a great sheen of moonshine and murmured a prayer of gratitude and aspiration that came straight from her heart. There was a thankfulness for the past and reverent petition for the future; and when she slept on her white pillow her dreams were as fair and bright and beautiful as maidenhood might desire.

CHAPTER XXXIII

THE HOTEL CONCERT

"PUT on your white organdy, by all means, Anne," advised Diana decidedly.

They were together in the east gable chamber; outside it was only twilight—a lovely yellowish-green twilight with a clear blue cloudless sky. A big round moon, slowly deepening from her pallid lustre into burnished silver, hung over the Haunted Wood; the air was full of sweet summer sounds—sleepy birds twittering, freakish breezes, far-away voices and laughter. But in Anne's room the blind was drawn and the lamp lighted, for an important toilet was being made.

The east gable was a very different place from what it had been on that night four years before, when Anne had felt its bareness penetrate to the marrow of her spirit with its inhospitable chill. Changes had crept in, Marilla conniving at them resignedly, until it was as sweet and dainty a nest as a young girl could desire.

The velvet carpet with the pink roses and the pink silk curtains of Anne's early visions had certainly never materialized; but her dreams had kept pace with her growth, and it is not probable she lamented them. The floor was covered with a pretty matting, and the curtains that softened the high window and fluttered in the vagrant breezes were of pale green art muslin. The walls, hung not with gold and silver brocade tapestry, but with a dainty apple-blossom paper, were adorned with a few good pictures given Anne by Mrs. Allan. Miss Stacy's photograph occupied the place of honour, and Anne made a sentimental point of keeping fresh flowers on the bracket under it. To-night a spike of white lilies faintly perfumed the room like the dream of a fragrance. There was no "mahogany furniture," but there was a white-painted bookcase filled with books, a cushioned wicker rocker, a toilet-table befrilled with white muslin, a quaint, gilt-framed mirror with chubby pink cupids and purple grapes painted over its arched top, that used to hang in the spare room, and a low white bed.

Anne was dressing for a concert at the White Sands Hotel. The guests had got it up in aid of the Charlottetown hospital, and had hunted out all the available amateur talent in the surrounding districts to help it along. Bertha Sampson and Pearl Clay of the White Sands Baptist choir had been asked to sing a duet; Milton Clark of Newbridge was to give a violin solo; Winnie Adella Blair of Carmody was to sing a Scotch ballad; and Laura Spencer of Spencervale and Anne Shirley of Avonlea were to recite.

As Anne would have said at one time, it was "an epoch in her life," and she was deliciously athrill with the excitement of it. Matthew was in the seventh heaven of gratified pride over the honour conferred on his Anne, and Marilla was not far behind, although she would have died rather than admit it, and said she didn't think it was very proper for a lot of young folks to be gadding over to the hotel without any responsible person with them.

Anne and Diana were to drive over with Jane Andrews and her brother Billy in their double-seated buggy; and several other Avonlea girls and boys were going, too. There was a party of visitors expected out from town, and after the concert a supper was to be given to the performers.

"Do you really think the organdy will be best?" queried Anne anxiously. "I don't think it's as pretty as my blue-flowered muslin—and it certainly isn't so fashionable."

"But it suits you ever so much better," said Diana. "It's so soft and frilly and clinging. The muslin is stiff, and makes you look too dressed up. But the organdy seems as if it grew on you."

Anne sighed and yielded. Diana was beginning to have a reputation for notable taste in dressing, and her advice on such subjects was much sought after. She was looking very pretty herself on this particular night in a dress of the lovely wild-rose pink, from which Anne was for ever debarred; but she was not to take any part in the concert, so her appearance was of minor importance. All her pains were bestowed upon Anne, who, she vowed, must, for the credit of Avonlea, be dressed and combed and adorned to the queen's taste.

"Pull out that frill a little more—so; here, let me tie your sash; now for your slippers. I'm going to braid your hair in two thick braids, and tie them half-way up with big white bows—no, don't pull out a single curl over your forehead—just have the soft part. There is no way you do your hair suits you so well, Anne, and Mrs. Allan says you look like a Madonna when you part it so. I shall fasten this little white house rose just behind your ear. There was just one on my bush, and I saved it for you."

"Shall I put my pearl beads on?" asked Anne. "Matthew brought me a string from town last week, and I know he'd like to see them on me."

Diana pursed up her lips, put her black head on one side

critically, and finally pronounced in favour of the beads, which were thereupon tied around Anne's slim milk-white throat.

"There's something so stylish about you, Anne," said Diana, with unenvious admiration. "You hold your head with such an air. I suppose it's your figure. I am just a dumpling. I've always been afraid of it, and now I know it is so. Well, I suppose I shall just have to resign myself to it."

"But you have such dimples," said Anne, smiling affectionately into the pretty, vivacious face so near her own. "Lovely dimples, like little dents in cream. I have given up all hope of dimples. My dimple-dream will never come true; but so many of my dreams have that I mustn't complain. Am I all ready now?"

"All ready," assured Diana, as Marilla appeared in the door-way, a gaunt figure with grayer hair than of yore and no fewer angles, but with a much softer face. "Come right in and look at our elocutionist, Marilla. Doesn't she look lovely?"

Marilla emitted a sound between a sniff and a grunt.

"She looks neat and proper. I like that way of fixing her hair. But I expect she'll ruin that dress driving over there in the dust and dew with it, and it looks most too thin for these damp nights. Organdy's the most unserviceable stuff in the world anyhow, and I told Matthew so when he got it. But there is no use in saying anything to Matthew nowadays. Time was when he would take my advice, but now he just buys things for Anne regardless, and the clerks at Carmody know they can palm anything off on him. Just let them tell him a thing is pretty and fashionable, and Matthew plunks his money down for it. Mind you keep your skirt clear of the wheel, Anne, and put your warm jacket on."

Then Marilla stalked down-stairs, thinking proudly how sweet Anne looked, with that

"One moonbeam from the forehead to the crown"[1]

and regretting that she could not go the concert herself to hear her girl recite.

"I wonder if it *is* too damp for my dress," said Anne anxiously.

---

[1] See Elizabeth Barrett Browning (1806–61), *Aurora Leigh* (1856). The quotation is apt, given the earlier comment by Diana on the parting of Anne's hair. "No one parts/ Her hair with such a silver line as you,/ One moonbeam from the forehead to the crown!" (4.1.1011–1013).

"'THERE'S SOMETHING SO STYLISH ABOUT YOU, ANNE,' SAID
DIANA."

"Not a bit of it," said Diana, pulling up the window blind. "It's a perfect night, and there won't be any dew. Look at the moonlight."

"I'm so glad my window looks east into the sun-rising," said Anne, going over to Diana. "It's so splendid to see the morning coming up over those long hills and glowing through those sharp fir tops. It's new every morning,[1] and I feel as if I washed my very soul in that bath of earliest sunshine. Oh, Diana, I love this little room so dearly. I don't know how I'll get along without it when I go to town next month."

"Don't speak of your going away to-night," begged Diana. "I don't want to think of it, it makes me so miserable, and I do want to have a good time this evening. What are you going to recite, Anne? And are you nervous?"

"Not a bit. I've recited so often in public I don't mind at all now. I've decided to give 'The Maiden's Vow.'[2] It's so pathetic. Laura Spencer is going to give a comic recitation, but I'd rather make people cry than laugh."

"What will you recite if they encore you?"

"They won't dream of encoring me," scoffed Anne, who was not without her own secret hopes that they would, and already visioned herself telling Matthew all about it at the next morning's breakfast-table. "There are Billy and Jane now—I hear the wheels. Come on."

Billy Andrews insisted that Anne should ride on the front seat with him, so she unwillingly climbed up. She would have much preferred to sit back with the girls, where she could have laughed and chattered to her heart's content. There was not much of either laughter or chatter in Billy. He was a big, fat, stolid youth of twenty, with a round, expressionless face, and a painful lack of conversational gifts. But he admired Anne immensely, and was puffed up with pride over the prospect of driving to White Sands with that slim, upright figure beside him.

---

[1] Cf. hymn by John Keble (1792–1866), poet and clergyman: "New every morning is the love/ Our wakening and uprising prove" (*The Christian Year* [1827; London: Dent, 1914]).

[2] Probably, "Mars La Tour, or, The Maiden's Vow" by Stafford MacGregor (1883). See *AA* 481–82. There are other candidates for this reference, including, as *AA* notes, "The Maiden's Vow" by Caroline Oliphant (1869).

Anne, by dint of talking over her shoulder to the girls and occasionally passing a sop of civility to Billy—who grinned and chuckled and never could think of any reply until it was too late—contrived to enjoy the drive in spite of all. It was a night for enjoyment. The road was full of buggies, all bound for the hotel, and laughter, silver-clear, echoed and re-echoed along it. When they reached the hotel it was a blaze of light from top to bottom. They were met by the ladies of the concert committee, one of whom took Anne off to the performers' dressing-room, which was filled with the members of a Charlottetown Symphony Club, among whom Anne felt suddenly shy and frightened and countrified. Her dress, which, in the east gable, had seemed so dainty and pretty, now seemed simple and plain—too simple and plain, she thought, amid all the silks and laces that glistened and rustled around her. What were her pearl beads compared to the diamonds of the big, handsome lady near her? And how poor her one wee white rose must look beside all the hot-house flowers the others wore! Anne laid her hat and jacket away, and shrank miserably into a corner. She wished herself back in the white room at Green Gables.

It was still worse on the platform of the big concert hall of the hotel, where she presently found herself. The electric lights dazzled her eyes, the perfume and hum bewildered her. She wished she were sitting down in the audience with Diana and Jane, who seemed to be having a splendid time away at the back. She was wedged in between a stout lady in pink silk and a tall, scornful looking girl in a white lace dress. The stout lady occasionally turned her head squarely around and surveyed Anne through her eyeglasses until Anne, acutely sensitive of being so scrutinized, felt that she must scream aloud; and the white lace girl kept talking audibly to her next neighbour about the "country bumpkins" and "rustic belles" in the audience, languidly anticipating "such fun" from the displays of local talent on the programme. Anne believed that she would hate that white lace girl to the end of her life.

Unfortunately for Anne, a professional elocutionist was staying at the hotel and had consented to recite. She was a lithe, dark-eyed woman in a wonderful gown of shimmering gray stuff like woven moonbeams, with gems on her neck and in her dark hair.

She had a marvellously flexible voice and wonderful power of expression; the audience went wild over her selection. Anne, forgetting all about herself and her troubles for the time, listened with rapt and shining eyes; but when the recitation ended she suddenly put her hands over her face. She could never get up and recite after that—never. Had she ever thought she could recite? Oh, if she were only back at Green Gables!

At this unpropitious moment her name was called. Somehow, Anne—who did not notice the rather guilty little start of surprise the white lace girl gave, and would not have understood the subtle compliment implied therein if she had—got on her feet, and moved dizzily out to the front. She was so pale that Diana and Jane, down in the audience, clasped each other's hands in nervous sympathy.

Anne was the victim of an overwhelming attack of stage fright. Often as she had recited in public, she had never before faced such an audience as this, and the sight of it paralyzed her energies completely. Everything was so strange, so brilliant, so bewildering—the rows of ladies in evening dress, the critical faces, the whole atmosphere of wealth and culture about her. Very different this from the plain benches of the Debating Club, filled with the homely, sympathetic faces of friends and neighbours. These people, she thought, would be merciless critics. Perhaps, like the white lace girl, they anticipated amusement from her "rustic" efforts. She felt hopelessly, helplessly ashamed and miserable. Her knees trembled, her heart fluttered, a horrible faintness came over her; not a word could she utter, and the next moment she would have fled from the platform despite the humiliation which, she felt, must ever after be her portion if she did so.

But suddenly, as her dilated, frightened eyes gazed out over the audience, she saw Gilbert Blythe away at the back of the room, bending forward with a smile on his face—a smile which seemed to Anne at once triumphant and taunting. In reality it was nothing of the kind. Gilbert was merely smiling with appreciation of the whole affair in general and of the effect produced by Anne's slender white form and spiritual face against a background of palms in particular. Josie Pye, whom he had driven over, sat beside him, and her face certainly was both triumphant and taunting. But Anne did not see Josie, and would not have cared if she had. She drew a long breath and flung her head up proudly, courage and determination tingling over her like an electric shock. She *would not* fail before Gilbert Blythe—he should never be able to laugh at her, never, never! Her fright and nervousness vanished; and she began her recitation, her clear, sweet voice reaching to the farthest corner of the room without a tremor or a break. Self-possession was fully restored to her, and in the reaction from that horrible moment of powerlessness she recited as she had never done before. When she finished there were bursts of honest applause. Anne, stepping back to her seat, blushing with shyness and delight, found her hand vigorously clasped and shaken by the stout lady in pink silk.

"My dear, you did splendidly," she puffed. "I've been crying like a baby, actually I have. There, they're encoring you—they're bound to have you back!"

"Oh, I can't go," said Anne confusedly. "But yet—I must, or Matthew will be disappointed. He said they would encore me."

"Then don't disappoint Matthew," said the pink lady, laughing.

Smiling, blushing, limpid-eyed, Anne tripped back and gave a quaint, funny little selection that captivated her audience still further. The rest of the evening was quite a little triumph for her.

When the concert was over, the stout, pink lady—who was the wife of an American millionaire—took her under her wing, and introduced her to everybody; and everybody was very nice to her. The professional elocutionist, Mrs. Evans, came and chatted with her, telling her that she had a charming voice and "interpreted" her selections beautifully. Even the white lace girl paid her a languid little compliment. They had supper in the big, beautifully decorated dining-room; Diana and Jane were invited to partake of this, also, since they had come with Anne, but Billy was nowhere to be found, having decamped in mortal fear of some such invitation. He was in waiting for them, with the team, however, when it was all over, and the three girls came merrily out into the calm, white moonshine radiance. Anne breathed deeply, and looked into the clear sky beyond the dark boughs of the firs.

Oh, it was good to be out again in the purity and silence of the night! How great and still and wonderful everything was, with the murmur of the sea sounding through it and the darkling cliffs beyond like grim giants guarding enchanted coasts.

"Hasn't it been a perfectly splendid time?" sighed Jane, as they drove away. "I just wish I was a rich American and could spend my summer at a hotel and wear jewels and low-necked dresses and have ice-cream and chicken salad every blessed day. I'm sure it would be ever so much more fun than teaching school. Anne, your recitation was simply great, although I thought at first you were never going to begin. I think it was better than Mrs. Evans'."

"Oh, no, don't say things like that, Jane," said Anne quickly, "because it sounds silly. It couldn't be better than Mrs. Evans', you know, for she is a professional, and I'm only a schoolgirl, with a little knack of reciting. I'm quite satisfied if the people just liked mine pretty well."

"I've a compliment for you, Anne," said Diana. "At least, I think it must be a compliment because of the tone he said it in. Part of it was anyhow. There was an American sitting behind Jane and me—such a romantic-looking man, with coal-black hair and eyes. Josie Pye says he is a distinguished artist, and that her mother's cousin in Boston is married to a man that used to go to school with him. Well, we heard him say—didn't we, Jane?— 'Who is that girl on the platform with the splendid Titian[1] hair? She has a face I should like to paint.' There now, Anne. But what does Titian hair mean?"

"Being interpreted it means plain red, I guess," laughed Anne. "Titian was a very famous artist who liked to paint red-haired women."

"*Did* you see all the diamonds those ladies wore?" sighed Jane. "They were simply dazzling. Wouldn't you just love to be rich, girls?"

"We *are* rich," said Anne staunchly. "Why, we have sixteen years to our credit, and we're happy as queens, and we've all got imaginations, more or less. Look at that sea, girls—all silver and shadow and vision of things not seen.[2] We couldn't enjoy its loveliness

---

[1] Tiziano Vecellio (c.1490–1576), Venetian painter. Titian's name is used adjectivally to refer to red hair.

[2] See Hebrews 11.1. See also Katherine Hankey (1834–1911), "Tell me the old, old story" (hymn, 1867): "Tell me the old, old story/ Of unseen things above,/ Of Jesus and his glory,/ Of Jesus and his love."

any more if we had millions of dollars and ropes of diamonds. You wouldn't change into any of those women if you could. Would you want to be that white lace girl and wear a sour look all your life, as if you'd been born turning up your nose at the world? Or the pink lady, kind and nice as she is, so stout and short that you'd really no figure at all? Or even Mrs. Evans, with that sad, sad look in her eyes? She must have been dreadfully unhappy sometime to have such a look. You *know* you wouldn't, Jane Andrews!"

"I *don't* know—exactly," said Jane unconvinced. "I think diamonds would comfort a person for a good deal."

"Well, I don't want to be any one but myself, even if I go uncomforted by diamonds all my life," declared Anne. "I'm quite content to be Anne of Green Gables, with my string of pearl beads. I know Matthew gave me as much love with them as ever went with Madame the Pink Lady's jewels."

CHAPTER XXXIV

A QUEEN'S GIRL

THE next three weeks were busy ones at Green Gables, for Anne was getting ready to go to Queen's, and there was much sewing to be done, and many things to be talked over and arranged. Anne's outfit was ample and pretty, for Matthew saw to that, and Marilla for once made no objections whatever to anything he purchased or suggested. More—one evening she went up to the east gable with her arms full of a delicate pale green material.

"Anne, here's something for a nice light dress for you. I don't suppose you really need it; you've plenty of pretty waists; but I thought maybe you'd like something real dressy to wear if you were asked out anywhere of an evening in town, to a party or anything like that. I hear that Jane and Ruby and Josie have got 'evening dresses,' as they call them, and I don't mean you shall be behind them. I got Mrs. Allan to help me pick it in town last week, and we'll get Emily Gillis to make it for you. Emily has got taste, and her fits aren't to be equalled."

"Oh, Marilla, it's just lovely," said Anne. "Thank you so much. I don't believe you ought to be so kind to me—it's making it harder every day for me to go away."

The green dress was made up with as many tucks and frills and shirrings as Emily's taste permitted. Anne put it on one evening for Matthew's and Marilla's benefit, and recited "The Maiden's Vow" for them in the kitchen. As Marilla watched the bright, animated face and graceful motions her thoughts went back to the evening Anne had arrived at Green Gables, and memory recalled a vivid picture of the odd, frightened child in her preposterous yellowish-brown wincey dress, the heartbreak looking out of her tearful eyes. Something in the memory brought tears to Marilla's own eyes.

"I declare, my recitation has made you cry, Marilla," said Anne gaily, stooping over Marilla's chair to drop a butterfly kiss on that lady's cheek. "Now, I call that a positive triumph."

"No, I wasn't crying over your piece," said Marilla, who would have scorned to be betrayed into such weakness by any "poetry stuff." "I just couldn't help thinking of the little girl you used to be, Anne. And I was wishing you could have stayed a little girl, even with all your queer ways. You're grown up now and you're going away; and you look so tall and stylish and so—so—different altogether in that dress—as if you didn't belong in Avonlea at all—and I just got lonesome thinking it all over."

"Marilla!" Anne sat down on Marilla's gingham lap, took Marilla's lined face between her hands, and looked gravely and tenderly into Marilla's eyes. "I'm not a bit changed—not really. I'm only just pruned down and branched out. The real *me*—back here—is just the same. It won't make a bit of difference where I go or how much I change outwardly; at heart I shall always be your little Anne, who will love you and Matthew and dear Green Gables more and better every day of her life."

Anne laid her fresh young cheek against Marilla's faded one, and reached out a hand to pat Matthew's shoulder. Marilla would have given much just then to have possessed Anne's power of putting her feelings into words; but nature and habit had willed it otherwise, and she could only put her arms close about her girl and hold her tenderly to her heart, wishing that she need never let her go.

Matthew, with a suspicious moisture in his eyes, got up and went out-of-doors. Under the stars of the blue summer night he walked agitatedly across the yard to the gate under the poplars.

"Well now, I guess she ain't been much spoiled," he muttered, proudly. "I guess my putting in my oar occasional never did much harm after all. She's smart and pretty, and loving, too, which is better than all the rest. She's been a blessing to us, and there never was a luckier mistake than what Mrs. Spencer made—if it *was* luck. I don't believe it was any such thing. It was Providence, because the Almighty saw we needed her, I reckon."

The day finally came when Anne must go to town. She and Matthew drove in one fine September morning, after a tearful parting with Diana and an untearful, practical one—on Marilla's side at least—with Marilla. But when Anne had gone Diana dried her tears and went to a beach picnic at White Sands with some of her Carmody cousins, where she contrived to enjoy herself tolerably well; while Marilla plunged furiously into unnecessary work and kept at it all day long with the bitterest kind of a heartache—the ache that burns and gnaws and cannot wash itself away in ready tears. But that night, when Marilla went to bed, acutely and miserably conscious that the little gable room at the end of the hall was untenanted by any vivid young life and unstirred by any soft breathing, she buried her face in her pillow, and wept for her girl in a passion of sobs that appalled her when she grew calm enough to reflect how very wicked it must be to take on so about a sinful fellow creature.

Anne and the rest of the Avonlea scholars reached town just in time to hurry off to the Academy. That first day passed pleasantly enough in a whirl of excitement, meeting all the new students, learning to know the professors by sight and being assorted and organized into classes. Anne intended taking up the Second Year work, being advised to do so by Miss Stacy; Gilbert Blythe elected to do the same. This meant getting a First Class teacher's license in one year instead of two, if they were successful; but it also meant much more and harder work. Jane, Ruby, Josie, Charlie, and Moody Spurgeon, not being troubled with the stirrings of ambition, were content to take up the Second Class work. Anne was conscious of a pang of loneliness when she found herself in a room with fifty other students, not one of whom she knew, except the tall, brown-haired boy across the room; and knowing him in the fashion she did, did not help her much, as she reflected pessimistically. Yet she was undeniably glad that they were in the same class; the old rivalry could still be carried on, and Anne would hardly have known what to do if it had been lacking.

"I wouldn't feel comfortable without it," she thought. "Gilbert looks awfully determined. I suppose he's making up his mind, here and now, to win the medal. What a splendid chin he has! I never noticed it before. I do wish Jane and Ruby had gone in for First Class, too. I suppose I won't feel so much like a cat in a strange garret when I get acquainted, though. I wonder which of the girls here are going to be my friends. It's really an interesting speculation. Of course I promised Diana that no Queen's girl, no matter how much I liked her, should ever be as dear to me as she is; but I've lots of second-best affections to bestow. I like the look of that girl with the brown eyes and the crimson waist. She looks vivid and red-rosy; and there's that pale, fair one gazing out of the window. She has lovely hair, and looks as if she knew a thing or two about dreams. I'd like to know them both—know them well—well enough to walk with my arm about their waists, and call them nicknames. But just now I don't know them and they don't know me, and probably don't want to know me particularly. Oh, it's lonesome!"

It was lonesomer still when Anne found herself alone in her hall bedroom that night at twilight. She was not to board with the other girls, who all had relatives in town to take pity on them. Miss Josephine Barry would have liked to board her, but Beechwood was so far from the Academy that it was out of the question; so Miss Barry hunted up a boarding-house, assuring Matthew and Marilla that it was the very place for Anne.

"The lady who keeps it is a reduced gentlewoman," explained Miss Barry. "Her husband was a British officer, and she is very careful what sort of boarders she takes. Anne will not meet with any objectionable persons under her roof. The table is good, and the house is near the Academy, in a quiet neighbourhood."

All this might be quite true, and, indeed, proved to be so, but it did not materially help Anne in the first agony of homesickness that seized upon her. She looked dismally about her narrow little room, with its dull-papered, pictureless walls, its small iron bedstead and empty bookcase; and a horrible choke came into her throat as she thought of her own white room at Green Gables, where she would have the pleasant consciousness of a great green still outdoors, of sweet peas growing in the garden, and moonlight falling on the orchard, of the brook below the slope and the spruce boughs tossing in the night wind beyond it, of a vast starry sky, and the light from Diana's window shining out through the gap in the trees. Here there was nothing of this; Anne knew that outside of her window was a hard street, with a network of telephone wires shutting out the sky, the tramp of alien feet,[1] and a thousand lights gleaming on stranger faces. She knew that she was going to cry, and fought against it.

"I *won't* cry. It's silly—and weak—there's the third tear splashing down by my nose. There are more coming! I must think of something funny to stop them. But there's nothing funny except what is connected with Avonlea, and that only makes things worse—four—five—I'm going home next Friday, but that seems a hundred years away. Oh, Matthew is nearly home by now— and Marilla is at the gate, looking down the lane for him—six— seven—eight—oh, there's no use in counting them! They're coming in a flood presently. I can't cheer up—I don't *want* to cheer up. It's nicer to be miserable!"

The flood of tears would have come, no doubt, had not Josie Pye appeared at that moment. In the joy of seeing a familiar face Anne forgot that there had never been much love lost between her and Josie. As a part of Avonlea life even a Pye was welcome.

"I'm so glad you came up," Anne said sincerely.

"You've been crying," remarked Josie, with aggravating pity. "I suppose you're homesick—some people have so little self-control in that respect. I've no intention of being homesick, I can tell you. Town's too jolly after that poky old Avonlea. I wonder how I ever existed there so long. You shouldn't cry, Anne; it isn't becoming, for your nose and eyes get red, and then you seem *all*

---

[1] Cf. Sir Lewis Morris (1833–1907), "An Ode to Free Rome": "And thou couldst bear/ To see her trampled under alien feet!" (223–224).

red. I'd a perfectly scrumptious time in the Academy to-day. Our French professor is simply a duck. His moustache would give you kerwollops of the heart. Have you anything eatable around, Anne? I'm literally starving. Ah, I guessed likely Marilla'd load you up with cake. That's why I called round. Otherwise I'd have gone to the park to hear the band play with Frank Stockley. He boards same place as I do, and he's a sport. He noticed you in class to-day, and asked me who the red-headed girl was. I told him you were an orphan that the Cuthberts had adopted, and nobody knew very much about what you'd been before that."

Anne was wondering if, after all, solitude and tears were not more satisfactory than Josie Pye's companionship when Jane and Ruby appeared, each with an inch of the Queen's colour ribbon—purple and scarlet—pinned proudly to her coat. As Josie was not "speaking" to Jane just then she had to subside into comparative harmlessness.

"Well," said Jane with a sigh, "I feel as if I'd lived many moons since the morning. I ought to be home studying my Virgil[1]—that horrid old professor gave us twenty lines to start in on to-morrow. But I simply couldn't settle down to study to-night. Anne, methinks I see the traces of tears. If you've been crying *do* own up. It will restore my self-respect, for I was shedding tears freely before Ruby came along. I don't mind being a goose so much if somebody else is goosey, too. Cake? You'll give me a teeny piece, won't you? Thank you. It has the real Avonlea flavour."

Ruby, perceiving the Queen's calendar lying on the table, wanted to know if Anne meant to try for the gold medal.

Anne blushed and admitted she was thinking of it.

"Oh, that reminds me," said Josie. "Queen's is to get one of the Avery scholarships after all. The word came to-day. Frank Stockley told me—his uncle is one of the board of governors, you know. It will be announced in the Academy to-morrow."

An Avery scholarship! Anne felt her heart beat more quickly, and the horizons of her ambition shifted and broadened as if by magic. Before Josie had told the news Anne's highest pinnacle of

---

[1] Latin textbook, probably *The Aeneid*. Virgil was a Roman poet of the first century BC.

aspiration had been a teacher's provincial license, Class First, at the end of the year, and perhaps the medal! But now in one moment Anne saw herself winning the Avery scholarship, taking an Arts course at Redmond College, and graduating in a gown and mortar-board, all before the echo of Josie's words had died away. For the Avery scholarship was in English, and Anne felt that here her foot was on her native heath.[1]

A wealthy manufacturer of New Brunswick had died and left part of his fortune to endow a large number of scholarships to be distributed among the various high schools and academies of the Maritime Provinces,[2] according to their respective standings. There had been much doubt whether one would be allotted to Queen's, but the matter was settled at last, and at the end of the year the graduate who made the highest mark in English and English Literature would win the scholarship—two hundred and fifty dollars a year for four years at Redmond College. No wonder that Anne went to bed that night with tingling cheeks!

"I'll win that scholarship if hard work can do it," she resolved. "Wouldn't Matthew be proud if I got to be a B.A.? Oh, it's delightful to have ambitions. I'm so glad I have such a lot. And there never seems to be any end to them—that's the best of it. Just as soon as you attain to one ambition you see another one glittering higher up still. It does make life so interesting."

CHAPTER XXXV

THE WINTER AT QUEEN'S

ANNE'S homesickness wore off, greatly helped in the wearing by her week-end visits home. As long as the open weather lasted the Avonlea students went out to Carmody on the new branch

---

[1] Cf. Sir Walter Scott, *Rob Roy* (1817), ch. 34: "My foot is on my native heath, and my name is MacGregor." See also *SJ* I 112.

[2] I.e., the easternmost provinces of Canada, with the exception of Newfoundland and Labrador, are designated the Maritime Provinces; thus Prince Edward Island, Nova Scotia, and New Brunswick.

railway every Friday night. Diana and several other Avonlea young folks were generally on hand to meet them and they all walked over to Avonlea in a merry party. Anne thought those Friday evening gypsyings over the autumnal hills in the crisp golden air, with the homelights of Avonlea twinkling beyond, were the best and dearest hours in the whole week.

Gilbert Blythe nearly always walked with Ruby Gillis and carried her satchel for her. Ruby was a very handsome young lady now, thinking herself quite as grown up as she really was; she wore her skirts as long as her mother would let her and did her hair up in town, though she had to take it down when she went home. She had large, bright-blue eyes, a brilliant complexion, and a plump showy figure. She laughed a great deal, was cheerful and good-tempered, and enjoyed the pleasant things of life frankly.

"But I shouldn't think she was the sort of girl Gilbert would like," whispered Jane to Anne. Anne did not think so either, but she would not have said so for the Avery scholarship. She could not help thinking, too, that it would be very pleasant to have such a friend as Gilbert to jest and chatter with and exchange ideas about books and studies and ambitions. Gilbert had ambitions, she knew, and Ruby Gillis did not seem the sort of person with whom such could be profitably discussed.

There was no silly sentiment in Anne's ideas concerning Gilbert. Boys were to her, when she thought about them at all, merely possible good comrades. If she and Gilbert had been friends she would not have cared how many other friends he had nor with whom he walked. She had a genius for friendship; girl friends she had in plenty; but she had a vague consciousness that masculine friendship might also be a good thing to round out one's conceptions of companionship and furnish broader standpoints of judgment and comparison. Not that Anne could have put her feelings on the matter into just such clear definition. But she thought that if Gilbert had ever walked home with her from the train, over the crisp fields and along the ferny byways, they might have had many and merry and interesting conversations about the new world that was opening around them and their hopes and ambitions therein. Gilbert was a clever young fellow, with his own thoughts about things and a determination to get the best out of life and put the best into it. Ruby Gillis told Jane Andrews that she didn't understand half the things Gilbert Blythe said; he talked just like Anne Shirley did when she had a thoughtful fit on and for her part she didn't think it any fun to be bothering about books and that sort of thing when you didn't have to. Frank Stockley had lots more dash and go, but then he wasn't half as good-looking as Gilbert, and she really couldn't decide which she liked best!

In the Academy Anne gradually drew a little circle of friends about her, thoughtful, imaginative, ambitious students like herself. With the "rose-red" girl, Stella Maynard, and the "dream girl," Priscilla Grant, she soon became intimate, finding the latter pale spiritual-looking maiden to be full to the brim of mischief and pranks and fun, while the vivid, black-eyed Stella had a heartful of wistful dreams and fancies, as aerial and rainbow-like as Anne's own.

After the Christmas holidays the Avonlea students gave up going home on Fridays and settled down to hard work. By this time all the Queen's scholars had gravitated into their own places in the ranks and the various classes had assumed distinct and settled shadings of individuality. Certain facts had become generally accepted. It was admitted that the medal contestants had practically narrowed down to three—Gilbert Blythe, Anne Shirley, and Lewis Wilson; the Avery scholarship was more doubtful, any one of a certain six being a possible winner. The bronze medal for mathematics was considered as good as won by a fat, funny little up-country boy with a bumpy forehead and a patched coat.

Ruby Gillis was the handsomest girl of the year at the Academy; in the Second Year classes Stella Maynard carried off the palm for beauty, with a small but critical minority in favour of Anne Shirley. Ethel Mair was admitted by all competent judges to have the most stylish modes of hair-dressing, and Jane Andrews—plain, plodding, conscientious Jane—carried off the honours in the domestic science course. Even Josie Pye attained a certain pre-eminence as the sharpest-tongued young lady in attendance at Queen's. So it may be fairly stated that Miss Stacy's old pupils held their own in the wider arena of the academical course.

Anne worked hard and steadily. Her rivalry with Gilbert was as intense as it had ever been in Avonlea school, although it was not known in the class at large, but somehow the bitterness had gone out of it. Anne no longer wished to win for the sake of defeating Gilbert; rather, for the proud consciousness of a well-won victory over a worthy foeman.[1] It would be worth while to win, but she no longer thought life would be insupportable if she did not.

In spite of lessons the students found opportunities for pleasant times. Anne spent many of her spare hours at Beechwood and generally ate her Sunday dinners there and went to church with Miss Barry. The latter was, as she admitted, growing old, but her black eyes were not dim nor the vigour of her tongue in the least abated. But she never sharpened the latter on Anne, who continued to be a prime favourite with the critical old lady.

"That Anne-girl improves all the time," she said. "I get tired of other girls—there is such a provoking and eternal sameness about them. Anne has as many shades as a rainbow and every shade is the prettiest while it lasts. I don't know that she is as amusing as she was when she was a child, but she makes me love her and I like people who make me love them. It saves me so much trouble in making myself love them."

Then, almost before anybody realized it, spring had come; out in Avonlea the Mayflowers were peeping pinkly out on the sere barrens where snow-wreaths lingered; and the "mist of green"[2] was on the woods and in the valleys. But in Charlottetown harassed Queen's students thought and talked only of examinations.

"It doesn't seem possible that the term is nearly over," said Anne. "Why, last fall it seemed so long to look forward to—a whole winter of studies and classes. And here we are, with the exams looming up next week. Girls, sometimes I feel as if those exams meant everything, but when I look at the big buds swelling on those chestnut trees and the misty blue air at the end of the streets they don't seem half so important."

Jane and Ruby and Josie, who had dropped in, did not take this view of it. To them the coming examinations were constantly very important indeed—far more important than chestnut buds or May-time hazes. It was all very well for Anne, who was sure

---

1   Another echo of Scott's *The Lady of the Lake*. See 91, note 4.
2   Tennyson, "The Brook" (1855), lines 11–14.

of passing at least, to have her moments of belittling them, but when your whole future depended on them—as the girls truly thought theirs did—you could not regard them philosophically.

"I've lost seven pounds in the last two weeks," sighed Jane. "It's no use to say don't worry. I *will* worry. Worrying helps you some—it seems as if you were doing something when you're worrying. It would be dreadful if I failed to get my license after going to Queen's all winter and spending so much money."

"*I* don't care," said Josie Pye. "If I don't pass this year I'm coming back next. My father can afford to send me. Anne, Frank Stockley says that Professor Tremaine said Gilbert Blythe was sure to get the medal and that Emily Clay would likely win the Avery scholarship."

"That may make me feel badly to-morrow, Josie," laughed Anne, "but just now I honestly feel that as long as I know the violets are coming out all purple down in the hollow below Green Gables and that little ferns are poking their heads up in Lovers' Lane, it's not a great deal of difference whether I win the Avery or not. I've done my best and I begin to understand what is meant by the 'joy of the strife.'[1] Next to trying and winning, the best thing is trying and failing. Girls, don't talk about exams! Look at that arch of pale green sky over those houses and picture to yourselves what it must look like over the purply-dark beech-woods back of Avonlea."

"What are you going to wear for commencement, Jane?" asked Ruby practically.

Jane and Josie both answered at once and the chatter drifted into a side eddy of fashions. But Anne, with her elbows on the window sill, her soft cheek laid against her clasped hands, and her eyes filled with visions, looked out unheedingly across city roof and spire to that glorious dome of sunset sky and wove her dreams of a possible future from the golden tissue of youth's own optimism. All the Beyond was hers with its possibilities lurking rosily in the oncoming years—each year a rose of promise to be woven into an immortal chaplet.[2]

---

[1] See Felicia Hemans (1793–1835), "The Woman on the Field of Battle" (1827): "Some, for the stormy play/ And joy of strife" (45–46).
[2] "A wreath for the head, usually a garland of flowers or leaves" (*OED*).

CHAPTER XXXVI

THE GLORY AND THE DREAM[1]

ON the morning when the final results of all the examinations were to be posted on the bulletin board at Queen's, Anne and Jane walked down the street together. Jane was smiling and happy; examinations were over and she was comfortably sure she had made a pass at least; further considerations troubled Jane not at all; she had no soaring ambitions and consequently was not affected with the unrest attendant thereon. For we pay a price for everything we get or take in this world; and although ambitions are well worth having, they are not to be cheaply won, but exact their dues of work and self-denial, anxiety and discouragement. Anne was pale and quiet; in ten more minutes she would know who had won the medal and who the Avery. Beyond those ten minutes there did not seem, just then, to be anything worth being called Time.

"Of course you'll win one of them anyhow," said Jane, who couldn't understand how the faculty could be so unfair as to order it otherwise.

"I have no hope of the Avery," said Anne. "Everybody says Emily Clay will win it. And I'm not going to march up to that bulletin board and look at it before everybody. I haven't the moral courage. I'm going straight to the girls' dressing-room. You must read the announcements and then come and tell me, Jane. And I implore you in the name of our old friendship to do it as quickly as possible. If I have failed just say so, without trying to break it gently; and whatever you do *don't* sympathize with me. Promise me this, Jane."

Jane promised solemnly; but, as it happened, there was no necessity for such a promise. When they went up the entrance steps of Queen's they found the hall full of boys who were carrying Gilbert Blythe around on their shoulders and yelling at the tops of their voices, "Hurrah for Blythe, Medallist!"

---

[1] See William Wordsworth (1770–1850), "Ode: Intimations of Immortality from Recollections of Early Childhood" (1807), lines 1–5 and 56–57.

For a moment Anne felt one sickening pang of defeat and disappointment. So she had failed and Gilbert had won! Well, Matthew would be sorry—he had been so sure she would win. And then!

Somebody called out:

"Three cheers for Miss Shirley, winner of the Avery!"

"Oh, Anne," gasped Jane, as they fled to the girls' dressing-room amid hearty cheers. "Oh, Anne, I'm so proud! Isn't it splendid?"

And then the girls were around them and Anne was centre of a laughing, congratulating group. Her shoulders were thumped and her hands shaken vigorously. She was pushed and pulled and hugged and among it all she managed to whisper to Jane:

"Oh, won't Matthew and Marilla be pleased! I must write the news home right away."

Commencement was the next important happening. The exercises were held in the big assembly hall of the Academy. Addresses were given, essays read, songs sung, the public award of diplomas, prizes and medals made.

Matthew and Marilla were there, with eyes and ears for only one student on the platform—a tall girl in pale green, with faintly flushed cheeks and starry eyes, who read the best essay and was pointed out and whispered about as the Avery winner.

"Reckon you're glad we kept her, Marilla?" whispered Matthew, speaking for the first time since he had entered the hall, when Anne had finished her essay.

"It's not the first time I've been glad," retorted Marilla. "You do like to rub things in, Matthew Cuthbert."

Miss Barry, who was sitting behind them, leaned forward and poked Marilla in the back with her parasol.

"Aren't you proud of that Anne-girl? I am," she said.

Anne went home to Avonlea with Matthew and Marilla that evening. She had not been home since April and she felt that she could not wait another day. The apple-blossoms were out and the world was fresh and young. Diana was at Green Gables to meet her. In her own white room, where Marilla had set a flowering house rose on the window sill, Anne looked about her and drew a long breath of happiness.

"Oh, Diana, it's so good to be back again. It's so good to see those pointed firs coming out against the pink sky—and that white orchard and the old Snow Queen. Isn't the breath of the mint delicious? And that tea rose—why, it's a song and a hope and a prayer all in one. And it's *good* to see you again, Diana!"

"I thought you liked that Stella Maynard better than me," said Diana reproachfully. "Josie Pye told me you did. Josie said you were *infatuated* with her."

Anne laughed and pelted Diana with the faded "June lilies" of her bouquet.

"Stella Maynard is the dearest girl in the world except one and you are that one, Diana," she said. "I love you more than ever—and I've so many things to tell you. But just now I feel as if it were joy enough to sit here and look at you. I'm tired, I think—tired of being studious and ambitious. I mean to spend at least two hours to-morrow lying out in the orchard grass, thinking of absolutely nothing."

"You've done splendidly, Anne. I suppose you won't be teaching now that you've won the Avery?"

"No. I'm going to Redmond in September. Doesn't it seem wonderful? I'll have a brand-new stock of ambition laid in by that time after three glorious, golden months of vacation. Jane and Ruby are going to teach. Isn't it splendid to think we all got through, even to Moody Spurgeon and Josie Pye?"

"The Newbridge trustees have offered Jane their school already," said Diana. "Gilbert Blythe is going to teach, too. He has to. His father can't afford to send him to college next year, after all, so he means to earn his own way through. I expect he'll get the school here if Miss Ames decides to leave."

Anne felt a queer little sensation of dismayed surprise. She had not known this; she had expected that Gilbert would be going to Redmond also. What would she do without their inspiring rivalry? Would not work, even at a co-educational college with a real degree in prospect, be rather flat without her friend the enemy?

The next morning at breakfast it suddenly struck Anne that Matthew was not looking well. Surely he was much grayer than he had been a year before.

"Marilla," she said hesitatingly when he had gone out, "is Matthew quite well?"

"No, he isn't," said Marilla in a troubled tone. "He's had some real bad spells with his heart this spring and he won't spare himself a mite. I've been real worried about him, but he's some better this while back and we've got a good hired man, so I'm hoping he'll kind of rest and pick up. Maybe he will now you're home. You always cheer him up."

Anne leaned across the table and took Marilla's face in her hands.

"You are not looking as well yourself as I'd like to see you, Marilla. You look tired. I'm afraid you've been working too hard. You must take a rest, now that I'm home. I'm just going to take this one day off to visit all the dear old spots and hunt up my old dreams, and then it will be your turn to be lazy while I do the work."

Marilla smiled affectionately at her girl.

"It's not the work—it's my head. I've a pain so often now—behind my eyes. Doctor Spencer's been fussing with glasses, but they don't do me any good. There is a distinguished oculist coming to the Island the last of June and the doctor says I must see him. I guess I'll have to. I can't read or sew with any comfort now. Well, Anne, you've done real well at Queen's I must say. To take First Class License in one year and win the Avery scholarship—well, well, Mrs. Lynde says pride goes before a fall and she doesn't believe in the higher education of women at all; she says it unfits them for woman's true sphere.[1] I don't believe a word of it. Speaking of Rachel reminds me—did you hear anything about the Abbey Bank lately, Anne?"

"I heard that it was shaky," answered Anne. "Why?"

"That is what Rachel said. She was up here one day last week and said there was some talk about it. Matthew felt real worried. All we have saved is in that bank—every penny. I wanted Matthew to put it in the Savings Bank in the first place, but old Mr. Abbey was a great friend of father's and he'd always banked

---

[1] I.e., domesticity. Compare Mrs. Lynde's opinion of the higher education of women with her earlier views on suffrage and women preachers. See 289, note 2 and 329, note 1.

with him. Matthew said any bank with him at the head of it was good enough for anybody."

"I think he has only been its nominal head for many years," said Anne. "He is a very old man; his nephews are really at the head of the institution."

"Well, when Rachel told us that, I wanted Matthew to draw our money right out and he said he'd think of it. But Mr. Russell told him yesterday that the bank was all right."

Anne had her good day in the companionship of the outdoor world. She never forgot that day; it was so bright and golden and fair, so free from shadow and so lavish of blossom. Anne spent some of its rich hours in the orchard; she went to the Dryad's Bubble and Willowmere and Violet Vale; she called at the manse and had a satisfying talk with Mrs. Allan; and finally in the evening she went with Matthew for the cows, through Lovers' Lane to the back pasture. The woods were all gloried through with sunset and the warm splendour of it streamed down through the hill gaps in the west. Matthew walked slowly with bent head; Anne, tall and erect, suited her springing steps to his.

"You've been working too hard to-day, Matthew," she said reproachfully. "Why won't you take things easier?"

"Well now, I can't seem to," said Matthew, as he opened the yard gate to let the cows through. "It's only that I'm getting old, Anne, and keep forgetting it. Well, well, I've always worked pretty hard and I'd rather drop in harness."

"If I had been the boy you sent for," said Anne wistfully, "I'd be able to help you so much now and spare you in a hundred ways. I could find it in my heart to wish I had been, just for that."

"Well now, I'd rather have you than a dozen boys, Anne," said Matthew, patting her hand. "Just mind you that—rather than a dozen boys. Well now, I guess it wasn't a boy that took the Avery scholarship, was it? It was a girl—my girl—my girl that I'm proud of."

He smiled his shy smile at her as he went into the yard. Anne took the memory of it with her when she went to her room that night and sat for a long while at her open window, thinking of the past and dreaming of the future. Outside the Snow Queen was mistily white in the moonshine; the frogs were singing in the marsh beyond Orchard Slope. Anne always remembered the silvery, peaceful beauty and fragrant calm of that night. It was the last night before sorrow touched her life; and no life is ever quite the same again when once that cold, sanctifying touch has been laid upon it.

CHAPTER XXXVII

THE REAPER WHOSE NAME IS DEATH[1]

"MATTHEW—Matthew—what is the matter? Matthew, are you sick?"

It was Marilla who spoke, alarm in every jerky word. Anne came through the hall, her hands full of white narcissus,—it was long before Anne could love the sight or odour of white narcissus again,—in time to hear her and to see Matthew standing in the porch doorway, a folded paper in his hand, and his face strangely drawn and gray. Anne dropped her flowers and sprang across the kitchen to him at the same moment as Marilla. They were both too late; before they could reach him Matthew had fallen across the threshold.

"He's fainted," gasped Marilla. "Anne, run for Martin—quick! quick! He's at the barn."

Martin, the hired man, who had just driven home from the post-office, started at once for the doctor, calling at Orchard Slope on his way to send Mr. and Mrs. Barry over. Mrs. Lynde, who was there on an errand, came too. They found Anne and Marilla distractedly trying to restore Matthew to consciousness.

Mrs. Lynde pushed them gently aside, tried his pulse, and then laid her ear over his heart. She looked at their anxious faces sorrowfully and the tears came into her eyes.

"Oh, Marilla," she said gravely, "I don't think—we can do anything for him."

---

[1] See Longfellow, "The Reaper and the Flowers" (1839): "There is a Reaper, whose name is Death" (1).

"Mrs. Lynde, you don't think—you can't think Matthew is—is—" Anne could not say the dreadful word; she turned sick and pallid.

"Child, yes, I'm afraid of it. Look at his face. When you've seen that look as often as I have you'll know what it means."

Anne looked at the still face and there beheld the seal of the Great Presence.[1]

When the doctor came he said that death had been instantaneous and probably painless, caused in all likelihood by some sudden shock. The secret of the shock was discovered to be in the paper Matthew had held and which Martin had brought from the office that morning. It contained an account of the failure of the Abbey Bank.

The news spread quickly through Avonlea, and all day friends and neighbours thronged Green Gables and came and went on errands of kindness for the dead and living. For the first time shy, quiet Matthew Cuthbert was a person of central importance; the white majesty of death had fallen on him and set him apart as one crowned.

When the calm night came softly down over Green Gables the old house was hushed and tranquil. In the parlour lay Matthew Cuthbert in his coffin, his long gray hair framing his placid face on which there was a little kindly smile as if he but slept, dreaming pleasant dreams. There were flowers about him— sweet old-fashioned flowers which his mother had planted in the homestead garden in her bridal days and for which Matthew had always had a secret, wordless love. Anne had gathered them and brought them to him, her anguished, tearless eyes burning in her white face. It was the last thing she could do for him.

The Barrys and Mrs. Lynde stayed with them that night. Diana, going to the east gable, where Anne was standing at her window, said gently:

"Anne dear, would you like to have me sleep with you to-night?"

"Thank you, Diana." Anne looked earnestly into her friend's

---

[1]   I.e., the presence of God; death. Cf. Kate Douglas Wiggin, *Rebecca of Sunnybrook Farm* (1903): "Ten minutes later Rebecca came out from the Great Presence looking white and spent" (278). For more connections with *Rebecca* see Constance Classen, "Is *Anne of Green Gables* an American Import?" *Canadian Children's Literature* 55 (1989): 42–50.

face. "I think you won't misunderstand me when I say that I want to be alone. I'm not afraid. I haven't been alone one minute since it happened—and I want to be. I want to be quite silent and quiet and try to realize it. I *can't* realize it. Half the time it seems to me that Matthew can't be dead; and the other half it seems as if he must have been dead for a long time and I've had this horrible dull ache ever since."

Diana did not quite understand. Marilla's impassioned grief, breaking all the bounds of natural reserve and lifelong habit in its stormy rush, she could comprehend better than Anne's tearless agony. But she went away kindly, leaving Anne alone to keep her first vigil with sorrow.

Anne hoped that tears would come in solitude. It seemed to her a terrible thing that she could not shed a tear for Matthew, whom she had loved so much and who had been so kind to her, Matthew, who had walked with her last evening at sunset and was now lying in the dim room below with that awful peace on his brow. But no tears came at first, even when she knelt by her window in the darkness and prayed, looking up to the stars beyond the hills—no tears, only the same horrible dull ache of misery that kept on aching until she fell asleep, worn out with the day's pain and excitement.

In the night she awakened, with the stillness and the darkness about her, and the recollection of the day came over her like a wave of sorrow. She could see Matthew's face smiling at her as he had smiled when they parted at the gate that last evening—she could hear his voice saying, "My girl—my girl that I'm proud of." Then the tears came and Anne wept her heart out. Marilla heard her and crept in to comfort her.

"There—there—don't cry so, dearie. It can't bring him back. It—it—isn't right to cry so. I knew that to-day, but I couldn't help it then. He'd always been such a good, kind brother to me—but God knows best."

"Oh, just let me cry, Marilla," sobbed Anne. "The tears don't hurt me like that ache did. Stay here for a little while with me and keep your arm round me—so. I couldn't have Diana stay, she's good and kind and sweet—but it's not her sorrow—she's outside of it and she couldn't come close enough to my heart to help me. It's our sorrow—yours and mine. Oh, Marilla, what will we do without him?"

"We've got each other, Anne. I don't know what I'd do if you weren't here—if you'd never come. Oh, Anne, I know I've been kind of strict and harsh with you maybe—but you mustn't think I didn't love you as well as Matthew did, for all that. I want to tell you now when I can. It's never been easy for me to say things out of my heart, but, at times like this it's easier. I love you as dear as if you were my own flesh and blood and you've been my joy and comfort ever since you came to Green Gables."

Two days afterwards they carried Matthew Cuthbert over his homestead threshold and away from the fields he had tilled and the orchards he had loved and the trees he had planted; and then Avonlea settled back to its usual placidity and even at Green Gables affairs slipped into their old groove and work was done and duties fulfilled with regularity as before, although always with the aching sense of "loss in all familiar things."[1] Anne, new to grief, thought it almost sad that it could be so—that they *could* go on in the old way without Matthew. She felt something like shame and remorse when she discovered that the sunrises behind the firs and the pale pink buds opening in the garden gave her the old inrush of gladness when she saw them—that Diana's visits were pleasant to her and that Diana's merry words and ways moved her to laughter and smiles—that, in brief, the beautiful world of blossom and love and friendship had lost none of its power to please her fancy and thrill her heart, that life still called to her with many insistent voices.

"It seems like disloyalty to Matthew, somehow, to find pleasure in these things now that he has gone," she said wistfully to Mrs. Allan one evening when they were together in the manse garden. "I miss him so much—all the time—and yet, Mrs. Allan, the world and life seem very beautiful and interesting to me for all. To-day Diana said something funny and I found myself laughing. I thought when it happened I could never laugh again. And it somehow seems as if I oughtn't to."

"When Matthew was here he liked to hear you laugh and he liked to know that you found pleasure in the pleasant things

---

[1]   See John Greenleaf Whittier, "Snow-Bound: A Winter Idyl" (1866), line 421.

around you," said Mrs. Allan gently. "He is just away now;[1] and he likes to know it just the same. I am sure we should not shut our hearts against the healing influences that nature offers us. But I understand your feeling. I think we all experience the same thing. We resent the thought that anything can please us when some one we love is no longer here to share the pleasure with us, and we almost feel as if we were unfaithful to our sorrow when we find our interest in life returning to us."

"I was down to the graveyard to plant a rose-bush on Matthew's grave this afternoon," said Anne dreamily. "I took a slip of the little white Scotch rose-bush his mother brought out from Scotland long ago; Matthew always liked those roses the best— they were so small and sweet on their thorny stems. It made me feel glad that I could plant it by his grave—as if I were doing something that must please him in taking it there to be near him. I hope he has roses like them in heaven. Perhaps the souls of all those little white roses that he has loved so many summers were all there to meet him. I must go home now. Marilla is all alone and she gets lonely at twilight."

"She will be lonelier still, I fear, when you go away again to college," said Mrs. Allan.

Anne did not reply; she said good night and went slowly back to Green Gables. Marilla was sitting on the front door-steps and Anne sat down beside her. The door was open behind them, held back by a big pink conch shell with hints of sea sunsets in its smooth inner convolutions.

Anne gathered some sprays of pale yellow honeysuckle and put them in her hair. She liked the delicious hint of fragrance, as of some aerial benediction, above her every time she moved.

"Doctor Spencer was here while you were away," Marilla said. "He says that the specialist will be in town to-morrow and he insists that I must go in and have my eyes examined. I suppose I'd better go and have it over. I'll be more than thankful if the man can give me the right kind of glasses to suit my eyes. You won't mind staying here alone while I'm away, will you? Martin will have to drive me in and there's ironing and baking to do."

---

[1] Cf. American poet James Whitcomb Riley (1849–1916), "Away" (1884).

"I shall be all right. Diana will come over for company for me. I shall attend to the ironing and baking beautifully—you needn't fear that I'll starch the handkerchiefs or flavour the cake with liniment."

Marilla laughed.

"What a girl you were for making mistakes in them days, Anne. You were always getting into scrapes. I did use to think you were possessed. Do you mind the time you dyed your hair?"

"Yes, indeed. I shall never forget it," smiled Anne, touching the heavy braid of hair that was wound about her shapely head. "I laugh a little now sometimes when I think what a worry my hair used to be to me—but I don't laugh *much*, because it was a very real trouble then. I did suffer terribly over my hair and my freckles. My freckles are really gone; and people are nice enough to tell me my hair is auburn now—all but Josie Pye. She informed me yesterday that she really thought it was redder than ever, or at least my black dress made it look redder, and she asked me if people who had red hair ever got used to having it. Marilla, I've almost decided to give up trying to like Josie Pye. I've made what I would once have called a heroic effort to like her, but Josie Pye won't *be* liked."

"Josie is a Pye," said Marilla sharply, "so she can't help being disagreeable. I suppose people of that kind serve some useful purpose in society, but I must say I don't know what it is any more than I know the use of thistles. Is Josie going to teach?"

"No, she is going back to Queen's next year. So are Moody Spurgeon and Charlie Sloane. Jane and Ruby are going to teach and they have both got schools—Jane at Newbridge and Ruby at some place up west."

"Gilbert Blythe is going to teach too, isn't he?"

"Yes"—briefly.

"What a nice-looking young fellow he is," said Marilla absently. "I saw him in church last Sunday and he seemed so tall and manly. He looks a lot like his father did at the same age. John Blythe was a nice boy. We used to be real good friends, he and I. People called him my beau."

Anne looked up with swift interest.

"Oh, Marilla—and what happened?—why didn't you—"

"We had a quarrel. I wouldn't forgive him when he asked me to. I meant to, after awhile—but I was sulky and angry and I wanted to punish him first. He never came back—the Blythes were all mighty independent. But I always felt—rather sorry. I've always kind of wished I'd forgiven him when I had the chance."

"So you've had a bit of romance in your life, too," said Anne softly.

"Yes, I suppose you might call it that. You wouldn't think so to look at me, would you? But you never can tell about people from their outsides. Everybody has forgot about me and John. I'd forgotten myself. But it all came back to me when I saw Gilbert last Sunday."

CHAPTER XXXVIII

THE BEND IN THE ROAD

MARILLA went to town the next day and returned in the evening. Anne had gone over to Orchard Slope with Diana and came back to find Marilla in the kitchen, sitting by the table with her head leaning on her hand. Something in her dejected attitude struck a chill to Anne's heart. She had never seen Marilla sit limply inert like that.

"Are you very tired, Marilla?"

"Yes—no—I don't know," said Marilla wearily, looking up. "I suppose I am tired but I haven't thought about it. It's not that."

"Did you see the oculist? What did he say?" asked Anne anxiously.

"Yes, I saw him. He examined my eyes. He says that if I give up all reading and sewing entirely and any kind of work that strains the eyes, and if I'm careful not to cry, and if I wear the glasses he's given me he thinks my eyes may not get any worse and my headaches will be cured. But if I don't he says I'll certainly be stone blind in six months. Blind! Anne, just think of it!"

For a minute Anne, after her first quick exclamation of dismay, was silent. It seemed to her that she could *not* speak. Then she said bravely, but with a catch in her voice:

"Marilla, *don't* think of it. You know he has given you hope. If you are careful you won't lose your sight altogether; and if his glasses cure your headaches it will be a great thing."

"I don't call it much hope," said Marilla bitterly. "What am I to live for if I can't read or sew or do anything like that? I might as well be blind—or dead. And as for crying, I can't help that when I get lonesome. But there, it's no good talking about it. If you'll get me a cup of tea I'll be thankful. I'm about done out. Don't say anything about this to any one for a spell yet, anyway. I can't bear that folks should come here to question and sympathize and talk about it."

When Marilla had eaten her lunch Anne persuaded her to go to bed. Then Anne went herself to the east gable and sat down by her window in the darkness alone with her tears and her heaviness of heart. How sadly things had changed since she had sat there the night after coming home! Then she had been full of hope and joy and the future had looked rosy with promise. Anne felt as if she had lived years since then, but before she went to bed there was a smile on her lips and peace in her heart.[1] She had looked her duty courageously in the face and found it a friend—as duty ever is when we meet it frankly.

One afternoon a few days later Marilla came slowly in from the yard where she had been talking to a caller—a man whom Anne knew by sight as John Sadler from Carmody. Anne wondered what he could have been saying to bring that look to Marilla's face.

"What did Mr. Sadler want, Marilla?"

Marilla sat down by the window and looked at Anne. There were tears in her eyes in defiance of the oculist's prohibition and her voice broke as she said:

"He heard that I was going to sell Green Gables and he wants to buy it."

"Buy it! Buy Green Gables?" Anne wondered if she had heard aright. "Oh, Marilla, you don't mean to sell Green Gables!"

---

[1]   Cf. Longfellow, "Maidenhood," the poem from which the title to Chapter XXXI is taken: "Bear through sorrow, wrong, and ruth,/ In thy heart the dew of youth,/ On thy lips the smile of truth" (40-42). See 281, note 1.

"Anne, I don't know what else is to be done. I've thought it all over. If my eyes were strong I could stay here and make out to look after things and manage, with a good hired man. But as it is I can't. I may lose my sight altogether; and anyway I'll not be fit to run things. Oh, I never thought I'd live to see the day when I'd have to sell my home. But things would only go behind worse and worse all the time, till nobody would want to buy it. Every cent of our money went in that bank; and there's some notes Matthew gave last fall to pay. Mrs. Lynde advises me to sell the farm and board somewhere—with her, I suppose. It won't bring much—it's small and the buildings are old. But it'll be enough for me to live on I reckon. I'm thankful you're provided for with that scholarship, Anne. I'm sorry you won't have a home to come to in your vacations, that's all, but I suppose you'll manage somehow."

Marilla broke down and wept bitterly.

"You mustn't sell Green Gables," said Anne, resolutely.

"Oh, Anne, I wish I didn't have to. But you can see for yourself. I can't stay here alone. I'd go crazy with trouble and loneliness. And my sight would go—I know it would."

"You won't have to stay here alone, Marilla. I'll be with you. I'm not going to Redmond."

"Not going to Redmond!" Marilla lifted her worn face from her hands and looked at Anne. "Why, what do you mean?"

"Just what I say. I'm not going to take the scholarship. I decided so the night after you came home from town. You surely don't think I could leave you alone in your trouble, Marilla, after all you've done for me. I've been thinking and planning. Let me tell you my plans. Mr. Barry wants to rent the farm for next year. So you won't have any bother over that. And I'm going to teach. I've applied for the school here—but I don't expect to get it for I understand the trustees have promised it to Gilbert Blythe. But I can have the Carmody school—Mr. Blair told me so last night at the store. Of course that won't be quite as nice or convenient as if I had the Avonlea school. But I can board home and drive myself over to Carmody and back, in the warm weather at least. And even in winter I can come home Fridays. We'll keep a horse for that. Oh, I have it all planned out, Marilla. And I'll read to you and keep you cheered up. You sha'n't be dull or lonesome. And we'll be real cosy and happy here together, you and I."

Marilla had listened like a woman in a dream.

"Oh, Anne, I could get on real well if you were here, I know. But I can't let you sacrifice yourself so for me. It would be terrible."

"Nonsense!" Anne laughed merrily. "There is no sacrifice. Nothing could be worse than giving up Green Gables—nothing could hurt me more. We must keep the dear old place. My mind is quite made up, Marilla. I'm *not* going to Redmond; and I *am* going to stay here and teach. Don't you worry about me a bit."

"But your ambitions—and—"

"I'm just as ambitious as ever. Only I've changed the object of my ambitions. I'm going to be a good teacher—and I'm going to save your eyesight. Besides, I mean to study at home here and take a little college course all by myself. Oh, I've dozens of plans, Marilla. I've been thinking them out for a week. I shall give life here my best, and I believe it will give its best to me in return. When I left Queen's my future seemed to stretch out before me like a straight road. I thought I could see along it for many a milestone. Now there is a bend in it. I don't know what lies around the bend, but I'm going to believe that the best does. It has a fascination of its own, that bend, Marilla. I wonder how the road beyond it goes—what there is of green glory and soft, checkered light and shadows—what new landscapes—what new beauties—what curves and hills and valleys further on."

"I don't feel as if I ought to let you give it up," said Marilla, referring to the scholarship.

"But you can't prevent me. I'm sixteen and a half, 'obstinate as a mule,' as Mrs. Lynde once told me," laughed Anne. "Oh, Marilla, don't you go pitying me. I don't like to be pitied, and there is no need for it. I'm heart glad over the very thought of staying at dear Green Gables. Nobody could love it as you and I do—so we must keep it."

"You blessed girl!" said Marilla, yielding. "I feel as if you'd given me new life. I guess I ought to stick out and make you go to college—but I know I can't, so I ain't going to try. I'll make it up to you, though, Anne."

When it became noised abroad in Avonlea that Anne Shirley

had given up the idea of going to college and intended to stay home and teach there was a good deal of discussion over it. Most of the good folks, not knowing about Marilla's eyes, thought she was foolish. Mrs. Allan did not. She told Anne so in approving words that brought tears of pleasure to the girl's eyes. Neither did good Mrs. Lynde. She came up one evening and found Anne and Marilla sitting at the front door in the warm, scented summer dusk. They liked to sit there when the twilight came down and the white moths flew about in the garden and the odour of mint filled the dewy air.

Mrs. Rachel deposited her substantial person upon the stone bench by the door, behind which grew a row of tall pink and yellow hollyhocks, with a long breath of mingled weariness and relief.

"I declare I'm glad to sit down. I've been on my feet all day, and two hundred pounds is a good bit for two feet to carry round. It's a great blessing not to be fat, Marilla. I hope you appreciate it. Well, Anne, I hear you've given up your notion of going to college. I was real glad to hear it. You've got as much education now as a woman can be comfortable with. I don't believe in girls going to college with the men and cramming their heads full of Latin and Greek and all that nonsense."[1]

"But I'm going to study Latin and Greek just the same, Mrs. Lynde," said Anne laughing. "I'm going to take my Arts course right here at Green Gables, and study everything that I would at college."

Mrs. Lynde lifted her hands in holy horror.

"Anne Shirley, you'll kill yourself."

"Not a bit of it. I shall thrive on it. Oh, I'm not going to overdo things. As 'Josiah Allen's wife' says, I shall be 'mejum.'[2]

---

1 Cf. 282, note 2 and 317, note 1.
2 I.e., medium, in the middle. "Josiah Allen's Wife" was one pseudonym of American writer Marietta Holley (1836–1926). According to *The Feminist Companion to Literature in English*, "[I]t was *My Opinions and Betsy Bobbet's*, 1873, that won her national fame as a humorist and popularizer of 'wimmen's rites.' It consists of loosely connected episodes in the life of Josiah Allen's wife Samantha, who expounds feminist views with vernacular humour" (533). Holley's writings appeared in collections of recitation pieces.

But I'll have lots of spare time in the long winter evenings, and I've no vocation for fancy work. I'm going to teach over at Carmody, you know."

"I don't know it. I guess you're going to teach right here in Avonlea. The trustees have decided to give you the school."

"Mrs. Lynde!" cried Anne, springing to her feet in her surprise. "Why, I thought they had promised it to Gilbert Blythe!"

"So they did. But as soon as Gilbert heard that you had applied for it he went to them—they had a business meeting at the school last night, you know—and told them that he withdrew his application, and suggested that they accept yours. He said he was going to teach at White Sands. Of course he gave up the school just to oblige you, because he knew how much you wanted to stay with Marilla, and I must say I think it was real kind and thoughtful in him, that's what. Real self-sacrificing, too, for he'll have his board to pay at White Sands, and everybody knows he's got to earn his own way through college. So the trustees decided to take you. I was tickled to death when Thomas came home and told me."

"I don't feel that I ought to take it," murmured Anne. "I mean—I don't think I ought to let Gilbert make such a sacrifice for—for me."

"I guess you can't prevent him now. He's signed papers with the White Sands trustees. So it wouldn't do him any good now if you were to refuse. Of course you'll take the school. You'll get along all right, now that there are no Pyes going. Josie was the last of them, and a good thing she was, that's what. There's been some Pye or other going to Avonlea school for the last twenty years, and I guess their mission in life was to keep school-teachers reminded that earth isn't their home. Bless my heart! What does all that winking and blinking at the Barry gable mean?"

"Diana is signalling for me to go over," laughed Anne. "You know we keep up the old custom. Excuse me while I run over and see what she wants."

Anne ran down the clover slope like a deer, and disappeared in the firry shadows of the Haunted Wood. Mrs. Lynde looked after her indulgently.

"There's a good deal of the child about her yet in some ways."

"There's a good deal more of the woman about her in others," retorted Marilla, with a momentary return of her old crispness.

But crispness was no longer Marilla's distinguishing characteristic. As Mrs. Lynde told her Thomas that night, "Marilla Cuthbert has got *mellow*. That's what."

Anne went to the little Avonlea graveyard the next evening to put fresh flowers on Matthew's grave and water the Scotch rosebush. She lingered there until dusk, liking the peace and calm of the little place, with its poplars whose rustle was like low, friendly speech, and its whispering grasses growing at will among the graves. When she finally left it and walked down the long hill that sloped to the Lake of Shining Waters it was past sunset and all Avonlea lay before her in a dreamlike afterlight—"a haunt of ancient peace."[1] There was a freshness in the air as of a wind that had blown over honey-sweet fields of clover. Home lights twinkled out here and there among the homestead trees. Beyond lay the sea, misty and purple, with its haunting, unceasing murmur. The west was a glory of soft mingled hues, and the pond reflected them all in still softer shadings. The beauty of it all thrilled Anne's heart, and she gratefully opened the gates of her soul to it.

"Dear old world," she murmured, "you are very lovely, and I am glad to be alive in you."

Half-way down the hill a tall lad came whistling out of a gate before the Blythe homestead. It was Gilbert, and the whistle died on his lips as he recognized Anne. He lifted his cap courteously, but he would have passed on in silence, if Anne had not stopped and held out her hand.

"Gilbert," she said, with scarlet cheeks, "I want to thank you for giving up the school for me. It was very good of you—and I want you to know that I appreciate it."

Gilbert took the offered hand eagerly.

"It wasn't particularly good of me at all, Anne. I was pleased

---

1 See Tennyson, "The Palace of Art" (1832):
      And one, an English home—gray twilight poured
        On dewy pastures, dewy trees,
      Softer than sleep—all things in order stored,
        A haunt of ancient peace. (85-88)

to be able to do you some small service. Are we going to be friends after this? Have you really forgiven me my old fault?"

Anne laughed and tried unsuccessfully to withdraw her hand.

"I forgave you that day by the pond landing, although I didn't know it. What a stubborn little goose I was. I've been—I may as well make a complete confession—I've been sorry ever since."

"We are going to be the best of friends," said Gilbert, jubilantly. "We were born to be good friends, Anne. You've thwarted destiny long enough. I know we can help each other in many ways. You are going to keep up your studies, aren't you? So am I. Come, I'm going to walk home with you."

Marilla looked curiously at Anne when the latter entered the kitchen.

"Who was that came up the lane with you, Anne?"

"Gilbert Blythe," said Anne, vexed to find herself blushing. "I met him on Barry's hill."

"I didn't think you and Gilbert Blythe were such good friends that you'd stand for half an hour at the gate talking to him," said Marilla, with a dry smile.

"We haven't been—we've been good enemies. But we have decided that it will be much more sensible to be good friends in future. Were we really there half an hour? It seemed just a few minutes. But, you see, we have five years' lost conversations to catch up with, Marilla."

Anne sat long at her window that night companioned by a glad content. The wind purred softly in the cherry boughs, and the mint breaths came up to her. The stars twinkled over the pointed firs in the hollow and Diana's light gleamed through the old gap.

Anne's horizons had closed in since the night she had sat there after coming home from Queen's; but if the path set before her feet was to be narrow she knew that flowers of quiet happiness would bloom along it.[1] The joys of sincere work and worthy aspiration and congenial friendship were to be hers; nothing

---

[1]   Cf. John Greenleaf Whittier, "Among the Hills" (1868): "Flowers spring to blossom where she walks/ The careful ways of duty" (361–62). Montgomery begins the sequel to *AGG*, *Anne of Avonlea*, with these lines as epigraph. This poem is an American settler poem which is also concerned with gender ideologies: the woman softens the rough life of the "homestead" in the poem.

"'COME, I'M GOING TO WALK HOME WITH YOU.'"

could rob her of her birthright of fancy or her ideal world of dreams. And there was always the bend in the road!

"'God's in his heaven, all's right with the world,'"[1] whispered Anne softly.

THE END.

---

[1]   *AGG* ends as it begins, with a quotation from Robert Browning, in this case from "Pippa Passes: A Drama" (184):

> *The year's at the spring*
> *And day's at the morn;*
> *Morning's at seven;*
> *The hill-side's dew-pearled;*
> *The lark's on the wing;*
> *The snail's on the thorn;*
> *God's in His heaven—*
> *All's right with the world!* ("Morning," Pippa's song, 221–28)

Appendix A: Selected Montgomery Stories before Anne

1. "Our Uncle Wheeler"

[From *Golden Days for Boys and Girls* 19.10 (22 January 1898): 145–46 (*R/W* 667).]

[This appears to be the earliest published version of the story that would be developed as Chapter XIX of *Anne of Green Gables*, in which Anne and Diana leap into the spare-room bed onto Miss Josephine Barry. This first version is closer to the "original" that Montgomery describes in her journal, where she indicates that the story had come from her father: in *AGG* Montgomery changes the gender of the jumpers, who are, here, boys. Montgomery writes:

> The scene where Anne and Diana jump into bed on poor Miss Barry was suggested to me by a story father told me of how he and two other boys had jumped into bed on an old minister in the spare room at Uncle John Montgomery's long ago. I worked it up into a short story, published early in my career in Golden Days; then used the idea later on in my book. (*SJ* II 43)

This early working-out in narrative is a compelling indication of Montgomery's writing practices of revising and reworking material and of negotiating particular domestic genres. While this version is arguably more concerned with administering moral advice to its readers about telling the truth than is the case in *AGG*, in both cases the story has to do with learning to take responsibility for one's actions.]

In reality he was our great-uncle, and we were very much in awe of him.

The rare times when he came to visit us—usually popping down unexpectedly at some particularly inconvenient moment—were periods of misery for us lively boys, for Uncle Wheeler was a very precise old gentleman, fidgety when boys were around, and with all an old bachelor's decided opinions as to the training and behavior of those unavoidable evils.

Consequently, as Rod used to say, we were "as unhappy as a cat on hot bricks" when Uncle Wheeler came.

He had befriended and aided father more than once in troublous times, for he was really kind-hearted at the core, and hence we were instructed to regard him with gratitude and respect. He was always "Uncle Wheeler" to us. Our other uncles were Uncle Tom, Dick or Harry, but we would as soon have thought of calling Uncle Wheeler "Uncle James" as of saying "hello" to the minister.

Rod and I were the oldest of our family, being fifteen and fourteen respectively. We were hearty, growing boys, and found it very hard to "tone down" during Uncle Wheeler's sojourn.

Nevertheless, we tried our best, for we really liked the old man, in spite of our fear of him. When it was decided that Rod should go to college if it could be managed, Uncle Wheeler wrote to father and mother a letter in which he denounced the project as "absurd nonsense," and railed at it for three pages. On the fourth he announced his intention of paying Rod's way through college if he were really bent on going, and hoped he wouldn't disgrace the family.

Rod was jubilant; but it behooved him to be very careful, for Uncle Wheeler was extremely touchy, and sometimes got offended at very trifling things. Therefore we made up our minds to be more than usually sedate and proper on the occasion of his next visit.

About two months after this letter, Rod and I received an invitation to a party at the house of one of our schoolmates. During the afternoon, Sydney Hatfield, a cousin of ours, arrived and decided to stay overnight, as he was going to Tracy's, too.

Mother intended to put him in the spare room to sleep; but about dusk a cutter drove up to the door, and in it were the three Winsloe boys from Bracebridge, who came in and said they were also bound for the party and would afterwards remain with us until the next day.

We were a big family, all told, so that mother said to us, just before we left:

"I think, boys, you'd better take Sydney up to your room to-night and let the Winsloe boys have the spare room. We can accommodate you all if you won't mind a little crowding."

Lou Winsloe said uninvited guests ought to be thankful to be taken in at all, and for his part he thought it jolly to sleep three in a bed, if it was a big one, and we all drove off to the party in high spirits.

It was late when we returned, and of course everybody was in bed. Mother had left a light burning for us, and we tip-toed in cautiously, so as not to disturb the sleepers.

While we were putting away our coats, I noticed Rod and Dave Winsloe talking earnestly, and when I went out to lock the back porch door Rod followed me.

"Say, Art, Dave's nervous; he's afraid of the ghost and doesn't want to sleep in the spare room. Of course he's a ninny, but arguing won't do any good. What's to be done?"

Dave Winsloe was a delicate boy of nearly fifteen, and we always regarded him as "babyish." He was extremely sensitive, and his nervous whims had to be indulged.

I don't know how he'd got wind of "our ghost," but he had. I may here remark that our spare room had the reputation of being haunted during the sojourn of the family who had preceded us. None of us had ever seen or heard anything worse than ourselves in it, and never felt in the least disturbed. We had good, healthy nerves and didn't worry about spooks.

But I knew Dave couldn't help his terror, so, feeling sorry, I said:

"Well, the three Winsloes had better go up stairs to our room and you and Syd and I will take the spare room. We're equal to any ghost who may be on the haunting trail to-night."

This arrangement suited all hands, so we showed the Winsloes up stairs and separated.

Our house was an old-fashioned one, and the spare room opened off the end of the parlor. The parlor was a long, narrow room, and the bedroom was also long and narrow, so that from the parlor door to the extreme end of the bedroom, where the bed was, was quite a distance.

Syd, Rod and I went into the parlor and found it deliciously warm, as there had been a fire in the stove. We supposed mother had lit it to warm the spare room for the Winsloes, and we thought it rather a good joke that Dave's ghostly terrors should have put him out of a warm sleeping room.

We undressed by the fire quietly enough, for we were tired;

but when we were ready for bed, Syd, who was always up to mischief, had a brilliant idea.

"Say, you chaps, let's start from the hall door and see which will get into bed first."

Rod and I thought it would be good fun, so we didn't make a noise. So, having taken a vow of silence, we put out the candle, for the moonlight was streaming in at the window, ranged ourselves by the hall door, and Syd gave the word, "Go!"

The bedroom door was open, so we flew down the parlor, shot through the door and the spare room, and the whole three of us, with one spring, bounded on the bed at the same instant.

There was one awful moment in which we realized what had happened, and then a wheezy, sleepy, well-known voice puffed out:

"Why, bless my soul, what's the matter?"

It was Uncle Wheeler!

We had jumped upon that bed pretty quick, but we jumped off three times quicker, dashed out of the room and scuttled through the parlor, never stopping for breath until we reached the kitchen.

Rod and I wished the floor would open and quietly let us into the cellar. Syd, being a stranger, of course didn't appreciate the situation so keenly.

"Say, you chaps, that old duffer must have got his breath most lammed[1] out of him. Who is it?"

"Uncle Wheeler," groaned Rod. "And, oh! what will he say? How ever did he come to be there, and why didn't mother leave some way for us to know?"

Just then we heard a gasp and sigh and a sort of groan in the little breakfast-room off the kitchen.

We all jumped.

"Great Scott! Is that one of Dave Winsloe's ghosts?" exclaimed Syd.

But I had got a lamp lit, and by its light we saw our eleven-year-old brother, Tad, come shuffling out of the breakfast-room, rubbing his eyes.

"Say, you fellows, have you got back? Mother told me to sit up and tell you—"

"Tell us what?"

---

[1] Slang: Beaten.

"That Uncle Wheeler'd come, and she'd put him in the spare room, and that the Winsloe boys must have your room, and you chaps would have to sleep in the kitchen loft. I meant to keep awake—honest, I did—but I got so tired, I went in there and lay down on the lounge.[1] I guess I went to sleep."

"I guess you did," growled Rod. "You've done for us now."

And after each of us had rated the still stupid and half-asleep Tad soundly by way of venting our ill humour, we crept off, shivering, to the kitchen loft.

We were too tired and cold and cross to talk it over then, but by dawn Rod and I were sitting up in bed, discussing our mishap in whispers, so as not to waken Syd.

"Nothing worse could have happened," lamented Rod. "Uncle Wheeler will be piping mad; you could hardly blame him, I suppose. What a rousing scare he must have got! But he won't listen to any excuse, and not a blessed cent need I expect for college if he finds out. Some men would just look on it as a joke, but Uncle Wheeler isn't that sort."

After forlornly admitting that we'd got into a scrape beyond doubt, we got up, put on some old clothes and went down to sneak Syd's suit out of the parlor for him, for needless to say, we hadn't stopped to get our clothes in our stampede of the night before.

On our way through the hall, we met the Winsloe boys tiptoeing down stairs, much to our surprise, for it was barely daylight.

"What's the rush?" asked Rod with an attempt at hilarity. "Been seeing any ghosts, Dave?"

"It's beginning to rain," announced Len, "and it's setting in for a big thaw, so we decided to get up, rouse you out if we could and start just as soon as possible. You know it's a long drive home, and a wretched road at the best of times. It'll be hardly passable in a thaw."

They passed on out to the stables. Rod and I looked at each other, both struck by the same idea.

"Nobody else will be stirring for an hour yet," said Rod, voicing my thoughts rather shamefacedly. "We'll light a fire and get some grub for the boys, and they'll be gone before mother or Uncle Wheeler come on the scene. They were supposed to be going to the spare room, and if we just hold our tongues, and get Syd to do the same, Uncle Wheeler will think it was the Winsloes."

---

[1] Sofa.

"But Tad?"

"Tad didn't appear until it was too late, so that won't give us away; and he was half asleep, and I'll bet a cent he'll never remember how many of us were there or that we hadn't our clothes on. It hardly seems fair, though, to put it on the Winsloes."

"That won't hurt. They're nothing to Uncle Wheeler, and he doesn't even know them, so it won't do them any harm, while it would do us whole heaps."

We talked it over and decided to go ahead. I left Rod to light the fire, while I went up, wakened Syd, explained the whole affair and easily got him to promise silence.

"We're not going to tell any fibs, of course," I said, virtuously. "If anybody asks us who it was, we'll have to tell straight out; but not likely any one will, and we'll just keep quiet. See?"

Syd thought it a good joke, and agreed to keep mum. The Winsloes came in; Rod and I got them a cold breakfast and they started off.

Just as they drove away, mother came out at the hall door, and Uncle Wheeler, in his dressing gown and slippers, emerged from the sitting room. He looked just as grumpy as Uncle Wheeler could look—and that is saying a good deal.

Mother didn't see him at first, and merely asked us why we were up so early and where the Winsloe boys were. We explained, and then mother saw Uncle Wheeler, and said she hoped he'd slept well and found his pillows high enough for him.

"Slept well!" growled Uncle Wheeler. "I wonder if you, or any one else, Amelia June Millar, could sleep well, if, just when you had dropped off to sleep, after a long and arduous journey, you were suddenly awakened by half a dozen great, lubbering[1] louts of boys coming down on you, like an avalanche, in the dead of night? I ask you how anybody could sleep well under such circumstances, madam?"

And Uncle Wheeler glanced at us boys, as if he knew we were the guilty ones. Mother was greatly distressed.

"Oh, dear me! The Winsloe boys went in, after all. Didn't Tad tell you that Uncle Wheeler was there?"

---

[1]   "A big, clumsy, especially idle person; a lout" (*OED*). Here, as adjective, descriptive of such a person.

"Tad went to sleep," said Rod, promptly, nudging me with his elbow, for fear I'd put in a word too many and complicate matters, "and didn't wake up till too late. When he appeared, the mischief was done. You might have known he couldn't keep awake, mother."

"There was no one else to leave," replied mother; "and I warned him not to go to sleep. I'm very sorry this should have happened, Uncle Wheeler."

Uncle Wheeler barely answered.

The Winsloe boys were gone, so he couldn't come down on them, and he had no excuse for blaming any one else, except Tad—who kept religiously out of the way that morning—so he felt defrauded of his rights.

He was as snappish and crusty as he could be all through breakfast, and kept making remarks about boys being out late at nights and gadding about to parties and coming home to disturb respectable folks at unseemly hours. He was never guilty of it, in his young days, and he felt very sorry to see that his nephews were; and, as for those three fools that had wakened him, he'd like to teach a lesson to boys who hadn't enough sense to get into bed properly, but must race and tear like a pack of wild cubs.

There was no doubt that Uncle Wheeler was in a fearful humour, and Rod and I realized that we had had a narrow escape.

Syd Hatfield, having no particular interest at stake, enjoyed the whole performance immensely, and afterwards remarked, in the seclusion of the kitchen loft:

"It's a jolly good thing for you chaps that your respected uncle doesn't know that it was you who disturbed his peaceful slumber. He doesn't seem particularly amiable this morning."

But, for all our success, I really didn't feel comfortable, and Rod looked awfully glum. Pretty soon he came out with it.

"I feel like an out and out sneak, Art," he confessed. "I never did anything like this before, and I never will again. We've deceived mother and Uncle Wheeler, and all I wish is that we hadn't."

"Same here, Rod," I said, heartily, for Rod had just put my own disquieting reflections into words.

Syd stared at us.

"You're a pair of geese! I think it is all a capital joke. Why, you didn't say a thing—never even stretched the truth itself; and it can't hurt the Winsloe boys one single mite."

"That isn't the question," replied Rod. "It's what we've done. I feel kind of dishonorable, but I suppose there's nothing more to be said now."

Still, we did feel mean. Uncle Wheeler got over his ill-humour by next day, and was as good as gold. Everything went well for a week outwardly, but Rod went about kind of grim and sulky, and as for me, I felt somehow or other that I was a pretty mean, sneaking sort of chap.

Rod and I had both been brought up to be strictly truthful and above board in everything, and we felt that we had come short of our mother's standard. It wasn't that our evasion was going to harm any one else, but we had simply lost our self-respect. Syd had gone home so we hadn't him to bolster up our consciences, and we got regularly blue and moody.

One night Uncle Wheeler had another cranky fit on. The wind was northeast and his rheumatism was always bad in a northeast wind. Finally, he remarked to mother:

"I'd a letter to-day from Henry Winsloe, the father of those rascals. He wants me to accommodate him with a loan for a short time. I shan't; I've worked hard for my money, and I'm not going to risk it in doubtful loans—not if he is honest and hard-up. I don't propose to help a man that can't bring his boys up better than he's done."

And Uncle Wheeler poked the fire viciously. The memory of the rousing-up he'd got that unlucky night was still vividly present with him.

Rod and I went softly out, leaving mother trying to intercede for Henry Winsloe, with no very good success, and went to our favorite roost in the kitchen loft.

"Here's a mess," said Rod.

"A bad one," said I. "What's to be done?"

"Done? Make a clean breast of it to Uncle Wheeler, of course. It'll ruin my chances with him, but I'm not going to have other people suffer for what isn't their fault."

"If only we'd told him at first!" I said, mournfully. "But even if he could forgive us for jumping over him, he never will for bluffing him about it. He'll think we were just fooling him for pure fun."

"It's a blue show," said Rod, gloomily, "but we deserve it—so I'm not going to flinch. After all, I don't know that I'm sorry we have to. I've felt like a regular sneak this week. Uncle Wheeler will be in a fury, of course, but I think worse of how mother will feel. She hates any crawly[1] business."

We made up our minds to beard the lion in his den as soon as possible. The afternoon of the next day we screwed up our courage and marched straight into the parlor, where Uncle Wheeler was writing letters before the table.

He shoved up his specs and looked at us sourly.

"What do you youngsters want?" he demanded, gruffly.

We both knew by experience that it doesn't do to beat about the bush with Uncle Wheeler. You have to come straight to the point and say what you've got to say.

Rod took a header right in.

"We've come, Uncle Wheeler, to tell you what we should have told you before. It wasn't the Winsloe boys who woke you up the other night. It was Syd Hatfield and Art and I."

Then we waited for the outburst. Uncle Wheeler gazed at us over his specs quite calmly. We knew he had a dozen different ways of getting mad, and this might be one; but, if so, it was brand new.

"It was you, was it?" he said, at last. "You young scamps—and you've the face to come and tell me so! And why did you say it was the other boys?"

"Please, sir, we didn't," I ventured to say. "Mother just thought it was because she had told them to go there. But Dave was scared of the ghost; so we changed rooms. Syd wanted us to race and see who'd get into bed first—that's all. We didn't know anybody was there, and we are awfully sorry. We were kind of scared, too; so we thought it wouldn't be any harm to let you all think it was the Winsloes. But it wasn't right, and we've felt mean ever since."

Uncle Wheeler glared quite fiercely.

"What do you think you deserve?" he asked.

And Rod spoke up manfully:

"Uncle Wheeler, we deserve a sound scolding for deceiving you, and we will get it when mother finds outs. But as for the rest, it was only in fun, and I don't think any one ought to regard it as a serious crime, although it was very silly of us. Most people would merely look upon it as a joke."

---

[1]   "Having, or like, the feeling of insects a-crawl on one's skin" (*Dictionary of Slang*). The implication here seems to be "sneaky."

"Oh, they would, would they?" said uncle, grimly. "Perhaps, when you get to be my age, young man, and don't find it so easy to get to sleep as you do now, you won't consider it much of a joke to have three great boys come sprawling over you in your first doze."

"We're sorry we disturbed you, uncle," said Rod, firmly, but respectfully, "and we apologize for not owning it up right off like men. That's all we can do, and I hope you'll forgive us."

"Humph! Go out, and tell your mother I want her."

That was all the satisfaction we got, but we went gladly, for we had escaped wonderfully well.

Mother went in, and was closeted with Uncle Wheeler for half an hour. When she came out, she looked amused over something, and though she tried to be severe, it was a failure.

"You deserve a scolding, boys, but I promised your uncle I'd let you off this time. He really seems in a good humour over it all, but I wouldn't advise you to repeat the experiment."

"What's he going to do about Mr. Winsloe?" broke in Rod, anxiously.

"He's going to help him, I think, since he found out the boys are not such 'louts' as he thought them."

Rod and I felt a good deal better then, you may be sure. Uncle Wheeler went home the next day, but he parted from us kindly, told Rod to be ready for college in the fall, and to remember mother's training in straightforwardness, and finally left an envelope in our respective hands. We found a twenty-dollar bill in each of them.

"Hurrah for Uncle Wheeler!" said Rod. "He's a brick!"

★   ★   ★

2. "A New-Fashioned Flavoring"

[From *Golden Days for Boys and Girls* 19.41 (August 27, 1898): 641–642 (R/W 674).]

[This story represents an earlier version of another episode in *Anne of Green Gables*, that of the liniment-flavoured cake in Chapter XXI. As with the Josephine Barry/Uncle Wheeler story, this narrative has an antecedent. Montgomery describes such an episode as this having "happened when [she] was teaching school at Bideford and boarding at the Methodist parsonage there. Its charming mistress flavoured a layer cake with anodyne liniment that day. [...] A strange minister was there to tea that night. He ate every crumb of his piece of cake" (*AP* 74–5). Montgomery clearly found this story to be a useful one: as well as working it into the narrative of *AGG*, she developed it in other, somewhat shorter versions, using the same narrative, with slightly different implications, and often using the same language and phrasing. See below, "The Cake that Prissy Made" and "Patty's Mistake." In all three of these stories, the emphasis is on the "housewifely" girl who is learning domestic skills. The conclusion of this story with a reward in the form of family reconciliation and money for education is characteristic of much of Montgomery's short fiction.]

When Mrs. Clay went to pay a long-promised visit to her sister it was not without some misgivings that she left her household in charge of Edmund and Ivy.

To be sure, Ivy could be trusted; she was fifteen, and had been her mother's right hand for years. But Edmund, who was sixteen and ought to have had more sense than Ivy, but hadn't, was prone to tricks and nonsense; and all the rest of the little Clays, a round half dozen in number, were noted for the numerous scrapes they contrived to get into daily.

Nevertheless, Mrs. Clay stifled her doubts and went away for a week, burdening Edmund and Ivy with so many charges and reminders that they forgot half of them before she was fairly out of the gate.

Edmund was deputed to kindle fires, chop wood, feed the pig, bring in water, and, last-but-not-least, he was to look after the youthful Clays and keep them in order.

Ivy was to do the housework and see that the children were kept comparatively clean and mended and keep a wary eye on things in general.

"And if anything dreadful should happen," warned their mother, "be sure to send for me at once. Be careful of the fires, Ivy, and, Edmund, never you try to light one with kerosene. I expect in the end to come home and find the house burned to the ground or half the children killed."

"That isn't the right spirit to go on a visit in, mother," said Edmund. He was sitting on the edge of the wood-box, whittling over the floor. "Just make up your mind to enjoy yourself. Don't worry about us. We'll be all right. I give you my word everything will go swimmingly. I'll keep the kids straight—and Ivy, too, if she gets fighting. You can depend on me, mother."

"I know just how much dependence can be placed on you, Edmund," replied his mother, severely; "now, *do* behave yourself while I'm away, and don't call your brothers and sisters 'kids.'"

"Well, I'm sure I can't call them lambs, anyhow. Just listen to that,"—as a crash and a scream sounded in an adjoining room. "Fan and Reeve have 'gone over' on the rocking chair again. There won't be a whole piece of furniture left in this establishment by another month."

Altogether, as has been said, Mrs. Clay did not leave home in a very easy state of mind. Nevertheless, the Clay household got on wonderfully well. Edmund behaved himself tolerably well and attended to his man-of-the-house duties with praiseworthy diligence. Moreover, he kept the younger Clays within reasonable bounds and refused to aid or abet them in making nuisances of themselves.

He studied hard in the long evenings after Fan and Reeve and Kitty and Jo and Frank and Bobby had been tucked away in their beds and Ivy had taken her knitting and sat down in the little sitting-room.

"I'd put more heart into it if I thought it would come to anything," he said mournfully; "but it won't. No college for me! I'll have to leave school in the spring and pitch into earning my own living and helping you folks along. It's tough on a fellow to be poor. Don't I envy Scott Dawson! He's going to college next fall."

"It's too bad you can't go, Ed," said Ivy, sympathizingly. "You're ever so much smarter than Scott Dawson. But I don't suppose we could ever manage it."

"I know that well enough. Let a fellow complain a bit, will you? It eases me. No. I won't whine when it comes to the point. I'll get all that done beforehand, and you'll see me grinning over the counter as if I were the happiest fellow in the world. If we were not so awfully poor, Ivy, or if the good old days of fairies and three wishes hadn't gone by, what would you go in for?"

"Music," answered Ivy, with a little sigh. "Oh, dear me! I'd just love to be a good violinist. But that costs money, too; so I needn't think of it."

"If that blessed Uncle Eugene of ours wasn't such a miserly old crank," continued Edmund, "he might help us along a bit. He isn't much like a story-book uncle, is he, Ivy? I'd like to meet him just to see what he's like."

"I wouldn't," said Ivy, emphatically, "if he's as cranky and particular as mother says he is. And he behaved abominably to father when they had that dispute over the property. No, I don't want to see Uncle Eugene. If I did I should be apt to flare out and tell him what I thought of him. It's a mercy there's no fear of us seeing him. He wouldn't come here for anything."

"You don't know. It's always the unexpected that happens," replied Edmund, oracularly. "Wouldn't it be a joke if he were to come now, when mother is away. If the kids—I beg your pardon! I mean my hopeful brothers and sisters behave as they usually do when we have company, how it would horrify him. Old bachelors generally know all about how children should be trained, and I've no doubt Uncle Eugene's an aggravated specimen."

The Clays were undeniably poor. Mr. Clay had died some five years before, leaving his family but scantily provided for. Mrs. Clay had hard work to make both ends meet. Being a woman of resource and thrift, she accomplished it, but luxuries were unknown in the little household. Yet they were happy in spite of their poverty. Edmund's college course had to be given up. He was to take a position as a clerk in a dry goods store in the spring. Ivy had her own deprivations, of which she said little. She buried music dreams in the recesses of her heart, and made over her dresses and wore her hats three seasons with smiling sweetness.

I think, on the whole, they enjoyed life quite as well as richer people; only, as Edmund said, a little more cash would not have been an overwhelming inconvenience.

"I tell you what, Ivy," said Edmund, on Saturday afternoon, as he banged down a load of wood with a deafening crash, and sent a shower of dust over the dishes Ivy had so carefully wiped, "I'm glad mother's coming home Monday, when all's said and done. We've got along tip-top, to be sure, but the cares of being at the head of family affairs have weighed me down so heavily this week that I feel like an old man. We've been fortunate so far in that we've had no visitors. But they'll be sure to come to-day—just our Saturday luck!"

"Mercy! I hope not. I'm so busy. I'm determined that mother shall find this house in spic and span order when she comes home, so I'm having a grand rummage. This cupboard has to be put to rights, and I've fifty other things to do. And I've got the most dreadful cold in my head. I can scarcely breathe. Goodness, Ed! That's never a knock at the door."

"But it is! Ten-to-one it's Aunt Lucinda Perkins come to stay over Sunday."

"Ed, you must go to the door," said Ivy, with dismayed remembrance of her wet apron and generally disorderly appearance. "And whoever it is show them to the sitting-room. Don't dare to take anyone into the parlor, for Reeve and Bobby got in there this morning to play shop before I discovered them, and it's in an awful mess."

Ivy listened anxiously as Edmund went to the door. The visitor's tones were masculine, and she breathed a sigh of relief that it was not Aunt Perkins anyhow; but her complacency was of short duration.

When Edmund had shown the caller into the sitting-room and returned to the kitchen, Ivy divined that the "something dreadful" had happened at last.

"Ivy, the Philistines be upon thee,"[1] said Edmund, with a solemnity belied by his dancing eyes that plainly indicated his enjoyment of the whole situation.

"Is it Aunt Perkins, after all?"

"It's worse than ten Aunt Perkinses. Ivy Clay, in that room, at this very minute, sits our respected Uncle Eugene."

"Mercy on us," exclaimed Ivy; and then collapsed, sitting down on the wood-box.

"Don't take a fit, sis. When I opened the door there he stood as grim as you please. 'Is your mother at home, boy?' he asked. 'No, sir; she isn't,' I replied. 'Well, I'm her brother-in-law, Eugene Clay,'

---

[1]   In the Old Testament, enemies of the Israelites. (See Judges 13–16, esp. 16.9: "The Philistines *be* upon thee, Samson.") A "philistine" has come to mean a person who is ignorant and uncultured *(The New Dictionary of Cultural Literacy,* Third Edition, ed. E.D. Hirsch, Jr., Joseph F. Kett, and James Trefil. [Boston: Houghton Mifflin, 2002.]) The phrasing here echoes Thomas Hardy's 1874 novel, *Far from the Madding Crowd,* ch. 9: "The Philistines be upon us."

he said, and 'I've come to see her as I have to wait a few hours here for my train.' Whereat I gasped out, 'Oh!' and towed him into the room, feeling decidedly faint. My part's done. Now, Ivy, it's your turn. Sail in gracefully and bid him welcome to the house of Clay."

"In this mess? I can't," declared Ivy.

"Well, no; you'll have to fix up a bit—brush your hair, and so forth. Do the thing up in good style, Ivy. I'm going to peek through the crack and watch the interview."

"Edmund," implored Ivy, beginning to recover her equanimity, "don't do anything dreadful now, will you? Don't make me laugh or anything like that?"

"Bless you, no! I'll be a model nephew. I'm properly scared, I tell you. Don't I look pale? All I'm afraid of, Ivy, is that Uncle Eugene will get alarmed and run, for all the kids are in the room above his head, and are making a most unearthly racket. If some of them come crashing through the ceiling, it's no more than I expect."

"Oh, Ed, do go and make them stop. My head is just in a whirl. Oh, if mother were only home! Do help me out of this scrape like a dear boy. What does he look like?"

"Who? Uncle Eugene? Oh, he's not too savage—more civilized looking than I had expected. Well, I'll go and make those little Clays up there tone down before his nervous system is utterly wrecked. You 'pretty' yourself up, Ivy, and beard the lion in his den[1] as if you liked it. Don't let him suspect what a martyr you are to family ties."

Poor Ivy hurriedly brushed her rebellious curls into place, replaced her soiled apron with an immaculate white one, and, with her heart in her mouth, but looking very pretty and housewifely, nevertheless, contrived, she never knew how, to get into the sitting-room and say:

"How do you do, Uncle Eugene? I am glad to see you," hoping she would be forgiven for the atrocious fib.

"Are you?" returned Uncle Eugene grimly. "So your mother isn't home, hey?"

"No; she's visiting Aunt Mary. She expects to be home on Monday."

"Was that your brother who opened the door?"

"Yes, that is Edmund, my older brother. Won't you take off

---

[1] See *AGG* 63, note 1.

your overcoat, sir? Of course, you'll stay to tea," said Ivy, devoutly hoping he wouldn't.

"Well, yes; I suppose I will, if you'll get me an early one. Train leaves at 4:30. I can't wait over. Sorry your mother is away! How many are there of you?"

"Eight."

"Humph! I should have thought there were four times eight by the noise that was going on overhead when I came in. So you're housekeeper at present? You look like your mother."

Uncle Eugene slowly divested himself of his handsome light overcoat. He was a tall man of about fifty, with grizzled hair and a clean-shaven face. He had a hard mouth and deep-set eyes.

Ivy, with a covert glance around the room, was thankful to see it was comparatively neat. A sudden calm had succeeded Edmund's entrance overhead. His measures, whatever they were, must have been sudden and effective.

"There," said Uncle Eugene, depositing himself comfortably in a rocker by the fire, "that will do. I daresay you're busy, so don't let me detain you. You needn't think you're in duty bound to entertain me; in fact, I'd prefer you wouldn't."

Thus abruptly dismissed, Ivy gladly left her grim uncle to the charms of solitude and hastened to the kitchen, where she found Edmund scrubbing the hands and faces of all the little Clays, not one of whom dared whimper under the operation, for they realized that Edmund meant business.

"Hello, Ivy! You didn't take long to dispose of him. Did he bite?"

"Oh, don't, Edmund. This is no joking matter."

"No, indeed! It's a serious case. Don't I look as if it were?"

"Ed, he's going to stay to tea, and he wants it early. What can we give him to eat?"

"What other people eat, I suppose. Or has he some abnormal appetite that craves—"

"I mean there's nothing baked in the house, only loaf bread. I was so busy this morning I thought I wouldn't make cake. And I've heard mother say what an epicure[1] Uncle Eugene was. I'm going right to work to make a layer cake; it won't take long, but I shall have to hurry. And there is the quince preserve. That'll have to do. You'd better go in with him, Ed."

---

[1]   A person devoted to pleasure and luxury.

"Not I. I have to fly round to the grocery for butter. Do you want anything else?"

"No; don't bother me," replied Ivy, who was scurrying in and out of the pantry with a bowl and a flour-scoop.[1] Edmund proved himself a tower of strength.[2] He finished putting the little Clays in order and then went around to the grocery with a rush.

On his return he found Ivy whipping up her cake energetically.

"It's all ready for the flavoring, Ed. Just hand me the bottle of vanilla out of the pantry, will you? It's on the second shelf."

Edmund dived into the pantry and returned with the vanilla bottle, rushing off again to settle a noisy dispute between Frank and Bobby in the hall. Ivy measured out and stirred in a generous spoonful of vanilla, filled her pans and triumphantly banged the oven-door upon them.

"Now, I do hope it will turn out well. I'll whip up a bit of frosting for the top. What a blessing those children are behaving so well! If they only keep it up at tea-time![")

Ivy began to set the tea-table, stepping briskly in and out of the room. She saw with dismay that Jo had strayed in somehow and was actually perched on Uncle Eugene's knee in earnest conversation with him.

Now, Jo Clay was six years old, and, not having arrived at years of discretion, was justly regarded as the infant terrible[3] of the family. He could not keep either his own secrets or those of other people, and Ivy was on thorns, for there was no knowing what revelations Jo might be making to Uncle Eugene. She hoped devoutly that he had not overheard any of her or Edmund's remarks, for they would be fatally sure to be recounted.

In vain she surreptitiously beckoned Jo out of the room. Jo refused to heed her, and once Uncle Eugene saw her and said:

"Leave him alone. We are all right." After which she gave up in despair, although in her pilgrimages in and out she caught scraps of Jo's remarks about "moosic" and "Ed wanting to go to college," that made her groan.

Ivy set the table daintily, with spotless cloth and shining china, and put an apple geranium in pinkish bloom in the centre. The

---

1   Appears as "flower-scoop" in *Golden Days*.

2   Cf. Shakespeare, *Richard III* 5.3 and Tennyson, "Ode on the Death of the Duke of Wellington."

3   From the French, *enfant terrible* (terrible child).

loaf-bread was cut in the thinnest of slices, the quince preserve was dished in an old-fashioned cut-glass bowl, and her cake came out of the oven as light and puffy as down.

"Just the best of luck, Ed," said Ivy, delightedly, as she clapped the layers together with ruby jelly, whisked the frosting over the top and sprinkled grated cocoa-nut on it. "Isn't that pretty? I hope it'll taste as good as it looks. Now, Ed, I'll take in the tea and you take in the children and get them settled in their places. Keep an eye on them, too. I'll have enough to attend to. And, oh, Ed! Jo's been sitting on Uncle Eugene's knee for an hour, and I know he's been telling him a fearful lot of stuff. Why couldn't you have decoyed him out?"

"Didn't dare! I'll bet Uncle Eugene knows everything about our family kinks by this time. Never mind! Come on! 'Charge, Ivy, charge! We'll win the day,' were the last words of Edmund Clay."

Edmund marshalled the little Clays soberly in and arranged them in order at the tea-table. Uncle Eugene sat down and Ivy poured out the tea with fear and trembling. But all went well at first. The tea and preserves were good and the children behaved beautifully.

Uncle Eugene said absolutely nothing. He evidently considered silence to be golden. Then Edmund, in obedience to a nod from Ivy, gravely passed the layer-cake to his Uncle, after which it went the rounds of the appreciative little Clays. Ivy took none. She was too tired and worried to eat; but Edmund helped himself to a generous slice.

When he had tasted it he laid down his fork, rolled his eyes, and opened both his hands in exaggerated dismay for Ivy's benefit. Bobby Clay followed with "Why, Ivy, what's the matter with the layer-cake?"

Edmund silenced him with such an awful look that none of the others dared open their lips, though each, after the first mouthful, left their cake uneaten on their plates. Uncle Eugene, however, appeared to taste nothing unusual, for he gravely ate his cake with an impassive face and finished the last crumb.

Frank sat to the right of the agonized Ivy, too far away to explain, but by his pantomime he conveyed the fact that something serious was the matter.

Finally, she took a peck of the triangle of cake on Reeve's plate next to her. She gave a gasp, a look at Edmund, and then, sad to relate, burst into a ringing peal of laughter, which, coming after the dead silence, was electrical in effect.

She caught herself up with a scarlet face, and in quick transition felt so much like crying that she might have done so if Uncle Eugene had not abruptly pushed back his chair and announced that he had had enough.

Ivy fled to the kitchen, whither she was followed by Edmund, with all the little Clays swarming after him.

"Ivy," demanded Edmund, tragically, "what in the world did you put in that cake? Never tasted anything like it in the cooking line before."

"Oh, Ed, how could you do such a thing?" cried poor Ivy, hysterically. "I can never forgive you. And after promising you wouldn't play any tricks, too!"

"Me!" exclaimed Edmund, too surprised to be grammatical. "Goodness, what have I done?"

"Oh, don't pretend innocence! I suppose you thought it a very smart trick to hand me out a bottle of anodyne liniment[1] to flavor that cake with—but I call it mean."

Edmund stared at her blankly for a minute, and then flung himself on the sofa and went off into a burst of laughter that made the kitchen re-echo.

"Oh," he cried, "Ivy Adella Clay! You don't mean to say you flavored that cake with anodyne liniment? Ho, ho, ho! If that isn't an original idea! I always knew you were a genius, Ivy."

"How could you, Edmund?"

Edmund sat up.

"Ivy, I give you my word of honor I didn't do it on purpose," he said, solemnly. "I thought it was vanilla—honest, I did. Why, it was in a vanilla bottle, and it's just the same color."

"Yes, don't you remember Reeve broke the liniment bottle last week and I put what wasn't spilled into an old vanilla bottle. Oh, dear me! This is dreadful!"

"You're to blame, then? Why didn't you put it out of the way? How was a fellow to tell? And how is it you didn't smell it?"

"I couldn't, with such a cold. Oh, Edmund, what must Uncle Eugene think?"

"Dear knows," said Edmund, going off into another parox-

---

[1]   See *AGG* 213, note 1.

ysm. "I suppose the poor man will think we were trying to poison him, unless he happened to recognize the taste. Fortunately, the liniment is for internal as well as external application, so nobody will die. Well, this is the latest! Flavoring a cake with anodyne liniment! Well done, Ivy!"

"Will we—do you think we ought to say anything to Uncle Eugene about it?"

"Goodness, no. Perhaps he didn't suspect anything amiss. He ate every crumb of it, so doubtless he imagined it was the newest thing in flavoring extracts. Your reputation as a cook would be gone forever if you let him know, Ivy."

"Well," said Ivy, disconsolately, "it's done now, and it can't be undone. Fortunately, as you say, it was harmless. But the whole thing is simply dreadful. What will mother say?"

"Accidents will happen, even in a well-regulated family like ours. Go and clear off the ruins, Ivy, and feed that liniment cake to the pig. Uncle Eugene will never be any the wiser."

Alas! When Ivy summoned up enough courage to return to the room and attack the table, what was her horror to find Jo delightedly telling all the details to Uncle Eugene!

Ivy caught the fatal word "lin'ment" and mentally collapsed. She must apologize somehow.

"Uncle Eugene," she stammered, with a scarlet face, her confusion not calmed in any degree by a glimpse of Edmund gesticulating wildly in the back hall. "I'm very sorry—that cake should have tasted as it did—I meant to put in vanilla, but Edmund made a mistake and somehow—well, I put in a spoonful of anodyne liniment instead. It won't hurt anyone, you know—it's sometimes taken internally—"

"But not in cakes," came in a stage whisper from the back hall.

Ivy gave up trying to explain, and, in spite of her efforts, gave vent to something that couldn't be called anything but a snicker. As for Uncle Eugene, his eyes twinkled quite genially, but all he said was:

"Accidents will happen."

And Ivy went out, considerably mystified as to what effect the disclosure had had on him.

Soon after he looked at his watch, said it was nearly train time, and put on his coat. He shook hands with Ivy and Edmund, told them to tell their mother he was sorry not to have seen her, and relieved the Clay mansion of his unwelcome presence.

"Thank goodness!" said Edmund, emphatically, when he had seen him safely out of the gate. "The old crank has gone. I guess he won't come back in a hurry. I should say liniment-flavored cake was an excellent preventative of unwelcome guests. What an opinion he must have of us! You are always doing something brilliant, Ivy, but you've surpassed yourself in this exploit."

When Mrs. Clay returned home on Monday she listened to the tale with a curious mixture of dismay and amusement.

"I wish I had been home," she said. "I can't think what induced him to come. He once said he'd never darken our doors again. I suppose I ought to be thankful to find you all alive and sound of limb, but it's a pity Uncle Eugene should have come when I was away. I expect he's gone for good, now, Ivy, after what you gave him to eat, poor man. I know how Uncle Eugene would regard anything like that."

But she didn't! Next week a letter came from her brother-in-law—short and abrupt, as was his fashion, but the contents were satisfactory.

It ran:

"Sister Martha:

"Doubtless this will impress you. I called at your house last week and found you away. However, your son and daughter entertained me very hospitably and I was much pleased with them both, but especially with the girl. The boy, I take it, is somewhat mischievous and likes to tease his sister. I dare say they think I'm a crusty old fellow and they are right; but I desire to make amends for the past if you will let bygones be bygones. I am a lonely man and I want to have some interests outside myself. Edmund and Ivy did not tell me about your concerns, but I picked up an inkling from little Jo. Tell Edmund he is not to go into that store, but to prepare for college next fall and I will put him through. I have nothing else to do with my money and you must gratify me in this whim. As for Ivy, you may tell her she is to take music lessons and I will send her the best violin to be had. She is a good, housewifely girl. Tell her also that her liniment cake seems to have had an excellent effect on her cranky old uncle for it appears to have made him well all over, even to his bones and marrow. I may pay you another visit soon.

"Until then I remain yours respectfully,
"EUGENE CLAY."

"Uncle Eugene is a brick," exclaimed Edmund, breathlessly,
"a regular brick! I repent in sackcloth and ashes[1] of anything I
ever said to the contrary."

"He is splendid," said Ivy, with shining eyes. "To think I am
to have music lessons—and a violin. It is too good to be true."

"You may well be grateful. It's not every uncle who would
behave so handsomely to a girl who gave him liniment cake to
eat. What an advertisement this would be for that liniment firm
if they got hold of it. A liniment warranted to cure, not only
every known bodily ailment, but those of the mind and heart as
well! They'd make their fortune. Mother, say something! Relieve
your feelings in some way!"

"I say, 'Long live anodyne liniment!'" said Mrs. Clay, laughing.
"Your experiment has turned out well this time, Ivy, but I
wouldn't advise a repetition. Uncle Eugene was always kind at
heart, although peculiar. And now, to prevent any further
mistakes, I'll go and put that new-fashioned flavoring of yours
out of the vanilla bottle into a more orthodox one. The next
time Uncle Eugene comes I'll make the cake myself."

★   ★   ★

3. "Patty's Mistake"

[From *Zion's Herald* (April 16, 1902): 494 (*R/W* 721).]

["Patty's Mistake" is a shorter and somewhat less developed
version of the cake-mistake narrative Montgomery produces in
"A New-Fashioned Flavoring." This story, published in 1902
(although possibly written at an earlier date), differs in some relatively minor ways from the more extensive and complex version.
The narrative is built around a cake-baking competition between
a pair of ten-year-old twin sisters. The eponymous "mistake"
involves the addition of saleratus (baking soda) to the cake's icing,

---

[1]   There are several occurrences of the image of repentance in sackcloth and ashes in
the Bible. See, for instance, Esther 4.1 and Daniel 9.3.

rather than anyodyne liniment for vanilla flavouring, as in "A New-Fashioned Flavoring" and *AGG*. This story, however, has other elements that are reproduced and reworked in *AGG*. For instance, Trudy dreams that "she was being chased all over the place by a fearful goblin with a big frosted cake for a head," just as Anne does in her cake-baking episode. The story, which was published in a Sunday School paper, has a predictable moral: Patty is rewarded for observing the "Golden Rule"—doing unto others as you would have them do unto you—by being forgiven for her own mistake in using the wrong ingredient in the icing. The story's domestic imperative for girls is evident in the basing of the competition on Uncle James' statement that "all little girls should learn how to cook."]

"Really *and* truly!" said Uncle James. "Well, well, well!"

Patty looked puzzled. Was Uncle James making fun of her? There was never any knowing just what he might mean when he said, "Well, well, well" in that tone of voice.

Uncle James pushed his spectacles more firmly on his nose, planted his hands on his knees, and bent forward to look into Patty's face.

"So you and Trudy have been learning to cook? Well, can either of you make anything fit to eat?"

"Indeed we can," declared Patty indignantly. "Papa says our cakes are as good as Nora's. You said when you were here last summer, Uncle James, that all little girls should learn how to cook. So Trudy and I learned. We had a *dreadful* time at first, and Nora said we'd be the death of her. But she's alive yet! And we thought you'd be so s'prised and pleased. We didn't s'pose you'd *laugh* at us."

"Bless your heart, child, I'm not laughing at you," said Uncle James. And indeed he looked solemn enough except for his eyes. "Go and bring Trudy here. I've something to say to both of you."

When Patty came back hand in hand with Trudy Uncle James looked at the two little ten-year-old maids as gravely as a judge.

"Bless me!" he said. "Which of you is which? It is a most confusing thing to have twins in the family."

"This is Trudy because she wears a red ribbon," exclaimed Patty, "and I'm Patty because I wear a blue one," she added, pulling her brown braids over her shoulder.

"Oh, I see! Well, for pity sake keep the ribbons in sight so that I won't get you mixed up. This is what I want to say to you: You tell me that you can make good cakes. But I have always believed that the proof of the pudding is in the eating[1]—likewise the proof of the cake. Now, I want each of you to bake a cake for me; and I will award a prize to the best one."

"Oh!" said Patty, and, "Oh!" said Trudy, both together.

"They must be very good cakes, you know," said Uncle James, more solemnly than ever. "They must have 'sugar and spice and all that's nice'[2] in them, and frosting all over the top. Don't forget the frosting, mind! The cakes must be made without any assistance from other people. The girl who bakes the best cake shall go to town with me next Tuesday and see the Park and the gardens, and eat ice-cream at Carter's, and go with me on the afternoon steamer excursion to Rocky Point. Now be off with you."

Patty and Trudy were wildly excited. Away they rushed to consult with mamma and Nora. It was agreed that they might make their cakes the next morning. For the rest of the day they thought of nothing else, and that night Patty dreamed that she had to stone a whole mountain of raisins before she could get one to put in her cake, while poor Trudy had a terrible nightmare, and thought she was being chased all over the place by a fearful goblin with a big frosted cake for a head.

Next morning Uncle James pulled straws to see who should bake her cake first. The lot fell to Trudy, who went promptly to work, sifting flour, stoning raisins, whipping eggs, and measuring flavoring extracts enthusiastically.

Patty sat by the kitchen table and watched her with very red cheeks and very bright eyes. She knew something. Trudy had forgotten the baking powder!

"I won't say one word," thought Patty. "She ought to remember it herself. It's very careless of her. But it's just like Trudy. She's so forgetful. If she doesn't put it in, her cake won't be any good at all, and mine will get the prize."

"But you know, Patty Reid," said a very little voice somewhere deep down in Patty's heart, "that if you were in Trudy's

---

[1]   Proverb. See Miguel de Cervantes (1547–1616), *Don Quixote* (1605–15), Part 2, Chapter 14.

[2]   Cf. the nursery rhyme: "Sugar and spice and everything nice; That's what little girls are made of."

place you'd like to be told. And the Golden Rule[1] says that you must do to others as you'd have them do to you."

"I don't care," answered Patty, resolutely. "I'm not going to tell her."

But the insistent little voice kept on, and finally had the best of it. Just as Trudy reached out for her bowl of flour, Patty spoke up:

"Trudy, you didn't put the baking powder in."

"Oh, dear me! neither I did," gasped Trudy. "How lucky you noticed it! Why, my cake would have been spoiled altogether."

So Trudy sifted the baking powder in and beat her cake thoroughly and poured it into the pan and baked it. It came out of the oven light as a feather and looking as good as a cake could look.

Then while Trudy made her icing Patty mixed her cake. And as she did it very carefully and baked it very carefully, she had good luck with it, too. She turned it out on the table by the window to cool and went into the pantry to make her frosting. The pantry was dimly lighted, for Nora had shut the blinds to keep the flies out. Trudy's cake lay in all its glory on a plate on the dresser. It certainly looked very toothsome.

Patty whipped up the white of an egg until the froth stood alone. Then she took a cup and crawled half way into the big dark cupboard below the dresser where the icing sugar was kept. An open paper bag full of it was in the corner. Patty scooped out a generous cupful and whisked it into her egg. Then she spread it on her cake and surveyed the result with satisfaction.

"It looks just as good as Trudy's, anyhow," she said, as she left it to harden.

That night at the tea-table Patty and Trudy were too excited to eat. A plate of Patty's cake was on Uncle James' right hand, and a plate of Trudy's on his left. When he finally took up the former Patty clasped her hands together under the table.

"Everybody must take a piece of this cake," announced Uncle James, "and then a piece of the other. And we will decide by vote which is the better."

The plate went round. Everybody except Patty took a slice. Everybody lifted the slice and took a mouthful. Everybody choked, gasped, spluttered, and rushed from the table.

"Oh! what is the matter?" cried Patty.

---

[1]   Do unto others as you would have them do unto you. Matthew 7.12.1.

She snatched the slice of cake which brother Bob had dropped, and took a big, brave bite. Then she burst into tears and fled from the room.

Patty had iced that cake with saleratus![1]

Upstairs in her own little room Patty cast herself face downward on the bed and cried stormily. Oh, it was dreadful! She had lost the prize, and Uncle James would laugh at her. And the boys would make fun of her forever. She could never look anybody in the face again. And Trudy would go to town and have the ice-cream, and she wished she had never learned to cook a thing, that she did, and her heart was broken.

Presently Trudy trotted into the room.

"Patty! Patty Reid!"

"Oh! go away, Trudy Reid," said Patty, with a fresh burst of sobs. She wriggled further down into the pillows and wouldn't look at Trudy.

"Don't be a goose," said Trudy, comfortingly. "Wait till I tell you. When the folks came back to the table they tried my cake and everybody said it was just elegant, and Uncle James said I had won the prize. And then I thought about the baking powder. And I told Uncle James how I had forgotten it, and you had reminded me of it; and I said I thought my mistake in forgetting it was just as bad as yours about the saleratus. And Uncle James said he thought so too, and he guessed the fairest way would be to take a piece of both cakes and cut off the icing and judge them that way. So they did, and they all said there wasn't a speck of difference, and one was just as good as the other. And then Uncle James said it was a tie, and we are *both* to go to town with him on Tuesday. So what do you think of that?"

Patty sat up and wiped the tears from her chubby cheeks.

"I think it's just splendid," she said happily. "But, O Trudy, wasn't that cake *awful*?"

Cavendish, P.E.I.

4. "The Cake that Prissy Made"

[From *The Congregationalist and Christian World* (11 July 1903): 59 (*R/W* 746).]

---

[1]   Sodium bicarbonate, or baking soda.

["The Cake that Prissy Made" appeared a year after "Patty's Mistake" in another Sunday School paper, and represents another version of the cake-mistake narrative Montgomery found so useable in her writing. This story is similarly short and undeveloped, and is based again on the confusion of icing sugar with saleratus; it has, however, a somewhat differently pointed moral than the one directed to a child reader, as in "Patty's Mistake." In this case the child's mistake leads to the reconciliation of two grown women who have been estranged since a quarrel. The child unwittingly and innocently teaches the adults forgiveness.]

"I am going to make a cake and take it over to the new minister's wife today," said Mrs. Wood. "I am sure she won't have had time to cook much when she's been so busy all the week getting settled down. And it's likely she'll have a strange minister or two to tea tomorrow, since that convention is being held over at Exbridge."

"May I help make the cake, mother?" asked Prissy.

"Of course you may, girlie. If it wasn't for the minister's wife I'd let you make it all by yourself."

For ten year-old Prissy was a famous little cook and very proud of the fact.

But just after dinner that day word came that Aunt Janetta Wood, over at Exbridge, had had another "spell." Mr. and Mrs. Wood hastily got ready and drove away, leaving Prissy in charge, with many directions and warnings.

When Prissy was left alone she remembered about the cake that was to have been made for the new minister's wife. Mrs. Wood had forgotten all about it.

"But I'll make it," said Prissy resolutely. "I know I can make it good and I'll take such pains."

So Prissy went to work in a housewifely fashion, tying a big frilled apron about her and looking as wise as a baker's dozen of little cooks. Very carefully indeed did she mix and measure and stir. Then came the baking, and Prissy hovered over the range until her jolly little round face was as red as one of the big peonies in the garden outside. But she felt repaid for all her trouble and worry when the cake came out of the oven light and puffy as golden foam.

"Now for the icing," said Prissy triumphantly, "and after tea I'll put it in the long basket and take it up to the manse."

By this time Prissy was a little tired, so she rather hurriedly beat up the confectioner's sugar for the icing and didn't even scrape out the bowl for her own sweet tooth, as she usually did.

After tea, when the icing on the cake was beautifully smooth and firm, Prissy dressed herself in her second-best blue-plaid gingham and started out to carry her gift to the manse, leaving brother Ted in charge of home affairs.

She was not sure just where the manse was. The Wood family had been living in River Valley only two months themselves, and Prissy had never been up the Exbridge road before and had not yet seen the minister's wife. When she had walked about a mile she met the little boy who sat at the desk next to hers at school and Prissy very politely asked him to direct her to the manse. And the little boy who sat at the next desk answered, just as politely, that she must take the next turn to the right, and the third house from the corner on the left hand side was the manse.

Prissy followed these directions and her nose, and soon found herself on the manse veranda. She rang the bell, asked the trim maid for Mrs. Stanley, and was whisked into the sitting-room, where a very pretty lady with brown eyes was arranging some books.

"Please'm," said Prissy, feeling horribly shy all at once, "please'm, I've brought you a cake—mother thought you might like it—because you've been so busy moving in."

The lady's brown eyes twinkled pleasantly.

"Sit down, dear," she said. "And so your mother has sent me a cake. It is very sweet and thoughtful of her. I haven't a bit in the house and I have been very much rushed. Now, which of my kind new neighbors is this nice mother of yours? And you'll tell me your own name, too, won't you?"

"Mother is Mrs. Chester Wood," said Prissy, "and my name is Priscilla Marian Wood. But everybody just calls me Prissy. Mother meant to bake this cake for you herself. But she had to go see Aunt Janetta after dinner—Aunt Janetta takes spells, you know—and so I made it myself. I hope you'll like it although, of course, it isn't as good as mother could make."

Prissy had not noticed the surprised expression which came over her hearer's face when she told her name. When the latter spoke there was a queer little tremor in her voice.

"It was very kind of your mother and very sweet of you. I— I—didn't expect it. Your cake looks so tempting that I am sure it is good and I'm going to get a knife and sample it right away. I feel really hungry for a bit of cake. I haven't had any for over a week you see."

She got a knife and cut a generous slice of the cake. She offered it to Prissy but Prissy declined politely. She was not sure whether it would be good manners to bring a cake to the minister's wife and then help to eat it. So her hostess took a big, brave bite of the slice herself. Then a queer look came over her face and she got up and whisked out of the room without a word. When she came back her face was very red but she ate up the rest of the slice and told Prissy that it was delicious. She did not eat the icing. She left that lying on her plate.

She asked Prissy a great many questions about her mother and herself and when Prissy went away she told her that she would come over the very next day and see her mother. Of course Prissy said politely that they would be very glad to see her but in her secret heart she did think it odd that the minister's wife should go visiting on Sunday.

She was at Sunday school the next day when the visitor came.

"Marian!" said Mrs. Wood in amazement.

"You expected me, didn't you?" said her caller. "I told Prissy I would come today. I couldn't wait until Monday. It was so good of you to think of me and of sending that cake, Julia. I understood it to mean that you wished to be friends again and were willing to forget that foolish old quarrel of ours which I have so deeply repented."

Mrs. Wood knew there was a mistake somewhere but it didn't matter. She held out her hands warmly to Marian and they kissed each other tenderly.

When Prissy came home her mother told her that the new minister's wife had never received the cake which had been so painstakingly made for her. Whether it was Prissy's mistake or the mistake of the little boy who sat at the next desk I don't know and nobody else knows. The manse was the third house on the right hand side. The house on the left hand side had just been rented for the summer by Mr. and Mrs. Stanleigh. And Mrs. Stanleigh had been Priscilla Marian Gray before her marriage.

"We were very dear friends, Prissy," said Mrs. Wood. "You were named for her. But we had a foolish, bitter quarrel some years ago and have been estranged ever since. I missed her greatly but our pride has kept us from seeking a reconciliation. We have forgiven each other now and all is well again, thanks to you, you blessed little blunderer."

But there are three things about this story that three people never knew:

Mrs. Stanley, the new minister's wife, never knew how narrowly she missed having a cake for her first Sunday tea.

Mrs. Stanleigh of the third house on the left hand side never knew that the cake she received was meant for somebody else.

And, Prissy never knew that she had iced that cake with saleratus!

Appendix B: Montgomery on Writing: "The Way to Make a Book"

[L.M. Montgomery used her 1917 autobiographical work, *The Alpine Path*, first published in the Toronto magazine *Everywoman's World*, to offer advice to would-be writers, but she is not as explicit in her recommendations there as she is in this earlier piece. This article appeared in *Everywoman's World* two years prior to the publication of the story of her career and presents a clear articulation of Montgomery's idea of the work of writing as a moral undertaking, as well as some information about her compositional practices. It is directed to aspiring female writers in particular. Given Montgomery's difficulties with her first publisher, an important element in this 1915 article is her advice to writers regarding contracts and royalties.]

[From *Everywoman's World*, Toronto (April 1915): 24–27. (This article is not noted in the Russell/Wilmshurst bibliography.).]

An old joke will probably be familiar to all who read this article. A woman who had one child was anxious to train it properly. Feeling herself to be very ignorant of such a subject, she appealed for instruction to a friend who had seven children.

"My dear," said her friend, "there is no use asking me how to bring up children because I really don't know anything more about it than you do. But just ask the first old maid you meet and she will be able to tell you all about it."

And it is just so in regard to the writing of books. Those who never write books can so easily tell how it is done and how it should be done. It is as easy for them as rolling off a log. For those of us who *have* written books it is an exceedingly hard thing.

My own experience is that books—real "live" books—are *not* written. Like *Topsy*,[1] they "grow." The function of the author is simply to follow the growth and record it:

---

[1] The reference is to Harriet Beecher Stowe's 1852 novel, *Uncle Tom's Cabin*. According to *Brewer's*, Topsy is a young African-American slave, who, when "questioned [...] as to her father and mother" responds thus: "[a]fter maintaining that she had neither father nor mother, her solution of her existence was 'I 'spects I growed.'"

"Perhaps it may turn out a song,[1]
Perhaps turn out a sermon."
Never mind what it turns out. As long as it grows out of your life it will have life in it, and the great pulse of humanity everywhere will thrill and throb to that life.

Before attempting to write a book, be sure you have something to say—something that *demands* to be said. It need not be a very great or lofty or profound something; it is not given to many of us [to] utter
"Jewels five words long
That on the stretched forefinger of all time
Sparkle for ever."[2]
But if we have something to say that will bring a whiff of fragrance to a tired soul and to a weary heart, or a glint of sunshine to a clouded life, then that something is worth saying, and it is our duty to try to say it as well as in us lies.

A book to be worth anything, must have a good central idea. I do not say a plot, for many very successful books have little or no plot. Certainly, a logical and well-constructed plot adds strength and charm to any book and increases the chances of its success. But a central idea—a purpose of some sort—a book must have. It is not to be flung in the reader's face; it is not to be obtruded in every paragraph or chapter; but it must be there, as the spine is in the human body, to hold the book together; and all that follows, characters, incidents and conversations, must be developed in harmony with this idea or purpose.

One should not try to write a book impulsively or accidentally, as it were. The idea may come by impulse or accident, but it must be worked out with care and skill, or its embodiment will never partake of the essence of true art. Write—and put what you have written away; read it over weeks later; cut, prune, and rewrite. Repeat this process until your work seems to you as good as you can make it. Never mind what outside critics say. They will all differ from each other in their opinions, so there is really not a great deal to be learned from them. Be your own severest critic. Never let a sentence in your work get by you until you are convinced that it is as perfect as you can make it.

---

1   Properly, a "sang." See "Epistle to a Young Friend" by Robert Burns (1759–96).
2   See Tennyson, *The Princess*, Canto 2.355ff., by Tennyson (1847). Properly, "Jewels five-words-long/ That on the stretched forefinger of all Time/ Sparkle forever."

Somebody else may be able to improve it vastly. Somebody will be sure to think he can. Never mind. Do *your* best—and do it sincerely. Don't try to write like some other author. Don't try to "hit the public taste." The public taste doesn't really like being hit. It prefers to be allured into some fresh pasture, surprised with some unexpected tid-bit.

An accusation is often made against us novelists that we paint our characters—especially our ridiculous or unpleasant characters—"from life." The public seems determined not to allow the smallest particle of creative talent to an author. If you write a book, you *must* have drawn your characters "from life." You, yourself, are, of course, the hero or heroine; your unfortunate neighbors will supply the other portraits. People will cheerfully tell you that they know this or that character of your books intimately. This will aggravate you at first, but later on you will learn to laugh at it. It is, in reality, a subtle compliment—though it is not always meant to be. It is at least a tribute to the "life-likeness" of your book people.

But no true artist ever draws exactly from life. We must *study* from life, working in hints gathered here and there, bits of character, personal or mental idiosyncracies [sic], humorous remarks, tales, or legends, making use of the real to perfect the ideal. But our own ideal must be behind it all. A writer must keep his eyes open for material; but in the last analysis his characters must be the creations of his own mind if they are to be consistent and natural.

Right here, let me say that a writer of books must cultivate the "note-book habit."[1] Keep a blank book; jot down in it every helpful idea that comes your way, every amusing or dramatic incident or expression that you hear, every bit of apt description that occurs to you. Be all eye and ear in your daily walks and social intercourse. If you meet a quaint personality write down its salient characteristic. If you see a striking face or feature describe it for future use; if you hear a scrap of native wit or unconscious humor or pathos, preserve it; if you see some exquisite, fleeting effect in sky or sea or field, imprison it in words before it can escape you. Some day you may create a character in whose mouth the long-preserved sentence of fun or absurdity may be appropriate—you

---

[1] Although Anne does not keep such a "note-book" in *AGG*, Emily Starr does, in the later "Emily" series (*Emily of New Moon* [1923], *Emily Climbs* [1925], *Emily's Quest* [1927].)

may stage your story in a landscape where the bit of first-hand description furnishes exactly the necessary touch of reality. I have, time and again, evolved some of my most successful tales or chapters from the germ of some such "bit," hurriedly scribbled in my note-book when I heard or saw or thought it.[1]

Write only of the life you know. This is the only safe rule for most of us. A great genius may, by dint of adding research and study to his genius, be able to write of other ages and other environments than his own. But the chances are that you are not a Scott or a Cooper.[2] So stick to what you know. It is not a narrow field. Human life is thick around us everywhere. Tragedy is being enacted in the next yard; comedy is playing across the street. Plot and incident and coloring are ready to our hands. The country lad at his plough can be made just as interesting a character as if he were a knight in shining armor; the bent old woman we pass on the road may have been as beautiful in her youth as the daughters of Vere de Vere,[3] and the cause of as many heartaches. The darkest tragedy I ever heard of was enacted by people who lived on a backwoods farm; and funnier than anything I ever read was a dialogue between two old fishermen who were gravely discussing a subject of which they knew absolutely nothing. Unless you are living alone on a desert island you can find plenty of material for writing all around you; and even there, you could find it in your own heart and soul. For it is surprising how much we are all like other people. Jerome K. Jerome[4] says: "Life tastes just the same, whether you drink it out of a stone mug or a golden goblet." There you are! So don't make the mistake of trying to furnish your stories with golden goblets when stone mugs are what your characters are accustomed to use. The public isn't much concerned with your external nothings—your mugs or your goblets. What they want is the fresh, spicy brew that Nature pours for us everywhere.

When you have shaped out your central idea and brooded over your characters until they live and move and have being for

---

[1] According to Montgomery, such a "bit" led to the writing of *Anne of Green Gables*. See *SJ* 1 330-31.
[2] Sir Walter Scott, cited repeatedly in *AGG*; James Fenimore Cooper, American novelist (1759–1851).
[3] A reference to Tennyson's poem "Lady Clara Vere de Vere."
[4] English humourist and playwright (1859-1927).

you, then write about them. Let them have a good deal of their own way, even if it isn't always your way. Don't try to describe them too fully; let them reveal themselves. As somebody has said, "Don't tell your readers that a certain woman growls; just bring the old lady in and *let her growl.*" See to it that your incidents and characters grow out of one another naturally, as they do in real life. Don't drag some event in, however dramatic or amusing it may be in itself, if it has no real connection with your plot or your idea. This doesn't mean that you must never indulge in any pleasant little by-way excursion to pick primroses. But your by-ways must always lead back to your main road. They must not stop short, leaving you and your readers to jump back.

Write, I beseech you, of things cheerful, of things lovely, of things of good report. Don't write about pig-sties because they are "real." Flower-gardens are just as real and just as plentiful. Write tragedy if you will, for there must be shadow as well as sunlight in any broad presentment of human life; but don't write of vileness, of filth, of unsavory deeds and thoughts. There is no justification of such writing. The big majority of the reading public doesn't want it; it serves not one good end; it debases a God-given talent. Never mind if some *blasé* [sic] critic sneeringly says that your book will "please the Young Person." You may be justly proud if it does. The Young Person's taste is well worth pleasing because, thank God, it is generally pure and natural, delighting in simplicity, not demanding salaciousness to spur a jaded appetite that has been vitiated by long indulgence in tainted food.

Don't spin your book out too long. The day of the three-volume novel[1] passed with the crinoline skirt[2] and the stage-coach. Don't make anybody too bad or anybody too good. Most people are mixed. Don't make vice attractive and goodness stupid. It's nearly always the other way in real life. Don't be content with writing pretty well; do your best; if you are only describing a stone wall, make your readers *see* that wall, see it

---

1 ("Three-decker.") "The dominant form in which full length new fiction was published from the mid-1820s until 1894: namely three octavo volumes [...] unillustrated. [...] Notoriously, the form encouraged narrative padding, especially a profusion of short-sentenced dialogue by which expanses of white paper could be used up with relatively few words" (*The Stanford Companion to Victorian Fiction*, ed. John Sutherland [Stanford: Stanford UP, 1989]).

2 "a stiff petticoat (undergarment) worn under a skirt to support or distend it; hence, a hooped petticoat" (*OED*).

yourself first; cut and prune, but—don't make things *too* bare. If you were a genius of the first rank you might present stark facts fascinatingly; but ordinary writers need a few branching sprays of fancy. Study and observe life that you may paint it convincingly; cultivate a sense of dramatic and humorous values; *feel* what you write; love your characters and live with them—

AND KEEP ON TRYING!

When you have your book written—what then? Send it to any publishing firm of good repute and standing you prefer. Don't worry over the fact that you are unknown and deduce therefrom the conclusion that your manuscript won't be read. It will be read; it may, and—if it is your first—very likely will, be sent back to you. Don't throw it in the fire; don't sit down and cry; just do it up and send it to the next firm on your list. If there is anything in it, it will find acceptance finally. Don't have anything to do with firms that offer to publish your book if you will pay half the expenses. Arrange to have it published on a royalty basis. On your first book you can't expect more than a ten per cent. royalty. Some firms offer to purchase a manuscript for a certain sum cash down. It is rarely advisable to accept this. If a book is anything of a success it will bring you in more on the royalty basis, and publishers seldom offer to buy a book outright unless they are strongly convinced that it will be a success.

When the book is published your publishers will send you half a dozen copies free. If you want more to present to admiring friends you have to buy them, same as everybody else. But what a day it is when your first book comes to you between covers!

"'Tis pleasant sure to see one's name in print—
A book's a book, although there's nothing in it."[1]

But if you have written it "for the joy of the working,"[2] there *will* be something it in [sic], and the praise of the Master of all good workmen will be yours.

---

[1] Byron, *English Bards and Scotch Reviewers* (1809) 1.51–52.

[2] Rudyard Kipling (1865–1936), British poet. "When Earth's last picture is painted, and the tubes are twisted and dried": "And no one shall work for money, and no one shall work for fame,/ But each for the joy of the working, and each, in his separate star,/ Shall draw the Thing as he sees It for the God of Things as They are!" *Complete Verse; Definitive Edition*, [New York: Doubleday, 1989] 1.10–12).

Appendix C: Montgomery on Gender

1. "The Thirty Sweet Girl Graduates of Dalhousie University"

[From *The Halifax Herald* (29 April 1896): 12 (*R/W* 1666).]

[This article written by Montgomery was published in *The Halifax Herald* in 1896 when she was twenty-two and was attending Halifax Ladies' College at Dalhousie College in Halifax, Nova Scotia. The article presents the full ambivalence of Montgomery's feminism, conveying her sense of the importance of "advancement" for exceptional women, and of the maintenance of the status quo for everyone else. In *AGG*, Marilla's argument for Anne's education has to do with the ability of women to support themselves; what Montgomery presents here is less career-focused, and makes the somewhat compromised point that an educated woman makes a better wife and mother—that is, that education for women is valuable for men and society, rather than for women as individuals. She does, however, also affirm the value of education for individual women with ambition and whose life work is better done with education, as, it is implicit, is the case for a writer. Characteristically, although Montgomery writes a journal entry on 29 April, 1896, she does not mention the publication of this piece, but describes her trip back to P.E.I. This article's appearance on the day of the conclusion of her academic career suggests that it is also interesting as a kind of valediction: Montgomery had wanted to continue her education, but was not supported in this desire by her grandfather.]

"Why, sirs, they do all this as well as we."[1]

    ★   ★   ★

"Girls,
Knowledge is now no more a fountain sealed;
    Drink deep until the habits of the slave,
The sins of emptiness, gossip and spite,
    And slander die. Better not be at all

---

[1]   See Tennyson, *The Princess*, Canto 2, 381.

Than not be noble."[1]

*   *   *

"Pretty were the sight,
If our old halls could change their sex and flaunt
With prudes for proctors, dowagers for deans,
And sweet girl graduates in their golden hair."[2]

Tennyson—"The Princess"

A Girl's Place at Dalhousie College

It is not a very long time, as time goes in the world's history, since the idea of educating a girl beyond the "three r's" would have been greeted with lifted hands and shocked countenances. What! Could any girl, in her right and proper senses, ask for any higher, more advanced education than that accorded her by tradition and custom? Could any girl presume to think that the attainments of her mother and grandmother before her, insufficient for her [sic]? Above all, could she dream of opposing her weak feminine mind to the mighty masculine intellects which had been dominating the world of knowledge from a date long preceding the time when Hypatia[3] was torn to pieces by the mob of Alexandria?

"Never," was the approved answer to all such questions. Girls were "educated" according to the standard of the time. That is they were taught reading and writing and a small smattering of foreign languages; they "took" music and were trained to warble pretty little songs and instructed in the mysteries of embroidery and drawing. The larger proportion of them, of course, married, and we are quite ready to admit that they made none the poorer wives and mothers because they could not conjugate a Greek verb or demonstrate a proposition in Euclid. It is not the purpose of this little article to discuss whether, with a broader education, they might not have fulfilled the duties of wifehood and motherhood

---

1   See Tennyson, *The Princess*, Canto 2, 90–94.
2   See Tennyson, *The Princess*, Prologue, 138–42.
3   d. 415, Alexandrian Neoplatonic philosopher and mathematician, a woman renowned for her learning, eloquence, and beauty. Little is known of her writings. Her fame is largely owing to her barbarous murder by a band of monks, said to have been encouraged by the archbishop, St. Cyril of Alexandria (a personal and political enemy of the prefect of Egypt, who was believed to have been Hypatia's lover.)" (*The Columbia Encyclopedia,* Sixth Edition [New York: Columbia UP, 2003]).

equally well and with much more of ease to themselves and others. Old traditions die hard and we will step very gently around their death bed. But there was always a certain number of unfortunates—let us call them so since they would persist in using the term—who, for no fault of their own probably, were left to braid St. Catherine's tresses[1] for the term of their natural lives; and a hard lot truly was theirs in the past. If they did not live in meek dependence with some compassionate relative, eating the bitter bread of unappreciated drudgery, it was because they could earn a meagre and precarious subsistence in the few and underpaid occupations then open to women. They could do nothing else! Their education had not fitted them to cope with any and every destiny; they were helpless straws, swept along the merciless current of existence.

If some woman, with the courage of her convictions, dared to make a stand against the popular prejudice, she was sneered at as a "blue-stocking,"[2] and prudent mothers held her up as a warning example to their pretty, frivolous daughters, and looked askance at her as a not altogether desirable curiosity.

But, nowadays, all this is so changed that we are inclined to wonder if it has not taken longer than a generation to effect the change. The "higher education of women" has passed into a common place [sic] phrase.

A girl is no longer shut out from the temple of knowledge simply because she is a girl; she can compete, and has competed, successfully with her brother in all his classes. The way is made easy before her feet; there is no struggle to render her less sweet and womanly, and the society of to-day is proud of the "sweet girl-graduates."

If they marry, their husbands find in their wives an increased capacity for assistance and sympathy; their children can look up to their mothers for the clearest judgment and the wisest guidance. If they do not marry, their lives are still full and happy and useful; they have something to do and can do it well, and the world is better off from their having been born in it.

In England there have been two particularly brilliant exam-

---

[1] To remain a virgin. See "Evangeline: A Tale of Acadie," Henry Wadsworth Longfellow (1807–82), Part 2, 713.

[2] The term used from the late eighteenth century to refer to female intellectuals and feminists.

ples of what a girl can do when she is given an equal chance with her brother: these are so widely known that it is hardly necessary to name them. Every one has read and heard of Miss Fawcett,[1] the brilliant mathematician, who came out ahead of the senior wrangler[2] at Cambridge, and Miss Ramsay,[3] who led the classical tripos[4] at the same university.

In the new world, too, many girl students have made for themselves a brilliant record. Here, every opportunity and aid is offered to the girl who longs for the best education the age can yield her. There are splendidly equipped colleges for women, equal in every respect to those for men; or, if a girl prefers co-education and wishes to match her intellect with man's on a common footing the doors of many universities are open to her. Canada is well to the front in this respect and Dalhousie college, Halifax, claims, I believe, to have been the second college in the Dominion[5] to admit girl students, if we can use the word "admit" of an institution which was never barred to them. Girls, had they so elected, might have paced with note-book and lexicon,[6] Dalhousie's classic halls from the time of its founding.[7] When the first application for the admission of a girl to the college was received, the powers that were met together in solemn conclave to deliberate thereon, and it was found that there was nothing in the charter

---

1 Philippa, only daughter of Millicent Garrett Fawcett (1847–1929), feminist and suffragist. She placed first in the mathematical tripos at Cambridge University, England.

2 Name for candidates placed in the first class in the mathematical tripos at Cambridge University, England, in this case at the senior level. The word appears to be printed as "wranglee" in the *Halifax Herald*.

3 Like Miss Fawcett, a student who achieved the highest score in her examinations, in this case, in classics.

4 Examinations for the B.A. degree with honours at Cambridge University, England. Women participated in these examinations from 1882.

5 I.e., Canada. According to Eugene Forsey in *The Canadian Encyclopedia*, "Dominion refers primarily to Dominion of Canada [formed in 1867]. The Fathers of Confederation wanted to call 'the new nation' the Kingdom of Canada. The British Government feared this would offend the Americans, whom, after the stresses of the American Civil War, it was most anxious not to antagonize. It insisted on a different title. Sir Leonard Tilley suggested 'dominion': 'He shall have dominion also from sea to sea, and from the river unto the ends of the earth' (Psalm 72:8). The Fathers said it was intended to give dignity to the federation, and as a tribute to the monarchical principle. The word came to be applied to the federal government and Parliament, and under the Constitution Act, 1982, 'Dominion' remains Canada's official title."

6 Word-book or dictionary.

7 Dalhousie University in Halifax, Nova Scotia was founded in 1818.

of the college to prevent the admittance of a girl.

Accordingly, in 1881 two girls, Miss Newcombe and Miss Calkin, were enrolled as students at Dalhousie. Miss Calkin did not complete her course, but Miss Newcombe did and graduated in 1885 with honors in English and English history,—the first of a goodly number who have followed in her footsteps. Miss Newcombe afterwards became Mrs. Trueman and is now on the staff of the Halifax ladies' college.[1] In 1882 Miss Stewart entered, took the science course and graduated in 1886 as B.Sc. with honors in mathematics and mathematical physics.

In 1887 three girls graduated, Miss Forbes and Miss MacNeill each took their degree of B.A., the latter with high honors in English and English history. The third, Miss Ritchie, the most brilliant of Dalhousie's girl graduates took her B.L., she then took her Ph.D., at Cornell university and is now associate professor of philosophy in Wellesley college. Then occurs a hiatus in the list, for we find no girls graduating till 1891 when there were four who received their degrees, Miss Goodwin, Miss McNaughton and Miss Baxter in arts; Miss Muir took the degree of B.L.

In 1892 Miss Baxter, who had graduated with high honors in mathematics and mathematical physics, took her degree of M.A., after which she went to Cornell and there gained a Ph.D.

Miss Muir took her M.L. in 1893 and has since been studying for a Ph.D. at Cornell. In 1892 three girls, Miss Weston, Miss Archibald and Miss Harrington, obtained their B.A. degree. Miss Archibald graduated with great distinction and took her M.A. in 1894. Afterwards she went to Bryn Mawr college, winning a scholarship at her entrance. Miss Harrington graduated with high honors in English and English literature and became M.A. in 1894. She also won a scholarship at Bryn Mawr, where she is at present studying.

In 1893 the two girl graduates were Miss McDonald and Miss Murray, the latter of whom took high honors in philosophy and is now on the staff of the Ladies' college. The graduates of 1894 were Miss Hebb, B.A., Miss Hobrecker, B.A., Miss Jamieson, B.A., and Miss Ross, B.A. Miss Hobrecker took honors in English and German. Miss Jamieson and Miss McKenzie each took their M.A. in 1895. Miss Ross graduated with high honors

---

[1] The affiliate of Dalhousie College which Montgomery attended in 1895–96.

in mathematics and mathematical physics.

In 1895 three girls graduated B.A. Miss McDonald took honor[s] in mathematics and mathematical physics; Miss Ross was the second Dalhousie girl to graduate with "great distinction," and takes her M.A. this year. Miss Best is at present studying for M.A.

It will be seen, from these statements, that, out of the twenty-five girls who have graduated from Dalhousie, nearly all have done remarkably well in their studies, and attained to striking success in their examinations. This, in itself, testifies to their ability to compete with masculine minds on a common level. This year there is a larger number of girls in attendance at Dalhousie than there has been in any previous year. In all, there are about fifty-eight, including the lady medical students. Of course, out of these fifty-eight a large proportion are not undergraduates. They are merely general students taking classes in some favorite subject, usually languages and history.

In all, there are about twenty-nine undergraduate girls in attendance this session. The number of girls in the freshman class is the largest that has yet been seen at Dalhousie. Out of the twenty-six girls, at whom disdainful sophs[1] are privileged to hurl all the old jokes that have been dedicated to freshmen since time immemorial, there are nine undergraduates. In the second year are eleven girls, eight of whom are undergraduates; and in the third year six out of the nine girls are also undergraduates.

There are also nine girls in the fourth year, seven of whom graduate this session. This is the largest class of girls which has yet graduated from Dalhousie. Several of them are taking honors and will, it is expected, simply sustain the reputation which girl students have won for themselves at the university. No girl has yet attempted to take a full course in law at Dalhousie. Not that any one doubts or disputes the ability of a girl to master the mysteries of "contracts" or even the intricacies of "equity jurisprudence;" but the Barristers' act,[2] we believe, stands ruthlessly in the way of any enterprising maiden who might wish to choose law for a profession.

However, we did hear a different reason advanced not long ago

---

[1] Sophomores. Students in the second year of study at college or university.
[2] In fact, women were first admitted as barristers by the Law Society of Upper Canada in 1895.

by one who had thought the subject over—he was a lawyer himself, by the way, so no one need bring an action against me for libel. "Oh, girls," he said, "Girls were never cut out for lawyers. [...] They've got too much conscience." We have been trying ever since to find out if he were speaking sarcastically or in good faith.

But, if shut out from the bar, they are admitted to the study and practise of medicine and two girls have graduated from the Halifax medical college as full-fledged M.D.s. One of these, Miss Hamilton, obtained her degree in 1894 and has since been practising in Halifax. In 1895 Miss McKay graduated and is now, we understand, practising in New Glasgow. There are at present three girl students at the medical college. One will graduate this year; of the other two one is in the third, and one in the first year.

Dalhousie is strictly co-educational. The girls enter on exactly the same footing as the men and are admitted to an equal share in all the privileges of the institution. The only places from which they are barred are the gymnasium and reading room. They are really excluded from the former, but there is nothing to keep them out of the reading room save custom and tradition. It is the domain sacred to masculine scrimmages and gossips and the girls religiously avoid it, never doing more than cast speculative glances at the door as they scurry past into the library. We have not been able to discover what the penalty would be if a girl should venture into [the] reading room. It may be death or it may be only banishment for life.

The library, however, is free to all. The girls can prowl around there in peace, bury themselves in encyclopedias, pore over biographies and exercise their wits on logic, or else they can get into a group and carry on whispered discussions which may have reference to their work or may not.

They take prominent part in some of the college societies. In the Y.M.C.A. their assistance is limited to preparing papers on subjects connected with missions and reading them on the public nights; in the Philomathic society they are more actively engaged. The object of this society is to stimulate interest and inquiry in literature, science and philosophy. Girls are elected on the executive committee and papers on literary subjects are prepared and read by them throughout the session.

They are also initiated into the rites and ceremonies of the Philosophical club and are very much in demand in the Glee club.[1] Once in a while, too, a girl is found on the editorial staff of the Dalhousie Gazette, and what the jokes column would do, if stripped of allusions to them, is beyond our comprehension.

The athletic club, however, numbers no girls among its devotees and it does not seem probable that [it] will—certainly not in this generation, at least. The question of the higher education of girls involves a great many interesting problems which [are] frequently discussed but which time [alone] can solve satisfactorily. Woman has asserted her claim to an equal educational standing with man and that claim has been conceded to her. What use then, will she make of her privileges? Will she take full advantage of them or will she merely play with them until, tired of the novelty, she drops them for some mere fad? Every year since girls first entered Dalhousie, has witnessed a steady increase in the number of them in attendance; and it is to be expected that, in the years to come, the number will be very much larger. But beyond a certain point, we do not think it will go. It is not likely that the day will ever come when the number of girl students at Dalhousie, or at any other co-educational university, will be equal to the number of men. There will always be a certain number of clever, ambitious girls who, feeling that their best life work can be accomplished only when backed up by a broad and thorough education, will take a university course, will work conscientiously and earnestly and will share all the honors and successes of their brothers. There will, however, always be a limit to the number of such girls.

Again, we have frequently heard this question asked: "Is it, in the end, *worth while* for a girl to take a university course with all the attendant expense, hard work, and risk of health? How many girls, out of those who graduate from the universities, are ever heard of prominently again, many of them marrying or teaching school? Would not an ordinarily good education have benefited them quite as much? Is it then worth while, from this standpoint, for any girl who is not exceptionally brilliant, to take a university course?["]

The individual question of "worth while" or "not worth while" is one which every girl must settle for herself. It is only in the general aspect that we must look at this subject. In the first place, as far as distinguishing themselves in after life goes, take the number of girls who have graduated from Dalhousie—say

---

[1] Singing club.

thirty, most of whom are yet in their twenties and have their whole lives before them. Out of that thirty, eight or nine at the very least have not stood still but have gone forward successfully and are known to the public as brilliant, efficient workers. Out of any thirty men who graduate, how many in the same time do better or even as well? This, however, is looking at the question from the standpoint that the main object of a girl in taking a university course is to keep herself before the public as a distinguished worker. But is it? No! At least it should not be. Such an ambition is not the end and aim of a true education.

A girl does not—or, at least, should not—go to a university merely to shine as a clever student[,] take honors, "get through" and then do something very brilliant. Nay; she goes—or should go—to prepare herself for living, not alone in the finite but in the infinite. She goes to have her mind broadened and her powers of observation cultivated. She goes to study her own race in all the bewildering perplexities of its being. In short, she goes to find out the best, easiest, and most effective way of living the life that God and nature planned out for her to live.

If a girl gets this out of her college course, it is of very little consequence whether her after "career" be brilliant, as the world defines brilliancy, or not. She has obtained that from her studies which will stand by her all her life, and future generations will rise up and call her blessed,[1] who handed down to them the clear insight, the broad sympathy with their fellow creatures, the energy of purpose and the self-control that such a woman must transmit to those who come after her.

★   ★   ★

2. "Famous Author and Simple Mother"

[From the *Toronto Star Weekly* (28 November, 1925): 44 (*R/W* 1835; as Norma Phillips Muir).]

[This article represents Mongomery's view of women and work in mid-life and mid-career, but her notion of women's responsibility to home and family is certainly pervasive in her writing for

---

[1]   See Proverbs 31.28.

her whole career. This article suggests that Montgomery's views were deeply traditional and arguably anti-feminist in 1925, more compellingly, perhaps, than they had been in the first decade of the century. One of the sub-headers that appeared in the first publication of this article makes this point: "Old Ideals Safe." This account of Mongomery's gender politics is interesting because of its clear articulation of domestic duty for women and the evidence it provides of the development over thirty years of the ideas of education for women she endorsed in 1896 in the *Halifax Herald* piece as well as of her continued sense of exceptional women who can move beyond conventional boundaries while not disturbing them—indeed, while actually reinforcing them, as she does for motherhood and work in this interview. These two articles together provide a way of understanding the maternalist narrative of *AGG* and all the "Anne" books.]

"Make it early Saturday morning, as early as you like," said L.M. Montgomery (Mrs. MacDonald) [sic], author of the "Anne of Green Gables" stories. "I'm going to take my son down town for lunch and then on to a movie. He's going to St. Andrew's now you know. I'm down for his football games."

This was in answer to our plea for half an hour of the time of this busy lady who combines the career of author with the no less arduous one of minister's wife, and manages to be a pal to her two sons and keep in touch with the ever turning wheels of the world.

Taking her at her word we were there shortly after nine on the Saturday morning, but we were not too early for Mrs. MacDonald. She was ready for us, and had given some time and thought to the matter on which we wanted her opinion: whether women can successfully possess themselves of careers and home lives at the same time.

"There are really two answers to that problem," she said smiling. "One is affirmative and the other is negative. I would say that a woman may successfully combine a profession of her own with the oldest one in the world, that of wifehood and motherhood, but only if she be able to pursue the career at home. It doesn't seem to me possible for a mother to be to her children what she should if they are only the recipients of her left over time, and are, for the major part under the care of paid help. [...]

"The writing of books, plays, poetry, painting and sculpture—

even a career in law is possible and consistent with the duties of wife and mother, but I don't think a woman can pursue any career which takes her away from her home, and still be what she should be to her husband and children. I know there are shining examples where women have been successful in the eyes of the world, and whose homes are supposedly ideally happy, but before I could say that the woman was a success in both phases I'm afraid I should demand the unbiased testimony of her husband and children."

"Think of the great actresses," we protested, "the women who have filled high executive positions, famous women doctors—they have not denied themselves husbands and children. Their very successes have made it possible for them to obtain nurses and governesses for their children—given them care and training which is scientifically perfect, and—"

"I am thinking," said Mrs. MacDonald quietly. "I'm remembering that the mortality rate in institutions which care for children is infinitely higher than it is in even the poorer class homes. Science is wonderful, but it is not as wonderful for a child as mother-love and mother care. Nothing can make up to a child for that. Children have died, and more will die for love. That is why I say give every woman who wants some interest in life in addition to her home life a hobby. Give her another interest so that the kitchen and the nursery may not pall, but let it be a hobby, an interest or a profession which she can follow at home."

Then, in answer to our questions Mrs. MacDonald smiled and told us, basing it on her own experiences, of how a woman can have her heart's desire, and no heartburnings and heartsearchings with it.

"The secret really is system," she admitted. "If one doesn't try to run one's life along any definite channels it will soon be like seed sown at random—and the harvest will be too difficult to bring in. Just take that homely old adage, 'A place for everything and everything in its place,' and add to it, 'and a time for everything and everything in its time' and you have the nucleus of success in whatever you are planning to undertake."

We pondered over this for a moment, and then, with a query here, a tentative theory there, the story took form.

It was while she was in her teens that L.M. Montgomery began writing, and like others to whom a large measure of success came later, she made her start in Sunday School papers. Then came serials, followed by "Anne of Green Gables," and with that book came the well deserved laurels. Later on romance, real and not the story book kind, came into the life of the young author, and she married Rev. Ewan MacDonald, and added a home, a husband, the parochial duties of a minister's wife to her authorship. Motherhood was added, and now two sturdy sons tell "mother" their youthful joys and sorrows. Leaskdale and Zephyr are the two charges over which Mr. MacDonald presides, and there are Sunday services, week-day meetings and week-night gatherings at which the minister and his wife are present, yet L.M. Montgomery's publishers are not disappointed or her public disillusioned when another book from her loved pen appears.

"It does keep me busy," she admitted. "But then there is nothing harder to do than nothing, is there? My day starts at seven in the morning and it lasts until twelve at night. There is breakfast to get and my younger boy's lunch to pack, routine work to see to—I just have a young maid—and then at nine o'clock I am at my desk and there I stay until twelve. Those three hours a day are all I can allow myself for actual writing, for I am connected with the various church organizations of both charges, president or member or committee worker, and that all takes time. Then there are the countless little things that have to be done about a home to keep it running smoothly, and while I do admit that well trained help could do most of these things as well if not better than the wife and mother can, there is still something about the fact that a man's wife, his sons' mother doing for her family that makes the little acts mean more than if they were twice as efficiently done by someone else. It is the love motif again.

"I think every woman should have an earnest interest outside or rather independent of her home interests, but one which does not take her away from the supervision of her home and the care of her children. The woman who has not children is in another position entirely, but I feel that while a mother is able physically and mentally, the care of her children should not be relegated to outsiders. [...]

"I think there are far too many girls in the world of business to-day for the good of the world of families," she said quaintly. "Girls have, if they be normal women, a desire for marriage in their hearts, and many of them realize that in the world of business they will have a better opportunity of finding for themselves the type of man they admire, and so—they don't spend the time learning to cook and play the piano and sew and be charming hostesses. They take a commercial course and enter an office and many times defeat their own purposes because the young men they meet are earning not much more than are the girls. They see the girls wearing expensive clothes, appearing well groomed and well content, and when they think, 'there's the kind of girl I'd like to marry,' they stop and think, and the result of the thinking is a decision that it is no use asking her to marry him. How can he suggest that they two get along on what she alone is making now? [...]

"Maybe he does ask and she says yes, with the proviso that she keep her position and pay for someone to look after the apartment. Maybe she makes another proviso, or maybe she just makes a resolve to herself, but the fact remains that she keeps her position and he keeps his, and when several Christmases have rolled around there are still no little sox [sic] to hang up as an enticement to Santa Claus.

"There are many girls working to-day who do not need to work, daughters of well-to-do fathers, girls whose mothers need them at home for companionship, but these girls are not content with the dullness and quietness of home. They want to be out in the world of rush and excitement, and so they go, and not being dependent upon what they make, they can afford to work for less, which means that the girl who is her own sole means of support is compelled to take a lower wage in competition with these other girls, and so the economic structure is shaken.

"There is one good thing about to come out of the license and disorder and horror—yes, to mothers and fathers it is horror—of to-day. The motor car, the dance hall, the remote road-houses, and clubs, the petting parties and flask parties— horrible as these are they will have their use, for the pendulum will swing backward again toward decency and normalcy. The girls and boys who are the fastest and the greatest danger to themselves with their desire to be smart and up to date—they are the fathers and mothers of to-morrow, and knowing the dangers that they encountered, the fine line of margin which they took, they will be stricter and more watchful with their children, and so the pendulum will swing backward.

"The secrets of life have been kept too much secrets," said

Mrs. MacDonald gravely, "and when these boys and girls, who because they realize that mystery has not paid and so have gone to the other extreme, have reached maturity and parenthood, they will see to it that youth learns the God-purpose of life in a very different way from the way in which they learned it, and that the mind and soul and body of their children shall be kept clean and healthy and happy and whole for the joys and purposes of life.

"This has grown to be a far cry from women and their careers in one way," she smiled as we rose to go, "but after all the relationship is close. Give a woman a profession which she will be interested in and devoted to, give it to her within the four walls of her own home and the knowledge that she is not neglecting her home, her husband or her children will give her greater strength and purpose for the career which will be satisfying her need of self expression, and will bring pride to her family, without any of the pain of renunciation."

Appendix D: The "Pansy" Novels of Isabella Macdonald Alden

[As has already been noted (see *AGG* 160, note 2), Alden's didactic and Christian stories for children were immensely popular. Mongomery refers to them in *AGG*, and indicates in her journal that she had read them (*SJ* 322). The first two of these three excerpts from "Pansy" novels consider the problem of Sunday School lessons that Montgomery also takes up in *AGG* in Chapter XI. Note the effects of "good" and "bad" instruction that are presented in these passages. The third excerpt, from *Ruth Erskine's Crosses*, takes up the question of "besetting sins" that Anne also discusses in *AGG* (see 242, note 1). Montgomery cites the "Pansy" novels in *AGG*: these sample excerpts suggest there are significant intertextual connections to be explored between the series and Montgomery's "Sunday School" novel.]

1. From *The Man of the House* (1883; 183–86)

All this made the lump come into Reuben's throat again, and swell larger than ever; but he resolved then and there he would never soil Bennie's overcoat by thinking a mean thought under it. It covered his worn and patched jacket to a nicety; covered even the patch on his pantaloons: and, with his shoes blacked and his hair combed, he felt, someway, as though the good times of his dream had begun to come, and he must attend to what was now going on, instead of looking for any more. New things were pouring in on him so fast they needed all his present attention. So he sat up straight in the end of the Barrows' pew, beside the gentleman; and though it was pretty warm, kept his overcoat on, tightly buttoned to his throat, and listened as well as he could to the sermon. But it was in the afternoon Sabbath-school that he did his best listening.

The class he was in was very unlike any that he had ever known about: at least, the teacher was. In the first place, she was a young and pretty lady. Reuben had a fondness for well-dressed people. He did not know it—at least he did not realize it—but he liked to look at them. He admired his teacher very much. The only other teacher with whom he was acquainted had been a man who read questions at him from a book: questions that he did not understand, and did not care about. This one did not seem to him to be talking about a Sabbath-school lesson at all.

"I wonder if any of you boys know how to manage a boat," she began, and some of them did, or thought they did, and others of them had questions to ask; and before he knew it, Reuben grew very much interested, and forgot all about the lesson.

"What do you think you would do in a storm?" she asked the boy who knew how to manage a boat. And that started talk afresh, and one told what he would do, and another criticized it, and at last, when Reuben was appealed to, he had to own that he knew just nothing at all about boats.

"Well, in any danger," said the teacher. "Suppose you are in some place where you know there is danger: you have done the very best you know, and yet you feel sure you are in great danger, and know of no way to help yourselves; what would you do next?"

"Why, there wouldn't be anything to do," declared one boy, "only to stand still and let it come."

"Or run away from it," said another.

"Suppose you couldn't run away from it" said the teacher; "suppose it would run away with you?"

"I'd find a way out somehow," said another.

"But we are supposing that you had tried all your ways out, and were *not* out, only felt yourselves getting deeper and deeper into trouble—what then? Think, all of you. Is there one in the class who has ever been in a great trouble, out of which he could not help himself?"

Quick as thought did Reuben's mind go back to that wild ride with Spunk and his drunken master, over dark and danger-ous roads, with the flying express train chasing them. He had kept pretty still until then, an eager listener, with little to say, but, at the memory of his danger and his escape, he drew a long, half-shuddering sigh, and said, almost before he knew it: "I tell you what it is, I've been there."

The boys turned and looked at him, and the teacher smiled on him and questioned: "In danger, my boy?"

"Yes'm."

"And did you know what to do?"

"Some things I knew, and did them; but there came a time

that there wasn't anything left to do only hold on, and that I did with all my might; but it didn't seem to be doing any good."

"And then what?"

"And then," said Reuben, in a slow, grave tone, his face paling over the memory of it all, "I told God about it."

"And did He answer?"

"Yes'm," said Reuben, simply.

The boys looked at him respectfully. His face was flushed now, and he looked down to the floor. He wasn't used to be talked with about such things.

"I am very glad," said the teacher, brightly. "You are better able, perhaps, than any of the rest of us, to understand how Peter felt when he got out on that water, trying to walk on it, and found that he couldn't; found himself sinking. It wasn't until then that he called out to the Lord. I wonder, Reuben, if you waited until you had done for yourself everything that you could think of before you called to Him?"

"Yes'm," said Reuben, going swiftly back over his experience; "I did just that."

"People are apt to," she said. "Peter did so too."

By this time every boy in the class wanted to know about Peter. Reuben had been placed in one of those trying classes where not a boy studied his lesson; and of course he hadn't. He never dreamed of such a thing; so they were all ignorant together, but eager to hear. Then began the story of the night ride on the lake, with hard rowing and contrary wind; and One walking on the water, of whom the sailors were afraid at first, and to whom Peter tried to go, and almost failed. It was a new story to Reuben; in fact, almost all Bible stories were new to him. He was very much interested; forgot that he was a stranger, and asked questions with such eagerness that the teacher found it a pleasure to teach.

2. From *Links in Rebecca's Life* (1878; 77–78)

Directly the hymn was concluded, the spirit of parade came over Miss Almina.

"We will not take time to repeat the Lord's Prayer this morning," she said; "you all know it so well there is no need of saying it every Sunday." Think of there being no need to pray because we all know the prayer so well! "You may rise and recite the Bible alphabet for Miss Harlow; I know she will like to hear you."

They recited it well; but Rebecca could not help wondering if they understood the hard words, and also what was the connection of ideas.

"A is for Advocate, Absalom, Adam. B is for Bethlehem, Benjamin, Boaz."

"They recite it nicely. Have you explained it to them? Do you think they attach any meaning to the words?" This she said when the pretty show that had been give for *her benefit* was concluded.

"Bless your heart, no," said the amused Almina. "They recite it just as parrots would. Why, they are nothing but babies. Do see how the sun fades this shade of lavender! Horrid, isn't it? Hush, children! Don't you know it is naughty to whisper in Sunday school? How many times I have told you you ought to be very quiet. Susie Marks, what *are* you talking about? That little tongue of yours is always busy."

"Well, Miss Ward[w]ell, she says her sash is widest, and I *know* it isn't, for I just measured the ends; and she won't believe me."

"Well, it's very naughty to talk about clothes in Sunday school. I'm astonished at you. That isn't being good children. Now we must have a lesson. Oh, first, have any of you a verse to recite?"

"I have," piped a dozen little voices. They liked to recite verses; that rested their dear little tongues. So the verses were heard.

What a pity, thought the practical visitor, since they are really fond of saying verses, that Almina didn't pick one out of the lesson and give it to them all to learn. Then they would have known something about it; but she will have to take the whole Bible for a lesson if she hits many of these verses.

Over the recitation of one verse the young teacher laughed.

"Kitty, you little witch!" she said, "I do believe you have recited that same verse to me fifty times; why *don't* you get a new one? Boys, why, the idea of fighting in Sunday school! I'm shocked!"

"He begun it," said the smaller boy.

"Well, he said I had red hair, and my hair is brown, ain't it, teacher?"

"Why, I guess so, a little. Anyway, it is very wicked to quarrel about it in Sunday school. The idea of the little mouse being sensitive as to the colour of his hair! Did you ever *hear* of such a thing?" This to the patient visitor.

"He is a perfect little mischief; always in a scrape of one kind or another; his temper is as fiery as his hair."

3. From *Ruth Erskine's Crosses* (1879; 183–86)

"Poor girl!" said Susan, tenderly. "Poor, tired heart. Don't you think that the Lord Jesus can rest you anywhere except by way of the grave? That is such a mistake, and I made it for so long that I know all about it. Don't you hear His voice calling to you to come and rest in Him this minute?"

"I don't understand you. I *am* resting in Him. That is, I feel sure at times. I feel sure now that He has prepared a place in heaven for me, and will take me there as He says. But I am so tired of the road; I want to drop out from it now and be at rest."

"Haven't you found His yoke easy and His burden light, then?"

"No, I haven't. I know it is my own fault; but that doesn't alter the fact or relieve the weariness."

"Then do you believe that He made a mistake when He said the yoke was easy?"

Ruth arrested her tears, to look up in wonder.

"Of course not," she said, quickly. "I know it is owing to myself, but I don't know how to remedy it. There are those who find the statement meets their experience, I don't doubt, but it seems not to be for me."

"But, if that is so, don't you think He ought to have said, 'Some of you will find the burden light, but others of you will have to struggle and flounder in the dark?' You know He hasn't qualified it at all. He said, 'Come unto Me and I will give you rest; take My yoke upon you, for it is light.' And He said it to all who are 'heavy laden.'"

"Well," said Ruth, after a thoughtful pause, "I suppose that means His promise to save the soul eternally. I believe He has done that for me."

"But is that all He is able or willing to do? If He can save the soul eternally cannot He give it peace and rest here?"

"Why, of course He could, if it were His will; but I don't know that He has ever promised to do so."

"Don't you? Do you suppose He who hates sin has made us so that we cannot keep from constantly grieving Him by falling into sin, and has promised us no help from the burden until we get to heaven? I don't think that would be entire salvation."

"What *do* you mean?" Ruth asked, turning a full, wondering gaze on her sister. "You surely don't believe that people are perfect in this world?"

"Pass that thought, just now, will you? Let me illustrate what I mean. I found my besetting sin to be to yield to constant fits of ill-temper. It took almost nothing to rouse me, and the more I struggled and tossed about in my effort to *grow* better, the worse it seemed to me I became. If I was to depend on progressive goodness, as I supposed, when was I to begin to grow *toward* a better state; and, when I succeeded, should I not really have accomplished my own rescue from sin? It troubled and tormented me, and I did not gain until I discovered that there were certain promises which, with conditions, meant me. For instance, there was one person who, when I came in contact with her, invariably made me angry. For months I never held a conversation with her that I did not say words which seemed to me afterward to be very sinful, and which angered her. This, after I had prayed and struggled for self-control. One day I came across the promise, 'My grace is sufficient for thee.' Sufficient for what? I asked, and I stopped before the words as if they had just been revealed. [...]"

"'My grace is sufficient for thee,'" Ruth repeated, slowly, thoughtfully. Then she paused, while Susan waited for the answer, which came presently, low-toned and wondering.

Appendix E: Selected Reviews

1. *The New York Yimes Saturday Review of Books* (18 July 1908)

A Heroine from an Asylum

A farmer in Prince Edward's Island [sic] ordered a boy from a Nova Scotia asylum, but the order got twisted and the result was that a girl was sent the farmer instead of a boy. That girl is the heroine of L.M. Montgomery's story, "Anne of the Green Gables," [sic] (L.C. Page & Co.) and it is no exaggeration to say that she is one of the most extraordinary girls that ever came out of an ink pot.

The author undoubtedly meant her to be queer, but she is altogether too queer. She was only 11 years old when she reached the house in Prince Edward's Island [sic] that was to be her home, but, in spite of the fact that, excepting four months spent in the asylum, she had passed all her life with illiterate folks, and had had almost no schooling, she talked to the farmer and his sister as though she had borrowed Bernard Shaw's vocabulary, Alfred Austin's sentimentality, and the reasoning powers of a Justice of the Supreme Court. She knew so much that she spoiled the author's plan at the very outset and greatly marred a story that had in it quaint and charming possibilities.

The author's probable intention was to exhibit a unique development in this little asylum waif, but there is no real difference between the girl at the end of the story and the one at the beginning of it. All the other characters in the book are human enough.

★ ★ ★

2. *Montreal Daily Herald* (21 July 1908)

Whether Miss L.M. Montgomery is a Canadian or not, we know not, but if she isn't she has taken a Canadian countryside, and peopled it, in a manner marvellously natural, and if she is a Canadian she has succeeded in writing one of the few Canadian stories that can appeal to the whole English-speaking world. "Anne of Green Gables" is a charmingly-told story of life on the north shore of Prince Edward Island, but the local coloring is most delicately placed on the canvas and in no respect weakens the impression created by the central figure, Anne. This waif from an orphan asylum in Nova Scotia, adopted by an old farmer and his maiden sister, is covered with a sensitive and imaginative mind and the story of her hopes, struggles and ambitions, will appeal to every reader, old and young. She is certainly one of the most attractive figure [sic] Canadian fiction has yet produced, while the characters of the farmer and his sister are drawn with a delicacy of touch that is most refreshing and charming. The book is an ideal volume for growing girls, being as pure and sweet as the wild flowers of the Island which Miss Montgomery describes so lovingly. In fact, one of the great attractions of the story is the author's love of nature which finds expression everywhere, without once appearing exaggerated or forced. The story is one which will give profit and pleasure to all its readers.

★   ★   ★

3. *The Globe*, Toronto, Saturday Magazine Section (15 August 1908)

The craze for problem novels has at present seized a large section of the reading public, and it must be confessed that several recent stories have not been healthy reading, and can serve no useful purpose that we can see. In these days of unhealthy literature it is, however, a real pleasure to come across a story so pure and sweet as "Anne of Green Gables," by L.M. Montgomery, from the press of Messrs. L.C. Page & Co., of Boston, Mass. There are no pretensions to a great plot in the story, but from the first line to the last the reader is fascinated by the sayings and doings of the girl child taken from a Nova Scotia home, adopted by the old Scotch maid and bachelor, brother and sister, who owned Green Gables, a Prince Edward Island farm, situated in one of the garden spots of the beautiful Island Province in the St. Lawrence Gulf.

The quaintness of the child, the funny scene when the old bachelor brother finds a girl waiting at the station for him, and not a boy, as ordered from the home, are pictured in irresistible drollery. Then the reader's interest is evoked as the author pictures how the poorly-trained and often hitherto harshly-treated little maiden develops into womanhood, under the strict yet kindly training of the strange couple who loved her so dearly, and who, Scotch like, could not find words to give utterance to that love. Every Canadian boy and girl who has had the happy chance of going to a rural school, and who has had ambitions to be something different to the ordinary individual, will take "Anne of Green Gables" to heart, and will laugh and cry with her in her school and home troubles, and many will easily call to mind people who are the very doubles of the tart, the gossipy yet always lovable characters sketched so faithfully by Miss Montgomery in her story; and those who have had the privilege to visit the Island Province will revel in the simple, yet splendid descriptions of the people and scenery of the island which are to be found on almost every page of this excellent story. "Anne of Green Gables" is worth a thousand of the problem stories with which the bookshelves are crowded today, and we venture the opinion that this simple story of rural life in Canada will be read and re-read when many of the more pretentious stories are all forgotten. There is not a dull page in the whole volume, and the comedy and tragedy are so deftly woven together that it is at time difficult to divide them. The story is told by an author who knows the Island of Prince Edward thoroughly, and who has carefully observed the human tide which flows through that island, as it does over all the places where human beings live. With the pen of an artiste, she has painted that tide so that its deep tragedies are just lightly revealed, for she evidently prefers to show us the placid flow, with its steadiness, its sweetness, and witchery, until the reader stands still to watch the play of sunshine and shadow as it is deftly pictured by the hand of the author of "Anne of Green Gables."

★   ★   ★

4. *Outlook*, New York (22 August 1908)

"Anne of Green Gables" is one of the best books for girls we have seen for a long time. It is cheerful, amusing, and happy. Anne is a sort of Canadian "Rebecca of Sunnybrook Farm" in her imaginativeness, love of high-flown language, and propensity to get into scrapes. But the book is by no means an imitation; it has plenty of originality and character. Moreover, it will please grown-up people quite or nearly as well as the school-girls for whom it is primarily designed. It ought to have a wide reading.

★ ★ ★

5. *Canadian Magazine* (November 1908)

In the whole range of Canadian fiction one might search a long time for a character study of equal charm with "Anne of Green Gables," a novel that easily places the author, Miss L.M. Montgomery, in the first rank of our native writers. The story of Anne, of her "ups and downs" in life is excellent in technique, development and consistency. It contains much genuine, quaint and wholesome humour, and it also appeals in a very intense way to the best human sympathies. Anne is indeed a most interesting and entertaining person, and she might well be placed with the best character creations in recent fiction. Her environment, a picturesque section of Prince Edward Island, is thoroughly Canadian, and Miss Montgomery presents it in a piquant literary style, full of grace and whole-heartedness.

Anne is an orphan who, owing to an error, is sent instead of a boy from an orphanage to live at "Green Gables" with Marilla Cuthbert, a spinster, and her brother, Matthew, a bachelor, both of rather set and precise notions of propriety. Anne is an extremely impetuous girl, and early in life she is bowed down in sorrow with red hair and freckles and an angular form, almost as angular as Marilla's. But she has a very accommodating imagination, a faculty that relieves her of many a heartache. She is continuously seeking "scope for imagination." On her first morning at "Green Gables" she looked out from her bedroom window and saw an apple tree in full bloom. Her delight was unbounded, and she expressed it generously to Marilla, whose appreciation of picturesqueness and romance is not very keen. [...]

The author is a resident of Cavendish, P.E.I., and is a young woman of unusual ability as a writer.

★ ★ ★

6. *The Bookman*, 29, New York (March–August 1909)

A [...] recent book, which has been showing striking vitality is Miss Montgomery's *Anne of Green Gables*, which, while it has not appeared often among the six best sellers, has attracted attention by the persistence with which it has been knocking at the door. It is the only book still a contender in the race for popularity that dates back to the end of last summer. One secret of this success is that it has an appeal both as fiction for adults and as a juvenile.

★ ★ ★

7. *Spectator*, London (13 March 1909)

We can pay the author of *Anne of Green Gables* no higher compliment than to say that she has given us a perfect companion picture to *Rebecca of Sunnybrook Farm*. There is no question of imitation or borrowing: it is merely that the scheme is similar and the spirit akin. To all novel-readers weary of problems, the duel of sex, broken Commandments, and gratuitous suicides, Miss Montgomery provides an alternative entertainment, all the more welcome because what we get in place of those hackneyed features is at once wholesome and attractive. As for Prince Edward Island, in which the scene is laid, no better advertisement of the charm of its landscapes could be devised than the admirable descriptions of its sylvan glories which lend decorative relief to the narrative. Miss Montgomery has not merely succeeded in winning our sympathies for her *dramatis personae*; she makes us fall in love with their surroundings, and long to visit the Lake of Shining Waters, the White Way of Delight, Idlewild, and other favourite resorts of "the Anne-girl."

The mechanism of the plot is simple enough. An elderly farmer and his unmarried sister decide to adopt an orphan boy and bring him up to assist them on the farm; but owing to a blunder on the part of an intermediary, a girl, and not a boy, is sent from the asylum in Nova Scotia. Anne Shirley, an "outspoken morsel of neglected humanity," with a riotous imagination, a genius for "pretending," a passionate love of beauty, and a boundless flow of words, bursts like a bombshell on the inarticulate farmer and his dour, honest, undemonstrative sister. But the law of extremes prevails. Matthew succumbs on the spot, and after a short space Anne casts her spell over Marilla as well, for in three weeks that excellent dragon admitted to her brother that it seemed as if Anne had been always with them:—

"I can't imagine the place without her. Now, don't be looking I-told-you-so, Matthew. That's bad enough in a woman, but it isn't to be endured in a man. I'm perfectly willing to own up that I'm glad I consented to keep the child, and that I'm getting fond of her, but don't you rub it in, Matthew Cuthbert."

The process of Anne's education both at home and at school is chequered and dramatic, and the way in which this little lump of human quicksilver and her grim but just mistress act and react on each other is brought out by scores of happy touches and diverting incidents. Anne is a creature of irresistible loquacity when we first meet her, and meeting with kindness and consideration for the first time after years of poverty and neglect, she expands in a way that is at once ludicrous and touching. Perhaps her literary instinct is a bit overdone, but otherwise Miss Montgomery shows no disposition to idealise her child heroine, and one can readily forgive exaggeration when it leads to such pleasing conceits as the child's suggestion that amethysts were the souls of good violets, or her precocious appreciation of the "tragical" sound of the lines:—

"Quick as the slaughtered squadrons fell
In Midian's evil day."

The book lends itself to quotation at every turn. [...]

Miss Montgomery has given us a most enjoyable and delightful book, which, when allowance is made for altered conditions, is in direct lineal descent from the works of Miss Alcott. It needed considerable restraint on her part to leave off where she did without developing the romantic interest hinted at in the last chapter, but the result is so excellent that we trust she will refrain from running the greater risk of writing a sequel. Having sown her wild oats, "the Anne-girl" could never be so attractive as the little witch, half imp, half angel, whose mental and spiritual growth is vividly set forth in these genial pages.

★ ★ ★

8. *The Mail and Empire*, Toronto (6 December 1913)

I wonder how many of my readers, says T.P.'s Weekly, have read "Anne of Green Gables" by L.M. Montgomery. It is a charming and delightful story of an imaginative young girl, an orphan, taken from an orphanage and brought up by a brother and sister—bachelor and old maid. There has been nothing so good since Louisa May Alcott gave to the world "Little Women," and, like "Little Women," "Anne of Green Gables" comes from across the herring pond. American writers—though this is a Canadian story—do these sentimental books full of tears and laughter and a quiet but insistent appeal to the Anglo-Saxon temperament much better than English writers. It is a book that will give pleasure to any girl between the ages of ten and twenty, and every person who has felt the pull at the heartstrings in the appeal of a child.

Select Bibliography

Currently, the best available bibliography of Montgomery's works is *Lucy Maud Montgomery: A Preliminary Bibliography*, which was prepared by Ruth Weber Russell, D.W. Russell, and Rea Wilmshurst and published in 1986 by the University of Waterloo Library in Waterloo, Ontario (referred to as *R/W* here). The bibliography of works on Montgomery in *R/W* is somewhat limited now, given the massive increase in critical studies of Montgomery and her writing since the 1980s. The most comprehensive current bibliography of critical works on Montgomery's writing and *Anne of Green Gables* is the "Ludlow Selected Bibliography," prepared by Heather Ludlow, and currently available on the CD-ROM, *The Bend in the Road: An Invitation to the World and Work of L.M. Montgomery*, issued by the L.M. Montgomery Institute at the University of Prince Edward Island in 2000.

What follows is a brief selection of critical material on *Anne of Green Gables*; the emphasis is on recent work and on studies in gender and culture. More extensive bibliographies can be found in the sources noted above.

Collections of essays

"L.M. Montgomery and Popular Culture," Special issue of *Canadian Children's Literature* 91.2 (1998).

Gammel, Irene, ed. *Making Avonlea: L.M. Montgomery and Popular Culture*. Toronto: U of Toronto P, 2002.

—— and Elizabeth Epperly, ed. *L.M. Montgomery and Canadian Culture*. Toronto: U of Toronto P, 1999.

Reimer, Mavis. *Such a Simple Little Tale: Critical Responses to L.M. Montgomery's* Anne of Green Gables. Metuchen, NJ and London: The Children's Literature Association and The Scarecrow Press, 1992.

Rubio, Mary Henley, ed. *Harvesting Thistles: The Textual Garden of L.M. Montgomery. Essays on Her Novels and Journals*. Guelph, ON: Canadian Children's Press, 1994.

Monographs

Ahmansson, Gabriella. *A Life and Its Mirrors: A Feminist Reading of L.M. Montgomery's Fiction*. Stockholm: Uppsala, 1991.

Elizabeth Epperly. *The Fragrance of Sweet-Grass: L.M. Montgomery's Heroines and the Pursuit of Romance*. Toronto: U of Toronto P, 1992.

Waterston, Elizabeth. *Kindling Spirit: L.M. Montgomery's* Anne of Green Gables. Toronto: ECW, 1993.

Articles and chapters (not included in collections listed above)

Careless, Virginia. "The Hijacking of 'Anne.'" *Canadian Children's Literature* 67 (1992): 48–55.

——. "L.M. Montgomery and Everybody Else: A Look at the Books." *Windows and Words: A Look at Canadian Children's Literature in English*. Ed. Aida Hudson and Susan-Ann Cooper. Ottawa: U of Ottawa P, 2002. 143–174.

Classen, Constance. "Is 'Anne of Green Gables' an American Import?" *Canadian Children's Literature* 55 (1989): 42–50.

Devereux, Cecily. "'Canadian Classic' and 'Commodity Export': The Nationalism of 'Our' *Anne of Green Gables*." *Journal of Canadian Studies* 36.1 (2001): 11–28.

——. "Writing with a 'Definite Purpose': L.M. Montgomery, Nellie L. McClung and the Politics of Imperial Motherhood in Fiction for Children." *Canadian Children's Literature* 99 23.3 (2001): 6–22.

——. "'Not one of those dreadful new women': Anne Shirley and the Culture of Imperial Motherhood." *Windows and Words: A Look at Canadian Children's Literature in English*. Ed. Aida Hudson and Susan-Ann Cooper. Ottawa: U of Ottawa P, 2002. 119–130.

MacLeod, Anne Scott. "The Caddie Woodlawn Syndrome: American Girlhood in the Nineteenth Century." *A Century of Childhood: 1820–1920*. Ed. Mary Lynn Stevens Heininger. Rochester NY: Margaret Woodbury Strong Museum, 1984. 97–119.

Robinson, Laura. "'Pruned down and branched out': Embracing Contradiction in *Anne of Green Gables*." *Children's Voices in Atlantic Literature and Culture: Essays on Childhood*. Ed. Hilary Thompson. Guelph, ON: Canadian Children's Press, 1995.

Rubio, Mary. "L.M. Montgomery: Where Does the Voice Come From?" *Canadiana: Studies in Canadian Literature*. Proceedings of the

Canadian Studies Conference, Aarhus, 1984. Ed. Jorn Carlsen and Knud Larsen. Aarhus: Canadian Studies Conference, 1984.

Siourbas, Helen. "L.M. Montgomery: Canon or Cultural Capital?" *Windows and Words: A Look at Canadian Children's Literature in English.* Ed. Aida Hudson and Susan-Ann Cooper. Ottawa: U of Ottawa P, 2002. 131–142.

White, Gavin. "Montgomery and the French." *Canadian Children's Literature* 78 (1995): 64–68.

Biographical

Bolger, Francis W.P. *The Years Before "Anne": The Early Career of Lucy Maud Montgomery, Author of "Anne of Green Gables."* 1974. Halifax, NS: Nimbus, 1991.

Gillen, Mollie. *The Wheel of Things: A Biography of L.M. Montgomery.* Toronto: Fitzhenry and Whiteside, 1975.

Rubio, Mary and Elizabeth Waterston. *Writing a Life: L.M. Montgomery. A Biography of the Author of* Anne of Green Gables. Toronto: ECW, 1995.

Montgomery's personal writing

Bolger, Francis and Elizabeth Epperly, eds. *My Dear Mr. M: Letters to G.B. Macmillan from L.M. Montgomery.* Toronto: Oxford UP, 1992.

Eggleston, Wilfrid. *The Green Gables Letters, from L.M. Montgomery to Ephraim Weber, 1905–1909.* Ottawa: Borealis, 1981.

Tiessen, Paul and Hildi Froese Tiessen, eds. *L.M. Montgomery's Ephraim Weber Letters, 1916–1941.* Waterloo, ON: Mir, 1999.

Montgomery, L.M. *The Alpine Path: The Story of My Career.* 1917. Markham, ON: Fitzhenry and Whiteside, 1997.

——. *The Selected Journals of L.M. Montgomery.* 4 vols. Ed. Mary Rubio and Elizabeth Waterston. Don Mills, ON: Oxford UP, 1985–2000.

The "Anne" Books by L.M. Montgomery

Anne of Green Gables (1908)
Anne of Avonlea (1909)
Anne of the Island (1910)
Anne's House of Dreams (1915)

Rainbow Valley (1918)
Rilla of Ingleside (1919)
Anne of Windy Poplars (1936)
Anne of Ingleside (1939)